Atlantic Crossing

★★★★★

Clarissa Swire

ISBN: 978-1-7167-8072-1 (sc)
ISBN: 978-1-7167-8082-0 (hc)
ISBN: 978-1-6847-4308-7 (e)

Library of Congress Control Number: 2020911945

Lulu Publishing Services rev. date: 09/14/2020

1

Charlotte at Home

Charlotte scowled at her notebook: *The fading light caressed the trees/Which crowned the earth, like nature's eaves.* Her brown eyes scanned the words twice before looking away in disgust. Pathetic, she thought, bracing herself for an attack of her imaginary critic. She saw it as a glossy crow, who materialized the minute she tried to write poetry. Sure enough, its claws dug into her shoulder now, its beady eye glancing at her scrawl. *Come on, Charlotte,* it squawked, *that metaphor of the tree as nature's house was hackneyed a hundred years ago. It's 1990, for God's sake, not 1890. Get a life.* Nodding silently, Charlotte ripped out the page and dropped it onto the threadbare carpet below. She picked up her pen, slashed through the first line and wrote two new ones:

A woman's fate? To be unseen/ And squelched, and bored, and lose her dream

To mutely watch men be rewarded/And clap while she herself is thwarted –

A voice from outside caused her to look up. In early spring, the London sky was nearly dark by late afternoon, and she strained to see the two sets of feet stationed outside her basement flat's window. Its subterranean location framed the lowest third of all pedestrians, giving her the perspective of a toddler. She could just make out a pair of men's loafers shuffling back and forth. The loafers faced a pair of black heels elevating two motionless ankles. The loafers paused, and she heard a man speak.

"Here we are. I'll ring you later."

The voice was muted, dulled by the single-paned sash window, whose rusted hinges had frozen shut years ago. Charlotte leaned forward, craning her neck upward. Her view ended at the brown loafers' knees. The black heel nearest the window rose to balance on its toe, shifting both ankles in the direction of the loafers, before descending and swiveling away. They moved out of Charlotte's view. The loafers turned toward Charlotte's window and she heard steps banging down the narrow metal stairway that led from the street to her front door.

Charlotte dropped her pen and rose, pushing her long brown hair out of her eyes with one hand as she crossed the room in a few steps. She opened the door to find her brother, Piers, tapping an impatient rhythm with his shoe, his eyes distracted under his messy blond curls, damp from the day's drizzle. Leaning forward to give Charlotte a distracted hug, he caught sight of a pile of clothes heaped onto the carpet. He pulled back and looked at his sister with mock outrage. "I suppose you've lowered your standards since moving to London?"

"I know – it's just as easy to hang it up," Charlotte said, imitating their mother's sing-song cadence. Piers walked in and Charlotte followed his eyes' rapid inventory of the room's sparse furnishings: two worn armchairs and a sagging sofa retired from service in the sitting room of the large house sitting on top of Charlotte's flat. The owner of the house, Lady Philippa, had pointed out the furniture's charms upon Charlotte's arrival a year earlier: *You'll be perfectly set up with all this,* she'd said, her gold bangles clanking as she waived her wrist at the half-tufted sofa. *Tough as old boots.* Charlotte's effort to update the sofa with two new cushions had only served to highlight its antiquity. Piers walked over to Charlotte's desk with an older sibling's easy assumption of territorial control. Charlotte watched his eyebrows rise as he read Charlotte's most recent lines.

"Jesus, Charlotte. I'm no poet, but isn't that a little melodramatic? You're not still upset about that would-be rock star, are you? The one who never played that guitar he lugged around?"

Charlotte flinched as Piers spoke, recalling the letter she'd received from her ex-boyfriend six months ago. *Dear Charlotte, I hope this won't upset you, but je suis tombé amoureux d'une femme Parisienne.* Charlotte still wasn't sure whether his use of French was meant to soften the blow or show off his newly-acquired language skills. She glared at her brother. "If you mean Alex, he's not a would-be rock star anymore. According to friends, he's still in France and becoming an accountant."

"Well good riddance, if you ask me."

"I didn't."

Piers shrugged, crossed the room, and flopped onto the faded patchwork quilt of Charlotte's single bed. His long legs stretched past its end, and his scuffed loafers dangled in the air. When he looked at Charlotte again, his expression had shifted from inquiry to aggrievement. "Well at least your whole career hasn't just been sacrificed to a horde of Swiss bankers descending from Zurich," he said, punctuating his last word by letting his briefcase thump to the floor.

"You've lost your job?"

"Well, no – not quite. But I may as well have. This morning, all the bankers were herded into a subterranean conference room – frankly, it looked like a bunker used during the war – to watch our chief exec glide around the stage and gloat about his latest brainwave: a merger with a Swiss bank. He kept nattering on about the importance of market share and economies of scale. He could barely contain his glee. He's calling it a merger of equals, but they're about twice as big as us—"

"As we are," corrected Charlotte.

"For God's sake, Charlotte, I'm losing my job and you're correcting my grammar? They're twice as big as *us*, and we're taking their name, so I'm sure all the English lads will be turfed out soon enough. Of course, senior management are making a bloody fortune out of the whole thing. It's just the galley slaves who've been thrown under the bus."

Piers threw himself back onto Charlotte's pillow, displacing a worn stuffed rabbit. His even features, drawn with a generous if not overly careful hand, struggled to maintain a look of woe. Impatience and affection clashed within Charlotte as she looked at her brother, and she struggled between a familiar urge to placate him, and a counter-urge to enjoy his setback. Why shouldn't he be dealt bad cards, and visit the land of insecurity and unfulfilled hopes in which she primarily resided? She yielded to the first and more generous of her responses. "I'm sorry, Piers. Maybe it won't be as bad as you think."

Piers picked up Charlotte's rabbit, who stared at him through the loose stitches of its face, and pulled at one of its bald, limp ears. "Poor little Bippity-Bob. We're none of us getting younger, are we?" Piers tossed the rabbit back onto the bed and stood up, rubbing his large hands together. "It's frigid in here. Doesn't Lady Philippa have central heating?"

"She turns it off when she's on holiday, which seems to be about half the year, given my plant-watering and post-collection duties. She seems to see me more as a concierge than a renter. I guess she feels her old friendship to Mother means I won't complain. Anyway, the cold isn't too bad. You know – *nothing a brisk walk won't solve.*"

Piers smiled faintly at this family maxim, brandished throughout their childhood against the Sussex damp penetrating every corner of their large, underheated house. He sat up and looked at his sister with new energy. "There's going to be a get-to-know-you event at the Hurlingham Tennis Club tomorrow to celebrate the bank deal. I suppose it's a Swiss ritual to host your victims before eating them. Perhaps they'll throw us into a fondue pot. Would you like to come? You don't have to play tennis – you can just wander around and drink Pims. Mother says you're not meeting anyone."

Charlotte digested her mother's betrayal, considering whether to refuse Piers's invitation as a matter of pride. She hesitated. "All right, if I don't have to play tennis."

Piers nodded at Charlotte's acceptance, as though it was a foregone conclusion, and Charlotte felt her irritation resurface. Piers's round, ruddy face had regained its characteristic good humor, and his blue eyes were once again clear and bright. He's like a child, Charlotte thought; all his troubles pass within minutes. Piers stood up and retrieved his discarded briefcase. "I'm off. Would you mind letting Mother know that I can't come down to the country next weekend? I'm busy."

Charlotte's thoughts turned to the pair of polished black heels outside her window. "Someone nice?" she asked.

"Not as nice as you," Piers said generously. He paused. "And also, would you mind telling Mother the news about the merger? You're so much better about telling her things, and she's always so worried about my career."

"That's nonsense, Piers. She adores you – she thinks you walk on water. And if she's anxious, it's just because, as she's constantly pointing out, *Piers is the man of the house now.*"

Piers scowled. "I didn't exactly sign up for the job, you know. Her faith might be shaken if she knew I could be sacked. And if she does dote on me, it's only because she knows I need more help than you. You're the clever, Oxford-educated one, remember?" He ran his eyes down his sister's lanky frame. "Are you eating anything? Tomorrow should be good for that. See you at noon."

By 3 p.m. the following day, Charlotte had lost interest in the tennis matches unfolding on the lawn courts below her. She'd arrived that morning cautiously optimistic, her spirits buoyed by the sight of the Hurlingham's expansive flower beds and meticulous lawns, all glistening under an uncharacteristically blue sky. Piers, looking relaxed and happy in his tennis whites, had ushered her through the crowds of guests toward a long buffet table piled with cold salads, sliced meats and sparkling drinks, where they'd piled their white porcelain plates shamelessly high before taking them to a table on a stone patio outside the Hurlingham's large Victorian club house. Without discussing it, she knew they both felt slightly awed by the presence of so much free, delicious food – their own childhood frowned on sensory indulgence, as morally suspect and financially difficult – and they ate with quietly embarrassed, complicit pleasure. That had been two hours ago. Since then, Charlotte had been perched on a western-facing bench in the full glare of the sun and was now hot and bored. She started to cast furtive glances at the linen-clad drinks table twenty feet away, tracking the progress of green-aproned waiters as they heaved silver urns of ice and bottles onto the table. Beads of moisture clinging to the urns sparkled in the light, increasing her thirst and impatience. Below her, Piers was finishing his third match, lunging to return a forehand launched by his Swiss opponent. The bluff pleasantries and banter punctuating the first two sets had given way to a series of grunts as the two men traded points. By the end of third set, Piers's mop of blond curls was soaked with perspiration, and his wide, good-natured eyes drooped at the corners.

Charlotte glanced sideways at the clusters of spectators watching neighboring matches. Piers had prepared her that morning for the crowd's mixed background: *There will be bankers from all of Europe and*

America – the City's become an absolute Noah's Ark, he'd said, frowning. Looking at them now, Charlotte saw only an undifferentiated mass of tennis whites and well-groomed heads. She plucked at the brown tweed skirt clinging to her stockinged thigh and started to feel resentful as Piers slammed a ball into the net. Why had he thought she would be at ease among all these tennis-playing bankers? Just because he had lived twenty-eight years without a moment's self-consciousness or doubt, did he really assume that she would slide into this crowd, where she knew no one and had nothing to say? Even worse, why was she the only person not dressed in tennis clothes?

The game had progressed to match point. Piers was taking a long time to serve, bouncing the ball on the chalked baseline with one hand while shoving back his untrimmed sweaty curls with his other. Charlotte glanced across the court to the Swiss man, admiring the sheen of his tanned skin, so different from the pale legs of the English bankers. Underneath the Swiss man's blue headband, a faint smirk registered Piers's stalling techniques.

Piers tossed the tennis ball in the air, and slammed it across the court, missing the line by a foot. He removed another ball from his pocket for a second serve. Bouncing it only twice, he served again. The ball landed a quarter inch beyond the service line. The Swiss man paused. "Fault," he called, in accented English.

"Sorry, in," countered Piers.

"No. Fault," repeated the Swiss man.

Piers swung his head toward the stands, looking for support. He looked past Charlotte, focusing instead on her neighbor, Katie, whom Piers had introduced that morning as his trading assistant. Together with Charlotte, Katie had sat through all three of Piers's matches, smiling each time he won a point. Piers beamed at Katie and called out, "Katie, what did you see? Was it in?"

Katie's glossy ponytail swung against her freckled neck as she nodded. "Absolutely," she said, turning to Charlotte for confirmation. "Didn't you see it, Charlotte?" Charlotte ignored Katie and stared at her brother. With his left hand, he was pushing his hair out of his eyes, the palm of his hand shadowing his face. She recognized the gesture as the one he'd perfected in childhood when charged with wrongdoing.

Charlotte waited for a moment for Piers to lower his hand and meet her look. He didn't.

"I wasn't watching," Charlotte said eventually, aiming her words in the direction of the drinks table, now circled by a growing ring of tennis players. From the far end of the court, the Swiss man snorted and slapped his racket against his thigh. He muttered something in German whose general, if not specific, meaning was unambiguous.

Piers shot an uninflected smile in his direction. "Sorry mate, looks like that's the match." The man's pale lips compressed and disappeared. With another snort, he gathered his belongings, threw a towel over his shoulder and stomped off the court. Piers walked over to the stands, his ruddy, broad face beaming with good health. "Drinks?" he called up to Charlotte and Katie. Katie ran down to the court and started to walk with Piers toward the club house. Charlotte labored after them, encumbered by her heels, which plunged into the lawn with each stride. By the time she reached them, Piers was handing around tall flutes of sparkling wine.

"Oh Char, don't be such a spoilsport," he chided her, extending a glass in her direction.

"It was out," she retorted, taking the glass from him.

"No, it wasn't. Well, perhaps just a touch. But isn't it enough they're taking over our bank, our jobs, and probably the City of London? Anyway, he wasn't such a charmer himself."

"That's not the point."

"But it is, my dear sister. It is *absolutely* the point. Oh – Simon, hello!" Piers turned toward a square-shouldered, short man whose greying hair was covered by a white cap emblazoned with the logo of a Swiss bank. He was the only person older than thirty-five Charlotte had seen all morning. The man turned a pair of steel-rimmed spectacles in Charlotte's direction with an inquisitive look. Piers threw a sweaty arm around Charlotte's back. "Simon, this is Charlotte, my little sister," Piers said, turning toward Charlotte with a hint of warning in his eye. "Simon is our trading desk's leader, widely considered one of the City's financial legends."

Simon acknowledged Piers's assessment with a deprecating chuckle. He turned his grey eyes toward Charlotte, running them over her inappropriate wool skirt and white silk blouse, both damp with perspiration. Charlotte took a sip of her champagne.

"It's good of you to support your brother," Simon said. "Didn't he play tennis at university? I suppose the matches were a piece of cake?"

Simon's sentence ended on an upward note of inquiry. Charlotte hesitated, and Piers broke in. "No trouble whatsoever."

Simon gave a complacent smile and he turned toward Charlotte. "That's what we like to hear. And you Charlotte, are you in the City as well?"

"No, I'm not. Advertising. Just to pay the rent."

Simon's eyes, which had been circling the room during Charlotte's answer, alighted briefly on her face, his eyebrows raised. "Really? And what is your true calling?" His elegant, playful tone held a note of irony, and Charlotte felt Piers stiffen beside her.

"Poetry. Lyric poetry, specifically."

Simon guffawed, the wrinkles around his eyes deepening with amusement. He turned toward Piers. "Looks like the family's fortunes rest on you, Piers."

Charlotte suppressed her irritation as Piers gave a hollow, uncomfortable laugh. "Oh no, Charlotte's the clever one – she'll be supporting me in the end." Piers's voice rose with his discomfort, and Charlotte saw a few heads turn in his direction.

Simon joined in his tone of hilarity. "Well, count me in for the subsidy when it arrives. I'm glad I'm not up against all these clever young women – it's enough to keep the Swiss boys happy." Simon wandered away, leaving Piers and Charlotte alone.

Charlotte turned toward her brother in anger. "Must you be so condescending?" she said.

Piers matched her look of irritation. "Lighten up, Char. It's not easy to resurrect a conversation after someone's declared herself a poet. Forgive me, a *lyric* poet. For the record, *he's* the one who was condescending, not me. Anyway, he's my boss. I had to say something."

"At my expense?"

"Don't be ridiculous. It's all in good fun. Anyway, let me introduce you to some others. Mother says you're not—"

"Meeting anyone," Charlotte snapped. "It's true. But I don't think Prince Charming is here, hiding in tennis whites. I'm off." Kissing her brother goodbye, Charlotte left.

2

Town and Country

C harlotte sprinted down the railway platform of Kings Cross, her weekend duffel slamming into her side as she ran toward her train. She jumped on board as the doors were banging shut, and the conductor was blasting his whistle with unfeigned satisfaction at the stragglers. Sinking into the first empty seat, she withdrew an anthology of poetry from her purse and placed it, unopened, on her lap, as her mind wandered toward the weekend ahead. It was so like Piers to ask her to break the news of his job situation to their mother. Piers dealt only in triumphs, never setbacks. Over the years, he had maintained his golden boy status with a combination of natural charm, seamless public relations and, when inescapable, actual achievement. The strategy had worked brilliantly on their mother, who, upon the early death of her husband, had transferred her appreciation of charming men from her late husband to her teenage son. In Charlotte's view, her mother had been only too willing to see it as entirely natural, indeed inevitable, that Piers should be Head Boy in school, captain of the rowing and tennis teams, and a top recruit to a private bank in the City (and this, Charlotte recalled with a frown, despite his appalling math A-levels). For years, Charlotte had felt that she was trudging unnoticed and unheralded in his glossy wake, ever reliable and unglamorous, a pallid contrast to her brother's easy radiance. Her early poetic efforts had lost their biggest champion when her father had been killed in a car crash when she was twelve, and her half-hearted teenage efforts to cultivate a more exciting image – the mildly risqué outfits, the endless repetition of Pat Benatar's *Heartbreaker* on her record player – had been met with a silence more puzzled than annoyed. Eventually, it had been easier to read about the great adventures of the past than to plot her own, and she had spent many comfortable hours tucked up in a nest of blankets, mesmerized by Shackleton's frozen race for the South Pole, and tales of England's missionaries sweating and dying in the furthest outposts of the Empire.

The train raced south and London's snaking urban ring roads receded, replaced by valleys of fields newly green in the early spring, and dotted by patches of crocus and daffodils. Overhead the clouds were sparse and thin, barely shading a pale yellow sun. Charlotte felt her spirits lift as she watched the blur of cropped hedgerows and low stone walls, long streaks of brown and gray framing the green of the fields. She loved the early spring, the yearly miracle of green leaves emerging from branches that looked all but dead. A line from a Wordsworth poem burbled up: *It was an April morning: Fresh and clear.* She let her anthology slide back into her purse and closed her eyes, repeating the words to herself over the monotonous hum of the train's engine. Fresh and clear, fresh and clear – she fell asleep.

A few hours later, Charlotte emerged at the diminutive station of her local village, whose claims to modernity ("capacheeno," £1, read the sign) were undermined by the octogenarian stationmaster, who glared at disembarking passengers from a chair nailed to the platform. Charlotte hurried through the ticket hall toward the taxi stand before being arrested by her mother's voice.

"Over here, Charlotte!"

Charlotte caught sight of her mother at the far edge of the parking lot. Her long, narrow figure was swathed in an ankle-length raincoat and wide-brimmed rain hat, between which only a pointy chin and lipsticked smile were visible. She was waving a well-worn leather driving glove in her direction. Walking toward her mother, Charlotte planted a kiss more dutiful than loving on her cheek.

"Mother, how did you know I would be on this train?" she said.

"Oh, Charlotte," said her mother, in a do-be-reasonable tone. "You always take this train. It isn't exactly as though you're a Russian spy, my dear. Though I must say," she continued, eying her daughter's hair, "if you're hoping to pass as one of the unwashed masses, you're doing awfully well. But you'll have plenty of time to wash and change before we host the Blooms for supper tonight. They're bringing their son, Horace. I'm sure you remember him."

Charlotte recalled a dour teenage boy hiding behind multiple barriers of lanky brown hair, dark sunglasses, and Dostoevsky anthologies. "Mother, not that ridiculous boy who pretended to speak Russian."

"I'm sure that's all done with, dear. Apparently, a gap year in Moscow shook that enthusiasm. He's down from London, too, and has brought a friend. An American."

"I'm to be trotted out like a prize pig?"

Her mother glanced sideways at Charlotte's tangled brown hair, limp cotton pullover and faded jeans. Charlotte felt an eyebrow arch behind her mother's hat. "Perhaps not a prized one," her mother replied, "But nothing a bath can't change."

That evening, Charlotte descended the stairs in black leggings and a thigh-length black cardigan with shoulder pads, an outfit copied from a picture of Princess Diana in *Hello!* magazine. The princess's hair had been sprayed into a blond wave cresting over her ear, but Charlotte's thick brown hair – an unwelcome legacy of her late father – had resisted all efforts at control, and Charlotte had conceded defeat, letting it spill forward onto her face and over her hazel eyes whose color, her mother said frequently, were their only shared feature. Midway down the stairs she paused, disconcerted by the sensation that her last year in London was a figment of her imagination. Everything in her childhood house was comfortingly, stiflingly exactly as she'd left it. She knew every picture on the wall next to her by heart: her parents' photograph as they boarded the Queen Mary ocean liner for their honeymoon to New York, their eyes glazed with anxiety; the posed baptismal portraits of Piers and herself, both of them obscured by her mother's wide-brimmed hat; and an oil painting of her, Piers and their cocker spaniel, whose habit of leaping on the painter had resulted in a canvas dominated by a meticulously observed frothing canine mouth, with two nondescript children sketched into the background. She squinted at the generic girl meant to represent herself at eight, wondering whether the subsequent years had made her image any more interesting or distinct.

She found her mother in the dining room, attempting to transfer two dozen pink tulips from a paper wrapper to a large glass vase. The stems of the tulips were spindly and kept flopping over in a disconsolate manner toward the polished wood sideboard.

"I don't know why tulips are traditional at Easter," her mother sighed, poking at the stems in irritation. "A flower less capable of resurrection I've never seen. Charlotte, could you try?" Charlotte leaned toward the vase, yanked out all the tulips and started again. As she hovered over the listless dripping pile, her mother sniffed audibly.

"Charlotte, what in the world is that smell?"

"What smell?" Charlotte said defensively.

"Your – I wouldn't quite call it perfume. Your – scent?"

"Oh, that! It's new. It's called Edge." Her mother said nothing for a long moment. Charlotte could feel her fighting, and losing, her battle for self-control.

"Charlotte, you smell like a wet muffler."

"It's supposed to be new and urban. People in the country aren't meant to appreciate it."

"Ah." Her mother pursed her lips and turned away. Charlotte stuffed the last of the tulips into the vase, causing another cascade of pink petals to litter the sideboard below. The rap of a door knocker interrupted her efforts. Walking toward the entry hall, she heaved at the front door. It seemed to stick more each year, as if begrudging the free flow of people across its worn threshold. She found Pamela and Richard Bloom beaming in her direction, wearing the matched smiles of long married couples, their bulky raincoats obscuring the two men hovering behind them.

"Why Charlotte, don't you look elegant! Quite the young lady, isn't she, Richard?" Pamela leaned forward to kiss Charlotte, before stepping aside to reveal a lanky young man whose dark hair flopped forward over a tense expression. "You know Horace, of course, and this is his great American friend, Paul."

"Patrick," corrected Horace, with a sidelong apologetic glance.

"Of course," said Pamela, vaguely. "All those early saints…" She and her husband moved forward in unison. Charlotte, Horace and Patrick remained still, the three of them marking out the points of a triangle on the landing's uneven flag stones. Horace glanced at Charlotte and ran a pale hand through his dark hair, a gesture she was surprised to recall from his teenage years. His dark eyes, no longer obscured by the sunglasses of his teenage years, studied her warily. Charlotte shifted her attention to his friend, whose well-tanned face was tipped well back as he surveyed the foyer behind Charlotte. Shorter and broader than Horace, he stood comfortably, his weight back on the heels of his shiny black shoes, his hands resting comfortably in the pockets of his dark wool trousers. His smooth blond hair caught the light of the dusty chandelier as he looked around with frank interest. Charlotte and Horace followed Patrick's gaze upward toward the coffered wood ceiling. Noting its patches of flaking paint, Charlotte looked down again.

"Have you just come down from London?" she asked.

Horace drew himself up as if to speak, but Patrick, lowering his chin, answered first. "We arrived this morning," he said, smiling easily. "Horace promised he'd show me England's country life. Didn't you, Horace?" Horace shifted his weight on the flagstones and ran his other hand through his hair. "So here we are," continued Patrick. "Your house must be one of the local highlights. This door is amazing. It must weigh fifty pounds." He took a step back and ran a bronzed hand over the filigree patterns etched into its peeling wood. "Fantastic. Could we see the inside of the house, too?"

"Of course, so sorry," said Charlotte, feeling subtly reprimanded. She stepped back and gestured toward a door standing open at the far end of the entrance hall. "It's just through there for drinks." Patrick moved forward, his shoes rapping against the flagstones as he crossed the front hall into a large sitting room punctuated by faded floral sofas and velvet armchairs of dull gold. Entering last, Charlotte noticed a few afghans newly draped across the armchairs to hide their bald patches. The Blooms were already nestled into the oldest and most comfortable of the sofas, deep in conversation with Charlotte's mother. Charlotte walked toward a sideboard holding a cluster of crystal liquor decanters on a silver tray. The decanters had sat in the same place for as long as she could remember, ready to oil the mechanics of countless social gatherings. Charlotte glanced backward.

"Horace? Patrick? Gin and tonic? Vodka?"

"Gin for me," said Patrick, "but poor old Horace is still on the prohibition bandwagon. Something to do with Lent?"

Horace gave a tight smile. "Just some tonic, if you don't mind, Charlotte."

Charlotte handed out the drinks and glanced at her mother, who was in full gale, recounting Charlotte's teenage effort to paint her bedroom aqua. Why was it that one's childhood and teenage years – such a series of small struggles and mortifications – were somehow all fodder to the older generation's conversational arsenal? Charlotte threw her mother a murderous look which went unnoticed.

"Such a comfortable couch, what a relief," said Patrick, patting the fabric's florid rose blooming next to his thigh. His glass was half empty, and a pink flush showed through his tanned cheeks. "I tried to find a couch last week for my new apartment – sorry, <u>flat</u> – and kept being offered things that felt like blankets pasted onto church pews. What does this country have against comfort, anyway?" Patrick punctuated his question with his glass, sloshing some of its contents onto the rose.

"I suppose we specialize in self-denial," said Charlotte, taking a large sip of gin and tonic. She glanced at Horace. "Do the two of you work together?"

Patrick nodded. "We do. You have in front of you about a tenth of Shorwell Capital's London office. Horace is our lead analyst, toiling away at his beloved numbers and spreadsheets, while I market his genius to pension funds around England. I just tell them we've hired one of your homegrown rocket scientists – was it physics at Cambridge? – and they all come running."

"Applied maths, Oxford," corrected Horace. "I don't think it's particularly relevant." Patrick waved his hand dismissively.

"It's the mystique that's the key. If you'd just let me take charge of your career, you'd be earning ten times as much. And then you could buy a house like this. Unless you're planning on marrying one?" Patrick turned to Charlotte. "And you, Charlotte, are you one of these terrifyingly over-educated English girls I keep meeting? I went to a conference the other day and nearly had my head bitten off by a self-professed <u>lady fund manager</u>."

"No, advertising," Charlotte began, "Just a stop-gap. But my brother Piers is in the City. His firm just merged with a Swiss one. He seems to think he might get sacked."

"Really?" said Patrick, looking at Charlotte with intensified interest. He placed his empty glass on the table in front of him, displaying a chunky gold signet ring. "Maybe he should speak to us. We're always looking for good people. What do you think, Horace?"

Horace, who had been staring into his tonic water, looked up. "Piers? I don't know. When I last saw him, he was mostly interested in rowing." Horace fixed his brown eyes on Charlotte. "Is Piers interested in equity sales? Or research?"

Charlotte paused; it hadn't occurred to her to link Piers's interests to his occupation. Besides which, what he did in his job was something of a mystery to her. She shrugged. "You know Piers – everyone loves him. I'm sure he's interested in anything where people can beam in his direction."

"There's a sister's recommendation for you," said Patrick. "I'd love to meet him, and I'll be sure to beam away. If you could just write down your number, we can all meet up next week in London." Patrick reached into a hidden breast pocket to produce a gleaming silver pen and small spiral notebook, placing them on the table in front of Charlotte, who glanced at Horace. He had returned to studying his ice cubes. Charlotte scrawled out a number and handed the pen back to Patrick, gripping it at its very tip to hide her ragged nails.

"Great," said Patrick. He looked up, where the Blooms were disappearing into the dining room. "Looks like dinner's ready. Should we join them?" Without waiting for a response, he rose and moved away, leaving Charlotte and Horace alone. From the next room, they heard Patrick praise the tulips to her mother, who repeated the joke about their non-resurrection. Charlotte toyed with her napkin, rolling it first into a tight cylinder, and then into a neat spiral. In her head, she heard her mother's voice: *Do stop fidgeting.* She dropped the napkin.

She looked up at Horace. His dark eyes, which had been trained on her restless hands, remain guarded, and his drink was untouched. "Do you think your friend really might help Piers?" she asked.

Horace hesitated. "He might. He's recruiting for the London office. But I don't know if it would suit Piers."

"Why not? Aren't all City jobs much of a muchness?" Charlotte said. "And you remember Piers, he's wonderfully malleable." She pronounced malleable with a heavy emphasis on "mal," making it sound like an illness. "I wouldn't have thought the content of the job would trouble him too much."

"No?" The corners of Horace's lips bent into a rueful smile. "You're right, I'm sure, all these City jobs are pretty much the same. Tilting at windmills." He paused. "But I'm not certain Patrick and Piers have too much in common. He might be happier elsewhere."

"I'm sure he'll be fine," retorted Charlotte. "He's always been amazing in looking after his own interests. And you're there, right? There must be something to recommend it. You're not buried in books, anyway. That's my last memory of you. Dostoevsky, right?"

"I've taken a break from him. All that philosophizing – I got tired of feeling shallow. I'm on to Tolstoy."

"Much more fun, I'm sure. Shall we go into dinner before mother subjects everyone to more awful Charlotte stories?"

"At least they delay the awful Horace stories," Horace said, laughing.

They entered the dining room, where Charlotte's mother was in the process of replenishing everyone's drinks. Patrick was seated between the Blooms, regaling his neighbors with the mortification of being an American in London.

"What it took me forever to realize," he said, raising his palm, as if making a pledge, "was that it is impermissible here to introduce oneself. I had no idea I needed a formal speech from a third party before saying good morning to my colleague sitting next to me, and preferably a formal speech preceded by a signed and stamped memo from a governmental agency!" Patrick banged his fist on the tablecloth as if stamping the memo. The party chuckled appreciatively. "Until I realized this," Patrick continued, his eyes circling everyone in turn, "I used to wonder whether I smelled particularly offensive. I would say good morning, and people would literally leap backwards. It was almost a party trick. So tell me, how does one get to know each other here?" His glance fell on Charlotte.

"I suppose we've simply always known one another," Charlotte stammered.

"Not very helpful to outsiders, is it?" said Patrick, feigning outrage.

"Oh, Patrick, you seem to be making out very well," rejoined Charlotte's mother. "Another drink?"

The following morning, Charlotte sat in the church foyer, sorting through a stack of charity greeting cards and humming the closing hymn of the service as she waited for her mother. It had been a hearty affair. The vicar, a small man swimming in the folds of his robe, had long ago abandoned his efforts to convey God's sanctifying powers, settling instead for a diet of short, common-sense sermons that confirmed his parishioners' existing views. Charlotte had devoted her energies to surveying the assembled crowd and looking at the stained-glass windows, partially destroyed during the war. As her eyes had flickered across a lurid depiction of the Last Judgment, she had been surprised to find Horace and Patrick squeezed into the back pew. Horace had his head down and seemed to be reading, but Patrick's clear blue eyes were in motion as they swept from the vicar, to the golden eagle on the Bible's lectern, to the fidgeting choir boys, and finally to Charlotte herself. Caught watching him, Charlotte had felt the blood rush to her cheeks as she gave him an embarrassed smile.

He wandered past now. "That was fun, wasn't it?" Patrick said, his voice echoing around the vaulted stone gallery. "What a great old place." He waved his arm in a gesture acknowledging the ancient floor, walls and ceiling before turning to Charlotte. "Is there somewhere to eat around here? Horace has abandoned me for *War and Peace*. He's on page fifty of roughly a million."

"There's the tea shop across the green," Charlotte said. "They do a reasonable fry-up."

"A fry-up. I have no idea what that is, but I'm sure it's perfect. Can you join me? Or are you tied down to these—," Patrick paused as he picked up a card imploring him to *Save Britain's Wildlife*.

"Charity greeting cards. Yes, I'm sure my mother can take over for me. Two ticks." Charlotte rushed off to find her mother, who was still in the pews chatting with friends. When she returned, she found Patrick leaning toward one of the stone walls, peering at the inscriptions of the Victorian tombstones embedded from floor to ceiling. His eyes were narrowed, and his face wore an expression of incredulity. He glanced at Charlotte as she approached before looking back at the wall.

"Look at this one," he said, nodding toward a stone rectangle of worn filigreed cursive. "William Poole, dead at 19 in 1835 and, according to this, a man of moral integrity, honor, selflessness and charity to the poor. I don't think I know any nineteen-year-olds who could manage any one of those things." He turned back to Charlotte with an ironic smile. "What do you think your commemorative stone will say? Are you as selfless and honorable as your dead villagers?"

"Absolutely," Charlotte said, defiantly tossing her head.

"We'll see about that," Patrick said. "Selfless is a pretty steep hurdle these days. I doubt young William Poole was trying to claw his way up the career ladder like the rest of us." Together they left the foyer and traced a patch through the gravestones hugging the Church walls, heading for the damp village green. The sky, having exhausted itself the previous day with an unusual show of sunshine, had reverted to grey. Low, leaden clouds threatened rain. Charlotte nodded to a few people, seeing them move their eyes furtively in Patrick's direction. Let them all gossip, she thought; it's about time I created a ripple of interest. She and Patrick entered a small tea shop on the main street of the village, its bells chiming as they opened the door. A harried woman with a fringe of frizzy red curls nodded toward Charlotte.

"Hullo, dear," she said, casting a discreet glance at Patrick, "How's London?"

"Fine, thanks, Mrs. Hall," answered Charlotte. "Just down for the weekend. Could we have a couple of fry-ups please?" Charlotte and Patrick squeezed past the other diners to sit at the last available table. The café was steamy and loud, and Charlotte found herself having to lean in toward Patrick to hear him, catching a scent of minty cologne as she did so. She saw his lips move but his words were lost in the chatter of the other diners.

"Sorry?" asked Charlotte, pushing her brown hair behind her ear and leaning further across the table.

"I asked you," he said, his straight white teeth four inches from her face, "what exactly you do in London."

"Oh, sorry! I work at an ad agency in Mayfair. Restaurants, home builders, that kind of thing. Have you seen the posters in the tube of DIY castles?" Patrick's face showed no spark of recognition, but his eyes continued to track hers attentively. Charlotte plowed on, buoyed by his attention. "Well, that's us. Right now, I'm working with a fish-and-veg restaurant chain. We're planning an anti-meat campaign. It's made me think about the ethics of eating animals." Charlotte paused, noticing that Patrick was slicing a sausage into neat discs. "But I'm just there until I make my next move." Patrick looked up. Despite the damp walk across the green and the humidity of the café, he looked fresh and neat, his blond hair sleekly combed straight back. His blue eyes rested on her face, in silent inquiry. Charlotte faltered.

"I haven't figured out quite yet what it will be. I used to want to be a poet, but I know that must sound ridiculous."

"No, not at all." His tone was non-committal.

"As a child, I used to want to be an explorer, and then a nun, and then a missionary to combine the two. Anything bold and courageous, you know. Something different – something other people might notice and respect. You know how it is." Embarrassed, Charlotte looked down at her scrambled eggs and stirred them with her fork. She wasn't used to talking about herself, and the effort confused her. Even the men she knew well were generally too busy talking about themselves to ask questions of others, and she barely knew Patrick. She beat a retreat. "Anyway, right now I'm too busy to plan the next step. We're pretty full-on at the agency."

"Really?" Patrick started to cut his bacon into sections. "I hope you're not too busy to go out sometime. I've hired a bunch of guys here to build out the new office, but they kind of stick to themselves. I can't tell whether it's their famous English reserve, or that they just see me as a social embarrassment – you know, the American dolt." Patrick gave a short laugh signaling the outrageousness of this perception. He wiped his mouth and placed his folded napkin on the table, lining it up with his plate. His movements were assured and precise. He smiled at

Charlotte. "Let's make a date for when we're back, okay? You can show me Charlotte Cheetham's London."

Charlotte felt a jolt of excitement. "Of course, I'd love to," she said, her voice higher than usual. "Ring anytime."

"Great. And I'd love to meet your brother too. We're always looking for guys with European expertise." Charlotte's eyes, which had been tracking Patrick's, clouded over. She fought back a flush of irritation. Must Piers intrude upon her every adventure? She forced a tight smile.

"Of course," she said. "Anytime."

A week later, Charlotte sat at a corner table in a dim West London pub. Her arms rested comfortably on her black poetry notebook, her elbows bracketing the handwritten title: <u>Works in Progress, C. Cheetham, 1988-</u>. Despite being two years old, the notebook looked fresh, and most of its pages were unused. Leaning her chin on the palm of her hand, she surveyed the scene – the usual combination of office workers popping in for a quick post-work pint, and regulars installing themselves along the bar. Above them all, Sky Television was blaring its new non-stop news channel. Glancing only briefly at the TV, her thoughts moved inward and landed, as so frequently in recent days, on what she'd begun to call the Puzzle of Patrick. She was bothered by her inability to evaluate, sort and place him within one of the hundreds of minutely nuanced social categories by which she categorized and navigated her world. It wasn't just his foreignness that formed a smokescreen; it was also his combination of enthusiasm and confidence that threw her, exactly the opposite of the ironic, gallows humor affected by her social circle. Equally foreign were his tan and gleaming straight teeth, without doubt the result of more enlightened dentistry. She replayed the scenes of Patrick's visit in her mind: stroking the front door of her house; slamming his fist on the dining room table; scoffing at the plaques of her village's deceased worthies; requesting to meet Piers. She frowned as she recalled Piers' overt skepticism when she'd suggested that he meet Patrick. It's as if he thinks the idea of me as a social conduit is ridiculous, she fumed. Feeling a touch on her head, she looked up to find her brother's easy smile beaming down. Her nascent irritation evaporated. It's hopeless, she thought; no one could hold a grudge against him. It's like trying to shiver in the sun.

Piers mussed her hair by way of greeting while glancing around the pub. "Why are you hiding in a corner, Char? Are you branching out into drug deals? And who is this guy, anyway? I'm missing my poker game."

Charlotte smoothed her hair into place before replying. "He's an American Horace Bloom brought home last weekend. They work together in the City. We were having drinks – well Patrick and I were, anyway, Horace seems not to drink – and your name came up. I mentioned that your firm had been taken over by the Swiss, and that your job was at risk." Piers winced, but Charlotte plowed ahead. "Patrick said he might be able to help you with a job – doing something – I don't know – City-ish." Charlotte watched Piers's face as it shifted from impatience to incredulity.

"You're promoting me as a job candidate?"

"Why not? He works with Horace."

"Horace! The Trotskyite who wears sunglasses in winter?"

"He's improved. And is that my thanks for trying to help you?"

"Help me?" Piers repeated, with heavy irony. "My little sister helping me with my career? Charlotte, that's charming, really, but you don't even know what I do."

Charlotte responded with indignation fueled by the truth of Piers's accusation. "That's nonsense. You sell things. Stocks, right? And bonds, and money, or currencies, and anyway, does it really matter?" A cough interrupted her outrage, and she looked up to find Patrick hovering above their table. A faint smell of mint drifted down from his clean-shaven throat, which disappeared into the tight knot of a navy and red striped tie and tailored grey suit. Charlotte lurched up from her chair in embarrassment. Piers rose more slowly, his features relaxing as his head rose two inches above Patrick's.

"Piers Cheetham," he said, extending his hand.

"The famous Piers! Great to meet you," said Patrick. "The family resemblance is unmistakable." Piers dropped Patrick's hand and threw a wary glance in Charlotte's direction. She missed it, her eyes focused on Patrick.

"Is lager all right? I'll get us a round." Patrick headed toward the bar without waiting for a response. Piers leaned toward Charlotte, who continued to watch Patrick as he made his way through the growing crowd.

"Stop staring, Charlotte, he's not a bloody pop star. And what does he mean, the famous Piers? What did you tell him about me?" Piers kept his voice low, his eyes darting between Patrick and his sister.

"Nothing," Charlotte whispered. "What do I know about you anyway? You never tell me anything."

"There's nothing to tell," Piers said, his voice rising in irritation.

"What about your new girlfriend? The one who walked you to my flat the other week?"

"Who, Katie? She's not my girlfriend!" Piers boomed. A pint of lager landed in front of him, neatly positioned by a large manicured hand. He looked up. "Oh – Patrick. Thanks."

"No problem," said Patrick, sliding into his chair and lifting a very full pint glass. "Cheers! I love these old English pubs." He dabbed at the foam dotting his upper lip with a bar napkin. "We just don't have places like this in New York. Our bars are glamorous, but anonymous." Piers glanced around the smoky room, seemingly baffled by Patrick's appreciation. To his right, a cluster of men in paint-splattered coveralls threw darts at a board hanging near the toilets. From behind the bar, the bartender watched Sky TV while rubbing pint glasses with a rag.

"I guess it's fine," Piers said, without conviction. "Where's home for you? Where are the glamorous bars?"

"The bars are in New York. But I'm from Minnesota. My dad's a farmer – corn, wheat, dairy. My grandfather too, and pretty much everyone right back to the 1850s when they got out of Ireland. I was supposed to help out, but I left." A pause ensued as Patrick drank more of his lager. Piers was already halfway through his pint.

"Do you miss it?" Charlotte asked.

Patrick gave a short, bitter laugh. "Farming? No way. The hours alone make Wall Street look like a walk in the park. And if that doesn't kill you, the sub-zero winters will. My dad works sixteen hours a day and spends the other eight worrying about the weather and government subsidies." Patrick replaced his pint glass on the table and sat back, his brow clearing. He turned toward Piers, who was drinking the last of his lager and eyeing a dark-haired woman whose knee-high leather boots dangled from a bar stool. Patrick followed his gaze, looking amused. "So Piers, Charlotte told me you might be looking around."

Piers turned back to Patrick with a shade of reluctance. "Possibly. We're merging with a Swiss firm, and all their boys are being shipped over to London and tossing out the locals." Piers shrugged with exaggerated nonchalance. "I'm sure something will turn up."

"That's too bad," said Patrick, keeping his eyes focused on Piers's face. "You'd probably be wasted there anyway. When have the Swiss taken any risks? And Charlotte tells me you're a good salesman."

"Really?" Piers raised his eyebrows in Charlotte's direction.

"Yes," Patrick continued. "I don't know whether Charlotte mentioned Shorwell to you? We're a New York investment group selling funds to pensions. Europe's a new market for us, and I was sent here last year to set up a team. My boss asked me to keep an eye out for someone who knows the European markets, someone who can help our guys in New York. It would be mostly sales. You'd get to fly around pitching our funds to Americans. You know – from sea to shining sea, all that. You might work. Another round?" Patrick stood up and headed back to the bar.

Piers looked his sister, puzzled. "Did he just offer me a job in New York?"

"Um – maybe?" Charlotte returned his baffled look, reverting to her childhood habit of matching her brother's expressions in moments of uncertainty.

Piers glanced away from his sister and toward Patrick, who was now chatting with the bartender. "Charlotte, do we even know who he is? And not that I lack faith in my abilities, but does he know anything about me?"

"No. But he's American, so we can't judge them by our standards. Aren't they known for moving at lightning speed? Operating on gut instinct and all that? Anyway, what's to lose? You could go see New York – and since you *don't* have a girlfriend here,"

"Who said I don't have a girlfriend?"

"So there *is* a girlfriend?"

Patrick reappeared above them, placing three new pint glasses of lager on the table. He moved with deft precision, arranging each glass with the handle pointing to the right. He pulled out his chair and sat down, smiling at Charlotte. "That bartender is awesome. Did you know his Irish grandfather started this place? It's been in the family for three generations." Patrick turned his blond head toward Piers and waited for him to swallow the first sip of his new pint before putting his elbows on the table and leaning toward Piers. "If you're interested, I can forward your resume to New York. I think the guys out there would love you, and your knowledge of Europe would really help the sales effort. And you're a rower, right? There's a rowing club right on the Hudson. Besides, I promise to look after Charlotte for you." Patrick leaned toward Charlotte and lay one of his hands on her fingertips, which were poised at the edge of the table. Startled, Charlotte felt a fleeting shock run up her arm. Piers, whose face had started to assume the melting quality of someone following an inner vision, regained its focus. He draped his arm around Charlotte in an awkward sideways hug, dragging her hand away from Patrick's.

"Oh, Charlotte can take care of herself," he said. "She's an expert." He released his sister and glanced at his watch. "Look, I'd love to learn more about Shorwell, but I'm afraid I have to bolt off. Thanks for the drink. I'll send you my resume." The two men rose and shook hands, and Piers walked rapidly out of the pub.

Patrick watched him depart and sat down slowly, a bemused look on his face. "He's very much the older brother, isn't he? Not that I would know – I never had a sister. Or brother. It must be great to have a built-in ally."

Charlotte hesitated, her brain whirring with a small storm of conflicting emotions. She nodded slowly. "Um, sort of," she answered.

3

London Calling

C harlotte sat at her office desk, a pile of scripts before her, gazing out of the large arched window to her left. Her ad agency, the vanity project of a socialite who'd lost interest long ago, occupied an 18th century townhouse whose floors had been converted into open plan offices. The rest of the street was populated by art galleries, clothing boutiques and a faux-French cafe. Charlotte's desk gave her a clear view of the café's street tables and the stream of non-faux French women who populated them throughout the day, slinging their glossy shopping bags across the cane back chairs. Since joining the agency a year before, Charlotte had spent many hours watching the shoppers glide by, speculating on the gulf between their lives and her own.

Looking at this morning's group of coffee-drinking expats, her thoughts turned to Piers. Fragments of his new adventure had filtered through to her answering machine over the past six weeks. It had all moved with surprising speed. Shortly after the meeting with Patrick, Piers had left his first update on Charlotte's answering machine: *They loved my background,* he'd said, his voice lit by enthusiasm; *I guess they're all great rowers over there. And Jerry, one of the sales guys, says they have a standing poker game every week.* A week later, another message had been left. *I'm flying over to meet them later this week. Tell Mother, will you?* And finally, a week later, a third message, this one groggily triumphant. *Hi Char. I'm back. New York was great – I can't wait to tell you all about it. They want me to move out there right away. I'm headed off in a few weeks. I don't think I'll be able to get down to see Mother beforehand. I'll ring her to say good-bye.*

Charlotte could practically see the glint of Manhattan's skyscrapers as she replayed the messages in her head, and she tried to ignore the wave of envy which accompanied her vision. He hadn't even bothered to thank her, she fumed. No doubt Piers saw this job as his rightful due, and was long past connecting it to her efforts. She watched a French woman sipping coffee at the café outside. Those women never eat anything, she thought, irritated.

A repetitive click disturbed her thoughts, and she looked up to see her colleague Annabelle hovering nearby, tapping her foot on the polished wood floor. Charlotte had often wondered whether Annabelle's habit of foot tapping was an unconscious act of impatience or a calculated effort to draw attention to her collection of stiletto heels. Today's were trimmed in fur.

"Right," said Annabelle, with a rap of her fur-clad toe. "The fish-veg chain just rang up and want to know whether we'd come up with an idea for a new series of ads. Any bright ideas?"

"Right!" Charlotte unconsciously imitated Annabelle's breathy urgency as she began to ad-lib. "I was thinking that we could interview – so to speak – various adorable cows and sheep from around the country. Live from the Dales, that sort of thing. We could do voice-overs and ask the animals about their lives: names, hobbies, favorite foods... at the end of each interview, we could sing a little song – you know, *Don't wish me dead, Try fish-veg instead!*" Annabelle looked at Charlotte with a blank expression and continued to tap her foot. Charlotte rushed on. "We don't have to use the word "dead," necessarily, but of course we want to get across the idea that eating meat is connected to killing the animals."

"I don't know," said Annabelle, pursing her red-glossed lips. "Do you think that might be overly – political?" A faint line appeared across her forehead. "We don't want to stir up a debate about the ethics of eating meat. It's supposed to be a light-hearted campaign. Nigel, what do you think?" She turned her head to a plump, fair man across the room perusing the weddings column of *The Daily Telegraph*. The son and presumed heir of the agency's founder, Nigel used the office primarily as a convenient place to change clothes as his day progressed, and for a comfortable chair during the many phone calls devoted to planning the logistics of his busy social life. Over the last year, Charlotte had found herself a captive audience to the intricacies of his schedule, a dazzling series of dinner parties, shooting parties, drinks parties, and weekends away across England and the continent. Her effort to disdain his idleness was entirely swamped by her envy of his social cachet. It didn't help that his manner to Charlotte, while unfailingly polite, remained distinctly hazy; Charlotte harbored a suspicion that Nigel, if pressed, couldn't recall her name.

Nigel tilted his smooth rounded cheeks upward toward Annabelle, his pale eyes vague. "Sorry? Cows? I wasn't listening." Annabelle pointed her fur stiletto in his direction and flicked her hair behind her shoulder.

"Do you think, Nigel" she said, balancing on one foot, "that it would be too *awkward* if we told our viewers that they shouldn't eat voice-overed cows and sheep?"

Nigel shrugged, uninterested. "I don't know. If you like, I'll call my uncle and ask him. He has acres of cows up north."

A smile streaked across Annabelle's face. "That would be super, thanks." The smile vanished as she turned back to Charlotte. "Maybe you could come up with a few more ideas for the clients so that they could choose. I'll help." She pulled a chair next to Charlotte's desk and wriggled into it comfortably. "Now, let's brainstorm. When I say fish-veg, what do you think of?"

Charlotte hesitated. "Hindus? South India?"

"What else?"

"Rivers? Fields? Hunter-gatherers?"

"Hunter-gatherers!" Annabelle pounced on this last desperate foray and wriggled her fingertips with anticipation. "Good! How about a series of ads showing Norsemen – really hunky, blond ones – spearing fish from a long boat? We could call it the Evolution of English Food, starting with the Vikings and leading up to our Fish-Veg Chain. One long continuous forward march of progress."

"I guess we would leave out the pillage and rape of the Anglo-Saxons along the way," Charlotte said.

"Obviously," Annabelle said, with a dismissive wave.

From across the room, Nigel interrupted. "I've just rung up Uncle Teddy. He's out shooting. My aunt said that his interest in cows extends only to his whether his steak is cooked through. Is that helpful?"

"Fantastically." Annabelle beamed at him.

"Good." Nigel returned to the day's *Telegraph*.

Annabelle turned back to Charlotte. "Well, that's settled. I have to run. Would you mind fleshing out our two main ideas? Just a few plots for each: settings, dialogue, jingles, that kind of thing. Won't take you two ticks."

Annabelle stood up and crossed over to her desk, where she retrieved a black cashmere cape draped across the back of her chair. With a sideways glance at Nigel, she hastened out of the office. Nigel, his phone nestled between his ear and shoulder, stood up as well. Charlotte listened to the end of his conversation.

"Elevenses with scones? Marvelous. See you in ten minutes." Replacing the phone handset into its cradle on his clean desk, he stretched in a leisurely manner before turning his pale eyes toward Charlotte.

"Well, I'm off. See you a bit later, uh, darling."

Charlotte gave him a perfunctory smile and turned toward her blank screen, whose cursor blinked expectantly. Was it possible that her education was really going to be sacrificed to the needs of a restaurant chain? Her father's worn volume of Wordsworth flashed before her: *Getting and spending, we lay waste our powers...We have given our hearts away.* Wasn't Wordsworth in love with someone called Annette? Episode One, Black Spotted Cow (Annette), she typed. Her phone rang.

"Yes?" said Charlotte, absentmindedly.

"Young man on the line for you, Charlotte," said Lucy, the agency's receptionist, adding with emphasis, "*American* man. *Not* a client, I wouldn't have thought."

Charlotte mustered her most professional tone. "Right, thanks. Put him through please."

There was a pause and a click. An energetic voice boomed into Charlotte's ear. "Charlotte? It's Patrick. I hope I'm not disturbing you? I called earlier but the receptionist said you were generally late on Mondays. She's quite a talker." Charlotte made a mental note to buy Cadbury chocolates to bribe Lucy into silence. Patrick continued. "Anyway, is there any chance you could be my date at some bankers' reception tonight? It's at some medieval guild hall – the Society of Ancient Something-or-Others. Weavers – no, that's wrong. Drapers? What's a draper, anyway? Whatever. It's at 8. Can you come?"

Charlotte hesitated, paralyzed by a sudden Olympiad of competing impulses. Leading the pack was the jolt of surprise at this unexpected invitation, and a vision of her new black chiffon dress. Next in line, plowing down the field with the easy assurance of past triumphs was her well-worn instinct of caution. Who was this American, anyway, who had already inserted his way into her life with such unaccustomed speed and nonchalance? The men she had known since childhood barely acknowledged her in the street unless quite literally pressed to the wall. She looked toward the last contestant of the race, making a heroic but doomed effort to compete: her pride. Was it simply too pathetic to be available at the last minute?

"Charlotte? Are you there?" Patrick's voice yanked Charlotte away from her internal race.

"Sorry. I'd love to join you," she said, watching her imaginary competitors collapse onto the track.

By the time Charlotte and Patrick reached the ancient half-timber walls of the Hall for the Society of Royal Drapers, the party was well under way, judging by the rosy, inebriated faces of the crowd. Charlotte, shivering in the thin fabric of her dress, scanned the dim hall for familiar faces, but found none among the groups huddled under the medieval tapestries and flags hung from the ceiling's wooden rafters. Outbursts of hilarity enlivened the clusters of guests at irregular intervals, and a small army of black-clad waiters circled the room, topping up champagne flutes. Patrick commandeered two glasses and handed one to Charlotte. He squared his shoulders beneath his navy blazer and grasped her elbow.

"Time to greet the troops and wave the Shorwell flag. Let's head that way." He gestured with his champagne flute toward a group of men huddled in front of an enormous marble mantlepiece.

"Do you know them?" Charlotte asked, but her question was lost in the din as Patrick steered them through the crowd. He glided smoothly through the chattering guests, and Charlotte struggled to keep pace in her strappy high-heeled sandals.

"Hello, boys," Patrick said, halting. Charlotte found herself being eased into a circle of four young men, all of whom seemed to stand taller upon Patrick's arrival. "Mark, James, Paul – and you know Horace already, of course."

Charlotte, who had been nodding to each one in turn, looked at Horace in surprise, a blush spreading across her cheek. "Oh, Horace! I didn't see you at first." Horace, matching Charlotte's surprise, took a rapid involuntary step backward, his eyes darting from her to Patrick and back again.

Patrick laughed at Horace's startled expression. "Oh, Charlotte and I are old friends by now," Patrick said, squeezing her shoulder. Charlotte felt her face flush and instinctively lifted her hands to her cheeks to hide the red blotches she knew were spreading across her pale skin. From earliest childhood, she had been mortified by her habit of blushing at the least provocation, feeling it as a betrayal of her body against her desire to present a coolly controlled exterior. "Um – new ones, I think," she said to both men. Horace, avoiding her eyes, said nothing, and Patrick didn't hear, his attention now directed to the rest of the party. Charlotte watched his eyes scan each cluster of chattering guests and settle on a group of glittering women at the far end of the room. He glanced at her.

"I'm off to drum up business," he said, striding away. Charlotte tracked Patrick's shining blond head as it moved across the shadowed hall.

From beside her, Horace coughed before leaning toward her ear to make himself heard above the noise of the room. "Have you heard from Piers since he reached New York?"

Charlotte hesitated before turning her eyes away from Patrick, who had eased his way into the group of young women. "He's left a few messages on my answering machine. He's mentioned poker games with someone called Jerry. Do you know him?"

"No," said Horace, rotating the champagne flute between his fingers. "The London office runs separately from New York. Our only contact is once a week, when we listen to our fearless leader deliver a pep talk over speaker phone." Horace attempted the broad vowels of an American accent. "Hey, guys! Great job on the stock picks! Keep it going!" Charlotte laughed, and Horace reverted to his own voice. "But actually, I've never seen the man, and I'm not sure I'd want to – he sounds a bit terrifying. In fairness, anyone would sound scary through the static of that phone. It's so bad, I think it may be bugged."

Charlotte tried to mimic Horace's American accent. "Great job, lads!"

"*Guys*, not lads," corrected Horace.

Giggling, Charlotte glanced across the room, where Patrick was now chatting with the tallest and most glittering of the women in his new group. Her head seemed to be thrown back in laughter, her chin pointed toward a tapestry of three golden crowns hung from the rafters above.

Horace leaned toward her again. "Are you going to be down in the country anytime soon?" he asked.

"Sorry?" Charlotte watched as Patrick leaned forward to light the tall woman's cigarette. "The country? Yes, no – I don't know." She thought she made out a flash of diamond as the woman waved her cigarette.

"We could go for a drink the next time you're there," Horace pursued.

Charlotte saw Patrick light the cigarette of another woman. Then, to her surprise, he glanced in her direction, as if expecting her to be watching him, waving her over. "Sorry, what? Would you excuse me?" Charlotte didn't wait for Horace's response as she crossed the room toward Patrick.

"Charlotte, meet Fiona," said Patrick, stepping back to admit Charlotte into their circle. Fiona extended a thin wrist, and Charlotte found herself momentarily blinded by a diamond bracelet, whose faceted stones caught the light of a chandelier as they shook hands.

"Fiona's just been telling me that she went to college – sorry, university – with your brother, but that he probably doesn't know her. I guess he was preoccupied with rowing?" Fiona flicked three shining red nails through her hair, beaming at Patrick. He continued. "Maybe it's different here in England, but back home we're able to row and still find time for good-looking girls. Charlotte, I'm sure if you asked Piers he would remember Fiona – sorry, what's your last name?"

"Deb-en-ham." Fiona pronounced each syllable very distinctly, as if throwing three small pebbles into the conversational space between them.

"Like the famous store," Patrick said. Fiona tilted her head in gracious condescension, and Charlotte glanced at Patrick in surprise. Piers wouldn't know the name of a shop if he were in it, she reflected. Fiona took another sip of champagne, as if toasting her family's good fortune.

"It was my grandfather's," she said, shrugging. "As a child, my sisters and I got to run up and down the escalators and try on the fur coats. It was such fun. But it was sold off when he died."

"That's a shame," Patrick said. "But maybe I can help your family have fun again. Shorwell Capital, my firm, is all about helping successful entrepreneurs diversify. I'd love to come tell your family about us. If you just tell them I'm a friend of Piers and Charlotte Cheetham, maybe they could spare a few minutes?" Patrick held a business card toward Fiona's diamond bracelet, holding her eyes until she secreted it in a fold of her dress. "Why don't you come meet some of the Shorwell guys?" Patrick placed a light hand on Fiona's shoulder and steered her across the room. Charlotte followed, landing again next to Horace. The level of champagne in his flute was unchanged since their last conversation, and its bubbles had gone flat.

Charlotte watched as Patrick introduced Fiona to the Shorwell men. In the din, their words were lost, but their motions were exaggerated, as if they were pantomiming a cocktail party. She shifted her weight back and forth on her heels to relieve an ache that had started to creep up her back. Next to her, Horace leaned toward her. His voice was inaudible against the room's noise.

"Sorry?"

He tried again, louder. "Can I drop you off at home? I think it's on my way." The ambient noise dipped for a moment and Horace's words rang out with unexpected volume. Charlotte felt a hand descend onto her shoulder. She turned sideways to see Patrick.

"I think I have the pleasure of getting Charlotte home tonight," said Patrick, keeping a grip on her shoulder as he turned toward the coat check. "Good night, all."

Horace retreated, and Patrick and Charlotte threaded their way through the hall, whose guests were starting to thin out. Outside in the chill air, Patrick hailed a cab and the two of them slid gratefully into its warm interior. Patrick yawned, leaned back against the seat cushions and shut his eyes and Charlotte, after a moment of surprise, turned her face toward the half-fogged window as the dark streets of the City slid past. The night's mist softened the edges of the office buildings into fuzziness, making them look like a stage set painted quickly in watercolor.

She glanced at Patrick, whose eyes remained lightly shut, and whose tanned, even features looked fresh and scrubbed, even after a night of drinking. A surge of pleasure, even triumph, burbled into her consciousness at the novelty of moving through the night streets with a man she barely knew – someone, at last, who was definitively outside the circumscribed circle of her university friends. Her thoughts drifted further from the man sitting next to her as she considered the evening's greatest pleasure: its narration the following day. Her colleague Annabelle would make a good audience, she decided. She started to formulate her script: *Oh, you know, just a typical City gathering – one of those ancient City venues – with a new friend. American, yes. Seems to run his office, and positively clung to my side during the party. He ran up to my flat for a very quick drink afterwards....* Her thoughts stalled as she considered whether to leave the after-party events ambiguous. Entirely absorbed in the possibilities of her story, Charlotte jumped when Patrick touched her arm. The taxi had stopped.

"Charlotte? Hello?"

Charlotte jumped. "Sorry! All that champagne, I guess."

"We're going to have to work on your drinking stamina. Anyway, that was fun. I'll call you." Leaning forward, he kissed Charlotte quickly on her cheek and sat back again. It took Charlotte a moment to realize that she was being dismissed. Fumbling for the internal handle of the door, she clattered onto the pavement, shivering as the night's chill enclosed her. Patrick had already retreated into the bubble of the warm taxi and Charlotte found herself calling out good night to its fading tail lights.

She entered her flat to the sound of her phone ringing. "Hello?" she gasped.

"Charlotte, it's Piers – I figured you'd be in."

"I'm just back, actually, from an evening with Patrick."

There was a pause on the other end of the phone and Charlotte heard mumbled male voices. Piers returned. "What? Sorry – just speaking to

Jerry about drinks later. Look, I was wondering, would you like to join me over here for a week or so? It would be fun to show you the city. And, to be honest, I was wondering whether you could help find me a place to live. I just don't have any time to visit apartments, and Shorwell won't keep putting me up in a hotel. I'd pay your ticket, and I'm sure you could stay with Mum's old friend Betsy – remember the one who married the American? What do you think?" Charlotte, surprised, said nothing and Piers continued. "Anyway, I've got to run. Just leave a message on my answering machine at work. It's 001 for America."

Piers hung up and left Charlotte standing in her flat, massaging the base of her back. Kicking off her shoes, she retrieved the keys that she'd left jangling in the door's keyhole. She considered Piers's offer. How hard could it be to find him a flat? A matter of a few hours, perhaps, and then she could wander around to all the places she'd heard about during her childhood when her parents had mentioned their honeymoon. It had sounded so romantic, the way they talked about getting off their ocean liner at New York Harbor and tried to find a taxi to take them to their small hotel. The smallest, dingiest room I'd ever seen, her mother always said, filled night and day with the sound of police sirens from the street below and the dishes clattering in the Chinese restaurant opposite.

A note in Annabelle's trademark violet ink greeted Charlotte when she arrived at her desk the next morning. In great, looping cursive, Annabelle had scrawled, *Client LOVES idea! Could you write two more scripts by the end of this week?* As Charlotte digested this message, Annabelle entered the office, crossing over to Charlotte with rapid steps, her grey cashmere stole floating behind her. She paused at Charlotte's desk.

"The client *loves* our idea of talking animals," Annabelle said, panting slightly. "They're keen to get started immediately. Could you track down some farmers who might let us film their animals? You'll have to traipse around with a tech crew once you find them – lots of mud and muck, but you're always wearing such sensible shoes, you should be fine." Annabelle rotated a leopard-skin stiletto as she spoke. "And it will be your account -congratulations! Oh – Nigel!" She swiveled on her heel toward Nigel, who had just wandered into the office with the affable expression of someone entering a cocktail party. In his brown suede shoes, corduroy trousers and blue wool cardigan, an early lunch at one of Mayfair's chic new gastronomical pubs seemed imminent.

Annabelle crossed the room, striking a pose above Nigel's desk and asking about his social engagements. Charlotte abandoned her effort to concentrate as her colleagues chatted. Their conversation wandered from a Bond Street gallery opening, to a new Thai restaurant (*amazing chandeliers*, enthused Annabelle), to a West End musical and finally to the Society of Drapers. Charlotte looked up, surprised. Annabelle and Nigel paused.

"Sorry – are we disturbing your work?" Nigel asked, turning a vague face toward her.

"I just thought I heard you mention the Society of Ancient Drapers. I was there last night, so it startled me."

"At the bankers' reception?" Nigel looked surprised, and his eyes narrowed, as if trying to bring Charlotte into focus. "I didn't see you. An old friend brought me along. City boys as far as the eye could see. Thankfully I dodged that bullet." He gave a short, pleased laugh.

"An American banker took me, a colleague of my brother's," she explained, enjoying this unprecedented degree of attention. "He's over here setting up an office."

"Well, well," said Annabelle, "Talk about burying the lede. Name? Age? Status?"

"Status?" Charlotte looked blank.

"Sta-tus," Annabelle repeated, as if to a slow child, "How many times have you seen him? Is he keen? Likely to play a role in the future?"

Charlotte smiled in what she hoped was a demure fashion, stalling for time. "Well, he certainly <u>seemed</u> keen," she said, hoping that her feigned shyness would be interpreted as a slew of romantic events rather than the reality of an abrupt dismissal from a taxi in the damp London night. Nigel and Annabelle continued to look at her, waiting for more information. When Charlotte remained silent, they returned to their previous conversation. Feeling her moment in the sun cloud over, Charlotte made an effort to regain their interest. "Sorry – Annabelle – I just wanted to let you know that I'll be taking the week at the end of the month off. Just in case you're setting up any appointments with the fish-veg client."

Annabelle swiveled toward Charlotte, an annoyed expression on her face. "If you just finish up a few new scripts, I'm sure we can work around it. Where are you headed?"

"Oh – just a quick jaunt to New York to see my brother. He's started up there at a new firm."

"Well, you're full of surprises this morning, aren't you?" She gave a short cackle like the cry of a toucan and rotated back toward Nigel's chair.

4

Bright Lights, Big City

Piers swore quietly as coffee from his paper cup dripped down his silk tie. Behind his seat on an American Airlines shuttle to Minneapolis, a little boy was throwing a tantrum, and one of his kicks had landed on the back of Piers's seat. Piers could hear the boy's mother gently scold the child, encouraging him to use his words. *Bloody hell*, thought Piers, *In England, a mum would just slap the little monster.* Dabbing at the coffee stains with a thin paper napkin, he opened the red folder that had landed on his desk in New York the day before. It held a glossy marketing presentation with Shorwell's logo splayed across its front: a red S trapped inside a tilting diamond. A paperclip held a sheet of notepaper to the presentation on which someone had written, in messy cursive, "Pre-Sales Briefing." Three bullet points followed: the location of the meeting; the name of his contact; and the meeting's objective: to sell Shorwell's pension product.

Piers turned to the presentation. It, too, was painfully thin, sketching out a brief history of Shorwell, the biographies of its key employees, and descriptions of its investment funds. Piers recalled the book-length presentations of his old bank, every word of which had been vetted by an invisible team of lawyers in Zurich. These lawyers – referred to dismissively by London as the seven dwarfs – had allowed no assertion to stand without inserting an asterisk directing the reader to a disclaimer at the end of the document. Despite the tiny font used for the disclaimers, their combined length had often stretched to more pages than the presentation itself. Piers had joked that the dwarfs would have required disclaimers for their own names.

Piers flipped to the page devoted to the investment fund he would be trying to sell at the meeting:

Our fund, designed for tax and volatility sensitive pen-
sion funds invests primarily, but not exclusively, in a
broad range of equities, bonds, and synthetic derivative
contracts that track the repo markets of western devel-
oped economies. It is designed to track a composite of
the S&P 500, MSCI and GMAB indexes while offering
a lower standard deviation of returns relative to these
indices.

Piers ran his eye over the spreadsheet that followed, showing the fund's historical returns, and a related graph which displayed a graceful curve rising smoothly upward. He looked across the aisle at Jed, the analyst who was accompanying him on the trip. Jed was considered the investment guru of Shorwell New York. Piers had seen him slouching around the office, a portly, fair man with bad posture, hooded eyes and untied shoes. Piers had attributed Jed's customary grimace to his undivided focus on the market and had so far steered clear of him. This wasn't difficult, as Jed rarely joined his colleagues' pizza lunches or post-work bar hopping, and kept his head buried in financial reports even while grazing the corridors. Piers had spoken to him for the first time the previous afternoon, when Jed had suddenly appeared at his cubicle for a five second pre-trip briefing. *Piece of cake – pension guys,* Jed had said by way of introduction, nodding in the direction of the folder on Piers's desk. *Just throw me any technical questions,* he'd added, shuffling away. Now, Piers saw, Jed was watching *Terminator 2*, the pupils under his heavy eyelids tracking Schwarzenegger on the seat-back's screen. Piers turned back to the presentation, and silently rehearsed a few sentences. He closed his eyes.

Two hours later, Piers and Jed entered a featureless conference room in downtown Minneapolis, where five men in pressed khaki pants and pale blue dress shirts were waiting for them. Piers tried to remember each man's name as he shook hands, but was quickly lost in the unvaried option of Bob or Rob. The youngest of the Bob-Robs handed them lukewarm coffee in Styrofoam cups.

The grayest of the men spoke. "We're glad to meet you, Piers, Jed. I'm Bob, the guy in charge of pension planning here. I'm responsible for making sure our guys keep getting paid once they stop working for us – and I better do a good job of it or those guys – and their <u>wives</u> – will come after me."

A muted chuckle circulated the room, and Piers smiled. He noticed that Jed's expression didn't vary from its habitual frown. The senior Bob continued. "As you know, it's getting tougher for us to fund our pension pool as our work force ages. While plain-vanilla investments have been okay in the past, we've decided, in consultation with our advisors, that we need to expand our investment horizons and take on a more diverse approach." He said the word diverse carefully, as if trying out a foreign language, repeating it as he continued. "A more *di-verse* approach that will boost returns in the future. We want to distinguish ourselves from the rest of the pension pack. We don't want to be another run-of-the-mill player." Bob's four colleagues nodded in agreement. "So," Bob continued, "we asked our New York pension consultants about firms focused on the pension fund market and Shorwell's name came up."

Piers took this as an invitation to begin. He smiled widely at the group, swiveling his head to make eye contact with every man in the room before coming to a rest at the most senior Bob. "Thank you, Bob. We are delighted to have this opportunity to meet you," he began. "Perhaps, in the interest of time, we should turn directly to a description of our main pension product." Piers had rehearsed this preamble, realizing on the airplane that he knew next to nothing about the history of Shorwell. He opened the presentation to its last page and held it up. "You can see, on this page, the product that was developed for investors such as yourselves. It is a bit complicated in its structure – relying on a chain of repo contracts whose yields are arbitraged by a series of hedge arrangements – but as you can see from the graph, it has generated steady returns with low tracking volatility for many years."

There was a long silence in the room, as all five men looked at the glossy page Piers held aloft. Senior Bob spoke first. "Now this looks really interesting, but I confess it has been a while since I took Econ up at U. of M. – and I know I speak for most of us when I say that if those classes didn't take place in my frat house, I may have missed this particular section." Another chuckle circulated the ranks. "So how about if you Wall Street whizzes just run us through what you mean by *synthetic derivative contracts that track the repo markets.*"

Piers smiled at Bob. "Absolutely. Excellent question. Perhaps this would be a good time to introduce the leader of our investment committee, Jed Miles, who will be delighted to answer all technical questions."

Jed, whose eyes had appeared all but closed until this moment, sat up and nodded to the senior Bob. For a few awkward seconds, he said nothing, and Piers felt his hands start to sweat. Then, without pleasantries, Jed began to speak. In a low monotone, he delivered a short lecture on the history of the creation of derivative contracts, their uses, and their growing popularity in the United States and internationally. Then, without pausing, he began to enumerate examples of derivatives and their synthetic variations.

Piers, who at first watched Jed attentively, started to steal glances at the rest of the audience, watching as the men's expressions progressed from mild attention, to bafflement, to boredom and, ultimately, defeat. Purposefully impervious or oblivious to the mood in the room – Piers wasn't sure which – Jed droned on, discussing the various indexes that had been developed to track these products. "GMAB is just one of many," he said, and Piers saw a look of desperation cross the table as Jed appeared poised to enumerate the many alternative indexes.

The most senior Bob capitulated. "Young man," he interjected, holding up both palms in Jed's direction, as if to block physically any further words. "A fine presentation. But I'm afraid we're out of time. Does anyone have questions?" A menacing light in the mild-mannered Bob's expression suggested that a positive response would be met by a demotion, at best. The men around the table barely drew breath in their desire to make no sound, and one corner of Jed's mouth edged upward before his eyelids once again sunk into his cheekbones. All the Bobs and Robs rose and filed past Piers and Jed, their lips compressed into tight smiles as they made their escape. Left alone, Piers looked at Jed, who again appeared to be near sleep.

"Thanks for the analytical support," Piers said.

"No problem," said Jed, not opening his eyes.

"Seems to have gone all right," Piers ventured.

"Oh, they'll bite," Jed said, lazily. "The more complicated the product, the better they like it. That way they can all point fingers at the next guy if it goes wrong."

"Right. Brilliant sales strategy." Piers hesitated. "I confess I still find the details a little baffling myself. Especially the points you made at the end. For instance, what's the GMAB index? I've never heard of it."

Jed eyes widened a fraction and glowed with atypical animation. "It's my own index," he said. "It stands for Give Me A Break. Our funds always beat it." Piers gave an uneasy laugh and glanced at Jed, waiting for him to retract or explain. Jed, his eyes once again almost closed, said nothing. Piers's eyes slid around the conference room before coming to rest on Jed's face. "Very funny. Do clients ever ask about it?"

Jed's eyes opened to give Piers a look of contempt. "Of course not. Is it different in the UK? Over here, we could show a graph of snowfall in Alaska and they wouldn't care as long as they get their promised returns." Piers felt Jed watching him as he pushed the hair out of his eyes with his left hand. Dropping his hand, he met Jed's eyes with a wan smile. "Got it," he said.

A week after the Minneapolis visit, Piers arrived at the office to find a white board mounted on the wall next to his desk. ASSET GATHERING: WHO WILL WIN? it screamed in red block letters across the top. A dotted line split the board in two: New York and London. The first entry in the New York column read Minneapolis, Piers/Jed, $100-$150m. Across from this entry were two in the London column: Birmingham, Patrick/Horace, £80m; Twickenham, Patrick/Horace, £30m. At the bottom of the board, someone had drawn an open treasure chest, out of which rose a nymph-like fairy with enormous breasts and a gold wand. Piers was staring at the fairy when Jed appeared, clutching a company's financial report.

Jed glanced at the white board. "I told you they'd bite. Looks like the back office got the news this morning. But Patrick's ahead, figuring in the exchange rate."

Piers felt his pulse accelerate. "Are results always public?"

"Oh sure," Jed said. "We're one big happy family, and we're all gunning for Dad to love us best – that's W. And we all want that treasure chest." He smirked at the sultry nymph with the wand. "There's a bonus for the guys who bring in the most by the end of the year. It's you and me against Patrick. You're the charm and I'm the wingman." Piers nodded as he took in Jed's words, encouraged by the simplicity and clarity of the game ahead. It was so straightforward, and so unlike the murky bureaucratic world he'd left in London. No more sucking up to useless bosses, he reflected; this was the real thing. Whoever rakes in the most wins. I can win this, no problem, he thought. He felt almost moved by the simplicity of the contest, flooded with anticipatory pleasure of his future success. He smiled at Jed, who was gazing at the white board, his fists deep in the pockets of his sloppy khakis.

"No problem." Piers said.

Jed's eyebrows rose a fraction. "Yeah, that's what Patrick's telling his guys right now," he said, turning away without a word. Piers's phone flashed. The LED display showed the extension of Angela, the personal assistant to Shorwell's CEO. Piers lifted the handset.

"W. will see you now," Angela said, and hung up.

Piers felt his good humor drain from his limbs. He had not yet met W., the founder of Shorwell Capital. According to office gossip, W. rarely came into the office, communicating instead via speakerphone from one of his homes in the Hamptons, Greenwich, or Palm Beach. No one seemed to know much, if anything, about the man who directed their firm. Office lore had it that he'd started out as a mail clerk on Wall Street, but this story, like all others related to W., was unsubstantiated. The initial W. supposedly stood for his rejected birthname, but no one knew what the discarded name was. Like a modern version of Rumpelstiltskin, Shorwell employees regularly bandied around possibilities when out drinking together, as if the truth would give them a leg up on their careers: Was it William? Wallace? Wade? Piers, fresh from a dutiful trip to the Metropolitan Museum of Art, had suggested Winslow, but this reference to Winslow Homer had met blank stares from his fellow traders, whose knowledge of art was limited to the beautiful young interns at Sotheby's they hoped to date. One of them snorted at Piers's remark. "Winslow, Win-slow, slow to win – I don't think so."

Glancing across the office, Piers drew himself up to his full height, flexed his biceps automatically and closed his eyes. *Come on, Piers,* he lectured himself, *it's just another field of play. You've won them all before. So he's American and rich and older, so what. He's just some guy further along in the game.* Opening his eyes, he strode down the corridor toward the double doors that led to W.'s office. He found Angela perched behind a blond wood desk that stretched almost the full width of the room, blocking the inner sanctum. Her dome of shellacked red hair was tipped over a spiral-bound desk calendar annotated with yellow Post-it notes. She looked up. Long dark eyelash extensions ringed her expressionless eyes, like a baroque gilt frame holding a blank canvas.

"Piers Cheetham," she said, her voice incurious. Piers nodded. Angela pressed a button on her phone's base and whispered into her handset. She replaced the handset and waved him in, looking down again at her calendar. Piers circled her desk and knocked on W.'s door. To his surprise, it was opened by Jed, who nodded at Piers and stepped aside. Piers blinked as his eyes adjusted to the light flooding in from the floor to ceiling windows. At the far end of the office, a lean, dark man sat behind a desk even larger than Angela's. His gelled, black hair was combed straight back from his tanned forehead, and he was grunting into a speakerphone as he drummed his fingers on the desk in front of him. Piers glanced around, searching for some clue to W.'s background. There was little to see. A blond leather sofa, a few matching chairs, and a wall of mahogany filing cabinets. Beige walls melted into a beige carpet. The only wall decoration was a framed oil painting of a lurid sunset glowering over the Manhattan skyline.

W.'s call finished and he stood up. "Goddamn lawyers," he said, crossing the length of the office toward Piers, a long arm extended like the rifle of a toy soldier. Piers saw that he was well over six feet, his height emphasized by the parallel lines of his crisp pinstripe shirt. He grasped Piers's hand. "Piers – our new London import. Welcome to New York. Please, sit down." He gestured to the sofa and sat down opposite them, moving his hand to his kneecap, which he started to massage methodically. There was a pause as all three men stared at the circular motion of his hand. "Too much squash. I had a court built out in the Hamptons and it's killing me." W. moved his hand upward toward his hamstring.

"You'll see the court when you come out for the summer party. Have you heard about it, Piers? It's an annual ritual. Big, big fun. Right, Jed?"

Jed nodded, echoing, "Big fun."

"Yup. It's a Shorwell tradition. You're gonna love it, Piers. I'm told you're already fitting in great. You're going to polish up our rough edges, right? Add some of that famous British charm?" Piers nodded uncertainly. W. continued. "I just know you and Jed are going to be a great team. You see out there, Piers?" W. twisted in his chair, unleashing a wave of ripples in his shirt as he gestured to the southeast window, through which the Empire State Building could be seen, its windows glinting in the sun. "How's that for a view? At Shorwell, it's going to be like that. You'll be looking straight up the whole time."

Piers stared at the iconic building and nodded, mesmerized, his pulse quickening. W. dropped his outstretched arm and turned back to the table. His manner became brisk. "As Jed already knows, Shorwell rewards individual merit. Your compensation is directly tied to the volume of business you generate. According to my lawyers, the most efficient way to do that is to turn you both into independent agents, so that your comp and bonus won't be net of all Shorwell's corporate over-head: insurance, legal, all that crap. Comprendo?" Piers and Jed nodded. W. jumped up and opened the office door. He leaned out the doorway.

"Angela? Would you mind bringing in the paperwork for Piers and Jed?"

In a moment, Angela was bending over the coffee table, the hem of her red wool miniskirt at eye level with the seated Piers and Jed. She placed a stack of documents in front of Piers, and a second stack in front of Jed. With moist red nails, she held out two Shorwell-logo ball point pens. "Just sign wherever you see a Post-it," Angela whispered, turning away.

Piers picked the pile of creamy white, watermarked pages and started to flip through them. Words popped out at him as he scanned the paragraphs of legalese: *independent contractor – relationship of parties – termination.* He looked over to Jed, who had begun to scrawl his name, an indecipherable clump of loops. He jumped as an unseen hand clapped down on his shoulder.

W.'s voice sounded from behind him. "It's just a lot of legal mumbo jumbo. You know lawyers – you worked for the Swiss, for God's sake.

I bet you signed a contract every time you ordered coffee." W. leaned down toward the back of Piers's head. Piers could feel W.'s breath on his neck, and he tried not to flinch. "Welcome to the Big Apple, Piers. Where the best and brightest win. Are you as excited as we are?" Piers nodded, his face still facing the stack of papers. W. squeezed his shoulder, leaving his hand there as he spoke. "You're going to be great, Piers. This is no cozy sinecure. This is the real deal, the real game." W. stood up and started to walk toward the door. "Sorry, guys, got to run. Just give the papers to Angela when you're done."

The two young men remained seated on the leather sofa. Jed quickly finished signing his name and leaned back, closing his eyes. Piers was still bent over the stack of papers, his ball-point pen poised next to the careful arrow that Angela had drawn on a yellow Post-it. The sofa's leather was slippery, and he had to keep yanking his body forward to read the print on the pages in front of him. He felt Jed watching him from under his hooded eyelids as he flipped through the document. One of the pages caught his thumb and a bubble of blood welled up. He rubbed it on his sock and continued to scan the text, one hand now clutching his ankle as the blood clotted. He paused when he spotted a section entitled *Hold Harmless. It read: The undersigned shall fully indemnify and hold harmless Shorwell Capital (and its officers, directors, employees and Affiliates) from and against any and all claims, demands, actions, settlements, losses and judgments arising out of or in connection with this Agreement, whether or not caused by negligence of Shorwell Capital or any other Indemnified Party, and whether or not the relevant claim has merit.*

Jed, whose eyes had fully opened at the sight of blood, leaned over Piers's shoulder to see what he was reading.

Piers sighed and turned to him. "Why do we have to sign all this?" Piers asked.

"Standard operating procedure. Welcome to the USA, land of the litigious. The good thing is, it means you're on your way to serious money. W. wouldn't fork over thousands of dollars to the lawyers to prepare all this crap unless he was certain of getting a return. Aren't you all fox hunters over there? You can get a whole pack of dogs when you're done here."

"You mean hounds?"

"Whatever. You can order a whole pack of wolves for all I care. Could you just sign so we can get out of here? Miss Post-it out there gives me the creeps."

Piers hesitated, considering Jed's impatient expression. It wouldn't take much, he knew, for that impatience to slide into irritation and contempt. He stared out at the Empire State Building, tilting his head up toward its metallic antenna, refracting the sun as it shot up into the cloudless blue sky. Gazing at it, he weighed Jed's disapproval against his misgivings in signing the unread contract. He glanced at Jed, who was staring at him, the slits of his eyes darkening into a gathering storm under his hooded eyelids. Piers swallowed hard. What the hell, he thought. In two minutes he had scrawled his name across five watermarked signature pages. He threw the ballpoint pen down, where it skittered across the glass table and fell off the far side. He didn't bother to pick it up. "Let's get out of here," he said to Jed, and walked out the door W. had left ajar.

Charlotte ran through Heathrow, her heart pounding. The loudspeaker had announced the final call for her flight to New York but she couldn't find the gate. Her feet were oddly heavy, barely moving despite her immense effort. Behind her, a people-moving cart kept honking, but Charlotte couldn't get out of the way. She was trying, trying – she waved her hands to signal her efforts, and banged her head. Opening her eyes, the airport vanished. She looked around, confused. Above her, a bright series of baseball pennants hung from the ceiling. Squashed against her cheek was a football-shaped cushion. She remembered where she was: Manhattan, lying in the narrow child's bed of Betsy's son, now twenty-six.

Images from the previous day repopulated her brain in a rush: the long and sleepless flight from Heathrow; the small village of Indian families, connecting from Delhi, who had engulfed her middle seat, the women's hennaed hands passing curries and restless children across her throughout the flight, their gold bangles clanging in her ears. Their voices had formed an unceasing wave of melodic speech that had flowed past Charlotte like a stream parting for a submerged rock. By the time she reached Manhattan via a bus that inched through city traffic, her exhaustion made her wonder whether the famed skyline was a mirage or reality.

The honking had not disappeared. Lifting the window shade next to her bed, she saw a truck trying to reverse down a one-way street. Behind it, a black Mercedes blocked its path. A red-headed woman in sunglasses leaned out the window of the Mercedes, yelling insults at the truck driver. Pedestrians wove between the truck and SUV without a second glance.

Charlotte let the window shade fall back into place, got up, and re-trieved a yellow envelope that had been thrust under the bedroom door. It held one piece of paper engraved with her hostess's initials. *Welcome, Charlotte. Hope you slept. Coffee in kitchen. Say hello to Piers. Betsy.* At this reminder of Piers, Charlotte dug out a notebook from her purse and walked down the hall to a sunny kitchen, where she found a wall-mounted phone. Still groggy, she found Piers's office number and dialed. After four rings, a woman picked up, her voice distracted.

"Shorwell, good morning."

"Hello. Piers Cheetham, please."

"Cheetham? Never heard of him. Hang on a sec, hon." Charlotte heard the woman muttering Chet-m, Chet-m and the sound of a key-board clicking in the background. Charlotte waited, eyeing the coffee pot across the kitchen counter. Steam puffed gently from its mouth, and Charlotte could smell the faintly acrid coffee. The receptionist's voice returned tinged with triumph. "Nope." she said, "No Chet-m in the phone registry."

Charlotte refocused on the phone. "Sorry? He must be there. It's C-H-E-E-"

The woman interrupted her. "*Two* Es?" She snorted. "Hang on." There was another long pause. Charlotte heard a muffled conversation on the other end of the phone. "Hey, Johnny – you running out? Grab me a coffee? Two sugars, extra creamer. And a jelly donut. Thanks, doll." She returned to Charlotte. "Sorry, miss, I still don't see him."

"It's C-H-E-E-T-H-A-"

47

"A? I didn't hear any A. All right, got it. CHEET-AM. CHEAT-HIM. Ha!" The joke seemed to revive her spirits. "Okay, hon, hang on, I'll transfer you over. Next time ask for extension 110."

There was a series of clicks and Piers's voice sailed through, sounding rushed. "Piers Cheetham."

"Oh Piers, finally. The gorgon at your front desk practically didn't let me through. She said you didn't exist."

"That's Doreen. She's an institution. We think she gets paid by how many calls she fends off. Can you come down to the office in an hour? I'll take you to lunch. Just grab a taxi. They're everywhere."

Piers put down the phone and stood up. From his corner cubicle, he could view the whole floor of Shorwell Capital New York. The open plan office on the fiftieth floor of a Midtown skyscraper was split into two rectangular sections: trading and research. The trading half of the floor held two long continuous rows of desks, with lines of young men permanently hunched over computers and phones, their faces tinted green by the glow of their stock market terminals. The sales and research side of the floor, where Piers sat, held rows of grey-walled cubicles in groups of four, like a series of village encampments. The cubicles had been erected with the intention of giving their inhabitants more privacy than the traders, but the structures' low sides and thin walls made a mockery of this idea. Piers had learned immediately that people retreated into one of the corner offices for any true privacy, and even then the offices' transparent walls ensured that one's every action was on view. The first and last time Piers had borrowed a corner office to make a phone call home, he was startled to see one of his cubicle-neighbors walk past him holding up a sign: "How's Mum in jolly olde England?"

Piers hadn't become Head Boy in boarding school without a shrewd facility for cultural adaptation, and by the end of day one he knew not to risk privacy again. Indeed, he now fell into his colleagues' habit of advertising publicly what only two months prior he would have considered private, making no effort to lower his voice whether in conversation with colleague, a potential date, or a pizza delivery man. It was thus with a sense of great ease that he finished speaking to his sister – loudly – and stood up to survey his new surroundings. As he stretched, he gazed down onto the desk of Jerry, whose cubicle backed up against his.

Jerry, as always, was hunched over a *Sports Illustrated*, engrossed by an article on baseball, his face entirely hidden by the New York Yankees cap he wore every day. Piers stared at the black curls escaping from his cap and waited for him to look up. Jerry only turned the page, entirely absorbed.

"Jerry? Jerry?"

Jerry grunted. Piers tried again. "Sorry to disturb your research."

"Ha ha," Jerry said, finally tilting back his cap, and leaving a short, fat finger to mark his place in the article.

"My sister has just landed in New York and will be here soon. Could you recommend a lunch place? I doubt she'll want to join Shorwell's trading floor for pizza. And could you give me the names of a few people who can show her some apartments? She's finding me one."

"Nice. Do sisters always do that kind of thing in London?"

"No, I just got lucky. And I paid her way."

"Got it." Jerry tilted his head back and scratched his neck as he considered Piers's question. "You could take her to the burger joint on the corner of 45th and 6th Ave. The one with the S&P ticker tape running along the bottom of the sports channel. The screens there are huge. You can see every muscle of Michael Jordan taking it to the rack. But I guess she might not be into basketball?"

"Not hugely, I wouldn't have thought."

Jerry missed Piers's note of irony, and nodded, reconsidering. "Well, girls like that Italian place on 47th. All those European dudes with their slicked-back hair swanning around with breadsticks and calling your date signorina. Girls always go for that crap. But the lasagna's not bad. And for an apartment, just tell her to walk into Midtown Mansions – ha, ha – on 58th. They'll set her up with someone to take her around." Jerry glanced back down at his magazine.

Piers took the hint. "Thanks, mate. I'll bring you back a breadstick."

"Very funny. But seriously, I could go for a take-out cannoli with extra whipped cream if you're offering." Jerry readjusted his cap and returned to his magazine, humming a little tune under his breath.

Pier's phone buzzed. It was Doreen, in reception. "There's a girl to see you, hon," said Doreen. "Should I send her back?"

Piers hesitated, briefly weighing the pros and cons of letting Charlotte meet his new colleagues. She might be impressed by his having a real office in a Manhattan skyscraper. And if wouldn't be unpleasant to show off his sister a bit. On the other hand, his cubicle, he had to admit, was no great shakes and he might be irritated by anyone who leered at her. His new Shorwell comrades were none too discreet, responding to the rare presence of women in the office with unveiled stares. Better not risk it on her first day. "No," he told Doreen, "I'll be right out."

Piers found Charlotte huddled in the corner of the reception's oversized black sofa, flipping through a magazine, and he could tell from her posture that she was exhausted. Piers paused, feeling a pang of guilt. *I should have picked her up directly from the airport*, he thought. Charlotte looked up. The skin under her eyes sagged with fatigue, and she was paler than in his memory.

"Piers!" she said, smiling.

Piers's guilt evaporated and he embraced his sister before leading her to the elevator and onto the street, where they joined the crowds of people disgorged by the steel and glass skyscrapers lining 6th Avenue. Piers took his sister's arm and steered her through the chaos, yanking her back to avoid a bike delivery man who careened across their path. "I know – it's a bit mad – this way," he said, turning into a side street and ushering her through a glass door. The noise of the street faded abruptly behind them, replaced by a scratched recording of Pavarotti singing Italian arias. At 12:30 p.m., the narrow trattoria was already bustling, and almost every narrow table was taken by diners shouting to make themselves heard. Charlotte eyes widened at the sight of two miniature poodles peeking out of brightly colored leather tote bags slung across the back of chairs.

Assessing them with an expert eye, the gelled-haired maître d' led them to a table in the very back of the room, positioned just next to the swinging door of the kitchen. Waiters flew in and out, fanning their table and providing glimpses of the chefs: four men in undershirts in a kitchen the size of a large closet, lobbing vegetables into a flotilla of sizzling skillets. Piers and Charlotte watched as one cook hurled a pan directly from the stove to the sink, missing the dishwasher's nose by two inches.

Charlotte plucked a bread stick from the glass vase centerpiece and looked at Piers, whose wide eyes were darting around the busy room. She leaned forward to make herself heard. "Piers, you're looking well. How are you liking it all so far?"

Piers turned to Charlotte, registering her appraising eye. "Don't worry, Char – it's the same old me. Don't look so worried. I'm having a grand time. You can't believe this city. It literally never, ever stops. I've been living in a hotel room near here and at any hour, it's like one long parade right below my window." Piers gesticulated with his breadstick as he spoke, his face alight with enthusiasm.

"And your job? Do you like your new colleagues?"

Piers shrugged, his eyes continuing to survey the room. Two women, both wearing poodles, squeezed into the table next to theirs. "They seem nice enough. Everyone has been super welcoming – I take it I'm seen as a kind of prized oddball. They keep taking me out to bars, and I've joined a gym used by some of the guys. And my first sales trip went well, I think. I went with our lead analyst, Jed, to help him with my expertise on the European markets and provide a little gloss on the sales process."

"They've hired you for your sophistication?" Charlotte was openly incredulous.

"Well, I'm not such a rube, my dear, though your faith in me is touching." Piers paused, and his eyes, laughing a moment before, lost some of their gleam. "The man who runs the firm is a bit odd, but he's not around a lot. I just met him, actually, for the first time today."

"Really? What's he like?" Charlotte leaned toward Piers, breadstick midair.

"Tall. He welcomed me, told me I'm doing great, and left me there with my colleague Jed to sign a stack of papers. Compliance stuff – standard operating procedure."

"Well, I'm sure you read it all first. Wasn't that what father used to say? *Never sign what you haven't read.*"

Piers gave a half-hearted laugh. "Of course, Char. Standard stuff. Anyway, let's talk about more important things. How about finding me a flat?"

Charlotte pulled out a notebook and started to take notes as Piers spoke: *10th -13th Street west of 6th Ave good, east until 4th Avenue less good, beyond 3rd Avenue NO (underlined); 80th-90th Street between Hudson River and Central Park okay (except 86th); nothing within three blocks of the UN; upper east side NO.* After ten minutes, she snapped shut her notebook and dropped her pen on the table. "Piers, while I don't doubt that you've got the whole city mapped after exactly eight weeks, if you want me to do this for you, you'll just have to trust my judgement."

Piers backed off. "Absolutely. I'm sure you'll be brilliant. Let's finish this delicious tiramisu and then we can go. And oh, remind me to ask the waiter for cannoli to go." Piers tucked his spoon into the gooey chocolate and rum dessert perched in a large wine goblet in front of his plate, rolling his eyes in bliss as he swallowed. "God, I <u>love</u> this town," he said, putting down his spoon and his credit card with two firm thumps.

The crowds had lessened by the time they left the restaurant, and they wandered back up Sixth Avenue in comfortable food-sated silence. As Piers vanished through the revolving doors of his building, Charlotte felt a moment of panic, but steadied herself with his parting advice. *Just look up to orient yourself, there's always some famous building you'll recognize.* Charlotte tilted her face to the sky and turned in a slow, dizzying circle. Her head whirled. In every direction, she saw flat expanses of mirrored glass glinting anonymously in the afternoon sun. She looked back down at the street. The only person not rushing by was a young woman applying lipstick while leaning against the wall of Piers's building. Charlotte watched her paint her full lips in bright red with deft, precise strokes, approaching when the woman was checking the results in a small hand mirror. "Sorry," Charlotte said, hesitating as the woman ignored her. "Could you tell me which way is north?"

The woman looked up from her mirror. "North?" Her red lips mouthed the word with distaste and her nose wrinkled. "I guess it depends which way you're facing," she said.

Charlotte soldiered on. "I mean, which way is uptown?"

The woman looked at her with scorn. "Oh, *uptown*. Yeah, sure, that way," she said, pointing her index finger toward Charlotte's right ear.

"Thanks," said Charlotte, but the woman had already returned to her mirror.

Three hours later, Charlotte stood in a dark stairwell, panting from the effort of climbing five flights of steps. She watched as Giancarlo, the real estate agent, emptied the contents of his jeans' pocket all over the stained grey carpet. At most twenty years old, and outfitted in Nike sneakers, a Nike zip jacket and a Nike baseball cap, Giancarlo had led Charlotte on a two-hour tour of cramped one-bedroom apartments while maintaining a stream of enthusiastic patter the whole time. Only Charlotte's hard-wired good manners enabled her to keep a straight face as Giancarlo sang the praises of each successive charmless location, pointing to their streaked windows with the enthusiasm of a medieval monk confronting the stained-glass windows of Chartres. Now on their tenth apartment, Charlotte trudged sullenly behind Giancarlo as he floated up five stories of an unlit stairwell in an apartment building on the Lower East Side. Rays of a setting sun filtered through the barred windows on each landing, and Charlotte tried to breathe through her mouth to avoid the faint smell of urine.

"It's so cool you're from England. The Queen, right? I gotta go there someday. I bet you've got some crazy great apartments over there. So let me tell you, I've saved the best for last. As the number one producing agent at Midtown Mansions – I mentioned that, right?" Charlotte nodded wearily. "I have a few special connections, and I hear about properties before other agents. This place just opened up, like minutes ago. I bet we're the first people to visit since the last guy moved out." Giancarlo finished spilling all the loose keys from his jeans and started testing them one at a time, letting the ones that didn't work fall onto the carpet while he continued his sales patter. "So this one is a five floor walk-up – no big deal for a young guy, right, unless he's planning to have kids soon, ha – in the heart of the East Village, absolutely the hippest spot in the whole city right now. Did you get a sense of the street life before we came in?"

Charlotte recalled a heavy, white-haired man sitting on the building's front steps, who had toasted them with an over-sized plastic mug as they entered. She nodded.

"So your brother – Paul, right ? – will think you're the coolest sister ever for finding this place. Got it!" Having found the right key at last, Giancarlo opened the door and stepped back to usher Charlotte in with a surprisingly graceful gesture. Charlotte blinked as her eyes adjusted to the small, dark room. Filtered light from the windows at one end dimly illuminated about half its narrow length; the rest was sunk in gloom. Giancarlo flicked a switch and Charlotte found herself in the center of a small circle created by a fluorescent light fixture overhead.

Giancarlo began his speech. "So this, obviously, is the living room, with a view of the street from the picture windows. There's a small kitchen over here with a fridge for take-out leftovers – I guess you've figured out that no one cooks around here, right, I mean even the chefs order in – and back here is the bedroom. I was told it has a great view of Tomkins Square Park."

Charlotte glanced at the tiny kitchen with its toy-sized stove, oven and sink, and dutifully followed Giancarlo back to the tiny bedroom. It was empty except for a rusted metal radiator which spat and hissed. She followed Giancarlo to the room's one window and tried to make out a spot of green through the grime on its glass. She saw only the windows of the apartments across the building's internal courtyard.

"I guess you have to kind of lean out for the park view," said Giancarlo. He hoisted up the bottom half of the window and thrust his head and shoulders through the open space. Charlotte watched him as he twisted his torso back and forth, his legs rising at an ever more precarious angle as he leaned forward. She was just wondering what she would do if he plummeted down toward the courtyard when she heard him exclaim, "I see it! Cool!" Agile as a cat, he jumped back lightly into the room, his jacket streaked in dirt. "I told you it had a park view," he said exultantly, "You can totally see the guys playing chess out there. Do you want to see it?"

"Um, no thanks," Charlotte said.

"No problem. So this property will get snapped up really fast. It's big, has a park view, a perfect location, and an incredible price – only $700."

"Per month?"

"Per week. Your brother would have to submit a letter of employment, first and last month's rent, and a security deposit pronto. What do you think?"

Charlotte looked around at the filthy window, the stained carpet and the blank walls. A thumbtack at eye level held a fragment of glossy paper from a ripped-down poster. Giancarlo stood next to her, also looking around the room, his face lit by enthusiasm. "It's lovely, Giancarlo, thanks. I just need to discuss it with my brother. Can I call you tomorrow?"

The young man sighed. "Sure, no problem, Charlene. But I can't guarantee it'll be here. This place is awesome. I have to warn you, it'll be snapped up."

"I understand," said Charlotte, "I'll run uptown now and talk to my brother about it. He'll call you first thing tomorrow morning."

Released, Charlotte ran down the five stories and ducked into the subway stop at the end of the street. When she emerged in Midtown twenty minutes later, people were flooding from office buildings onto the narrow sidewalk, and Charlotte found herself shuffling north on Fifth Avenue, encircled by a mass of pedestrians. Through their bobbing heads, she tried to see the shop windows, whose artful displays seemed more exciting than London's – the mannequins' dresses brighter and tighter, the mannequins themselves skinnier, their frozen expressions meaner. The crowd carried her to the entrance of Bergdorf Goodman, the glossiest of all the stores. On an impulse, she dodged left to push open its heavy glass door. Immediately, an orchestral arrangement of Madonna replaced the noise of the street, and she found herself facing a saleswoman in a white fur suit sitting behind a jewelry display counter. Charlotte walked past her and glided up two floors on the escalator. She found herself surrounded by an amphitheater of shoes arranged on raked metal shelves, all of them illuminated by hidden lights. A pair of crocodile-skin boots stood at the center, rising like an altar before her. Glancing around, Charlotte cautiously lifted a boot to read its handwritten price tag: $5000. Gasping, she replaced the boot, but not before catching the smirk of a plump waist-coated salesman rounding the corner.

Charlotte left the store, her mind disturbed, her emotions a muddle of envy and outrage. Brought up to be suspicious of sensory pleasure and material excess, New York's unabashed celebration of luxury both repelled and fascinated her. As a child, she had watched her mother greet leaking roofs, inadequate heating and threadbare sofas with cheerful nonchalance, tales of post-war rationing and Spanish sherry, bought in bulk. Charlotte hadn't been particularly bothered; as a child, she had dreamed away her young years in books, and at university, her intellectual friends had scorned money as an objective. Now, surrounded by the unending flow of sleek, post-work New Yorkers strutting up Fifth Avenue, Charlotte found her convictions falter. Would it be such a crime, she wondered, to pursue the money that funded every elegant outfit, and clung invisibly to every highlighted head of golden hair?

She found Piers by pre-arrangement on a bench near the Central Park zoo. He was deeply absorbed in a book, impervious to the flow of traffic generated by the pretzel and hot dog stands next to him. His long legs were sprawled out, and his briefcase lay casually open by his side. Only when Charlotte flung her purse on the slats of the bench did he look up, his startled expression turning to embarrassment as he stuffed the book, *Ten Steps to Success in Sales,* into his briefcase. Charlotte raised her eyebrows as its title flashed by. "Just something Jerry tossed over the cubicle wall – required reading for Shorwell guys," Piers said defensively, slamming shut the leather case.

Together, they meandered up the twisting path of the park, through the stone arch that marked the entrance to the children's zoo. The light was fading quickly, and diagonal shadows from the grand apartment buildings lining Fifth Avenue fell across their path. Charlotte shivered as she ran her eye over the silhouette of the buildings' roofline, feeling dwarfed by their bulk. Next to her, Piers was looking at the buildings as well, his blond curls resting on his starched shirt collar as he tilted his broad face upward. "It's fantastic here," Piers said. "Do you think mum and dad walked on this path on their honeymoon?"

Charlotte hesitated, oppressed by the mixture of sadness and discomfort she always felt when Piers mentioned their father. Piers seemed to see him as a kind of mythic superhero – an unseen champion who could be summoned at any moment to support Piers's activities, a kind of heavenly cheerleader. Charlotte, by contrast, remembered her father primarily during her darkest moments, when her uncertain future made her yearn for his support and guidance. Piers continued. "You know," he said, "I feel like being out here is what Dad would have wanted me to do. He liked risks, you know – Mum always said he struck out on his own after university. I know it sounds silly, but I feel like he's out there rooting me on. Maybe it's a good thing that my old firm sold out to the Swiss. It's led me here – the new world, the wild of the frontier." Piers gestured grandly to Fifth Avenue, whose soaring Art Deco apartment buildings gleamed through the barren trees.

"The frontier of Fifth Avenue – very daring. You're an absolute pioneer." Charlotte's voice dripped with sarcasm.

Piers only laughed. "You better believe it, Char. Come on, let's grab a taxi. The Shorwell guys are downtown."

Hailing a taxi on Fifth Avenue, they hurtled downtown in the darkening night. Charlotte found herself being ushered into a crowded bar in Tribeca, whose interior was lit only by a central circular bar, with liquor bottles gleaming like jewels on back-lit glass shelves. A velvet banquette, low mahogany tables and leather club chairs ringed the room's periphery. Piers pointed to a few of his colleagues and moved in their direction. Charlotte, trailing behind, could almost feel the enthusiasm which flowed from his buoyant stride; the noise, crowd, and even the crush at the bar all seemed to feed his excitement.

Piers found Charlotte a chair and introduced her to his colleagues before leaving to buy drinks. Turning to her right, Charlotte found an unshaven young man with wide-eyed, boyish features sipping a tumbler of scotch and staring at her.

"Charlotte, right? I'm Bill, one of Shorwell's traders. You're Piers's sister? You don't look like him."

"I know," Charlotte answered. "He got the height and blonder hair."

"Tough luck. I should know – I'm short and dark myself," answered Bill affably, swirling the scotch in his tumbler. "Most of the Shorwell guys are. Piers is our new outlier. I think that's why he got sent over. It's management's diversification push: tall people."

Charlotte laughed, warming to him. "I won't tell Piers. He thinks he was hired for his skills."

"Yeah, everyone thinks that for a while," said Bill. "Then they get smart and realize that skill is pretty irrelevant. It's more about sucking up and knowing the right people. But hey – Piers looks like a natural – he's already met Shorwell's number one marketer." He nodded in the direction of the bar.

Charlotte swiveled her head around to follow his gaze. She spotted Piers's profile across the bar, facing a tall woman whose bare arms were splotchy with the colors of the glowing liquor bottles above her. The woman's eyes were trained on Piers, whose normally reserved expression had relaxed as he returned her look. Charlotte watched as her brother leaned toward the woman's colorless face to say something, his lips inches from her cheek. The woman's mouth broke into a wide smile as she laughed, flicking her hair back behind her shoulder strap. Piers took a sip of his drink (he forgot mine, Charlotte thought, irritated) and his lips moved again, eliciting another look of delight. Piers's smile widened.

Charlotte looked away in disgust. Really, she thought, it was too awful to watch the people one knew best – their every emotion written as clearly across their faces as the subtitles of a foreign language film. It was embarrassing, almost prurient to know another person that well; people's desires were too raw to withstand such unwanted intimacy. She turned her head away from Piers and regarded the strangers around her, losing herself in speculating about their lives. When she glanced again at Piers, he was facing the bartender and the face of his companion, un-watched, had lost its animation and gone dark, like an actor off-stage. Then Piers turned back to her with fresh drinks and Charlotte watched, fascinated, as the woman's face transformed, re-animated. It was as if she'd flicked a light switch, Charlotte thought, torn between contempt and awe at her seamless performance.

Piers placed two tall glasses on the bar. Flamboyant sprigs of mint sprouted lushly from their mouths. "Here you are, Miranda – a fresh mojito. Cheers."

Piers lifted his own drink and took a large sip. Miranda smiled at him and started to transfer the bouquet of mint onto a cocktail napkin. As she removed each branch, she slowly tilted her head back and forth, and then rotated it in a slow circle. Mesmerized, Piers watched her blond hair flop against her neck and chin, suppressing a desire to reach out and stroke it. Miranda tilted her chin straight upward in his direction. Piers stood up straighter, trying to remember whether his morning shave had been thorough.

"I get the worst neckaches from being at my desk all day," she said, rotating her head in a clockwise direction. "I hold the phone between my ear and shoulder for hours as I take notes from clients. By the end of the day, my neck is just killing me. I bet I practically qualify for disability at this point."

Piers stared at Miranda's neck, a pale pink column rising smoothly above a gold chain resting on the points of her collarbones. Miranda started to circle her head in the opposite direction, keeping her eyes on Piers during its slow rotation. "The Shorwell clients keep me pretty busy. We're growing fast. When did you join?"

"A few months ago. I met Patrick, who was sent out to London. He recommended me. Do you know him?"

Miranda's eyes widened, and she hesitated. "Slightly. From Minnesota, right? Sort of mid-height and blond hair? I think we spoke once or twice. How's he doing out there, anyway?"

"From what I hear, he's like a duck to water," said Piers. "Picking up clients right and left and a huge social success. He was down at my mother's house a few months back. Everyone loved him."

"How nice," Miranda said, without enthusiasm.

Piers watched her smile fade and her eyes shift to a point beyond his right shoulder. He turned to see Charlotte forcing her way in their direction, her lips continuously mouthing "sorry" as she squeezed through the impervious drinkers.

Miranda took a sip of her mint-free mojito as she watched Charlotte's determined progress. "Woops. It looks like you're ignoring your date. Should I disappear?"

Piers looked bewildered. "My date?"

Charlotte reached Piers and glared at his mojito, ignoring Miranda as she turned to her brother. "Piers, I have been waiting *thirty* minutes for something to drink. I have learned all about your trading operations from someone called Bill, all about the Mets from someone called Jerry, and was about to be subjected to someone's story about his grandparents' trip to London,"

"That would be Phil," said Piers.

"Before, understandably, fleeing yet another monologue. Where's my drink?"

"Sorry, Char," Piers said, rumpling her hair. "I'll get on it. In the meantime, meet Miranda. She's one of Shorwell's marketers. She knows Patrick."

Piers turned away to engage the attention of the bartender while the two women exchanged very brief, very cold smiles. Miranda made no effort at subtlety as her eyes slid down the length of Charlotte, from her thick brown hair, frizzed by the heat of the room, down to her flat brown loafers. "I'm sorry," Miranda said. "I didn't know I was keeping Piers from his date."

Charlotte looked blank, before laughing. "His date? I'm not his date. I'm his sister."

From his post at the bar, Piers twisted his head around. "Oh, Charlotte wouldn't date me even if I weren't her brother. She likes foreigners. Didn't Patrick take you to a drinks party or something?" Piers returned to his futile effort to win the attention of the bartender, whose red beret was hunched over the tattooed forearm of a customer.

Miranda looked at Charlotte with more attention. "You know Patrick?" she asked, watching Charlotte carefully.

Charlotte, checking on the progress of her drink, missed the warning light in Miranda's eye. "Somewhat," she said.

"Somewhat? What does that mean?"

"Bloody hell," interrupted Piers, throwing up his hands in frustration. "It looks like you need a tattoo around here to get a drink." Miranda and Charlotte both turned toward the bartender, whose entire upper half was now resting on the bar counter as she displayed a tattoo on her neck.

Miranda leaned toward the bartender. "Excuse me!" she screamed. "When you're done with the tattoo show-and-tell, could we get a drink?" There was a momentary hush at the bar as everyone's head swiveled in Miranda's direction. Miranda smiled at the crowd and returned to her mojito. "Sometimes you just have to be a little forceful," she said to Piers. "It's an American thing." Utterly composed, Miranda started to pluck leaves from a piece of mint.

Charlotte stared at Miranda with a stunned expression before looking at Piers. He, too, was staring at Miranda, but with a look of utter awe and admiration. Charlotte registered Piers's look and turned away. "I'll get my own drink," she announced, pressing her way back through the crowd to her table. Miranda watched her stomp off.

"It doesn't look like I impressed your sister," she said to Piers.

"Oh, don't worry – she'll recover. We just don't tend to do things like that in England. That's quite a party trick."

Miranda gave a demure smile. She played with the corners of her cocktail napkin and arched her back slightly. Piers felt the bristles of hair on his arms stand up as he watched her. "I'm afraid I have to go meet a friend at a restaurant," Miranda said, frowning at her watch. "But you're welcome to join us."

Piers hesitated, briefly wrestling with his conscience. He sighed. "Thanks, but I can't abandon my sister. Can I call you?"

"Of course," said Miranda. "My number is in the office directory. I'm on floor forty-nine, the one just beneath yours." She took a last sip of her drink and slung a gold lamé purse over her shoulder. Leaning toward Piers, she brushed her cheek against his and turned toward the exit. Piers watched her narrow frame navigate its way to the door. *What a stunner*, he said to himself. *God, how I love New York.*

The rest of Charlotte's time in Manhattan passed quickly. Having convinced Piers to take the last of the apartments she had visited ("It has a park view!" she enthused), Charlotte turned toward exploring the city. Armed with a map and a half-dozen subway tokens, Charlotte chose stops at random, wandering through whichever neighborhood appeared when she emerged from underground's stairs. Wherever she went, the noise of the city never faltered, nor the crowds. People of all colors and ages, speaking languages she couldn't identify, were everywhere, filling the sidewalks, the cafes, the shops, and the buses, most of them stuck motionless in traffic. By the second day, she'd given up muttering "sorry" when someone bumped into her, and by the fourth day she was bumping into others without apology.

At first, Charlotte was appalled by the city's noise, dirt, and crowds. Channeling years of her mother's rants about American vulgarity – how her mother knew this was never quite clear – it was all too easy to find evidence for this prejudice. After a few days of wandering the streets, however, Charlotte found that her dismissal began to be tinged with other feelings: envy, curiosity and fascination. A traitorous, unwelcome thought started to push its way into her consciousness: New York was simply more fun than London. It was alive and colorful and direct, compact and immediate. Almost despite herself, Charlotte started to collect souvenirs: a tourist map of Ellis Island, a toy model of the Empire State Building. She went to the clothing stores in the West Village and bought a blue denim shirt with snap buttons and, then, egged on by the saleswoman, a pair of vintage cowboy boots. She went to the rooftop garden of the Metropolitan Museum of Art and took pictures of Central Park from every direction. She walked across the Brooklyn Bridge and into Wall Street, asking a Japanese couple to take her picture in front of the famed bull. And she began to flirt. Whereas once she had blushed when a man stared at her on the street, now she stared right back. Why not? she thought, experimenting with her bold, new response. She'd never see any of these people again anyway. It was as if her time in New York was off the record, without any of the social, familial or cultural consequences that reined in her behavior at home. For the first time in her life, she felt free. When, after ten days, she bought a box of expensive chocolates for her hostess, she found herself writing a note of great enthusiasm. *Dear Betsy,* she wrote, *Thank you so much for letting me stay here. I have had the most marvelous time. I love New York! Charlotte.*

5

Trading Partners

London did not seem like a dear old friend to Charlotte upon her return. After the crisp cold air of New York, London's damp, bone-chilling fog enveloped her like the embrace of an unwanted suitor. Everything and everyone looked grey: Heathrow's charmless concrete terminal, the grimy tube stuffed with moist, pushing passengers, and the poky semi-detached houses that lined London's ring roads. Even the larger Victorian houses on Lady Philippa's tree-lined street seemed to hunker down, stolid and uninviting, behind the spikes of their black iron fences. Letting herself into her basement flat, Charlotte was greeted by the damp mustiness of unheated rooms, flamboyantly desiccated house plants and a bathroom wall growing mold. Her effort to foist her jet-lagged misery onto her mother was foiled when her phone call reached a coolly impervious answering machine.

After twelve hours of dreamless, stunned sleep, Charlotte rose with a missionary's zeal to bring the pace of Manhattan to London. Wearing a trench coat plucked from a West Village boutique, she arrived at her office early and started to review the pile of papers that had mounted during her absence. Setting aside the organizational pleas ("employees are reminded <u>not</u> to drink the bottled water designated "Guest" in the office refrigerator"), she turned to the scripts she had written before leaving. She was deep into a vision of Annette-the-cow's exploits when she heard Annabelle's distinctive stiletto tap, augmented by a loud hum: Madonna's *Like a Virgin*. Charlotte looked up as Annabelle, swathed in her black cashmere cape, was settling herself onto the edge of Charlotte's desk. A scent of musk and jasmine wafted from her neck. Annabelle ran her eyes up and down Charlotte.

"Here bright and early, I see. Has your trip to America made you a workaholic? Mustn't let those nasty habits rub off." She glanced at Charlotte's new trench coat, whose camouflage fabric and shoulder epaulets already seemed defeated by the office's yellow damask curtains. "New coat? Very, um, functional."

Charlotte adopted a brisk tone. "Thanks. Could you bring me up to date with the fish/veg client? I thought a lot about various scenarios while in New York, and I think I've got some good new ideas."

Annabelle hesitated, twirling a section of blond hair with a manicured nail. "We did speak to the fish/veg people," she said after a moment, avoiding Charlotte's eyes. "Well, I spoke to them, actually. They wanted to move ahead immediately. So, as you were gone, I said I'd oversee filming the first script, the one on the farm. My shoes were utterly ruined by the mud. But it went brilliantly. They asked me to do the rest." Annabelle gave a fluttery little laugh. "Your name will still be on the account too, of course, in a supporting role."

Annabelle withdrew her finger from her piece of twisted hair, which bounced down to her shoulder like a sprung coil. Charlotte watched its oscillations as her cheeks start to burn. She picked up the pile of scripts on her desk and thrust them at Annabelle. "I expect you'll need these," she said.

"No worries," Annabelle answered. "I've already made copies. Oh, Nigel!"

Annabelle turned toward the main door of the office, through which Nigel was lugging a large canvas satchel stuffed with tennis rackets. Moving with impressive speed in her heels, Annabelle raced to help him.

Charlotte dropped the stack of scripts on the floor as her phone rang. "Yes?" said Charlotte, making no attempt to hide her irritation.

"Well, we're *not* in a good mood today, are we?" said Lucy in reception. "Your American is on the line."

There was a series of clicks, and Patrick's American accent shot into Charlotte's ear. "Charlotte – Patrick here. I know you're always busy," Charlotte could have sworn his voice held a shade of irony, "But do you want to have lunch today? I have something I want to ask you. There's a good Thai restaurant in Jewry Lane, near my office. I think it's called Hi-Thai. Women in mumus, that kind of thing, but good crispy duck."

"Um," Charlotte hesitated, surprised.

"Great. 12:30 okay? See you then."

Three hours later, Charlotte was trying to extricate a piece of meat from the deep-fried leg of a duck. An immaculately groomed waitress in a tight kimono dress had already replaced her chopsticks with a fork and knife, revealing a swell of pale breast as she bowed regretfully. The western utensils were no better however; even in death, the bird seemed unwilling to part with its flesh. Charlotte gave up and sat watching Patrick dissect his own bird with methodical efficiency.

"Delicious," he said, manipulating his chopsticks expertly. "It's great to see you, Charlotte. I hear you went to visit Piers in New York ? The guys out there told me. They love him. I knew they would." Patrick waved his chopsticks, as if brushing away a sentiment that was almost too obvious for comment. "I was wondering," continued Patrick, "if you know anyone else who might want to join our firm. I'm supposed to double our team here, and I've realized it's more efficient to find good people through contacts than through your local head hunters. I've already asked all the guys working for me, and I thought I'd ask you, too. And, I'll admit, it's nice to see you." He paused in his dissection of the duck and looked at her, chopsticks midair. "It gets sort of lonely here sometimes. And it's always dark. I mean, in Minnesota, growing up, it was freezing, but at least the sun came out sometimes."

Patrick lowered his chopsticks and returned to dissecting his duck. Charlotte considered his question as she watched him make two vertical stacks of duck and rice, their edges not touching. She shuffled through the people she knew from university. Most of them were by now ensconced in fields ranging from accountancy to art school, depending on their appetite for novelty and, crucially, their level of parental subsidy. None of Charlotte's friends had landed in the City, which was dismissed as a destination for people who were socially reactionary, intellectually thick, or both. When Piers had joined a bank, her friends had turned a blind eye, understanding it as an unfortunate necessity of her family's finances following her father's untimely death.

Now, for the first time, Charlotte questioned her friends' collective scorn. Patrick was by no means conventional and dull, she argued inwardly, and Horace was widely considered a math wizard. Maybe City jobs were more interesting and important than her friends realized. What did they know of them, anyway? She herself knew nothing except that the people holding them seemed to earn an awful lot – far more than the pittance she earned at the ad agency, being condescended to and ignored by Annabelle and Nigel. If people were earning such a lot of money, surely they were doing something worthwhile, weren't they? An image of Miranda, utterly self-assured as she screamed at the bartender, flashed through her mind as she wrestled internally. Perhaps, she thought, her assumption that badly paid work was morally worthy was all wrong. Perhaps it just meant that you were too stupid to complain or too lazy to move. On an impulse, she tilted her body forward across the table toward Patrick, who looked up from his duck leg, now stripped bare of flesh.

"Patrick, how about me?"

"You?" He looked up from his duck.

Charlotte colored but pressed on, fearful of reconsidering. "I mean for your office. How about me? I have a lot of experience in advertising and I'm sure you need to promote Shorwell here, don't you? And I've just finished with my main client at the ad agency."

Patrick's expression made a rapid transition from blank to amused to thoughtful. Charlotte held his eyes, reeling from her unconsidered suggestion.

"That's an idea," said Patrick, nodding his sleek blond head slowly. "You're right; we don't have anyone promoting our brand here yet." He hesitated, his face impassive, his mouth pensive and his eyes whirring with calculations. "You want to give Piers a run for his money? Show him that you're not just the little sister?"

Charlotte's poise broke. "No, that's not it at all – I just thought I could be useful."

Patrick interrupted her protests with a laugh. He waved his hand dismissively. "Just joking, Charlotte, don't get – what's the expression here – don't get your kickers in a twist?"

"Knickers," Charlotte muttered.

66

Patrick shrugged. "Right. Knickers. Jesus Christ, what a country. Anyway, sure, why not? I've got a big hiring budget and it's worth a try. You're a lot more fun than all the guys I work with. Did I mention that we're all guys, no girls? That won't bother you, will it?" Charlotte thought of Annabelle, perched at the edge her desk, explaining the defection of the fish/veg client to her. She shook her head.

Patrick glanced at his watch. As if on cue, the kimono-wrapped waitress materialized at their table, placing a bill beside Patrick with a deep bow. Glancing at the waitress but not the bill, Patrick handed over his credit card and rose from his seat, standing as he signed the receipt. He leaned forward to kiss Charlotte on the cheek.

"This will be fun, Charlotte. I'll leave any details on your answering machine, okay?"

Two weeks later, Charlotte found herself squashed against a grimy cement wall at Bank Street Tube, watching a stream of grey-faced City workers shuffle past her in the main concourse. Delivered by invisible escalators from every direction, like tributaries feeding a churning sea, Charlotte watched them thread their way through the packed hall before being ejected into the city streets, shoulders hunched under the sky's drizzle, feet obscured by the steam rising from subterranean boilers. In this roiling sea of humanity, she was the only fixed point.

She recalled the route she had memorized the night before when looking at the A-Z London map: East on Cheapside, south on Milk Street, through the Church graveyard and north on Bread Lane. Or was it north on Milk Lane, through the cloisters and south on Bread Street? Charlotte pulled a scrap of paper from her pocket on which she'd written down the address. The words had been blurred by the wet lining of her coat.

Twenty minutes later, having crossed and re-crossed both a grave-yard and cloisters, Charlotte reached her destination: a metal door with a hand-written sign saying Shorwell Capital taped to its front. Entering, Charlotte found a bare reception area with one desk, occupied by a young woman reading Tatler magazine. Charlotte pasted her lips into a polite half-smile as she waited to be acknowledged. The receptionist yawned and turned to the next page. *Bloody hell, you'd have been sacked at the ad agency*, Charlotte thought.

Pushing past her, Charlotte walked down a short hallway at the far end of the foyer and opened another door. The light shifted, and she paused to let her eyes adjust. In front of her, under patchy fluorescent lights, lay an open-plan, windowless office. Rows of identical metal desks covered in computers stretched out in front of her, separated by thickets of tangled black wires. A group of young men – perhaps twenty, she guessed – sat motionless, staring at the screens. Not one head turned at her entrance. Charlotte waited, and coughed politely, but the slight noise was lost in the unceasing burble of the two televisions suspended overheard. Charlotte glanced up and saw that they were tuned to competing financial news channels. She hovered at the doorway and started to dig her fingernails into the palms of her hands.

Years ago, she'd stood at another doorway in mounting panic. That one had led to a classroom in the Sussex primary school she'd joined following her family's move from London. At nine, she had been old enough to feel the full misery of being a new girl, but too young and unsophisticated to parlay her urban roots into social capital. The headmistress of the Sussex school had led her and her mother to the threshold of her new classroom, where she was meant to introduce herself to her new teacher. Instead, Charlotte had frozen at the doorway, paralyzed by the grid of desks and unknown girls in front of her. From behind her, she could hear her mother's foot tapping a rhythm of impatience into the linoleum floor. *Go on*, her mother had hissed, *you'll be fine.* Charlotte had taken one faltering step before feeling her gut contract, and the taste of vomit rise from her esophagus. She'd turned and dodged past her mother and headmistress, running headlong through the school hallways before bolting out the school's main exit. She'd made it far as the school's vegetable garden before retching into the corner of a rotting fence.

Charlotte's face flushed and she started to breathe more rapidly. Scanning the impervious men, she spotted a familiar profile at the far end of one of the rows. Relief swept through her. "Horace!" she cried.

All the heads in the room swiveled in her direction, but Charlotte looked only at Horace, whose head was the last to rotate, a vague expression on his face. After a moment, his features sharpened in surprise.

"Charlotte – what on earth?" Rising, he loped toward her, his feet expertly dodging the coiled wires that swam across the floor. One foot away from her, he came to an abrupt stop with his arm partly extended and his torso canted in her direction, as if uncertain whether the occasion demanded a social kiss, a handshake or no contact at all. His fingertips just missed Charlotte's forearm as he turned to face their mute audience. "Everyone – uh – this is Charlotte Cheetham. She's Piers's sister and she's," he paused, turning back toward Charlotte with a questioning look. "Sorry, you're–?"

"I'm here because Patrick hired me. Didn't he tell you?"

Horace's eyes widened in incredulity. "No. Sorry, I mean, not exactly." Horace turned again to his colleagues, speaking to the whole group. "Did Patrick happen to mention to any of you that he'd hired someone new?" There was no response, and Charlotte saw that most of the men had returned to their computer screens. Horace tried again. "Does anyone happen to know where Patrick is?"

A muted chuckle swept through the ranks, and a baby-faced red-haired man called out, "Does anyone *ever* know where Patrick is?"

Horace looked at Charlotte apologetically. "No worries, Charlotte, I'm sure we can get it all sorted – we're a start-up. Just a bit disorganized, as you can see. Mind the wires," he said, leading her to an unused desk at the back of the room. "Why don't you sit here for now? There's a phone, a fax machine and a computer, not yet a Reuters terminal I'm afraid." He paused, and asked delicately, "Will you be needing a Reuters terminal? I hadn't realized you were interested in the financial markets."

"I'm not," answered Charlotte. "Or not yet, anyway. Patrick has hired me to head up advertising for Shorwell London. I'll be publicizing your brand."

Charlotte watched Horace's eyes widen briefly. "Of course – our brand. Brilliant. I'll just leave you to settle in. There's a kitchen if you need a cup of tea. Oh, and any product documents you might need are over there." He nodded toward a line of filing cabinets against the wall.

As Horace retreated, Charlotte looked around, trying to maintain an unruffled expression despite the lurching feeling in her stomach. The momentary interest her arrival had aroused had evaporated, and the men's focus had returned to the flickering screens in front of them. From her desk in the corner, she could make out columns of numbers and graphs on their computers. She felt a surge of longing for the comfortable upholstered office she'd left behind in Mayfair.

Rising, she picked her way through the wires toward the file cabinets Horace had indicated. Opening a large metal drawer at random, she found rows of file folders labeled by industry: Oil, Paper, Metals, Trucking, Retail, Utilities: Electric and Water; Commodities (Coal). Her mind went numb. Why had she thought she wanted to do this? She opened another drawer, this one filled with files on companies: Marks and Spencer, British Telecom, Tate and Lyle. She opened a third drawer, half-filled with file folders labeled Client Presentations/Leads. Removing these, she returned to her new desk. She began to read:

Shorwell Capital is the leader in offering pension plans access to synthetic derivative contracts comprised of equities and asset-backed debt. Underlying assets to this product are investment-grade AAA/ Aaa (per S & P and Moody's), ensuring unusually low credit risk and volatility, while offering above average alpha and tax efficiency through leverage associated with Shorwell Capital's unique derivative structure.

Charlotte felt a flutter of desperation. Was this English? She had a sudden recollection of being asked to translate Flaubert in school. The exercise had been a humiliating disaster, as she'd scanned the passage for the simplest of words, before turning in a translation comprised mostly of startling homonyms. Now she took a similar tack, searching the paragraph for words she recognized. "Debt" was clear enough, although its association with "synthetic" – surely some kind of nasty material? – seemed odd. Charlotte continued to the next paragraph.

Shorwell Capital's industry-specific pension fund products enable asset class diversification that not only reduces standard deviation of returns relative to underlying market performance, but also adds significant additional alpha.

A colorful graph followed. Tangled red, blue and green lines angled up from the horizontal axis like a flock of tropical birds careening into a sky of statistics. Charlotte stared at the lines, beating back a whiff of panic. A polite cough interrupted her thoughts, and she looked up to see Horace, his dark brown eyes cautious. He deposited a stack of folders on her desk.

"I thought these might be useful. They're marketing presentations and client reports. I see you're reading one now. Can I help at all? Sometimes the language is a little obscure." He pulled a chair up to Charlotte's desk and sat down, pushing his dark hair away from his temples as he glanced at the page in front of her before turning in her direction. "That seems pretty clear. Are there any points I can explain?"

Charlotte paused. It was too embarrassing to ask for an explanation of every word, so she chose the picture instead, pointing to the cheerful lines fluttering across the graph. "Maybe you could just clarify this graph, if you wouldn't mind," she said. "The text seems straightforward enough."

"Absolutely," Horace said, with an encouraging smile. He folded his hands in his lap, paused to collect his thoughts, and began a short lecture on the definition of standard deviation. Charlotte trained her eyes on him and tried to follow his words. She nodded crisply whenever a word came up that she recognized – risk, return – noting that his face brightened each time she did so. She nodded more frequently, and Horace continued to talk. As he spoke, fewer and fewer of his words seemed to Charlotte connected to any recognizable meaning, and her tenuous understanding became wholly unmoored. She stopped listening. His eyes were what, she thought – brown? or perhaps hazel? If he'd just trim his hair, one could see them better, and perhaps if he got glasses that weren't so black and owlish. And was he blinking for emphasis, or was that repetitive twitch at the corner of his left eye a physical tic? It seemed to accelerate when she nodded a lot. It was sweet, she mused, her thoughts wandering further, that he seemed so keen on imparting all this information to her, though it was not particularly impressive that he'd failed to see that she wasn't following along at all. Her polite smile wavered. It was so like men, she reflected, to be completely impervious to the reception of their words. Charlotte's face clouded and Horace paused, his left eye giving a larger than usual twitch. He picked up a pen lying on Charlotte's desk.

"I know, that particular definition of standard deviation is a bit thorny. Maybe – if you'll just bear with me – I could just sketch out a few equations that would explain its arithmetic basis, and then you'll see why it's such a useful tool. It's really quite fascinating." He bent over Charlotte's desk and started to make a neat series of equations.

"I think you've got the x in the wrong place, Horace." There was a loud chuckle overhead, and Charlotte looked up to see Patrick's blue eyes shining down at them, his tanned face split by a wide grin.

"I do?" Horace squinted at his equation to discover his error. Finding none, he looked up and saw Patrick's look of hilarity. A faint pink flush spread from his neck to his face, and his left eye twitched badly. In one motion, he dropped his pen, shoved the hair out of his eyes and stood up.

Patrick beamed at him, unruffled. "Sorry to interrupt the math lesson – or do you say maths here?" continued Patrick, "but I wanted to give Charlotte the heads-up on a phone call I've scheduled for her with the head of marketing in New York." Patrick rested a hand on Charlotte's shoulder.

"Of course," muttered Horace. He edged backward, tripping over one of the wires coiled near Charlotte's desk.

"Thanks, Horace," Charlotte said, watching him disentangle the black wire. "That was fantastically helpful." Horace threw aside the cable with a violent gesture and returned to his desk.

Patrick looked down at Charlotte. "Good first day? You certainly brighten up the office. I brought you the name of the head of advertising in New York. She's sort of an all-purpose public relations point person for us. She's expecting your call." Patrick placed a yellow Post-it note on Charlotte's desk. "Just tell her you're heading up branding over here and she'll give you lots of good ideas."

Patrick turned away, and Charlotte watched as he approached the cluster of traders huddled in the center of the room. He circled behind their desks, chatting with each one briefly and exchanging jokes. His tanned hands were in constant motion, patting shoulders, slapping backs, and gesturing toward the glowing screens. Charlotte watched the reserved expression of the British men slacken and melt in the glow of Patrick's attention. Like the circular beam of a lighthouse, he illuminated all his colleagues in turn, flooding them in a brief and intense light before shifting his gaze inexorably to the next person. A low, happy hum filled the room while Patrick made his cheerful rounds. After fifteen minutes of animated chatter, Patrick threw a navy blazer over his tailored check shirt, waved a cheerful goodbye and exited the room. As though a light switch had flicked off, the happy burble ceased and the traders' faces resumed their glum contemplation of the flickering screens in front of them.

Charlotte looked at the Post-it Patrick had left. *Davina Dooly*, it read, followed by a New York phone number. Charlotte dialed.

"Yes?" barked a woman's voice.

"This is Charlotte Cheetham, from the London Shorwell office, calling for Davina Dooly, please."

"Davina here."

"Oh – good. Patrick told me to ring you. I'm heading up branding for the London office and he said you run the marketing department in New York and that we should discuss strategy." Charlotte paused, waiting for a response. None arrived. "So," Charlotte continued, "if this is a good moment, perhaps we could have a chat." Charlotte wasn't sure whether she heard static or an exaggerated sigh on the other end of the line.

"What would you like to know?"

Charlotte rolled her eyes. "Patrick said that we might be able to coordinate a marketing strategy for the brand. Perhaps if you could tell me how you're advertising yourself, I could use that as a starting point for the London office."

"Sure. The strategy is simple. We sell investment products to pension plans through consultants. So I get to know the consultants. First, I cold-call them, then I take them to lunch, and then I take them out to drinks after work, and listen to them complain about their wives, and then – well, I'm sure you can figure it out. Or are things done differently over there?"

Startled, Charlotte tried to adopt what she hoped was an insouciant and knowing tone. "Oh, it's the same everywhere, of course – ha ha – but actually I was just wondering whether you had any particular logos, or themes to your advertising campaigns?"

"Sure. All our print ads say *Shorwell: Invest with the Best*. I thought it up – very to the point. You can use that if you want."

"Very catchy. Over here, I might need something a bit more subtle," said Charlotte. There was dead silence on the phone. "Less boastful, perhaps."

"Less boastful?" Davina sounded dubious. "Like what?"

Charlotte scanned her mind for advertising slogans, mentally reviewing the posters that currently plastered the walls of London's tube stations. A glistening slab of raw meat advertised by Sainsbury's floated into her mind. "Perhaps something like, *Shorwell: A Bit More, for a Bit Less*."

Davina snorted. "A bit more for a bit less? You've got to be kidding. But whatever works. Frankly, it's the drinks that really matter anyway. Ask Patrick what your expense budget is. That's the key."

"Thanks, Davina, it's kind of you to –" Charlotte stopped short, as she heard a dial tone announcing that Davina had hung up.

Over the next weeks, Charlotte found herself fighting off waves of nausea as she grappled with her new job. Everything about it felt foreign and threatening: the office's half-hidden location, the brutally unadorned workspace, the largely mute herd of young men. Worst of all were the pages of turgid financial jargon through which she plowed each day, searching for fragments of meaning. Unwilling to risk another humiliating lecture from Horace, she bought a dictionary of financial terms in a bookstore and hid it in her desk drawer, furtively searching for definitions to help her decode the stock market reports and Shorwell presentations piled in front of her. After one particularly inscrutable report on the derivative markets, she began to compile a mental list of metaphors to describe her sensation. Was she a shipwreck survivor clinging to a raft on a churning ocean? An astronaut whose rocket ship had spun out of orbit? A baby dove who had imprinted upon a family of vultures?

Charlotte's internal panic made no mark upon the unchanging rhythms of the office. The young men around her remained politely impervious to her existence. Her daily entrance at 8:30 a.m. – making her the last of the employees to arrive – elicited no comment from their ranks, and Charlotte trained herself neither to offer nor expect pleasantries. Clutching her takeaway coffee, she simply nodded at the sleepy blond receptionist before plunging forward each morning, trying not to flinch at the aroma of cleaning fluids that hung over the under-ventilated office. Avoiding eye contact with anyone, she retreated to her desk and made a show of reading the financial section of the newspaper while she waited for the caffeine in her coffee to prod her brain into semi-consciousness.

Each day, she surreptitiously watched her colleagues to decode their behavior and discover clues to their personal lives. It was a futile exercise. Whereas her colleagues at the ad agency had blatantly treated the office as a decorous backdrop to their social lives, Shorwell London's employees appeared united in doing the opposite. No family photos, revealing knick-knacks or even Post-it lists dotted her colleagues' desks. Just heaps of paper, screens, and stacks of folders, all of it illuminated by the flickering fluorescent lights and dueling television pundits overhead.

Charlotte evolved from bewildered to bitter. Perhaps they have no personal lives at all, she thought. After all, they're here when I arrive and when I leave – maybe there *are* no families, girlfriends, or hobbies. She gazed at the stocky, baby-faced redhead who sat closest to the exit. His pale thick fingers sat immobile, like defrosting sausages, as he stared at his computer. Was he thinking about the flashing numbers in front of him, lost in some reverie? She shifted her gaze to his right, where his sallow, narrow-eyed neighbor pulled at a fraying shirt collar as he rifled through a stack of papers. No clue to him, either. At least Horace had the good grace to look alive, she thought, watching him stretch and shift his lanky frame as he typed on his computer.

Only Patrick was unchained to his desk. He wafted in and out of the office unpredictably, his unanticipated arrivals jolting his colleagues out of their individual circles of concentration or torpor. "Hello lads and lady!" Patrick would call out, his American accent lingering on the word "lady," as he bowed ironically in Charlotte's direction. At these moments, a murmur of acknowledgment rumbled through the room, and everyone sat up straighter. Even the crop-haired man by the toilets whose fingers seemed surgically attached to a coffee mug – the most stolid and taciturn of them all – would brighten, his eyes widening as he followed Patrick's entrance.

Within a few weeks, Charlotte thought of the office hours as two distinct entities: with-Patrick, and without-Patrick. From her desolate corner, monitoring Patrick's breezy entrances and exits, she was galled to realize that she tracked Patrick's presence just as intently as the rest of her colleagues. Too humble to imagine that he'd hired her out of romantic interest, she nonetheless tried to gauge his attentions toward her, trying to interpret whether his casual wave in her direction denoted any special affection, and parsing each of their short conversations for an indication of his favor. Focused entirely on interpreting Patrick's intentions, her own desires went unexamined, lost in the pleasure of his casually administered charm.

After her first month, it seemed to Charlotte that her appraisal of Patrick was her strongest reason to go to work. Her few efforts to call potential clients had yielded nothing, and she had read through all the Shorwell client presentations with neither interest nor understanding. With the occasional exception of fleeting smiles from Horace, her colleagues had consistently ignored her existence. By her fourth Friday, she arrived at her desk sunk in self-pity. Only this sad, decaying plant needs me, she thought morosely, as she poured a plastic beaker of water into a potted fern that someone had stuffed into the corner near her desk. The plant's delicate leaves were shriveled and brown, drooping toward the floor. Poor thing, it's as desperate for attention as I am, she thought, as she broke off the dead ends of its desiccated fronds.

A warm hand clamped down on her shoulder and made her jump. Whirling around, she found Patrick beaming down, his minty scent wafting around him. Charlotte dropped the fragments of fern.

"I've got something for you," Patrick announced. With a magician's dexterity, he produced a stiff envelope from the breast pocket of his navy blazer and waved it at her. "It's your first paycheck, just processed by New York. I thought I'd hand-deliver it." He waved the white rectangle back and forth in front of Charlotte's nose, creating a small breeze. She sneezed, and Patrick dropped the envelope onto her desk. Charlotte ran her index finger under its seal and pulled out the piece of paper inside. Her eyes widened and she inhaled sharply.

"Did I forget to tell you about the signing bonus? It's a Shorwell tradition. Welcome to the club, Charlotte. Our motto is: To those who have, comes more. Maybe Horace can translate that into Latin for us to make it respectable." He gave a mocking look at Horace's back, which looked suspiciously tense and still. Patrick's voice dropped, and his brilliant blue eyes looked at Charlotte intently. Even under the fluorescent lights, they were very clear, the color of an unsullied lake. She stared back at him, mesmerized. He spoke with quiet intensity, dropping his usual bantering tone. "I know the first weeks anywhere are tough, Charlotte. And these guys" – he gestured to the cluster of desks in the center of the room – "are not exactly court jesters. But we'll hit the road with client presentations, and you'll start having fun. OK?" Charlotte nodded, not taking her eyes from his face. "And in the meantime," he said, pointing at the paycheck, "you can spend that."

"Thanks," said Charlotte. "It's a lovely surprise. And I'm doing fine, really." She tried to smile. "It's just that no one seems to want to talk to me when I ring them. They don't know Shorwell, and they're not interested."

Patrick nodded. "Selling is tough. My favorite book is <u>How To Sell in Ten Easy Steps</u> – it's on my bedside table. Maybe you'd like to come over and read it sometime?" Charlotte blushed, wondering furiously whether Patrick was mocking or propositioning her. His laughing blue eyes were inscrutable. "What about your friends from college? I bet everyone you knew there is related to a potential client."

Patrick turned away and Charlotte sat down, staring at the paycheck in front of her. *Five thousand pounds sterling*, it read in italicized print. *Crikey*, Charlotte thought. I haven't even done anything yet. She stole a glance at her colleagues. Patrick was making his rounds, cracking jokes with the sallow-faced collar puller. Her thoughts raced: No wonder they're here all the time. If I'm getting this after four weeks, what are they earning? She took a breath and, for the first time, didn't flinch at the office's perennial odor of stale food and cleaning detergent. She looked up at the babbling television commentators with newfound interest. Perhaps they were onto something after all.

Charlotte tapped her fingers on the desk, seized by a new sense of purpose. Right, then, she thought. *Surely I met someone useful at Oxford.* She closed her eyes and called up an image of the long, wood-paneled hall in which she'd eaten stringy beef and overcooked beans for three years. Her pupils swiveled under her eyelids as she saw the rows of oil portraits: stern, white-haired men in black robes glaring down from their gold-framed posterity. *Not you,* she told them impatiently; *I need graduates who are alive.* She shifted her mind's eye to her neighbors at the long oak tables, trying to make out the identities of the fuzzy-featured undergraduates. She saw first her best friend, Henrietta, who now spent her days alternately threatening and cajoling students into learning Latin. She moved her inward gaze down the table to Adrian, Henrietta's boyfriend. *Wasn't his father the chief exec of some large company? Trucking? Paper?* Charlotte cursed herself for not having paid more attention. *Well, Henrietta would know.* She opened her eyes, and the dark hall vanished. She dialed Henrietta's phone number, left a long and cheerful message on her answering machine, and sat back to ponder other people. Closing her eyes again, she sank into a pleasant reverie of her university days.

When she got back to her dank basement flat that night, the red light of her answering machine was flashing. *Adrian said he'd be delighted to help,* Henrietta said, her voice marked by the overly enunciated consonants that signaled a long day of flogging Latin into the heads of bored teenagers. *I asked him just after inviting him for a home-cooked supper this Friday.* In rapid Latin, Henrietta relayed Adrian's phone number, adding that she hoped Charlotte's new position in finance hadn't yet rotted her brain.

Charlotte played the message four times over before translating Henrietta's words into what she hoped was Adrian's phone number. In another few minutes, Charlotte had explained her situation to Adrian and was thanking him for his offer to introduce her to his father.

"Not at all, Charlotte. I'm sure my father would be delighted to see you. I haven't heard, though, of Shorwell Capital. Is it new?"

"It's American. The London office just opened a year ago," Charlotte explained. "I'm doing their marketing. Piers, my brother, is working for them in New York."

"Two Cheethams! It's bound to do well. Anyway, I'm sure I'll come across it soon. I'm toiling away at the financial regulator's office checking up on all you Mammon worshipers. I've traded in my goal of being an actor for being a Member of Parliament instead. I can't say it seems much different. Anyway, I'll get back to you as soon as I speak to my father. He doesn't think much of me, but he adores Henrietta. I'll tell him you're her best friend."

Two days later, Adrian left a message for Charlotte saying that his father would be glad to meet her in Kent, where he managed a food manufacturing company. Elated, Charlotte threw herself into planning the trip, cobbling together a new sales presentation from old ones left in the filing cabinets; adding a page of her own jaunty prose detailing Shorwell's success in the United States; and briefing Patrick and Horace, who would be joining her. In less than a week she was standing at Charing Cross Station, rehearsing an introductory speech and watching the station's large departure board, whose numbers and letters filled the station with loud shuffling noises as they scrambled their way into brief moments of coherence: Dover, Rochester, Ashford. She shifted the weight of her heavy satchel as she watched the flickering board, mesmerized by the race of black and white letters in the cool morning light.

She pulled back the cuff of her navy suit to check the time on her wrist watch, a gleaming gold-rimmed oval purchased with the proceeds from her first paycheck. Its alligator leather band matched her new Italian shoes, whose gold buckles were now rubbing blisters into both feet. She scanned the crowds of morning commuters spilling out from the trains, a sea of grey suits, pastel shirts and tightly furled umbrellas. Turning her head back and forth, Charlotte spotted Patrick and Horace approach from opposite directions: Patrick stepping buoyantly from the south, his blond head thrown back; Horace loping hunch-shouldered from the north. They reached her simultaneously.

Patrick ran his eyes over her outfit and gave a low whistle of approval. "You look great, Charlotte. New suit? Very nice, don't you think, Horace?"

Horace grunted. The three boarded the train and settled themselves in seats that faced each other across a folding metal table. Charlotte began her daily labored reading of the *Financial Times* while Horace studied a Shorwell presentation. Patrick scanned a tabloid, quoting out loud from the most absurd of its articles, and openly appraising the bare-breasted model on page three.

One hour later, they disembarked at a small station lined by curlicued iron railings and hanging pots of red petunias. Rousing the sleeping driver of the station's one taxi, they drove through a series of hedge-lined roads before turning into a gravel driveway leading to a solid brick Victorian mansion. A neat young woman led them down a series of corridors to a cavernous, badly lit ballroom with heavy velvet curtains, a parquet floor and leaded glass French doors. Two enormous, unlit chandeliers hung from a coffered plaster ceiling. On a twenty-foot-long dining table, a silver tea tray lay waiting with a large plate of shortbread biscuits.

Looking around, Charlotte saw that every available surface – the grand marble mantelpiece, the oval conference table, even the top of the draped grand piano – held towers of cardboard boxes wrapped in cellophane, clustered together like apartment complexes.

Patrick approached a small side table and picked up a box from one of the stacks. "Whitely's Wheat Wafers," he read in a bemused voice. He picked up the next box. "Whitely's World Famous Lemon Biscuits."

Horace put down his sales presentation and walked toward another side table, leaning over to scan the boxes. He turned toward Charlotte in excitement. "Whitely's Whipped Chocolates!" he exclaimed. "Do you remember these? We used to get them as a treat."

"We loved those," answered Charlotte, with equal enthusiasm. "Although we liked the lemon cream ones even more. Did you get those?"

"I can't remember," said Horace, pulling at the cellophane. "Do you think we could open a box?"

"By all means, go ahead." A quiet, cultivated voice answered Horace from the far end of the room. They looked up and saw a short man in a formal dark suit poised at the entrance. His pale eyes swept across them as he moved forward, his hand outstretched. "I assume you're Charlotte? I am Charles Whitely, Adrian's father." His voice was surprisingly deep and resonant for a small man.

"Thank you for meeting us," Charlotte said, walking toward him to shake hands. The older man held hers for a long moment, looking at her intently. "Your father and I were in school together," he said, releasing her hand gently. Startled, Charlotte said nothing, staring at him mutely as she took in this information. Patrick stepped forward and Charlotte cursed herself for having missed her chance to deliver her introductory speech.

Patrick began. "Mr. Whitely, I'm Patrick Connolly, head of Shorwell London. And this is Horace Bloom, our senior analyst. Before we get started, may I offer you something? Just a small thank you for agreeing to see us today." Patrick dove into his briefcase and extracted a bright red baseball cap emblazoned with the Shorwell logo. He waved it back and forth, nearly displacing a nearby stack of cartons, before extending it to Mr. Whitely, who took it with two fingers and placed it upside down on the chair next to him.

"Too kind," the older man murmured. "Tea?" Mr. Whitely started to fill the bone china teacups with practiced assurance, and the aroma of Earl Grey spread across the table. Patrick handed out the glossy copies of the Shorwell presentation and Mr. Whitely, distributing the steaming cups, nodded to him to start. Patrick cleared his throat and began to outline the history of the firm and its success in the U.S. market. He was just starting on Shorwell's international ambitions when Mr. Whitely, now finished with his tea duties, glanced down at the presentation for the first time.

"Forgive me for interrupting," he said, pouring a few drops of milk into his cup. "But I don't understand why you are selling your products here, given that you're doing so brilliantly at home." Charlotte, hearing the softest note of irony, glanced in his direction, but Mr. Whitely's expression was obscured by his cloudy glasses, steamed over by the tea.

Patrick answered, his voice scrupulously polite. "As you know, sir, the UK has many pension plans that are underfunded, and the government is unlikely to step in, as it might do in France or Germany. We thought the British – the most forward-thinking of their managers, at any rate – would want to diversify their investments to make up the gap."

"I see. You are hoping to save us," Mr. Whitely said, his tone dry. He flipped through to the next page of the presentation, where a graph showed the steadily rising returns of the Shorwell funds. He shifted his body toward Horace. "Are you the analyst who chooses the investments?"

Horace, whose eyes had been glued to his own presentation, lifted his head for the first time. "Just one of them. We have a team here and one in America."

Patrick smiled across the table and slapped Horace on the back. "Horace is just exhibiting your famous English modesty. He's really our secret weapon, our resident rocket scientist. He can tell you anything about any of our investments or strategies."

Mr. Whitely nodded and started to ask Horace a series of questions. Horace took careful notes in the margins of his presentation as he listened, angling his head toward Mr. Whitely's soft voice. Then, pausing to collect his thoughts, he answered each question with a barrage of technical language. His voice, at first hesitant, became more fluid and animated as he spoke, and he began to wave his pen midair, as though conducting his own remarks. For twenty minutes, Mr. Whitely and Horace talked while Patrick and Charlotte listened. Finally, closing the presentation, the older man turned the conversation back to Patrick.

"So, Patrick Connolly? Your family is Irish?"

"Yes, sir. They left during the famine."

Mr. Whitely nodded. "Terrible times. Happily, you're back under better circumstances. Your rocket scientist here is very convincing," he continued, gesturing to Horace, whose face had resumed a guarded expression. "But I will have to consult with our Board of Directors. All investment decisions are subject to their approval."

"Of course. We look forward to being in touch."

Mr. Whitely rose and the three young people shot up from their seats. He shook each one's hand, lingering an extra moment with Charlotte. "Please, help yourselves," he said, gesturing toward the biscuit boxes. The door shut behind him with a quiet click.

Patrick spoke first. "Well done, troops! I told you your university

friends would help you, Charlotte." Charlotte beamed as she luxuri-
ated in his praise. Glancing around the grand, decorated room, she
felt an absurd desire to dance. Raising her arms, she turned a clumsy
half-pirouette toward Patrick, immediately feeling like an idiot as her
narrow skirt constrained her movement and the buckles on her new
shoes dug into her feet. She collapsed into a sofa and leaned over to rub
the blisters through her stockings, blushing as she knelt over. She felt
Patrick's arm land across her back. His voice sounded in her ear.

"Great job getting the meeting, Charlotte. Who could resist the
lovely Charlotte Cheetham?"

Charlotte looked up Patrick, her hand still holding her foot, her
hazel eyes bright under her dark hair. She scanned his face for irony as
her mind raced. Was he just pleased about the new prospective client, or
did he actually admire her? Could she risk letting herself fall into a real
infatuation? Was this, finally, a kind of declaration? She registered the
weight of his arm resting across her back but was too immersed in her
own calculations to enjoy it. She let go of her foot and sat up.

"Thanks," she said, cursing herself for being so tongue-tied.

Patrick, seemingly relaxed, didn't register her answer. He was
looking at the back of Horace, who had crossed the room to a new
stack of biscuit boxes. "Horace? Do you think it went well?" Horace
kept his face averted from the two of them and shrugged, moving
further away to the immense marble mantelpiece, where even more
boxes were piled.

Turning slowly, Horace glanced at Charlotte. His hands were occupied in prying open a brown and orange striped box which he held
up to Charlotte. "Cocoa Crumbles – I loved these. Remember them,
Charlotte? Anyway," he said, still not looking at Patrick, "I think it was
all right. He's a clever chap. Hard to say, really." He turned back to the
mantelpiece.

A silence fell over the group. Patrick withdrew his arm from
Charlotte and returned to the table to collect the presentations. Patrick
and Horace left the room, while Charlotte lingered, casting a last look at
the beautiful room, and the expanse of green lawn stretching out beyond
the leaded glass French doors.

Her thoughts were still on Patrick when she left the room and ran into Horace. He had stopped in a narrow hallway and was looking at a painting, his dark hair practically brushing the canvas as he leaned forward. Charlotte followed his gaze, squinting in the dim light and balancing on her toes to see clearly. The painting showed an eighteenth-century frigate in a storm whose sails listed at an impossible angle. A spear of lightening shot down from the heavens, piercing the very top of its mast. Horace glanced down at Charlotte, and she saw his left eye twitch.

"Look at this, Charlotte – pretty grim. It's hard to believe England's wealth was created by these flimsy boats sailing around the world. I made a model of one like this when I was about twelve for a school project. It took me a month to get the rigging right."

Charlotte stared at the painting, making out a few tiny figures clinging to the tilting mast, waving a Union Jack. She laughed. "I know – and here we are, selling American investments for a living. Not a very impressive following act. What would those brave sailors think?"

"Probably that we're bloody lucky not to be risking our necks. And that Whitely's Crumby Crumbles are a far sight better than scurvy and rotten fish. Have one?"

Charlotte took a biscuit from the box Horace offered. "Delicious," she said, turning away, and making sure not to drop any crumbs on the carpet.

When Charlotte opened the door to Shorwell's office the following morning, she was startled to see several heads swivel in her direction. Their synchronized movement was brief and wordless, to be sure, but it was nonetheless a sign that her presence had been noted. After stopping short in surprise, she nodded back with an equally brief and mute gesture, trying to suppress the small smile which crept across her face. She had arrived.

Reaching her desk, she found the light on her phone blinking. She dialed into her voicemail and heard Piers's familiar jesting voice pour through her handset. *Congratulations, Charlotte. I hear you've started to arrange sales calls on the parents of your university friends. Clever of Patrick to hire you, I must admit.* Charlotte wondered how Piers had already learned about her meeting and made a mental note to ask Patrick whether he was reporting on her activities. She refocused on her brother's voice: *...and I am having a brilliant time over here while you become the darling of the London office. Have you heard about our big win with the Minnesota utility pension fund? $80 million dollars, and that brings us up to $450 million since I reached New York. If I'm not mistaken, I think we're ahead of your boy Patrick?* Charlotte heard Piers's familiar happy chuckle. *Anyway, Char, give my love to mother when you see her next, will you? I'll try to make a flying visit in the next few weeks if I can tear myself away from the Big Apple. We're pretty busy with sales, and I'm going to the Hamptons for the weekend with some buddies. There's a big party at W.'s house. Everyone says his parties are amazing. Cheerio!*

Piers's voice stopped, replaced by a long dial tone. Charlotte put down her handset. She felt her earlier sensation of well-being eke away. She frowned. Just as she was finally making progress at Shorwell, Piers had to trumpet his lead. She tried to think of what she'd heard about the Hamptons but drew a blank. Wasn't it some sort of beach community? She envisioned the houses her family had rented during a series of soggy holidays in Cornwall, shivering in recollection of their bare, chilly rooms, always gritty from sand tracked in from the sodden beach. It was hard to imagine why a holiday house along the coast would be so wonderful.

Under the flickering fluorescent lights of New Jersey's SEC headquarters, investigator Joseph O'Brien looked at the free calendar sent to him by the National Board of Tourism. *Destinations 1990!* was splashed across its cover in red letters. With short fingers stained by tobacco, O'Brien rifled through the months, registering the predictable images of Yellowstone, the Golden Gate Bridge, and autumnal Vermont, followed by the Grand Canyon, the Tetons and Yosemite. At July he paused, recognizing the Montauk Lighthouse on the tip of Long Island. *The Hamptons, America's best-loved playground*, read the caption. O'Brien's habitual look of irritation deepened as he dropped the calendar into the wire trash can next to his desk. *America's best-loved playground if you're a crook and a billionaire,* he thought.

Sitting down at his desk, he started to sort through a stack of manila folders stuffed with papers and yellowing newspaper articles. Each folder was labelled with the name of a hedge fund and represented an ongoing investigation for possible fraud. O'Brien had started stuffing these folders with documents five years ago when, riding high after three years of tracking drug dealers for the U.S. Attorney's office, he'd won the hedge fund beat in the financial fraud division of the SEC. That he knew nothing about finance didn't worry him; in his experience on the drug beat, criminals were a dime a dozen. His bravado had quickly faded. First of all, there was a thicket of financial jargon that O'Brien didn't understand and about which he was too proud to seek help. Second, the funds were protected by book-length legal documents which numbed him with boredom. Finally, there was the frustration of gathering concrete information; between the secure computer networks and encrypted phone lines, it simply wasn't a fair fight, in his view. For five years, he toiled away, opening investigations into any hedge fund that offered a crumb of wrongdoing, and filling folders with newspapers clippings and the testimony of disgruntled employees whose whistle blower information always proved impossible to verify.

It had all led nowhere. After the first few years, O'Brien lost his jaunty swagger and avoided making eye contact with the colleagues he passed in the badly lit corridors. His humiliation and anger grew daily. What had started as a mild interest into financial fraud evolved into a full-blown obsession, fueled by O'Brien's growing realization of the huge fortunes being made by this unregulatable industry. The sums taken home by the players literally took his breath away, at first with awe, and then with fury: $200m, $500m, $1 billion? Denied any tangible prize, and stuck on a government salary, his envy morphed into moral outrage, and he became convinced that the whole business was crooked. Exactly how, he wasn't yet sure.

6

Trouble in the Hamptons

Piers pulled a Mets baseball cap over his eyes to shield them from the sun that beat down on the long white beach. He scanned the flat expanse of sea stretching before him, massaging his right shoulder, sore from his new obsession with squash. Digging his long pale toes into the sand, he sighed in pleasure as its warmth enveloped his feet. Now *this* was a beach, he exulted, almost overwhelmed by the purity of its impeccable manifestation. This was nothing like the dripping, ragged offerings of the Cornwall coast in England, where the rain forever hovered, and ruined one's laboriously constructed sandcastles. He scoffed as he remembered himself as a child, damp and bedraggled as he and Charlotte had hauled wet sand toward their sad little fort. Pathetic, he thought, dismissing the memory without nostalgia. Inhaling the salt air, he swelled with pride, as though he himself had reached down from the heavens and personally created every grain of sand.

The weeks since Charlotte's visit had gone well. He and Jed had begun to travel every few days to meet pension fund managers across the country, and Piers had become expert in rushing through La Guardia airport, coffee cup in hand, just as the flight gate was closing. After a few hours in the air, he and Jed would land in a midsized American city where interchangeable groups of men in blue dress shirts and khaki pants waited in oak-paneled conference rooms of new-built office buildings. With carefully modulated deference and charm, Piers would introduce Shorwell Capital before Jed launched into his lecture.

At first, Piers had been puzzled by how attentively these earnest, sober people listened to Jed's interminable monologues, but eventually he realized that their attention was not intellectual but emotional; all their pension funds lagged far behind the requirements of their aging employees, and all were desperate to find a miraculous solution to make up the gap. To them, Piers realized, he and Jed were not salesmen but potential saviors, whose magic wand might dig them out of their holes. When Jed droned on about the use of contracts or synthetics or the various indexes – occasionally inventing a few on the spot, Piers noted – the listeners would nod silently as if confirming an incantation, and Piers was reminded of Church sermons from his boyhood, half expecting someone to murmur And Also with You in response to Jed's most inscrutable statements and optimistic projections.

The columns on the white board had grown longer. The Piers/ Jed team ("Pierced," according to an anonymous whiteboard jokester) now included Des Moines, Ann Arbor, Portland and Austin, and had commitments totaling $400 million. On the London side, Patrick and Horace ("Porous Hat-trick") had made gains as well, winning mandates in Birmingham, Leeds and Norfolk. Piers, invigorated by the rivalry, had thrown himself daily into researching and cold-calling potential clients. While the name of Shorwell Capital was unknown, Piers soon realized that the people he called were sufficiently intrigued by his British accent to give him enough time for an initial sales pitch. Never one to squander an advantage, Piers had reined in the various American expressions that had begun to creep into his speech, reverting to a kind of Beatrix Potter parody. "Hullo!" he would bellow into the phone, "Piers Cheetham here, *terribly* sorry to bother you." His Anglicized bluster rolled down the telephone wires in all directions, from Washington State to Florida, from Maine to Hawaii. More often than not, these unabashed recitations of top-ten British expressions led to a hesitant invitation, if only from the listener's curiosity to meet a person who could toss off "Right-Ho!" with such cheerful nonchalance.

Piers turned his head toward the dunes, where Jed had established a festive encampment of beach towels, a large umbrella, and collapsible fabric chairs. All were striped in a jaunty blue and red ("Decorator," Jed had muttered). From the center of this striped nest, Jed sat drinking a beer, his eyes shut against the sun. Drinking beer on the beach was his weekend ritual, he had told Piers that morning as he drove them in his red BMW convertible past the faded strip malls of Long Island. With atypical expansiveness, he'd listed his top three activities for the weekend: drinking beer on the beach; going out to drinks at a restaurant on the beach; and watching the gorgeous girls on the beach. We'll just drop our stuff off at my cottage first, he said. Piers was startled when Jed turned into a long driveway lined by neatly pruned fruit trees ("Apple?" Jed had said uncertainly, in response to Piers's question, before adding "Gardener"). They reached Jed's "cottage," a sizable shingled house with a pool house in back.

"Nice," Piers said.

"Wait 'til you see W.'s," Jed said. "He lives *south* of the highway."

Piers wandered up the beach to Jed, who nodded wordlessly at him and gestured toward the cooler. Piers helped himself to a beer and sat down in one of the beach chairs. He picked up the front section of the *Wall Street Journal* and began to skim the headlines. Jed sat silent and unmoving, his eyes closed. After twenty minutes, Piers let the paper flutter down into a heap on the hot sand and leaned back, his mind numbed by the heat. He closed his eyes and started to drift off, lulled by the repetitive splash of the waves.

"So tonight." Jed's voice cut through his haze. Piers's eyes whipped open. "So tonight," Jed repeated, "Everyone from Shorwell will be there. W. throws the Labor Day blow-out every year. It's casual – khakis, the usual. But you might want to bring a change. They can get a little wild. People usually end up in the pool."

"Even W.?" Piers asked, recalling the older man's impeccably tailored shirt and handmade leather shoes.

"W. doesn't actually attend the parties. Sometimes he makes an appearance, but it's brief. He just throws them and makes sure everyone has fun. *A lot* of fun." Piers swiveled his head with a questioning look, but Jed's face was expressionless, his heavy lids shut as firmly as black-out shades. Piers stared at him for a moment, nodding as he digested Jed's statement. Now fully awake, he retrieved his newspaper from the ground to read about NATO's latest negotiations with the Saudi government.

Six hours later, Piers and Jed were sailing along a leafy avenue in high good humor. Their two hours of luxuriating on the beach had evolved into two hours of lunching at a nearby beach café, followed by two hours of drinking beer by the edge of Jed's pool. Piers was practically numb with the unvaried diet of relaxation, and had to prod himself toward consciousness with a chilly shower. Now, casually dressed, carefully shaven and mildly bronzed, he felt ready for his first Shorwell party. Jed had said nothing more about it after his laconic comments on the beach, and Piers approached the event with an equal mix of anticipation and anxiety, both of them muted by the steady quantity of alcohol they had been consuming all day.

They felt the party before they heard or saw it. As Jed raced his car along narrow lanes of dense foliage, Piers felt a repetitive vibration move through his torso. A few seconds later, he heard a series of thumps and a high screech. He winced as the wailing voice, its gender uncertain, rose in pitch and volume. Piers looked over at Jed, who was grinning from the driver's seat.

Jed yelled over. "W.'s favorite band. Post-punk-rock-African fusion. The Ghana Screamers." He spun the car into a long driveway, passing through a set of glossy wrought-iron gates, decelerating as the wheels shifted from asphalt to gravel. Piers squinted into the setting sun and made out the silhouette of a sloped slate roof punctuated by massive brick chimneys and symmetrically placed dormer windows. Jed swung his car to the left of an enormous oval lawn lined with odd shrubs, whose asymmetric outlines cast freakish shadows on the grass. Puzzled, Piers stared at them, realizing they were a series of bizarre topiaries. Jed slowed the car to a crawl and nodded at the one closest to them.

"That one is a bull, for the obvious reason. There used to be a bear, too, but W. ripped it down when a real bear market hit. And that one's Buddy." Jed nodded at what looked like a pit bull the size of a horse. He was lunging forward, his meticulously clipped leafy ears and tail at high alert.

"He looks a bit terrifying for that name, even as a hedge," Piers screamed back.

"Yeah. Luckily the actual dog lives in the stables with the horses and trainers. Nice house, huh? Supposedly W. went over to France to see the chateaux with some girlfriend and got pissed off when some old count wouldn't sell him their favorite. So he had an exact replica made, and sent a picture of it to the count." They passed a topiary of a hunchbacked man leaning on a cane. "That bush is the count. W. sent him a picture of that, too."

Jed parked his car at the side of the house. About fifty other cars were already there, most of them sporty two-seater convertibles, like Jed's. The two men entered a large foyer and fought their way through the crowd to a drinks table set up on the far wall where a deeply tanned bartender presided over an array of liquor bottles, mixers, and crystal glasses, a crisp white linen shirt rippling against his skin as he swayed to the deafening music. Next to him, wearing a matching shirt, was a small woman whose dark hair and translucent skin made her look like a black and white version of her colleague's color photo. She stood frowning at the crowd, her pale hands hovering in space above the liquor bottles.

"Excuse me?" Piers shouted over the music. The woman looked at him without expression. Her eyes were large and watchful, and she made no effort to please. "Could I have a vodka tonic?"

The woman titled her head a fraction, before picking up one of the bottles and checking its label before pouring out twice as much vodka as necessary and adding a small dollop of tonic water. She handed it to Piers with a level gaze. Piers, feeling his cheeks flush, turned away. He scanned the crowd, trying to find someone he knew. In every direction, clusters of bronzed young men and women stood drinking cocktails and screaming at each other. The guests were dressed with near uniformity, as if in accordance with an unseen memo: the men in khakis, polo shirts and the occasional blazer; the woman in tight sleeveless dresses and low heels. Even their hair matched, Piers noted, the men's combed straight back in an unspoken tribute to W., the women's shoulder length, bone straight and tawny with golden highlights. A mixture of desire and unease collided in him, and he took another long drink of his vodka tonic, draining it to the end.

He threaded his way through the crowd. The room was rapidly darkening as the sun descended, and he smiled uncertainly at a few people whose features looked familiar in the dark, receiving equally tentative smiles in return. He pressed on toward a set of massive French double doors which were propped open to a terrace where another very tanned bartender in a linen shirt and Bermuda madras shorts was lining up a series of tall frosted drinks. Piers swooped down on one and walked to the edge of the terrace. The noise from here was deafening, and he realized that the band had been set up on an island in the middle of an artificial lagoon extending from the back of the house. The lagoon twisted and curved around a series of miniature islands which were connected by narrow wooden footbridges. The islands were dotted by palm trees and circular bamboo huts with thatched roofs. Was this meant to be a bad historical joke, Piers wondered: the pretend count wandering out to oversee the pretend tropical colony?

A presence materialized at his elbow and Piers turned to see Jed, his pale heavy cheeks reddened by alcohol. Jed screamed to make himself heard. "Cool, isn't it? But the real party goes on in the inner sanctum – those huts down there." Jed waved his drink at the lagoon, whose water reflected the rising moon. "Come on." Piers followed Jed down a curving staircase to a lower terrace that extended to the edge of the water. A small pier jutted out, with a few miniature rowboats moored to its railing.

"You've got to be kidding," Piers said to Jed, watching Jed lower his heavy frame into the nearest rowboat, causing it to lurch dangerously to one side. Leaving his empty glass on the dock, Piers climbed in after him. Jed had seized the oars and was straining to move the boat. "I think you have to untie first," laughed Piers, unwinding the boat's rope from its cleat. Jed began to row and they lurched forward, each drunken stroke splashing water into the boat. In five minutes they reached one of the miniature islands. Jed careened toward its dock, smashing into another miniature rowboat. He hoisted his graceless frame onto the dock.

A short path lined by swinging lanterns led them to the entrance of the circular hut. Piers paused and closed his eyes, sniffing the air. He caught the musky scent of marijuana, with an incongruous overlay of over-sweet lilies. In front of him stood a doorway hung with strings of crystal beads and seashells. He pushed through them and paused in the thick haze of smoke, his eyes smarting. Through the darkness, he could make out a low cushioned bench ringing the walls and a group of people huddled around a large glass hookah. One of the men glanced up, and Piers recognized a trader who spent his days motionless in front of a Reuters terminal, a phone all but glued to his ear. The trader waved a silver-tipped hose in his direction.

"Hey, Sir Lancelot – ever seen one of these on your side of the pond? Try it." The trader put the long silver mouthpiece between his lips and inhaled, before slumping onto the cushioned bench. Piers felt a touch on his right arm. A woman with dark straight hair stared up at him with eyes lined in black kohl. A silky white sleeveless dress cascaded down her long narrow body and puddled onto the floor, mermaid-like. She appeared to be waiting for an answer to an unheard question, and Piers angled his ear down toward her mouth, catching again the heavy scent of lilies.

"Are you here for the game?" Her hand was on his right bicep, each narrow finger flashing the color of a different stone.

Piers flexed his muscle without thinking. "Game?"

"It's a tradition at W.'s parties. There's a different treat in each hut. Whoever tries them all wins a prize." She nodded toward the shimmering glass bong, with its circle of traders, their clean-shaven jawlines slack under the drug's effect.

Piers hesitated. "What are the treats?"

"Different things – to create different experiences. All the highest quality, of course – W. makes sure of that."

Piers watched as Jed settled himself on the cushion at the far end of the hut and picked up one of the silver mouthpieces. Piers leaned down again to the woman near him, whose hand still lingered on his arm, in equal measures flirtation and command. "What's the prize?" he asked.

The woman's hand tightened, and her clinging dress rippled in his direction. "You'll have to find out," she said, her lips practically touching his ear. Piers nodded and walked over to the bong and picked up one of the unused hoses lying on the ground, wiping its silver tip on his damp pant leg. He glanced at the mermaid woman, who was watching him with an enigmatic expression under her black-rimmed eyes. He slid his eyes down her body to the pool of white silk puddling at her feet and inhaled. Warm smoke filled his throat and he felt the heat float down into his lungs and up into his skull, lulling him into a half sleep.

The woman shook his arm. "You're Piers, right? Come on, you have two more huts to go."

Piers opened his eyes reluctantly. It took him a moment to register what she had said. "How do you know I'm Piers?"

The woman looked down, playing with a yellow-stoned ring. "W. always tells us about the new guys. We're supposed to make sure they have a good time." She covered Piers's hand with her own, and he stared at her bejeweled hand, groggy. The woman tightened her grip with surprising strength. "Come on, let's go."

Piers roused himself and followed the shimmering white dress out of the hut. The moon was higher now, and Piers could see the silhouettes of the party guests in the main house. The black outlines seemed far away. Piers rubbed his eyes as one of the silhouettes appeared to be removing its clothes and climbing up on the balustrade above the lagoon, teetering briefly before falling into the water below. The other silhouettes pumped their fists into the air, like grotesque Javanese shadow puppets.

"Come on," the woman urged, dragging Piers onto a wooden bridge. Piers turned away from the house, where more silhouettes were now tumbling into the water. Piers followed her up a gentle slope to another circular hut. Inside was a crowd of people dancing underneath a mirrored disco ball that was emblazoned with Shorwell's S-shaped logo. Still clinging to his bicep, Piers's mermaid guided him around the crowd to the back of the room, where a table was set up with three large silver boxes. Piers watched the woman lean over and flip open the lid of each box. Through her gleaming curtain of hair, he saw neat stacks of unused bills in different denominations: $100, $1000, and £50 sterling. Piers picked up one of the pale pink UK banknotes. It showed an engraved Sir Christopher Wren in a curling wig, crooking an elegant finger at the floorplan of St. Paul's Cathedral. Under his massive domed head, he stared at Piers with arrogant complacence. Piers felt subtly rebuked. What in the world am I doing here, he wondered through the fog of his brain.

The mermaid tugged at his sleeve. "Is that the one you want first?" she asked.

"First? What do you mean?" She pointed to the boxes, and he realized that each one held a second, smaller box nestled near the stacks of money. One was filled with white powder, and two with small white pills. She looked up at him and smiled. "These are the treats," she explained, as if to a child. "The bills are W.'s idea of a straw for the coke. The pills are ecstasy." Piers stared at the table, trying to mask his amazement at the overt profusion of money and drugs. He watched a young woman detach herself from the crowd of pulsing flesh and approach the table. Without looking at him, she extracted a $100 bill, deftly curled it into a narrow cylinder and bent over the box of powder. Her straight blond hair fell forward as she inhaled. Standing up, she pocketed the bill in her sundress.

Piers's mermaid tugged at his sleeve in impatience. "Try the ecstasy – you know, the *love* drug. It makes everything you touch – *anyone* you touch – more exciting. Want to try it together?" She tipped one of the small white pills into the palm of her hand and held it out to him. Her nails grazed his chin.

"Is this the treat? Or the prize?" he asked. The word prize came out pies, as he fought the layers of liquor, marijuana and sheer unease. If the woman heard the slip, she showed no sign. She nodded to the polished table, laden with drugs and money, all of it glimmering and swirling under the disco ball. "Those are the treats," she said. She arched her back toward him. "And, obviously, I am the prize."

There was no contest, ultimately, between the clash of apprehension and excitement that collided within Piers. It would have been a moral failure to back down: a betrayal of the tenacious, if loosely considered, values that governed his life. What hero would retreat in the face of a green-eyed, half-naked woman? What future titan of Wall Street would hesitate from a few unknown and illegal drugs when they were laid out, like cakes at a tea party, in full view of a crowded room? Physical desire for his seductress stirred within him faintly; but the romance of his role – of being the foreigner who conquered a mysterious woman at a Hamptons bacchanal – moved him deeply. Piers wrapped one arm around the woman's waist and took the pill with his other. Choking it back, he leaned down to her upturned mouth, choosing to ignore her enigmatic expression. He hesitated as her scent of lilies made him feel faint. Pulling himself together, he continued his descent and kissed her.

He woke up the next day to the sound of a motor roaring. Half-conscious, he opened his eyes a fraction and peeked through the venetian blind next to him. Two men in matching t-shirts were on Jed's lawn, pushing diesel-powered lawn mowers back and forth. Piers lay back and looked down at his body. His damp khaki pants clung unpleasantly to his legs, and an ache that started in his esophagus stretched upward to enclose his whole head. Fragments of the previous night started to re-emerge like a movie whose scenes had been purposefully scrambled. The white dress; the rowboat; the topiary of the count; the darkened room. Piers hit pause on his brain's slideshow of images and tried to picture the darkened room. What had happened? He willed his brain to rewind. He remembered kissing the mermaid for a long time before following her to a room downstairs. It had been warm and very dark, with only pinpricks of light overhead, like clusters of artificial stars. Squeezing his eyes shut, he tried to envision her body and couldn't. He remembered only the feel of her ropey muscles under her skin, and the smell of salt and lilies that rose from her neck as he'd burrowed into it. He had a hazy memory of feeling powerful – conquering – exultant, emotions that now, in his shattered state, seemed incomprehensible.

Desperate for water, he maneuvered himself into a sitting position, and stood up, keeping his hand on the mattress for balance. The pain in his head intensified. He walked into the living room. Jed was sprawled on a long black leather sofa, his mouth open, the pale hairless expanse of his soft, fleshy stomach rising and falling with his snores. Piers grimaced and went into the kitchen, where the LED displays of the answering machine and microwave were flashing, their beeps ricocheting off the granite counters and marble floors. A half empty glass of whisky sat near the sink, its aroma still hanging in the air. Piers looked at it, winced, and retreated to the bathroom, turning the shower on maximum.

When Piers reached the office at 8am on Monday, Jerry was already hunkered down at their shared cubicle, his Mets baseball cap slung low over the latest copy of *Sports Illustrated*. Piers walked toward him but offered no greeting; he had learned that Jerry's cap only touched the magazine when one of his teams had suffered a momentous loss. Piers settled down with his *Wall Street Journal* and began reading about the approaching Treasury bill auction. Ten ominous minutes passed before Piers heard Jerry's chair creak backwards, and his fist hit the desk. Jerry's voice came through their shared felt wall, fully audible.

"15-1 to the fucking *Red Sox*." Piers said nothing, giving him a chance to settle down. Jerry's intimate, tortured relationship to the Yankees was common knowledge. Another five minutes passed, and Jerry's voice sounded again. "So I hear you scored." Piers maintained a diplomatic silence, resisting the impulse to draw a comparison between his success and the Yankees' failure. Two more minutes passed. Jerry tried again. "Good party at W.'s chateau?" He pronounced the word chaw-toe. "I couldn't go. My grandma turned eighty. You can't believe the stack of cannoli my mom made. I ate so many I practically passed out." Jerry paused. "I hear you practically passed out, too."

Piers looked up from his paper and stared at the grey felt wall in front of him. "Where do you get your information?"

"Oh, word gets around. You know. One big happy family and all that. Anyway, I hear you're one of us now. Poor you. I'll send your mother a condolence letter."

"Very funny."

Rattled, Piers stood up and glanced at the white board, only to find more evidence of his new notoriety. The anonymous cartoonist had been at work since the party in the Hamptons. W.'s chateau, jutting upward in a frenzy of turrets and chimneys, now covered half the board. Mythic beasts poked their fanged heads out its moat. Miniature rowboats tossed on the moat's waves. Once again the mermaid appeared, this time sitting on a little island next to the chateau, her long hair flowing decorously, if ineffectually, over her bare breasts. Her trunk of gold coins had been joined by a stick figure waving a Union Jack flag. Piers glowered at the image. Was all information here public? On the other hand, he reasoned, wasn't he the one sitting with the gold coins and the buxom mermaid? Wasn't that the point of the hero's adventure? Walking to the white board, Piers picked up a red marker from its tray and swiftly annotated the picture, giving the stick figure a grotesquely muscled torso, and enlarging the mermaid's breasts. He looked at his work, satisfied, and returned to his cubicle, where his phone was flashing with a new voice mail. Dialing into his mailbox, he heard Charlotte's familiar voice floating through his earphone.

"Piers, sorry to bother you," Charlotte said, with no noticeable note of apology, "I have been ringing Miranda about a document needed by one of my clients," – *bloody hell*, thought Piers, _your_ clients? – "and she doesn't seem to be getting my messages. Could you help? She's the one I met at the pub, right? The screamer? She seemed effective enough when it suits her. Also, Mother's been asking me about you. Could you ring her soon?"

Piers hesitated, and then dialed Miranda's office extension. It rang four times before a breathless voice answered. "Miranda here," she said, with the usual absence of pleasantries that Piers now expected from his American colleagues.

"Miranda, it's Piers here. My sister, Charlotte, the one you met at the bar –"

"Of course! She seemed super sweet."

"Yes, well – I guess you know that Patrick hired her in London and she's working on sales and marketing over there. I gather she's spoken a few times to Davina about it?" There was no answer. "Anyway, she asked if I could help her track down a client report she needs from you. I don't know whether you've heard from her directly?"

"No, not a word."

"I guess she's still learning the ropes. It would be great if you could call her. You know, she's new, and doesn't yet know all the procedures." Piers paused lamely, waiting for Miranda to join his brotherly conde-scension. She didn't take the bait. Instead, after a long pause, her voice re-emerged, as clear and uninflected as a referee's whistle.

"Of course! No problem. Just tell her to call me, okay?" Miranda hung up, and Piers felt doubly irritated, as if both women had manipu-lated him successfully. What a pain in the neck they were, he thought. Even that mermaid girl at the Hamptons – who was she, anyway? What he needed, he reflected, was a lot more squash. And mates. And money. He picked up his phone and jabbed the number of a potential client, causing the base of the phone to lurch across the desk.

7

Patrick's Spell

Charlotte entered the Embankment art gallery and stopped short at an enormous painting hung in the foyer. A group of men suspended by golden parachutes floated above the Manhattan skyline at dusk. Their bodies were shown as silhouettes, cartoon-like, and their faces were blank. Above them, dollar bills rained down from a black blimp. Walking into the gallery proper, a featureless white room, Charlotte looked at the next painting. This one, in a similar style, showed a man in a superhero cape astride Wall Street's famous bronze bull, his fist pumping the air. A wallet had replaced the man's nose.

Charlotte scowled. A contemporary art gallery had seemed the perfect venue for her first marketing event – chic and new, and suggestive of Shorwell's Manhattan origins. Although the gallery owner had warned her that the exhibitions could be edgy, Charlotte had dismissed the comment, imagining a series of provocative nudes or Andy Warhol-inspired soup cans. It had not occurred to her that the backdrop would be a screed against capitalism. Well, it couldn't be helped; the guests were due in thirty minutes.

Charlotte marched past the rest of the artist's silhouettes and started to arrange brochures advertising Shorwell's funds on a table near the back of the room. She fanned out two dozen glossy brochures that still smelled of the print shop's ink. Their text had caused her hours of frustration, as she'd tried to distill from her inarticulate colleagues the essence of their investment strategy.

"What would you say is the key advantage we bring to our clients?" she'd asked one day after the market closed, standing at the edge of the traders' horseshoe of desks, a pen poised above her ringed notebook. If she had asked them to announce their most depraved sexual fantasies, they couldn't have looked more alarmed. After a long and startled silence, when the traders realized that she wasn't leaving, a few answers had floated forth.

"Uh – we focus on mispriced securities?" offered the sallow red-haired collar puller.

"We're focused on client requirements?" said his neighbor. Charlotte scribbled down these answers and nodded. She continued to hover.

"We have lower than average volatility," Horace had thrown in, without looking up.

"And don't forget our culture of transparency!" added Patrick from across the room, where he was chatting with the lead trader.

Charlotte had retreated and spent the next few hours trying to string these meager offerings into a coherent investment philosophy. Even without a background in finance, she could tell that the result was hardly inspiring: Had there ever been an investment firm espousing a different set of strengths? Horace had come to the rescue, creating a few impressive graphs of the Shorwell funds' performance based on data sent by New York. With these graphs and an artsy photograph of the trading floor – Patrick's smile gleaming into the camera, his arms draped across the backs of the traders – she had produced Shorwell London's first marketing brochure in preparation for their inaugural event.

The guest list, an undiluted lineup of pension fund consultants and company financial directors, was another problem. Charlotte had tried to leaven the mix by inviting every university friend she could possibly justify, spending a long evening leaving increasingly desperate invitations on answering machines across London: *You won't even notice the financiers, I promise, and there will be free drinks.* A small handful had answered her plea. The first to arrive was her best friend, Henrietta, who swept in trailing a bedraggled knit shawl, her clever brown eyes drooping after a day of drilling Latin conjugations into unwilling teenagers. The fraying leather satchel slung across her body was crammed with black exam books and banged against her hip as she made a beeline for the table where wine glasses were set out. Without slackening her pace, she glanced at the paintings with an amused expression.

"Please tell me you're not responsible for the art, too," she said, embracing Charlotte, before pulling back to examine her tailored black suit and leopard skin heels. "You look *incredibly* smart," she said. "Maybe selling one's soul is worth it after all. One more day with my thickest students and I might just offer up my soul for free. Where's the promised drink?"

Charlotte directed Henrietta to a box of Chardonnay bottles underneath the table and handed her a corkscrew. When she looked up, the Shorwell traders had arrived and were huddled in the foyer. As a group, they shuffled toward the back of the room. Charlotte beamed in their direction. "Thanks so much for showing up," she said. "The consultants and potential clients will be here any minute. I'll make a quick speech of welcome, and then I'd be grateful if you could fan out to answer questions." Charlotte received a few mute nods, as the traders continued their approach to the drinks table.

Henrietta, holding a very full glass of white wine, sidled up to Charlotte and said in a loud whisper, "Jolly lot, aren't they? Make my sixth formers look like jesters."

"You're an angel for coming, Hen. But they're not so bad. If you're really stuck for conversation, ask them about the spread between triple and double B bonds. Look, it's Adrian." Charlotte nodded toward a thin young man with receding blond hair who was making his way toward them. Henrietta brightened.

Adrian kissed Henrietta before turning to Charlotte. "Who could have imagined that we'd all meet at a drinks party promoting American financiers? Gosh, Charlotte, you do look amazing, doesn't she, Henrietta? Not the frumpy classics student I knew at university – just kidding, of course. Who are all these people?"

Charlotte glanced around the gallery. The room was filling rapidly now, as a steady stream of pale-cheeked, suited young men filed through the door, glanced at the art and headed toward the drinks. The noise level was rising in the uncarpeted space, and it was getting warmer. Among the crowd, she recognized only a few consultants. Adrian continued. "They don't look like criminals, at any rate, which is the main thing. Now that I'm a government employee in Her Majesty's Royal Service – regulating you and your colleagues, young lady," he said, giving Charlotte an ironic smile, "I have to keep my eye on these things."

The sound of a bell interrupted Charlotte's response. Turning her head, she saw that Patrick had arrived and was tapping a silver spoon on the edge of a wine glass to silence the crowd. She glanced at him in surprise; they had agreed that she was going to make the first speech of welcome. Had he forgotten? Alarmed, she tried to catch his gaze, but he was hovering three feet above everyone on a stepladder left behind by the gallery's installation crew. Behind him, at waist level, hung the painted Wall Street bull. The crowd hushed and looked at Patrick expectantly. His elevated position made him look broader and taller than usual, and his blond hair shone under the gallery's lights.

"Welcome, everyone, and thank you for being here. I am Patrick Connolly, fresh from your former colony of New York," – a general chuckle circulated the room – "by way of your other former colony, Ireland." The chuckle evaporated. Patrick pressed ahead. "Our goal tonight is to introduce you to our firm. All of our traders are here, waiting to answer your questions." Patrick gestured with his wine glass to the pack of men standing in a tight cluster near the drinks. "As you can see, they are strategically placed near the wine! Please, help yourselves to drinks, and ask them any detail about the markets. We look forward to working with you. Cheers!" Patrick raised his glass to the crowd before jumping down from the ladder, his face flushed. He headed toward Charlotte, who made space for him in their small circle. She turned toward her friends. "Henrietta, Adrian, this is Patrick, who heads up the London office."

Patrick leaned forward to shake hands. "Thank you for coming to our inaugural party. Charlotte's party, I should say. She did all the arrangements." He squeezed Charlotte's shoulder familiarly. "Great job on getting people to show up. What did you promise them, anyway?"

Henrietta said brightly, "Free drink. And no financiers."

Patrick's eyebrows lifted a fraction, but his genial expression didn't waver. "Gosh, are we that bad?" He used his most exaggerated farm boy drawl, but Henrietta didn't laugh, and his face shadowed. "Well, Charlotte doesn't seem to mind us so much," he said, letting his hand slide down from Charlotte's shoulder to her waist.

Henrietta's eyes tracked Patrick's sinking arm. "*De gustibus non est disputandum*," she said, eliciting an embarrassed chuckle from Adrian and an annoyed glance from Charlotte.

Patrick's arm dropped to his side. He looked at Henrietta, baffled. "Excuse me?"

"Oh – it's just a joke classics students tell," said Adrian, evenly. "Much more useful is the phrase *Tempest Bebende*: time to drink. Shall we?" Adrian directed this question at Patrick, before turning into the crowd.

"Great idea." Patrick said, swiveling on his heel and following him into the sea of suits. The two women stood alone, unspeaking. Henrietta's lower lip was pushed forward mulishly, while her eyes registered a kaleidoscope of shifting emotions.

Charlotte stared at her. "What in the world inspired that?"

Henrietta's face settled into truculence. "He doesn't speak Latin. Don't worry about it."

"But he'll figure it out, and he's my boss, and he's—"

"What, your boyfriend? Don't be ridiculous." Charlotte hesitated, not wanting to concede to Henrietta or to herself that Patrick's feelings toward her remained frustratingly inscrutable. Henrietta's instant contempt, fueled by her own insecurity, filled her with rebellious fury. She stood, fuming, staring straight ahead at the mingling guests.

Henrietta touched her arm. "I'm sorry, Charlotte – dearest Charlotte – but don't tell me you've fallen for an American who pretends he's fallen off a hay wagon."

Charlotte turned her head toward Henrietta. "I think he's charming," she said.

Henrietta's expression hardened. "Clearly, he does too, so I guess you share one thing in common."

Patrick followed Adrian to the drinks table, where a half-dozen wine bottles already stood empty. On the far side of the table, Horace wrestled with the recalcitrant cork of a new bottle. Adrian stood watching his progress, an empty wine glass dangling from his hand.

Patrick joined him in watching Horace. "I guess it will be a while before we are bebending, or bebonding, or whatever it was you said. At least we've escaped Charlotte's guard dog over there. Sorry – she's not your girlfriend, is she?"

"Oh, don't mind Henrietta," Adrian said, unruffled. "She spends her days drilling Latin and Greek into the children of Arab and Russian oligarchs, who either bribe or threaten her to get their offspring into the right schools. She practically requires a security detail to go to work. It hasn't left her too enamored of businessmen."

Horace uncorked the bottle with a loud pop. There was a cheer from around the table, and Adrian held out his glass. Patrick waited until it was filled it before speaking again. "So, what brings you here? Are you part of Charlotte's welcoming committee as well?"

Adrian swirled the wine around in his glass before looking up to reply. "No; that's just Henrietta. I'm here because my father, Charles Whitely, mentioned to me that our family's firm has invested some of our pension with you." Adrian took a sip of wine. "Also, I'm working for the government agency that regulates foreign investment firms in the City. You could consider my appearance tonight entirely professional."

Across the room, still standing next to Henrietta, Charlotte scowled. Why did Henrietta always have to be so dogmatic? At university, impressed and intimidated by Henrietta's social confidence, she'd accepted her friend's standards as a matter of course. For three years of easy friendship, their interactions had followed a pattern, with Charlotte relaying anecdotes and conversations on which Henrietta would pass judgment. But now, less cowed by Henrietta's stature, and less convinced of her friend's omnipotence, she felt a rebellious rage. What did Henrietta know about Patrick, anyway?

Charlotte glanced at Henrietta, whose eyes were sweeping the room, assessing the people in it. Henrietta's face had regained its usual equanimity, and Charlotte knew that she felt certain her cutting remark had been the last word on the subject. Henrietta's steely confidence infuriated Charlotte further.

She turned toward her friend. "I'm sorry you feel that way, Hen. We can't all be as morally upstanding as you, devoting ourselves to the conjugation of Latin and Greek all day. I think Patrick is charming, despite his being American. I am terribly sorry to have put you out by asking you to come to this party."

Henrietta looked at Charlotte in amazement and hesitated, as though giving her friend a chance to retract and retreat. Charlotte did neither. There was an uneasy pause between them, an eddy of silence amidst the rolling conversational sea surrounding them. The two women looked at each other, each face registering a poisonous mix of anger, pain and pride. Henrietta was the first to look away.

"Well, Charlotte, allow me to be the first to wish you joy." She gave her knit shawl a vicious yank and marched off to the drinks table. Charlotte stood rooted to the ground, breathing hard, no longer seeing the people around her.

Patrick's face appeared in front of her, blurred by the tears she was fighting to hold back. "Earth to Charlotte? Come in, please."

"Sorry," she said automatically. She rubbed her eyes on her sleeve and Patrick's face came into view, his cheeks glowing with the wine and noise. He looked happy and buoyant, and perfectly at ease. Charlotte cursed herself for being so affected by Henrietta's words. Why shouldn't she feel as liberated as Patrick? It was her party, after all, and a success by any measure. An unfamiliar breeze of recklessness wafted through her. Damn Henrietta and her social snobbery; she was going to have a good time. She edged closer to Patrick and stared directly into his face, hoping that her incipient tears hadn't smudged her mascara. She looked up at him, angling her head to one side.

"Enjoying the party?" she asked.

Patrick's eyes widened as he caught her look. He snaked an arm around her waist and leaned over to speak into her ear. "Loving it, Charlotte – great job. What do you say we have our own party afterwards? Say in about half an hour?" His grip tightened on her waist. Charlotte looked past him to see Henrietta's tall figure stalk out of the room and slam through the gallery's door.

She refocused on Patrick's questioning face. "Absolutely. Half an hour should be perfect." Charlotte returned to the drinks table and picked up a handful of brochures. Keeping half an eye on Patrick, she turned to one of the guests who was drinking by himself in a corner, giving him a brochure and launching into a rehearsed speech about Shorwell. Charlotte was aware of speaking too quickly and smiling too much. She could see Patrick across the room, laughing with a group of people she didn't know. On autopilot, she continued to talk as her mind raced. Should she back down – perhaps run after Henrietta and apologize, or tell Patrick that she'd changed her mind? Her eyes flicked back to Patrick across the room, his face now in profile, his chin tipped upward as he threw back his head to laugh at his own joke. No, she thought, she couldn't retreat now.

Forty-five minutes later, the party had all but fizzled out. The guests had one by one left their empty wine glasses on the table, grabbed a Shorwell brochure, and retrieved their coats. Only the traders remained, clustered around the wine table, doggedly working through the last of the bottles. Patrick turned to Charlotte and lifted his eyebrows. She nodded and went to find her coat and purse before joining Patrick by the drinks table. He smiled at her and together they turned toward the street. She could feel the eyes of the traders tracking them as they walked through the gallery's anti-capitalist paintings toward the exit.

Reaching the door, Patrick turned back to wave at the group. "Drink up, boys! A great success. Well done!"

"Well done *you*," called out one of the traders, grinning in Charlotte's direction. Charlotte could feel her cheeks turn bright red as Patrick ushered her out the door. Hailing a taxi, Patrick gave the taxi driver his address: a new steel high-rise south of the Thames that had replaced a decayed fish processing warehouse. By the time they pulled up to its flood-lit metal door, the alcoholic buzz and moral outrage fueling Charlotte's courage had worn off, and she was only half listening to Patrick chat about the success of the party, her mind preoccupied with visions of Henrietta stomping out of the gallery. When they entered his flat, she all but lunged at the tumbler of scotch he held out.

"Thanks, that's brilliant," she said, clasping the glass with both hands, like a golden bauble.

"I didn't know you were such a scotch fan," Patrick said. He set down his own glass onto a granite coffee table and reached for the re-mote control of a television propped up on a stack of phone directories across the room. Enormous helmeted men in blue and white spandex appeared hurtling down a football field. Patrick sat down on a grey sofa and leaned toward the screen, fully engaged.

Charlotte lowered herself down next to him and sipped her whiskey, ignoring its burn as she swallowed. She surveyed the room's few features: some matching grey furniture, seemingly unused, a granite coffee table, and a beige polyethylene rug. To her left, a framed poster of grey and beige spirals leaned against a wall. She glanced back at the TV, where the football players were huddled around a grizzled man whose windbreaker hugged his round torso like a sausage casing, its elasticized waist riding up as he waved his arms. Feeling the beginnings of a headache, Charlotte looked away from the TV and back at the poster.

Patrick followed her look. "Like it?"

Charlotte thought it was the ugliest poster she'd ever seen. She searched for a neutral answer. "It matches the sofa," she said.

"It should, since the lady at the furniture shop threw it in for free when I got the furniture." Patrick waved his arm around the room. "She said it would tie it all together." He glanced back at the TV, which was now on commercials. Looking back at Charlotte, he nudged closer to her and reached over to Charlotte's glass, now empty, taking it from her and placing it on the table. Turning back, he encircled her torso with both his arms, pressing her arms against her sides. Charlotte leaned into him, heady with the faintly minty smell coming from his neck.

His voice was quiet and near. "What do you think, Charlotte? Do you feel nicely tied together because of the poster?" Charlotte ignored the silly question as she closed her eyes, leaned further forward, and tilted her mouth upward, anticipating his kiss. Suddenly, the TV erupted with the roar of a crowd. Patrick let go of Charlotte and swung his head toward the screen. She opened her eyes: A man in a tusked-Viking helmet was leaping up and down, punching the air with a fake trident.

"Touchdown!" said Patrick, leaning toward the screen, his expression rapt. Charlotte took a belated breath and stared at him, confused and humiliated. The golden skin of his profile glowed with enthusiasm as he looked at the screen. Just below the hem of her skirt, one of his hands, its nails neatly trimmed, rested casually on her knee, his large signet ring pressing into her skin. Charlotte remembered the night they'd met, and how she'd thought it was odd to see a ring on a man's hand. Somehow, it seemed less odd now, she thought, feeling the light touch of metal through her stocking. She heard her mother's voice in her head, *Don't be difficult, darling.* Her irritation melted into resignation.

Rising from the sofa, she wandered into the narrow galley kitchen and turned on the light. White laminate cabinetry and appliances gleamed at her. On a granite counter sat a heap of plastic-wrapped cutlery and a box of glass tumblers, two of them still mummified in paper packaging. She opened the nearest cabinet, whose internal light flicked on to reveal four empty shelves. She turned to the stainless-steel refrigerator: also empty, except for six cans of Guinness.

Charlotte peeked back toward the sitting room and saw that Patrick remained absorbed in the game. She began to snoop with abandon. She tiptoed into the bedroom, where a double bed with a coverless duvet and a side table sat in the corner. There was nothing else. Charlotte looked around, incredulous at the room's emptiness. It's impossible, she thought; everyone has at least something from home, at least one memento. Her eye fell on the side table, a grey industrial cube with one drawer. Casting a swift glance over her shoulder, Charlotte nudged open its drawer, which glided forward on steel runners to reveal a stack of books. Charlotte felt a burble of victory as she knelt to examine them. The Great Gatsby was on top, a hardback edition with F. Scott Fitzgerald's name engraved in gold cursive. Its heavy cream pages looked untouched. Placing it beside her, she turned back to the drawer and picked up two paperbacks both with unbroken bindings: Ireland's Great Potato Famine, and Horatio Alger's Only An Irish Boy. Underneath the books was a plastic folder which held a Richie Rich comic book, its faded cover showing a tuxedoed boy perched on a pile of diamonds, waving a cigar. Charlotte shook her head in disbelief and turned to the final book. It was the only one to display signs of wear: How To Sell, by Wilson Weld, America's greatest salesman.

Glancing again over her shoulder, Charlotte sat down on the bed and ran her thumb over its pages. The book fell open to a page heavily underlined in pencil. She began to read. *The key to selling is to estab-lish a relationship of trust between you and your buyer. Do you have a social connection in common, even at two or three steps removed?* Charlotte paused, diverted by a vision of Patrick introducing her to the Debenhams heiress at the drinks party. She pushed away the image. *Are you both members of a hobbyist, political, social or other affinity group? If not, how else might you create the illusion of friendship? Try, as a start, this strategy. When meeting a buyer for the first time, arrange to have someone interrupt your meeting two or three times. Each time you re-enter the room, the buyer will see you as an increasingly familiar face. Success will not be far off.*

Mesmerized by the text, and foggy from whiskey, Charlotte didn't hear Patrick until he was hovering above her in the doorway. She dropped the book and gave him a brilliant smile, trying to look cheerfully indifferent. Patrick's forehead was creased, and his eyes were shadowed with irritation that cleared only slowly as his face regained its usual genial expression. It was like watching an actor arrange his features before walking onstage, she thought, wondering, despite herself, what the effort must have cost him. Patrick lowered himself onto the bed and picked up the book, flipping through the pages.

"This was given to me by the first guy who gave me a job when I got to New York," he said, speaking more slowly than usual. "The Wall Street shops wouldn't talk to me because I didn't come out of their Ivy League club, so I went out to Long Island and found this guy. He was a bond trader who wouldn't have cared if I hadn't even gone to college. He taught me a lot. But after a while, I realized his whole deal was just about sucking up to clients. When his trades went the wrong way, he stopped taking their calls. It was my job to pick up the phone and tell people he wasn't there. I got sick of listening to them scream at me." Patrick paused, and looked at Charlotte. "Do you know what I mean? I guess not – you've always been around nice people, I guess."

"Oh, no – of course there are questionable people everywhere." Charlotte faltered as she thrashed her memory for disreputable people she had encountered over the years. She drew a blank. "I'm sure it must be much more difficult in America," she concluded, lamely.

"Well, I don't know about that. But in any case, I tired of his crap. That's why I joined Shorwell. What an uptick." Patrick put down the book and turned his clear blue eyes toward Charlotte. "What about you,

Charlotte? Are you having fun yet? You've been great so far, you know." He put his arm around her waist. Charlotte could feel the separate pressure of each one of his fingertips. Shifting his weight toward her, he spoke into her ear. "I promise this won't change anything between us at the office, just in case you're worried."

"Of course not," Charlotte lied, her heart beating faster.

Patrick leaned forward and kissed the edge of her ear, before angling her body backward with his weight. The discarded book on selling dug into the base of Charlotte's spine as he lay on top of her. She ignored it as desire, fueled by the thrill of adventure, moved through her. This is it, she thought; this is just what my life in London was supposed to be. Damn Henrietta, Piers and the rest of them. She put her arms around Patrick, drawing him closer to her, feeling the warmth of his skin through his shirt.

He whispered into her ear. "You're so beautiful, Charlotte. You know, I've never met anyone like you. It's like you come from a book where everyone is so innocent and sweet." He stopped talking as his mouth shifted down from her ear to her neck. His hand, which had been stroking the small of her back, paused as his index finger ran across an inch-long raised welt. Charlotte stiffened as she felt Patrick's finger retrace the scar. He shifted his body upwards. "Did a bull gore you?" he asked. The stubble on his jaw scraped her neck as he spoke.

"No, not a bull – a doctor. I had spinal surgery for scoliosis. They put a metal bar in my spine when I was fourteen." Charlotte shifted so that she could look directly at him. His clear blue eyes looked earnestly down at her, his expression concerned. "It was awful," she continued. "The mean girls at school called me Char-Bar."

The corners of Patrick's mouth twitched. "Poor you," he murmured, starting to tug at her blouse. In a sudden panic, Charlotte tried to remember whether she'd put on her best lingerie that morning. She reconstructed the start of her day, seeing herself lurch out of bed, late, and reaching toward a heap of clothes discarded the previous night. She swore at herself inwardly.

Patrick's hands paused again. "Hey, are you okay?"

Charlotte gave what she hoped was a credible sigh of passion. "Never better. I was just wondering, could we turn off the light?"

"The light?"

"The overhead light. It's a little blinding."

Patrick rolled to his side and stared down at her flushed face. He looked bemused. "No problem." Getting up from the bed, he stretched across to the light switch, flicking it off with a neat motion. Charlotte saw that he was still wearing his highly polished dress shoes and looked remarkably neat in contrast to her rumpled state. He was leaning over her again when his phone rang in the living room. Enjoying herself, Charlotte pulled Patrick to her. "Let it ring. The answering machine will pick up, right?"

But Patrick was staring in the direction of the phone, his body tense under her hands. He started to shift his weight away from her when Charlotte yelped in pain. He froze. "What is it?" His voice registered equal parts concern and irritation.

"My earring – I think it's caught on your collar." Patrick sighed and lowered his torso back down, his head still turned toward the ringing noise, his body tense. Charlotte fiddled with her earring as she tried to disentangle it from his neck. She yanked on the unseen wire, feeling intensely ridiculous. Patrick's body, coiled with impatience, hovered four inches above hers. The phone rang again and Patrick made an annoyed sound. Charlotte managed to disengage the wire from his collar just as the answering machine in the next room clicked on. She heard a woman's voice speak, her flat American vowels carving out a plaintive tone. Patrick leaped up and bounded into the next room. Charlotte sat up and tilted her liberated ear in the direction of the phone. She thought she heard a woman saying "Patrick, it's me," before Patrick picked up the handset.

"Patrick, it's me," repeated Miranda, her voice clearly irritated. "Where have you been? I thought you said you'd be in tonight."

"Sorry, doll – I was just in the next room. How are you? It's kind of late here, even for me. Can I call you tomorrow?" Patrick covered the phone with his hand as he spoke, and turned his neck turned the bedroom.

"You sound like you're in a cave. Is British Telecom that bad?" Miranda started to laugh at her own joke and stopped short. "Is someone there, Patrick?"

Patrick could practically feel her outrage and suspicion pulse through the coiled phone cord. "Of course not, doll. It's just been a long day. I'll call you tomorrow, okay?"

There was a long pause, and Patrick could feel her weighing his words, considering whether to continue her campaign of accusation. He held his breath, casting another quick glance in the direction of the bedroom.

Miranda abandoned the effort. "Okay Patrick. But you better remember."

Patrick retreated to the bedroom, where Charlotte was still lying on the bed. He sat down next to her and touched her neck lightly, tracing his finger toward the earring that had prevented him from picking up the phone in time. "Where were we?" he said.

"Who was that?" Charlotte asked. Her tone was light, and Patrick couldn't see her expression in the darkened room.

"Just a friend from home," he said, leaning over her. "No one in particular."

Miranda slammed the phone down and pushed back her rolling chair. She glared out the window next to her cubicle. It was only early September, but a freak storm had rolled across the Atlantic, hitting the Eastern seaboard that day. Miranda watched as the drops hit the outside of her window, clinging briefly to the glass before capitulating to gravity and racing downward. She stood up with an angry sigh and held herself very straight, sucking in her abdomen to the count of five, just as she had learned over ten years of ballet training during her childhood in the sprawling suburbs of New Jersey. Her ballet classes had been the primary influence of her young life, leaving her with an unyielding belief in good posture and careful breathing. So far, she hadn't encountered too many problems that couldn't be solved by rolling back her shoulders and tightening her abdominal muscles. Today, though, the magic wasn't working. She stood up straighter, realigned her neck, and began to run through her barre exercises. Placing her left hand on the back of her chair, she kicked off her heels and flexed her feet outward, starting with first position. Her colleague Davina looked up from the other side of their shared cubicle. She watched Miranda move through all five positions.

"Patrick not behaving?" she asked with a smirk. Davina's job as head of client marketing had left her no illusions about male behavior. For three years, Davina had spent her days cold calling pension fund consultants, and her evenings entertaining them. She was long beyond trying to reestablish her psychological wellbeing through ballet or any other form of exercise, having discovered a far more efficient source of equilibrium in the liquor with which she plied potential customers.

Miranda ignored this barb, splaying her feet outward and jamming her heels together to start again at first position. Over the past two years, she had told Davina about her on and off again relationship with Patrick, sharing only the glamorous tidbits that highlighted his pursuit. She had been less forthcoming about the long gaps between phone calls and dates, and her ongoing suspicion that he was stringing her along while seeing other women. Many times, Miranda had decided to drop him as a point of pride. But then, he would drop by her desk with a giftbox from Barneys, or take her to a Japanese sushi bar, or kiss her beneath the plum blossom trees in Central Park, and she would relent, telling herself that she could string him along, too, and see other men on the side. Except that other men seemed boring and predictable compared to Patrick, and she had found, to her annoyance, that he had become the yardstick by which she measured them. None of this, naturally, she had confided in Davina, who had dated enough men in finance to assess them with an expert, unsentimental eye, and scorned women who behaved otherwise. Miranda reached fifth position and dropped her arms to her sides.

"No, he's fine. Just busy." Davina gave a skeptical snort and returned to her work. Miranda sat down and stared at her daily to-do list, covered with her neat, loopy handwriting. Each item was crossed out except for one: Fax Charlotte valuation reports for Welsh shipping client. She frowned. The reports had been sitting on her desk for two weeks, during which time Miranda had stalled, resenting the fact that Charlotte had now been inserted into the marketing process. Charlotte's unfailingly polite voice mail messages requesting the reports had only increased Miranda's irritation. Why couldn't she just demand things like a normal person? She and Piers were like some parody of a children's book. Fuming, Miranda recalled the answering message that Patrick had left for her just before Piers's arrival in New York. It had been typically brief. *Hey babe,* he'd said, sounding rushed. *I'm sending over an English guy named Piers for the sales team. Could you help ease him in? Go for a drink or something? W. asked me to find someone who looked and sounded good – someone who could impress the pension clients. This guy seems okay. Thanks, doll. I owe you.*

Miranda examined a chip on the nail of her index finger, considering whether to send the report before leaving the office for a manicure. Maybe a different brand of nail polish would last longer? Her phone rang. She glanced down and recognized Jed's extension. Her muscles relaxed. She and Jed were on the same page: no pleasantries, no niceties, no illusions. She picked up the phone and tucked it between her ear and shoulder, rotating her hand to see the chip from a different angle. "Hey Jed."

"Hey. You know that valuation report for the shipping guys in the UK? It turns out the one I gave you has some wrong numbers. Computer glitch. I'm sending you the right one now. Fax it to Charlotte, okay? Unless you're not talking to Patrick's new girlfriend?" Jed gave a short and brutal laugh.

Miranda gripped the handset so tightly that her nails dug into the palm of her hand. "Girlfriend?" She made her voice as light as possible.

"Yeah, you know Patrick, right? One of the traders out there called me about something and said they'd left some marketing party together. Whatever. Anyway, tell her the one I'm sending you now is the right one, okay?"

Jed hung up the phone and Miranda let the handset dangle from her hand as outrage surged through her. That lying bastard, she thought. I'll – I'll – she hesitated, as she considered how best to wreak revenge. She sucked in her cheeks, biting down on them with her teeth as she considered. After a few minutes, she nodded to herself. Got it, she thought: I'll screw them both at once. I'll just send the wrong report and make them both deal with their angry client. She picked up the pages that Jed had left on her desk a few days ago. Writing very neatly in her school girl cursive, she wrote a cover page to Charlotte: *Hi Charlotte! Sorry this is a little late. Jed took a while. Here is the report you needed. Thanks, Miranda.* She stared at her note with satisfaction, adding a smiley face beneath her signature. She picked up the report and headed over to the fax machine. The report zipped through in a minute. Miranda put on her coat and slung her purse over her arm.

She turned to Davina. "I've had it. My nails need me more than this place. Good luck with your latest consultant. Anyone interesting?"

Davina waved without looking up. "No. Some new guy from Omaha. Forty-five minutes for a drink, max."

8

Horace at the Bridge

Charlotte wobbled on the uneven cobblestones as she returned from her lunch break. Hobbled by high-heeled boots and a narrow skirt, both new, she struggled to maintain her balance as she picked her way down the medieval lane, tilting to one side to keep a shopping bag from slipping off the shoulder pads of her raincoat. Ten feet from the office, she stopped to consider what to do with her bag, a large pink rectangle which screamed *Agent Provocateur: Fine Lingerie* across its side. She didn't fancy giving the traders another reason to smirk at her; already that morning, she had noticed a few smothered grins in her direction when she'd struggled into the office an hour late, exhausted by her 2 a.m. departure from Patrick's flat the night before.

Charlotte removed her raincoat and wrapped it carefully around the bag. Balancing the lumpish bundle on her left hip, she walked a few steps and stretched her right hand toward the building's metal door just as two of Shorwell's traders burst through from the other side, knocking her off balance. Her raincoat and bag fell onto the street, the bag's contents scattering. On the damp black cobblestones, her new lace-edged white camisole gleamed like a snowflake.

"Sorry, Charlotte. Let me help." The sallow collar-tugging trader knelt and reached toward the overturned bag. Turning toward the camisole, he stopped, withdrawing his hand abruptly.

Charlotte lurched forward. "Thanks – I'm fine." Feeling her cheeks flame, she reached toward the sodden camisole. The trader sprang backwards with an inarticulate apology, his eyes wide in alarm. The two men retreated down the lane, their hasty steps echoing off the street. Charlotte re-wrapped the bag, crushed it mercilessly under her arm, and marched into the office.

A voice mail had arrived during her shopping expedition. It was from the secretary to their client in Cardiff. Her soft Welsh voice sounded young and anxious. *My boss needs to ask you something, could you ring this afternoon? It's something to do with the portfolio holdings report you faxed over.* Charlotte looked down at the report, still lying on her desk, and scanned its small type impatiently. It looked like all the other reports faxed over by Miranda since she'd started.

Wondering which of her colleagues to consult, she glanced around. Most of the traders sat in their usual self-enclosed pools of silence, staring at their screens as they ate ham and cheese sandwiches from triangular plastic boxes. Patrick was nowhere to be seen. Circling the room, her gaze fell on Horace. From her desk, she could just make out the top of his head, his thick dark hair falling forward as he studied a newspaper on his desk. She picked up the report and walked slowly toward him, pausing when she reached his chair. He continued to study the article in front of him.

Charlotte tapped his shoulder with one cautious finger. "Horace?" He jerked backwards, his head swinging up toward Charlotte, his dark eyes brightening before clouding over a split second later. Charlotte felt a pang as she watched the rapid transition. What had she done to merit such caution? She hovered over his right shoulder, shifting her weight back and forth. "Horace," she repeated. "I wonder if you could help me? It's about the report I sent over to our shipping client this morning – the one Miranda faxed from New York. The client has some questions about it. There are so many things I still don't quite understand. Would you mind glancing at it before I ring them?"

For a moment, Horace said nothing, his face neutral and unmoving except for the twitch of his left eye. "Why don't you ask Patrick?" he said at last, his voice edged by an atypical note of sarcasm.

Charlotte shifted her weight again, flinching as the unbroken leather of her new boots dug into her heel. "I would, Horace, but for one thing, he isn't here, and I gather from the assistant that it's a bit urgent; and for another, you're the resident rocket scientist when it comes to all this. Of course, if you don't have time…" She paused, and let the words hang in the air. She gave him a beseeching look. "Please, Horace?" Her voice was practically a whisper.

Horace looked away. "All right, Charlotte. Just leave it on my desk." He picked up his newspaper.

Charlotte whispered her thanks and slunk back to her desk in the corner of the office. Once seated, she looked up at the financial pundits on the televisions overhead. Both were talking about oil, whose price had skyrocketed after Iraq invaded Kuwait. One pundit pointed to a map of Iraq, while the other displayed photos of oil wells in Saudi Arabia.

Charlotte stared at the babbling men in irritation. Don't they ever just shut up? She glared at the anchorman nearest her desk, a young man whose hairless baby face puckered as he explained the politics of OPEC. I bet he's never even visited the Mideast, Charlotte thought. Closing her eyes, she envisioned the white painted bookcase of her childhood room. As a teenager, she had filled it with nineteenth century travel logs written by missionaries sent out to proselytize across the British Empire. From under her patchwork quilt in rural England, she had read with fascinated horror about India's blistering heat and China's freezing winters, villages with no running water, medicine, or sanitation. Year after year, they recorded their unceasing efforts to fund new schools and hospitals; the infants they lost to unknown diseases; their rare spiritual victories, their many failures.

Charlotte was alternately humbled and baffled by the patience of England's ideological foot soldiers. At least they had been working toward a goal, she reflected sourly. Why were concrete goals so elusive? The few toward which she had aspired had been brief and mortifying failures. At ten, awed equally by her Communion ceremony and her new white satin dress, she had followed her mother to the garden to announce her intention of becoming a nun. Her mother had not even looked up from planting tulip bulbs as she told Charlotte not to be ridiculous. A few years later, impressed by a TV documentary about a socialite-turned-nurse during the Great War, Charlotte had visited a nearby hospital to volunteer her time. The nurse at the reception desk had glanced at her school uniform and told her to return in ten years.

She opened her eyes and looked at Horace, who remained hunkered down in front of his newspaper, a pool of light illuminating his hunched shoulders. He looked so studious and alone, she thought. It was impossible to imagine him reading a book on how to sell. She closed her eyes again and saw Patrick on the bed next to her the night before, his fingers leafing through the book's pages. She felt again his tanned hand on her thigh and smelled his minty breath on her face. A warm glow suffused her, and the babbling television pundits receded.

The noise of loud male laughter interrupted her luxuriant daydream, as Patrick and a few of the traders banged open the door after what had clearly been a boozy lunch. Jolted out of her reverie about the night before, Charlotte bolted out of her chair, a delighted cry of "Patrick!" escaping from her.

A dozen male heads swiveled in her direction, their laughter extinguished by her outburst. Charlotte stood alone in her corner, her expression of adoration turning to one of utter embarrassment. A low, suppressed laugh started to rumble from somewhere within the group of men and she crumpled into her chair, overcome by a wave of mortified nausea. She squeezed shut her eyes as she fought back tears, lacerating herself mercilessly. How could you stand there screaming his name like some teenager worshipping a pop star? You bloody idiot. Cracking open her wet eyes, she stole a look at the men, who had descended into their usual positions, their faces carefully blank, Charlotte's exclamation ignored and smoothed over by years of social training.

Only one face failed to reestablish its normal appearance. Horace, from his end of the horseshoe, had watched Patrick's entrance and Charlotte's reaction, and had heard the laughter of his colleagues. He didn't join in. Instead, he grabbed the report Charlotte had left on his desk and strode across the office to where Charlotte sat in her isolated circle of misery, her face tilted down toward her desk. Her inflamed cheeks were still blotchily red, and her eyes were smudged with mascara set afloat by her escaped tears. Without warning, he dropped the report onto her desk, where its pages scattered in a messy heap. Charlotte turned her wrecked face toward him in surprise. His eyes were focused two inches above her head toward the wall behind her. "It looks like Patrick is back. I suggest you ask him instead."

Horace retreated to his own desk and picked up a thick analyst's report. Charlotte glared at his retreating back before gathering up the disordered pages and rearranging them. After three minutes, she found that her sea of humiliation had been displaced by anger. I'll bloody well call the client myself, she thought, banging the pages on her desk to align them properly.

She gripped the report with fingers still moist with tears. The numbers on the fax were fuzzy and small, and she squinted at them with bloodshot eyes ringed in streaked mascara. <u>Monthly Valuation Report, Cardiff Shipping Pension Fund (A)</u>, she read. The report was in four sections, listing the fund's holdings in each asset class. Charlotte ran her eye over the list, familiarizing herself with each name before dialing the client. The woman who answered sounded even younger and more uncertain in real life than in her message. Charlotte forgot her misery as she listened to the fluid lilt of the woman's voice.

"Charlotte Cheetham of Shorwell? I'm sorry to trouble you, but my boss, Mr. Penry, said it was important, and you just can't imagine what he's like when he's in a foul temper. I mean, it's not that he's unfair as such, but he's like a dog with a bone until he gets what he wants. Men can be so *difficult* – I'm sure you know what I mean?" Charlotte murmured something inarticulate, and the young woman hurried on. "I was having a perfectly lovely morning – the weather's beautiful down here for *once*, and I was so pleased to find the report you sent me sitting in the fax machine this morning, Mr. Penry's been asking for it again and again, and then I nipped out for a biscuit at the new corner Tesco's – you know the little ones popping up everywhere? And when I got back he was just pacing back and forth saying that the report looked wrong and could I please get you on the phone. Anyway, now you've rung back which is very kind but," she paused for a much-needed breath, "I'm afraid he's gone out."

Charlotte, mesmerized by the soft, lisping consonants of the woman's voice, and rendered semi-comatose by the length of her remarks, took a moment to respond. "No worries," she said. She felt an almost motherly concern for this garrulous young woman. "If you could just tell me the problem, I'll have it fixed. I'm sure he'll be much happier when he learns you've sorted it all out."

"It's very kind of you to say so. People around here are always saying how snooty Londoners are and the English generally, if you'll forgive me, you'd almost think they'd all forgotten we were part of the UK if you know what I mean – for all they go on, you'd think Wales was the absolute center of the whole island – but anyway I've never found that, I mean the English people I've met on holiday here seem perfectly nice. A little tongue-tied, perhaps. Anyway, about the report, I'm sure I don't really know, he just muttered something about the numbers not matching up to the ones he has. He read maths at university, you know, and is absolutely a bore about numbers always having to match up to the penny. That's his favorite expression you see, to – the – penny. Just to needle him sometimes I say, not to the *penry*, Mr. Penry? He hates that."

"How irritating," said Charlotte sympathetically, abandoning all professional pretense. "How annoying for you."

"Oh well, Mother always says I should just ignore it and feel grateful I have a proper job and that I'm not stuck down in the coal mines like my grandad and his brothers." Both women paused as they observed a moment of silence for the miners. The Welsh woman spoke again, resuming her cheerful patter. "Ah well, life moves on. I shall tell Mr. Penry you called and I'm sure he'll be glad to hear all about our conversation." Charlotte felt a spasm of sympathy for the unknown, penny-counting Mr. Penry.

She said briskly, before her unknown interlocutor could continue, "Well, I'll check into the report on our end. I'm sure it will all be straightened out in no time, Miss—"

"Burton. Like the famous actor, the dark one who went off to America and married that child actress, the one with all the husbands. I watched National Velvet eight times, I was horse mad."

"Miss Burton. Very nice to speak to you. Goodbye." Putting down the phone, Charlotte found that her spirits had lifted considerably. Humming the theme song to National Velvet, she picked up her purse and headed to the ladies' room to repair her makeup. I think I'll pop out to Tesco's as well, she thought, as she headed for the door.

A few weeks later, Charlotte returned to her flat to find a message from Henrietta on her answering machine. The two friends hadn't spoken since Henrietta's angry exit from the party at the art gallery and Charlotte, accustomed to Henrietta's unyielding opinions, had resigned

herself to a long period of frosty relations. Previous disagreements between them had always resulted in Charlotte backing down after a few
days of awkward silence, rationalizing her capitulation as the price of a
sophisticated and exciting friend. For years, the friendship had bumped
along in this fashion. This time, however, Charlotte had resolved not to
extend an olive branch. *I'm done with backing down,* she told herself, *I
don't care how much I miss her.* It was with pleased surprise, therefore,
that she heard Henrietta's familiar, cultivated voice on her answering
machine one evening: *Charlotte – it's Henrietta – I know, the awful, un-
forgivable Henrietta who stomped out of your party in a huff. Please forgive me, dearest Char. I'm planning to have a little dinner party for some
friends in a few weeks, after the Christmas holidays, and I hope you'll
come. Do bring Patrick. I'm sure he's charming upon better acquaintance.*
Charlotte replayed the message to make sure she'd heard it correctly. It
wasn't like Henrietta to reconsider a social judgement; was it possible
that Henrietta was mellowing with age? With this happy idea in mind,
she played the message a third time, hearing in Henrietta's voice a new
element of warmth.

Pleased, she turned from the answering machine and shivered, realizing that Lady Philippa, once more in France, had shut down the
house's central heating. Pulling on a wool cardigan, she considered
Henrietta's invitation. Now that she had gained her point, and her rift
with Henrietta appeared over, she was able to consider the situation
with a cooler head. To her surprise, she discovered that she was not,
in fact, wholly looking forward to inviting Patrick. She considered this
new thought as she wandered over to her refrigerator and stared at its
meager contents: half a container of hummous, a pint of milk, and two
pots of strawberry yogurt.

Images of Patrick passed through her mind, and she started to
smile. There was Patrick with his arm loosely draped on the back of
his lead trader, his neat golden head shining next to the lanky hair of
his English colleague. There was Patrick's straight white teeth, always
visible through his easy smile and set off by his face, somehow tanned
throughout the year while everyone around him remained ghostly pale.
Her involuntary smile grew as she recalled his smooth broad back, his
shoulder muscles moving underneath her hand on the night after the art

gallery party. The discomfort of lying on top of his book, <u>How To Sell</u>, had faded from memory. She shook her head, clearing her imagination like the etch-a-sketch game that had fascinated her as a child.

Her thoughts wandered to the cafe where she and Patrick had eaten lunch a few times in the weeks following the night they'd spent to-gether – always rushed, always last minute. Twice, Patrick had material-ized at her desk with his jacket already on: What do you say, Charlotte? Lunch? At one of these lunches, he'd tossed onto the table a small flat box, wrapped in glossy silver paper and stamped with the name of a nearby shop. It held a silk scarf of blue and orange hibiscus flowers. *It's beautiful*, she'd said, certain that her pale skin would look even more faded against its vivid colors. Patrick had shrugged and said, *I thought I'd brighten you up.*

She dragged her teaspoon around the bottom rim of the yogurt pot. The image of Patrick's even features and easy smile started to dim and flicker in her mind, like a lightbulb in its last seconds of life. She shivered in the cold flat again, as the glow of her memory receded. Why wasn't she more excited about inviting him to Henrietta's dinner party? She could count on him to be charming with the other guests, she knew; charm was the prominent quality which Henrietta had so held against him. But would he be charming to her? Charlotte paused. It was true that he had taken her to lunch, and given her presents, and spent a night with her in his featureless flat. But did he care about her at all? She sighed, realizing that she had no idea how to answer this crucial question. She envisioned Henrietta's eagle eye watching Patrick's behavior at the forthcoming party and winced as she registered her lack of confidence. Walking over to her minute kitchen, she threw the yogurt pot into the rubbish bin.

The fact was, she was stuck. Having won her point against Henrietta, she couldn't falter now. Wrapping a scarf around her neck, she picked up a half-read novel and flung herself onto Lady Philippa's cast-off sofa, losing herself in the adventures of the novel's heroine, whose tragic fate, blissfully, was entirely out of her control.

9

A Game of Squash

Piers swore under his breath. He'd seen the ball hit the lower corner of the squash court and rebound against the wall behind him, but then he'd lost track of it. Breathing hard, he held the racket outstretched in his right hand and whirled around, looking wildly for the small black rubber ball. He looked up just as it slammed into his ankle. Wincing, he swore again, this time audibly. From three feet away, W. laughed. "My point, Brit."

W. wound up to serve the next ball. The older man was dressed in an immaculate white polo shirt and shorts, their matching Nike swooshes neatly highlighting his toned physique. W. was in superb condition, a fact which he never failed to point out when Piers or Jed missed a shot. "I'm fifteen years older than you guys," he would scream, elated by victory. "Move it!"

Piers and Jed moved it. Squash games with W. in his private club were one of the more painful distinctions to which their success entitled them. Jed, whose motions in the office were limited to ponderous walk-abouts, surprised Piers with his skill as a squash player. With his usual laconic competence, Jed hit the ball with efficient and hard strokes, rarely missing, and exhibiting no emotion whatsoever whether he won or lost a point. Piers, by contrast, worked twice as hard and half as effectively, careening across the court as he tried to adjust from twenty years of tennis to the manic rhythms of squash. He lashed out at the ball, alternating between total misses and startling successes, swearing quietly throughout.

His winning streaks were undermined by his anxiety about the unspoken politics of the games: Was he meant to give W. a hard game and then lose, without appearing to give it away? Or would that be considered an act of cowardice? Would W. be outraged and insulted if he won? Jed's own behavior on this question was no guide, as Jed's efficient game never actually threatened to beat W.'s expensively coached and rehearsed bursts of competitive fury.

Tonight, W. was winning fair and square, leaving Piers no time to consider his approach to competition vis-à-vis his boss. Piers's natural athleticism couldn't offset the onslaught of bars and clubs to which his body had been subjected. Never before had Piers's social life been so extensive or intense. With the other traders at Shorwell, he now made nightly rounds of SoHo and TriBeCa, occasionally venturing south toward Brooklyn or north towards Harlem when they were feeling particularly adventurous. He was long beyond feeling flattered by the attentions of the ubiquitous beautiful women who flocked toward the group of financiers like exotic, expensive birds; he now expected to be fawned over whenever he walked into a darkened room. Whereas in London, the men worked hard, if ineffectually, to impress the scarce women, in Manhattan, the reverse was delightfully, deliriously true: The women – to his eye, all gorgeous, all incredible – flocked toward the men, provided they were in finance and would foot the bill for drinks. In the rare instances when he felt he was failing to impress, Piers had learned to dial up his British accent and expressions to full tilt, with a success equal to that of his client list. The quiet self-disgust that accompanied this technique fell silent under the combined effect of alcohol and the smooth, golden hair illuminating every darkened bar.

Piers lost the last point and W. slapped him on the back. Piers winced.

"Good game, Piers," W. said with complacence, not bothering to feign sympathy for his loss. "Drinks?"

Piers nodded, and turned to Jed, who was waiting for them just outside the court, having lost to W. during the previous game. The three men turned toward the showers and steam rooms, W. branching off toward a special VIP members' area for a massage first.

An hour later, they reassembled in the club's private bar and dining area. W. was waiting for them, stretched out comfortably on a leather banquette, and nursing a scotch.

"Gentlemen," he said, with a hint of irony, as they approached the table. "Drinks?" W. summoned a waitress with a nod. A young woman in a skin-tight black knit wraparound dress slithered toward the table, a diamond crucifix glinting from the recesses of her cleavage. Her blond hair was teased upward into a gleaming golden pyramid, and her heavy mascara suggested a curtain rising on a long-running theatrical performance. W. tilted back his head, his hair slicked back after his shower, and smiled at her guarded eyes.

"Ah, Maureen," he said, grasping her hand and holding it while he spoke. He turned to Jed and Piers. "Maureen has been taking care of me since I joined the club." He looked up at her with a knowing smile. "I think my friends here will join me in a scotch – right, boys?" Without waiting for their answer, he dropped her hand in dismissal. Watching W. from across the table, Piers's depleted body coiled with the tension of a small animal tracking an unpredictable predator.

W. drummed his manicured fingers on the polished mahogany surface in front of him while glancing around the room, an expanse of leather club chairs, low tables and geometric abstract paintings, all dimly lit by faux candle sconces. The drinks for Piers and Jed arrived, and all three men lifted the heavy cut glass tumblers of scotch.

"Gentlemen," W. repeated, "Congratulations. Let's celebrate." Without elaborating, W. took a swig of his drink, his smoothly shaved neck expanding and contracting as the liquid descended. He drained half his glass before replacing it on the table with a muted thud. Piers followed his lead, feeling the alcohol hit his tired body with a jolt. His muscles relaxed very slightly. W. smiled across the table in a satisfied, almost paternalist fashion. Reaching into his blazer's breast pocket, he withdrew a small silver box and placed it on the table next to a squat arrangement of spiked tropical flowers. Piers felt Jed shift his weight forward. W. pressed a small button on the side of the box to flip open its lid, before tossing two crisp $100 bills across the table.

"A quick pick-me-up before dinner – think of it as an aperitif." Jed twisted one of the bills expertly and leaned over to inhale. He pushed the box in Piers's direction. Piers looked at the smooth white powder and felt a wave a nausea. His dehydrated brain ached. He shook his head slowly.

"No, thanks. I'll stick to liquor tonight."

W. looked at him for a moment, and then shrugged. "No problem," W. said, replacing the box into his breast pocket with a smooth motion. He shifted his hand upward and started to tap a syncopated rhythm on his collarbone, nodding his head in time to the beat. "I used to play drums for a band in college. We were called the Poison Pistols – very post-punk. I used enough gel to make my hair into a perfect sphere. It didn't even move when I danced. God, I miss those days – girls rushing the stage, enough free drugs to last forever – well, almost."

He gave his collarbone a final tap before raising his index finger in the air to signal another round of drinks, not checking to see whether Maureen was watching. He continued. "I saw the new client wins report, and I am impressed. I don't know what you're promising in your sales meetings, and I don't want to know, but it's working. You guys are my top two lieutenants – my team *numero uno*." W. raised his glass in a mock salute and drained it.

He looked at Piers. "Piers, I told you when you joined that you and Jed would be an awesome sales team and that the sky was the limit. I meant it. Your buddy Jed is tapped out with the data side of the client reports—" W. swiveled his eyes toward Jed, who nodded, expressionless, "but I have a new business line for you. It's going to be a perfect fit." W. stared at Piers meaningfully. Piers met W.'s look head-on, hoping he looked more eager than wary. His body, which had cooled down since the squash game, started to pick up heat again.

W. caught his apprehension and laughed. "Piers, don't worry, buddy. You're gonna love this. Here's the deal. There are in this city, within one-half mile of us *right now*, hundreds of seriously rich women who are bored out of their minds. Some of them are widows, some aren't, but may as well be for all they ever see their Wall Street husbands. And those guys aren't much to look at when they do show up. So here's the plan: You, Piers Cheetham, are going to be their new thing. You're going to show up at their parties where they're swanning around as hostesses chairing museum galas, gallery openings and opera fundraisers – whatever. You grab a few champagne flutes from a waiter, you offer one to whichever woman is loaded down with the most seriously outrageous jewelry, you talk up Shorwell and within six months – I guarantee it – we have a serious new private client business."

Piers hesitated. Was W. setting him up to be a kind of salesman gigolo?

"And don't get me wrong," W. continued, seeing his uncertain face. "It's all going to be above-board – no after-party visits or anything like that. Just a lot of dressing up, using your exquisite British manners and plying your natural charm and you're done. And, by the way," W. paused for emphasis, "whatever new income you bring in, you get a one-third cut."

Jed, whose head had sunk into its usual attitude of reptilian lethargy, lifted his chin. His eyeballs swerved in Piers's direction as he spoke. "One-third? I'll get my Hamptons broker to call you."

W. smiled at Jed and reached across the table, grasping one of Jed's and Piers's hands at the same time. The three men sat linked as W. looked from one to the other for a long and awkward moment. W. squeezed hard and released their hands. "Guys, this is it. This is the future. It's going to be awesome. Now, if you'll excuse me, I'm finishing my evening with someone even better-looking than either of you."

W. stood up and stretched, massaging his lower back. Giving the table a final syncopated tap, he left the room with an energetic stride. Jed and Piers remained seated, unspeaking, each one staring into his own drink and adjusting to the release of pressure after W.'s departure. Jed stood up. "I'm off," he said.

Piers, lost in his own thoughts, nodded. He continued to sit, waiting for his head to clear from its increasingly familiar alcohol-induced fog.

Thirty minutes later, he found Sixth Avenue slick from a recent rain shower. In the darkness, the lights from the skyscrapers overhead created shiny reflections in the shallow, oily puddles at the street corners. The usual cacophony of honking horns and screeching tires assaulted his ears, but Piers, now accustomed to New York's unrelenting noise, didn't register it. He stuck his arm out for a cab – he'd stopped using the subway after his first paycheck had cleared – and barely retreated when a car swerved in his direction.

He settled himself on the cab's black bench seat, his mind glowing from the squash game's endorphins, the large tumblers of scotch, and W.'s praise. W.'s words ran in continuous loop in his head. *Doing great – top lieutenant – rich widows – exquisite British manners.* He listened to these words over and over again as the cab careened down Fifth Avenue, flying past Rockefeller Center, the stone lions of New York's public library and Madison Square Park. Around twenty-fifth street, the loop halted at *exquisite British manners* and Fifth Avenue slid away, replaced by the dining room of his childhood house, where his eight year-old self sat across from his parents at dinner, fuming at his mother as she corrected his use of his knife and fork. *It doesn't matter*, he protested, throwing his silverware onto the clean tablecloth. His father, usually so mild mannered, put down his own knife and fork and looked at Piers. *Oh yes, it does, Piers*, he said. *You'll find that in the end, things like knives and forks and please and thank you and all the rest of it matter a great deal.*

The vision of his father vanished, replaced by W.'s tanned, handsome face, staring at him from across the table. *Exquisite British manners...* Piers squirmed internally. He wasn't sure that chatting up old rich widows was in his narrative of American conquest. He wanted to succeed on talent and hard work – perhaps more talent than hard work, if he were honest – but W.'s new business venture seemed dodgy and possibly disreputable. Piers sighed. What would his father have said? He reached out in his imagination to this longed-for font of avuncular wisdom cut short by his father's early death. Piers strained at his memory, grasping for clues. He replayed the supper table. *In the end, knives and forks ... are what matters.* Could this have been a premonition of the talents Piers would use to rise in the world? Was his father anticipating this very moment in his future? Piers knew, rationally, that this was absurd, but the idea tugged at him seductively. Maybe he was meant to use his charm to great effect, he thought; maybe this was one of the tools his father had discerned within him from an early age. So what if it was a bit sleazy? He would be selling them financial products that couldn't hurt them, after all, and they had more than enough money to burn, and perhaps it might be a fun new thing for them, too. He heard Jed's flat voice: *I'll have my Hamptons broker call you....*

By the time the cab delivered him to the door of his apartment building on east 13th Street – Piers thrusting a $20 bill at the driver without bothering to wait for the change – his mind was settled and clear from doubt. It had taken only twelve blocks for him to reinterpret his father's comment about proper table manners into a posthumous directive to pursue this new opportunity with enthusiasm. Excited, and grateful to a man who had been in his grave for over ten years, Piers bounded up the five flights to his apartment. Grabbing a chilled bottle of beer from his doll-sized refrigerator, he kicked off his shoes and flicked on the television to watch a college basketball game, losing himself in the exertions and combat of other men.

One week later, on a chill Thursday night, Piers stood at the base of the stone steps of the Metropolitan Museum of Art. He stood straighter than usual, conscious of the starched tuxedo that he had donned in the men's room of Shorwell's offices. It had arrived on his desk that after-noon from W.'s personal tailor, a grizzled Russian in midtown who eyed Piers's shoulders and ran a tape measure up the inside of his leg before dismissing him with a grunt.

Piers gazed up at the museum's soaring sandstone columns. Huge floodlights were placed at their base, leading the eye upward to the sculpted crowned heads which peered down from the roofline. Piers felt his heart leap at the magnificence of the great structure and the symmetrical beauty of its façade. He glanced at his watch: 8 o'clock. He looked around for Jed, who had agreed to accompany him on this first foray into New York society. *I'll be your wingman,* Jed offered, wryly; *no one will feel threatened with a guy as unimpressive as me next to you.* Piers, accustomed to Jed's sarcasm, hadn't bothered to answer.

Jed materialized from the shadows of the pavement. His thick blond hair had been combed back from his wide forehead for the occasion. With eyes fractionally more open than usual, he looked Piers up and down. "You clean up well," he said, laughing.

"You too, mate," grinned Piers.

The two men crossed over to the main entrance, where a red carpet cascaded down the museum's stone steps and onto the pavement. Piers put a tentative shining black leather shoe onto the red carpet, half-expecting to be repulsed as an imposter. At the entrance, a delicate young man wearing a diamond earring glanced at them in a cursory fashion as he checked their names from a long list, his eyes shifting quickly to the guests behind them.

Inside, the noise of the soaring entrance hall was intense, as New York's elite competed against a full orchestra staged on the balcony directly overhead. Women in floor-length sparkling dresses greeted each other with shrieks of enthusiasm, sweeping past the tuxedoed men, who stood in clusters like rock formations in a foaming sea. Piers glanced around the room, pausing as he caught sight of a woman with a sheaf of shining black hair. The draped folds of her red silk dress hugged her with loving adoration, outlining the curve of her hips and breasts in voluptuous radiance. Jed followed Piers's eyes and jabbed him in the side. "Focus, Piers: old, bored, loaded with jewelry. Don't screw this up. After you get the one-third cut, you can chase as many red silk dresses as you want."

Piers felt a tap on his arm, and he turned to find a short blond woman looking up at him with an impatient stare. A triple strand of pearls illuminated a practical, no-nonsense mouth. She ran an efficient eye over Piers and Jed. "Piers and Jed? From Shorwell?"

"Yes," said Piers, inclining his head, "and you are?" He offered her his hand, which she ignored.

"Dee Brown. I write a society column for the New York Post. I know W. from ages ago – before, let's just say, he lost the rest of his name. He asked me to introduce you to someone. As a favor. I'll take you there, and then you're on your own. You're welcome."

The woman rotated on her heel and started to maneuver deftly through the crowd, not checking whether Piers and Jed were keeping pace. They had crossed the width of the great hall when Piers realized that they were at the entrance to another, smaller room. Dee whispered a few words to the young man guarding its entrance – this one even more elegant than the first, and with a larger diamond in his ear – and Piers found himself being scrutinized yet again, this time more slowly, and with more overt curiosity. Piers squirmed, and tried to match the impassive expression of Jed, who stood one step behind. The man turned to Dee with a minute shrug of his shoulders and wearing an expression of indifference. He stood aside to let the three of them pass into the inner sanctum, his eyes staring beyond Piers and Jed as they entered.

The noise of the inner room was even more intense. Piers smelled something sweet, and he looked up to see masses of red tropical flowers hanging upside down from the ceiling, their orange stamens leering at him. The women in the room had matched their dresses to the flower motif and rustled by in swathes of orange, red and pink. With rapid steps, Dee moved to the center of the room, where the largest dress of all was stationed, a swirl of crimson taffeta rising in waves to a vertical collar that ring-fenced an emaciated face, once beautiful. The skin of the woman's face was stretched back like cellophane over her bones, emphasizing her disproportionately plump, orange stained lips. Dee leaned over to kiss the air three inches from the woman's hollow right cheek, whispering something into the cluster of diamonds that pulled down her sagging earlobe. Piers saw the woman's eyes widen within their rings of black eyeliner and swivel in his direction. Jed nudged him. Taking a deep breath, Piers stepped forward with his hand outstretched and a polite smile on his face.

Dee turned to him with a perfunctory smile and cool eyes. "Elena Rothschild, may I present Piers Cheetham? He's one of your greatest fans." Elena Rothschild's face remained impassive as her jet-black eyes swept over Piers's face.

"Indeed, I am Mrs. Rothschild," Piers said lamely, frantically wondering what to say next. He turned for help to Dee, but she had disappeared.

"Call me Elena. All my fans do." The woman's voice was surprisingly low and brusque, and she pronounced the words very precisely, in the manner of someone who had learned English as an adult. "What do you like most? My theater or my film work?"

"Film," Piers said, added a silent prayer, *please don't ask me which.*

"And which," Elena Rothschild said, "is your favorite?"

"Saved from Paradise. Although its sequel, Banished from Paradise, was great too." Piers and Elena Rothschild both turned to look at Jed, who had emerged from his shadow behind Piers. His blond hair was still slicked back from his forehead neatly, and his heavy-lidded eyes looked directly at the older woman.

Elena Rothschild tilted her head a fraction to acknowledge this tribute. "Another fan, I see."

"Oh yes. We're always talking about great actresses at Shorwell Capital," Jed said.

"Absolutely," echoed Piers, taking up the thread. "We are great film buffs. A love of movies is one of our hiring requirements. We especially love the classics, right, Jed?" The woman's dark eyes flashed. Piers realized that all her emotions emanated from these two black wells, as the skin on her face had been stretched too tightly to allow any mobility of expression.

"I hope I am not," she said with her distinct, foreign vowels, "yet old enough to be considered a classic." Her eyes swiveled past Piers, starting to focus on the people around him.

Piers felt a panicked jolt of adrenalin that had powered him through many hard-won tennis matches. "Of course not," he said, "We love contemporary beauties as well. We're thrilled to meet you – we came to this party hoping to get to see you. Jed and I are Shorwell Capital's biggest movie fans. Do you know Shorwell? It's an investment firm. Lots of our clients are in the arts, like you."

Elena Rothschild waved a dismissive hand emblazoned with diamond rings. "I never think about money," she said.

"Of course not," Piers replied. "That's what we're for. An actress – an artist – shouldn't be distracted from her craft." He reached into his pocket and produced a card, holding it out with a shallow bow, and his most winning smile. "If you'll just take this, we won't impose on you any longer. No doubt there's a long list of admirers waiting to pay tribute." Elena Rothschild glanced down at the card, pinching its edge between her wrinkled thumb and index finger, and sequestering it in an invisible pocket hidden within the billowing folds of fabric. Piers swiftly produced a second card and a ball point pen. "And – if it's not too great an imposition, would you consider signing this one for me? I collect autographs of great actors."

A smile of gracious condescension crossed the woman's face. She reached for the pen. "What did you say your name was?"

"Piers."

She nodded, scrawling a few words on the card before handing it back to him and turning away. Piers looked at the card and grinned. In a pinched script, it read, "To Peter with affection, Elena." Underneath these words was her phone number.

10

Missed Signals

Charlotte stood on the ground floor of Fortnum and Mason, humming along to the Christmas carols broadcast by hidden speakers. The famous store was festooned for the holidays, its famous green walls draped with leafy garlands and red taffeta bows. Outside, tourists crowded around the store's bowed glass windows, filled with scenes from the Nutcracker ballet, complete with miniature porcelain dancers who whirled through snow blown by an unseen fan.

Charlotte looked down at her Christmas list, torn from a page of her poetry notebook. It was short: a matching spade and fork for her mother from Fortnum's famous gardening department, a book of photographs of New York vistas for Piers, and a scarf, perhaps, for Patrick. Henrietta was off the list this year. Mounting two flights of stairs, she entered the men's department and found a glass display case of scarves, each folded with meticulous precision. They looked lush and elegant, and wickedly expensive. As she bent over the case, trying to spot a price tag, she heard the voice of a woman demanding assistance. With a start, she recognized the voice as Annabelle's, her ex-colleague from the ad agency. She kept her eyes cast firmly downward.

"Charlotte! Charlotte Cheetham!" Annabelle's cawing voice sliced through an orchestral rendition of Silent Night.

Charlotte lifted her eyes slowly from the scarves. "Annabelle! I didn't see you."

"Nonsense, Charlotte, you were never a good liar. Nigel and I always knew exactly when you were eavesdropping when you were pretending to work. But that's all over with now that you're a City girl. I don't suppose you ever give us a thought." Charlotte started to demur, but Annabelle had already turned again to the sales assistant, a tall Polish woman with wide pale eyes. In a loud voice, using exaggerated consonants, Annabelle asked to see a large travel bag elevated on a glass shelf behind the cash register. Silently, the saleswoman turned to the bag and hoisted it down onto the counter.

Annabelle ran a manicured nail over the sumptuous leather before turning to Charlotte. "What do you think, Charlotte? Nice enough for our Nigel?" Annabelle peered at Charlotte's face, eager for a reaction.

Charlotte kept her face as impassive as possible. "It's lovely, Annabelle. Are you going somewhere?"

Annabelle's face took on a smug look of victory. "Don't you read the engagements column in the Telegraph? Really, have you fallen off the map entirely since decamping to the City? Nigel and I are engaged. You needn't wish me joy – I'm overflowing already. We're off to Bermuda." Annabelle paused, and stroked the leather again. "And you? Whatever happened to your American boy? Peter?"

"Patrick."

"Well?"

Charlotte decided to match Annabelle's smug look. "He's fine. As it happens, I'm just looking for a Christmas gift for him now. This woolen scarf, I thought." Charlotte recklessly pointed to the most luxurious of the lot, an oversized cashmere scarf woven in shades of moss green and brown.

Annabelle turned to the saleswoman, who continued to stand on the other side of the counter. "My friend would like that one," Annabelle said to her, clicking her nail on the glass of the display case. Charlotte started to protest but the sales lady, suddenly deaf, had removed it in a flash and was already folding it into a box lined with tissue paper. Annabelle, still stroking the leather travel bag, watched as the woman secured the box with a wired fabric bow.

Carrying the box to the cash register, the saleswoman regained her hearing and turned to Charlotte. "Cash or credit, madam?"

"Credit," Charlotte croaked.

The saleslady rang up the purchase, and all three women stared at the register's display: £250. There was a moment of silence.

"That should do the trick," said Annabelle. "Allow me to wish you joy, too. And don't worry: From now on, all the expenses will be on him." Charlotte extended her credit card and stood numb as the saleswoman rang up the purchase.

Annabelle pushed the leather travel bag back across the counter. "I'll keep looking," she said, before turning to Charlotte. "I'll tell Nigel you said hello."

The next day, Charlotte was back at her desk, frowning at her nails as she listened to the complaints of her Welsh client, Mr. Penry, who was unhappy with the portfolio report Charlotte had forwarded from Miranda. *May I remind you, Miss Cheetham, that I read maths at university, and my numbers are calculated very carefully – to the penny, one might say. Moreover, there are a few positions whose values I cannot independently ascertain at all.* Charlotte sighed as he began to list all the stocks whose valuation he was questioning. As she listened, her heart went out to Miss Burton; even from afar, it was clear that theirs must be an aggravating relationship. She envisioned the guileless Miss Burton: a red-haired, blowsy, Rosetti-like young woman in scarves, scarcely able to sit still as a balding man read instructions from a yellow legal pad. Miss Burton's loose hair would be decorated by fresh flowers – no, not flowers, Charlotte thought, reining in her imagination; even she wouldn't go so far. Mr. Penry reached the end of his long list and stopped. The imagined Miss Burton evaporated, and Charlotte promised to get back to him as quickly as possible. Putting down the phone, she approached Patrick, who was poised behind the chair of his head trader.

"Our Welsh client is upset. He says our numbers don't match his."

Patrick didn't look up. "No problem, Charlotte. It's probably just a currency issue. Or a reporting glitch. I'll call Miranda after lunch. New York's not open yet."

"Good luck with that," Charlotte said, her voice heavy with sarcasm. "She never answers."

Patrick flicked his head sideways to grin at Charlotte. "She's what you call a boy's girl. Leave her to me."

Charlotte retreated to her desk. Boy's girl or not, she didn't believe Patrick had any intention of sorting out her problem with Mr. Penry. I'll call Piers, she thought. He's always boasting about how early he starts work; maybe he's in the office now. She dialed Piers's number.

"Piers Cheetham," said Piers. His voice sounded unused and weary.

"Good morning, Piers! Were you out late last night? More bars and Manhattan nightlife?"

A hollow laugh made its way across the Atlantic. "Yes, dear Charlotte – it's a constant party on this side of the pond. Are you ringing me at the crack of dawn to discuss my social life?" He paused, and his tone sharpened. "Is it Mother? Is anything wrong?"

"No, she's fine, and looking forward to your arrival home for Christmas. I expect you've already bought her a present?" There was no answer. "I'm ringing because the Welsh shipping client is upset that the report Miranda faxed through doesn't match his internal numbers."

"Oh, for God's sake."

"And Miranda won't return my calls, and I promised him I'd sort it out. So I thought I'd call you, big brother. Tell me, where does Miranda get her reports?"

"I don't know," said Piers, mulishly.

"I thought you knew everything. Aren't you and Miranda friends? Shall I call her again?"

"No," Piers said quickly. "No, for God's sake stop bothering Miranda. The reports are probably from Jed."

"So I should call Jed?"

A long pause greeted this suggestion, ending in a sigh. "No. That wouldn't go well. Jed is – difficult. Let me speak to him for you. But Charlotte,"

"Yes?"

"After this, could you just drop it please? It's getting hard to be a Cheetham around here, with my sister hassling my colleagues all the time."

"I'm not hassling them, Piers. I'm just trying to do my job."

"Yes, and I'm just trying to do mine, and it's getting a lot more difficult with you around."

Piers and Charlotte hung up, each convinced that the other was unreasonable and difficult. Charlotte stomped out of the London office for a brisk lunch and walk, but Piers, at 8 a.m., was left to stew in irritation. He started to make a wisecrack about women before remembering that Jerry no longer sat two feet away. Instead, his former neighbor was halfway across the floor, still sitting in the cubicle Piers had abandoned when he'd been moved to a private office. True, it was the smallest of the private offices, and faced the neighboring buildings rather than Central Park or the Empire State Building. Still, Piers had been flattered and excited by this sign of approval, and had spent a happy afternoon peering through his new floor-to-ceiling windows, fascinated by the bird's eye view of his neighbors' rooftops, and trying to peer into the windows of the tall apartment buildings nearby. Angela had even left a Post-it note on his desk with the name of an art gallery W. patronized, instructing Piers to choose something for his large blank wall. Piers had rushed down after the close of the market to a gallery in the heart of Soho, a brilliantly lit white room emblazoned with large acrylic abstracts, whose screaming neon colors stopped him dead upon entry. It was only after a restorative club soda offered by a willowy blond saleswoman – W.'s contact – that he was able to select which of the blinding canvases to hang on his office wall.

He squinted at the swirling mass of red and yellow paint now and felt his head begin to ache. Swiveling his chair away from the painting, he gazed out the window. The day was again wet and grey, and a thin mist hung over Sixth Avenue, fifty floors below. A constant muted honking floated up, as taxi drivers vented their fury on the sea of black umbrellas that surged into every gap of the street, blocking their progress. Piers watched the street drama for two long minutes, a sodden, frustrated mass of humanity in miniature. It was like looking into the wrong end of a telescope, he thought. He turned to his phone and dialed Jed's extension.

"Jed here."

"Hey, Jed. Piers. Sorry to call so early."

"No problem. Is this a thank you call for the apartment broker I sent you? I told you she was hot. Did you find a new apartment to replace that dump you're in?"

"She's gorgeous, Jed, and all the apartments look good with her in them. But look," Piers hesitated before continuing. "My sister just called from London with a problem. Our Welsh shipping client has been complaining that the most recent valuation report we sent him doesn't match his numbers. Apparently he keeps his own internal spreadsheet."

"What the fuck. Which report?"

"She said it came from Miranda last week by fax." There was a long pause on Jed's end of the phone. Piers continued, rattled, "Sorry to bother you about this Jed, but Miranda's not returning any calls and Charlotte can be like a dog with a bone..." Piers's voice trailed off.

A few moments passed before Jed spoke. "No problem. I'll deal with it."

"Thanks, buddy. I owe you." Jed hung up. Frowning, Piers began to skim the headlines of the *Wall Street Journal*. His phone rang again.

"Piers?" A light and musical woman's voice floated into his ear. "It's Monique Divine, the real estate broker."

"Monique! What a nice surprise." Piers sat up straighter.

"I just wanted to let you that two more amazing apartments have come onto the market overnight, a duplex loft in the West Village, and a two-bedroom conversion in TriBeCa. They're only a little past your price range, but that's okay, right, for a young man on the rise? Are you free to see them tonight?"

"I'd love to, Monique. But I have a symphony gala I've got to attend."

Monique Divine gave an exaggerated laugh. "I've been blown off before, but never that blatantly. Finance guys don't go to the symphony. Prove me wrong. I'll be your date." A fleeting, tantalizing image of Monique Divine in a clinging evening dress passed through Piers's mind, her bare arm brushing his as he handed her a champagne flute. In a flash, her fresh face was displaced by Elena Rothschild's, whose eyes mocked him behind her fleshless, surgically immobilized face. "I would love that, but I'm there on company business."

"Company business at the symphony? I thought I'd heard them all. But no problem, Piers – call me when you're free. But those two properties will probably get snapped up tonight."

Piers hung up. He tried to visualize Monique Divine as she'd looked last night, sleek and black as a cat as she showed him two available apartments in the West Village, a coy smile on her glossy lips as she raised a suggestive hand toward the empty bedrooms. They were stage sets waiting for the actors to enter, he'd thought, actors who were locked up in high-rise office buildings in Midtown and Wall Street, staring at their screens all day while their stylish, expensive, empty stages remained empty. Piers tried to hold onto her image but couldn't; it was too thin. Annoyed, he wandered out to his old cubicle. Jerry sat at his desk, his Yankees baseball cap bent forward over his newspaper. Piers leaned over his shoulder and saw that the newspaper had been turned to the sports section.

"Glad to know you're not risking any real news – you had me worried for a second."

Jerry looked up and laughed. "Not a chance. What are you doing out here with the *hoi polloi*? You're not missing us, now that you've been bumped up to the big leagues, are you?" Jerry's laugh held a bitter edge, which Piers chose to ignore. He gave a friendly smile to Jerry and wandered back to his office. He picked up his newspaper again, but had trouble focusing on the headlines. Jerry's remark stung. The fact was, he was lonely. With all the excitement of coming to New York, he hadn't dwelt much on his past life in London but now, sitting in this sleek, temperature-controlled glass box high above the earth, watching the grey fog drift past his expanse of windows, he wondered about his former colleagues. They'd be downing a quick pint of beer right now, delaying their return to the office after lunch. He saw them clearly, men at the tail end of their first youth, conservatively dressed in muted pin-striped suits whose waistlines were starting to feel snug. In London, he'd chafed at their predictable banter and jokes, all familiar from years spent with similar boys at school and university. Now, their very predictability seemed their charm. At least you knew where you were with them, he thought. He considered the people he'd met since coming to Shorwell. What did he know about any of them? Who were they, anyway? He shut his eyes, seeing a life boat bobbing on an ocean. This was his life, he thought: in uncharted waters and without a compass, praying that he could navigate by following the stars that blinked brightest.

Sighing, he switched on the TV that hung in a corner of his office. The CNBC anchorman was talking about oil, whose price had been rising steadily since Iraq had invaded Kuwait. Behind the sleek anchorman, a red graph showed its rise, an angry diagonal line that inched upward as he spoke. Oil was hitting new highs, the anchorman said, his smooth forehead taking on a concerned crease. Piers listened to his commentary without much interest.

He'd just muted the sound and turned to his newspaper when Jed appeared, his large frame filling the entrance to Piers's office. Jed was holding a marketing presentation for their next meeting, and his face wore its usual dour, inscrutable expression: hooded eyes almost shut, his mouth neither smiling nor frowning. Piers, glad to have the company of another person, looked up at him with a smile. Jed started to approach Piers's desk when he stopped, his attention caught by the television. His eyelids sank even further into his cheeks.

Piers stood up and reached for the document in Jed's hand. "Oil again. Getting boring."

Jed, watching the crimson red line pointing to the oil price trajectory, didn't answer.

Piers looked at him, surprised. "The funds don't own oil, right?"

Jed turned away from the screen and looked at Piers, but his eyes seemed focused on a point beyond Piers's head. Piers, accustomed to Jed's habit of long pauses between sentences, waited. After a few seconds, Jed's eyes appeared to register Piers. "No, the funds don't." His skin, which remained cool and colorless even during squash games, was flushed pink. He handed Piers the marketing document for the meeting in Atlanta the following day.

Piers flipped through its pages and looked up. "The usual?"

"Yup. Two hours with the pension fund committee and back here by 6. I'll see you at the airport."

Jed left, and Piers flipped through the presentation. He and Jed had become a well-oiled team over the past months, and he no longer felt any anxiety about presenting Shorwell's funds. During the first handful of meetings, he'd felt a fleeting moment of unease when Jed mentioned an imaginary benchmark or promised returns that seemed aggressive, if not impossible, but Jed had brushed aside his concerns with laughing contempt. *We're masters of the universe, buddy, remember?* Piers had nodded, and with each account win, Jed's easy formulation had seemed ever more justified. Piers gave the new presentation a cursory glance and tossed it aside, his thoughts on his conversation with Charlotte. Perhaps he should buy something for his mother after all. Something that would show her how well he was doing in New York. He scanned his memory for the stores where the best-looking women shopped, the ones in tall leather boots and expensive handbags, the ones whose straight blond hair flicked across the fur collars of their coats as they walked down Fifth Avenue. What was that store they were always entering? He searched his memory. Bergmans? Bergers? No, Bergdorf's, that was it. He would go find some ravishing seductress behind the jewelry counter there. She would be sure to know what to buy his mother for Christmas.

11

Coal in the Stocking

Charlotte's mother was waiting for her at the train station, her tall frame engulfed by a raincoat that stretched from her scarf to the tips of her green rubber boots. The bright afternoon light emphasized the worry lines stretching across her forehead, and Charlotte felt a pang of guilt as she leaned forward to be kissed. Following her mother to the family's station wagon, she found its back seat lowered to accommodate an enormous thicket of holly branches, whose jagged leaves, red berries and sharp thorns stretched into the front seats. Charlotte sat down warily, her weekend bag stuffed onto her lap.

Her mother gestured toward the holly. "Very festive, don't you think? You can help me decorate before Piers arrives this evening. The man down in the village gave me a discount for taking the rest of his branches. I think he was eager for his tea. I must say, every year, they seem to have more thorns and fewer berries."

They swung into the high street, and Charlotte gazed out the window with a vague sense of oppression. The village seemed never to change, she thought; even the windows of the Oxfam charity shop appeared to have the same ragged display of used clothes on its two mannequins. She felt her mother watching her, gauging her appearance and waiting for an opening. Leaving the town behind, they began to climb a long hill.

Her mother coughed. "You're looking well, Charlotte. London seems to be agreeing with you." Charlotte nodded, saying nothing. They continued upward, her mother grinding through the car's gears as she coaxed its laboring engine, *You can do it, old thing.* She gave the steering wheel an encouraging tap and Charlotte gave her a sharp look. Since when had her mother talked to the car? Fifteen minutes later, crunching into the pebbled driveway of their house, Charlotte instantly felt her life in London recede as her childhood house appeared, smaller than in her memory, its red brick façade disappearing behind an ivy vine that was creeping across her bedroom window. She felt a moment of panic as she envisioned being trapped inside, her adult life erased out of existence. She stroked her new black cape in an unconscious reminder of her London life.

Her mother glanced over. "What a lovely cape that is, Charlotte. You must wear it to the Blooms' party this evening. They're so excited to see you and Piers. They want to hear all about his new job in America."

"Mother, I have a new job as well," Charlotte answered, crossly.

Her mother glanced sideways with a look Charlotte recognized, even in profile, as her don't-be-difficult-darling expression. The car came to a halt, her mother praising it, *Well done!* Sulkily, Charlotte threw open the passenger door and slung her weekend bag over her shoulder. She started to mount the familiar stairs to the front door.

Behind her, her mother called out. "Darling, I'll need help with the holly. Bring down some scissors and work gloves, will you?"

Three hours later, Charlotte stepped back to survey her decorating efforts. Her mother had left the tree for her, a fourteen-foot fir that stood, as always, in the bow window of the sitting room. Charlotte had covered its branches with decorations stored in molding cardboard boxes she'd hauled up from the basement. Miniature gold lights, thick red ribbons and hand-painted ornaments collected over twenty years of jumble sales and antique mart strolls covered every branch. She pressed her nose into the tree's trunk and inhaled the fresh, sharp smell of the pine. A rush of past Christmases washed over her in a wave of pain and nostalgia. Without thinking, she touched her throat, feeling the gold necklace her father had hung on a branch of the tree when she was twelve, its gold heart pendant obscured by the spiky pine needles.

Her mother entered the sitting room holding the bundle of holly at arm's length, craning her neck to the side to avoid its spiked leaves.

"I've never understood why this attacking plant is considered festive," she said, laying the branches down in the center of the faded rug. "Even the berries look poisonous."

"They are," said Charlotte.

"Really?" Her mother looked vague. "Well let's get on with it, then."

Donning gardening gloves, they attacked the bristling pile, thrusting jagged holly sprigs into vases and wrestling branches into wreaths. Charlotte left the field of combat first, retiring to a sofa to examine a series of red welts left by the holly's thorns. Her mother's eyes followed her, before returning to the heap of leaves remaining on the floor. She kept her eyes focused on the holly while speaking to Charlotte. "Lady Philippa says you've been out a good deal lately."

"Does she? She's hardly in herself, I would have said, with all the jaunts to France."

"Oh, I expect that France isn't so frequent, is it?" Her mother manhandled a holly branch into a ceramic urn. "She says there are nights when you're back quite late."

"Mother, she's my landlady, not my prison warden."

"Of course not, dear. What an idea, Philippa as warden!" She laughed lightly. "And she says there's been the same young man who's dropped you off in a cab." Charlotte's mother dropped an unyielding branch of holly as she said this, looking straight at her daughter. Charlotte mumbled something inaudible and rose from the sofa. She was mounting the stairs when she heard a loud knock. Turning back toward the front hall, she opened the front door to find Piers. A taxi rumbled away behind him, crunching its way down the long drive.

"Piers!" she said, engulfing him in a hug. "Mother, Piers is here!"

Piers smiled at his sister, looking both pleased and embarrassed. His even features drooped from fatigue, and a one-day stubble of hair grazed the lower half of his face. "You didn't expect me to sit in my office in New York for Christmas Eve, did you?" He turned toward his mother, who had coming rushing toward the door at Charlotte's call. Her face was lit in a glow of delight, the worry lines across her forehead erased. She threw her arms around her son, who accepted her embrace with a fond kiss to her greying hair. Moving into the sitting room, Piers duly admired the bedecked Christmas tree and the strategically placed clusters of holly, deflecting his mother's repeated offers of tea and sandwiches with good grace. It was all so familiar and comfortable, Charlotte thought, except that it was all different and strange; between her and Piers now hovered the silent transcript of their recent phone calls across the Atlantic, and their mutual irritation. Piers's accent had changed, too, Charlotte noticed: His vowels sounded flatter, and he peppered his speech with expressions never before heard in their sitting room. Their mother looked on, happy and faintly bewildered, as Piers recounted his long plane journey from New York earlier that day. Sitting on the faded floral sofa, he propped up his feet on a cushion embroidered by a long-dead relative.

"Of course, it was lovely just to chill out after all the months of working so hard, Mother. But of course, I'm always on a plane these days making sales calls around the States. It will be *awesome* to have some time off, away from the grind."

Piers kept talking, comfortable in knowing that he was with the woman who loved him most. Within ten minutes, Charlotte found herself suppressing her desire to make ironic comments in response to his monologue. By the time Piers volunteered his impression of the British Airways flight attendants ("Wearing uniforms that must have been modelled after our Girl Guides in the war"), she rose and said that she would take a rest before the party that evening.

Her mother nodded, her eyes not leaving Piers's face. "Of course, darling," she said, as Piers paused in his description of W.'s Hamptons chateau. Charlotte heard the word "topiary" as she moved up the stairs.

Christmas morning dawned clear and cold. Charlotte was up early, making a large pot of tea and cutting slices of grain bread from the Village's new organic food shop. Taking the thickest slice, she walked toward the far end of the kitchen, where a large window looked out over a fallow field, sullen in the low light. Low stone walls and clusters of leafless trees marked the borders of further untended fields. Charlotte sighed, torn by the combination of comfort and claustrophobia that defined home. Staring out at the bleak view, her thoughts shifted to the party the night before. Horace had been there, his pale face looking drawn and oppressed as he dutifully made the rounds of his parents' friends, a champagne bottle in hand.

"Oh, Charlotte," he'd said, as he breezed past her during one of his circles through the inebriated guests. "Merry Christmas, of course. Piers back, I see. How nice. More champagne?" Efficiently filling her glass, his eyes down, he'd scooted off with his graceful lope, leaving Charlotte with a full flute of champagne and not one word suggesting that they sat ten feet from one another each day in a London office. Somewhere behind her, she'd heard Piers's voice, somewhat slurred. "Oh well, in New York you know, we'd just be getting started. The hours run much later there. Masters of the universe and all that –"

A noise sounded from behind her and she turned to see her mother enter the kitchen, a cheerful red and green Christmas hat perched on her head. "Piers is muttering about jet lag in his sleep. I don't think Christmas mass is in his plans. Shall we go?"

They returned from church three hours later, full of self-conscious pride for having attended early Christmas mass. Piety was not a virtue much emphasized in the Cheetham household, and Charlotte's self-congratulations in the wake of her visits was magnified by their rarity. She stood in the front hall, ostentatiously humming a hymn. Piers, pajama-clad and unshaven, passed by on his way to the kitchen.

He frowned. "Could you turn down the piety until I've had some toast?"

Charlotte took the high road, beaming at his retreating back. "Of course! Merry Christmas!" She went into the sitting room and gazed at the tree. Its pine needles were still healthy and green, though their sharp aroma was starting to fade. Looking down at the small hill of gifts, she saw that two new boxes covered in heavy red paper had appeared, gleaming like peacocks amidst a flock of wrens. Charlotte knelt and picked one up. An oblong gold sticker said *Bergdorf's*.

Piers entered the room, his face fuzzy behind a steaming mug of tea.

Their mother followed, wearing a smile Charlotte recognized as equal parts good cheer and stoicism. The three of them stared down at the gifts: their mother's, in wrapping paper of cherubs and trumpeters sold by the Women's Aid Society; Charlotte's frosty green paper, Fortnum and Mason's unchanging offering; and Piers's shiny red boxes from Manhattan. There was a pause.

Charlotte rallied first. "Shall we?" she said. The small family sprang into motion. Piers put down his mug on a doily-covered side table and her mother handed out two trumpet-and-cherub boxes. Christmas morning started. Charlotte unwrapped a wool cardigan, a scarf, and a box of notecards from London's National Gallery. Piers received a striped tie, a crewneck blue sweater and a complete set of Sherlock Holmes mysteries to replace his tattered childhood copies. Charlotte passed out her Fortnum and Mason boxes of pale green and watched as her mother unveiled the shining silver trowel with its handle of enameled flowers.

"Charlotte, dear, it's lovely, but far too grand for actual use." The gleaming spade was laid aside with a deprecating murmur.

Piers dove under the tree to retrieve the red boxes. "Here," he said, handing one to each woman. "Straight from the Big Apple."

Charlotte turned her box over, looking for a seam but not finding one. Ripping the paper with her nail, she uncovered a white box, which held a black velvet drawstring bag. She glanced at Piers, who was absorbed in watching their mother. Loosening the bag's string, a handful of cold unpolished aqua rocks linked by a silver chain fell into her hand. She looked up at her mother, whose lined hands were raising a choker of similar stones.

Piers smiled at his mother's startled expression. "Do you like it? The stones are mined in Vietnam, apparently. They're selling like hotcakes at Bergdorf's. Here, let me help you." Piers lifted the choker from his mother's suspended hands and fastened its silver clasp around her narrow neck. The rocky choker sat across her collarbones like an archipelago, covering the gold chain she always wore. Charlotte watched her mother raise a cautious hand to her throat. Piers beamed and turned to Charlotte. "You've got the bracelet version. You'll be the first in the

City to have one." His eyes narrowed. "Unless Patrick has imported one for you?"

Charlotte's mother's head swung toward her daughter, like a hound catching the scent of a fox. "Patrick? Is that the young man Lady Philippa saw?"

Charlotte threw an infuriated look at Piers. "No, mother." She busied herself with stuffing the rocks back in their velvet bag. Her mother waited for a further explanation and, receiving none, retrieved a large rectangular box from under the tree which she handed to Piers. He unwrapped it quickly, his large deft hands balling up the Christmas trumpets and dropping them onto the carpet. He lifted the expanse of white tissue paper and paused. A dark leather briefcase lay inside. Its clasp was a dull antique brass, and the leather of the case itself, though newly polished, was worn at the corners where the stitching had come loose. Looking up at his mother, who was gazing at the briefcase, he faltered. "Mother–"

Charlotte interrupted. "But that's father's!"

Her mother detached her eyes from the briefcase and looked at Charlotte. The faint mist that had risen to her eyes cleared as she spoke. "Yes, it is. And now that Piers has a big job in America, he can put it to good use." She turned toward her son, and her tone softened. "Can't you, Piers?"

Piers gave a tense smile. "Of course, Mother. Thank you." He spoke slowly, shaken from his usual equanimity. He stretched out his arms, encased in a fraying bathrobe rescued from the closet of his old bedroom, and pulled the briefcase from the box. He stroked its leather before grasping the handle and swinging it back and forth, at first slowly, and then more rapidly, like a metronome picking up speed. His mother watched him with a far off, vague smile, and Charlotte knew that she was seeing her husband of thirty years ago, whom Piers so resembled. Charlotte's felt a stab of anger and envy. Wasn't she the one her father had called his best and brightest child? Hadn't she got into Oxford and ground out a first in classics while Piers spent his university years rowing and on the tennis courts? And here was their mother, basking in Piers's presence because of an accident of gender. It was appalling, monstrous. At the top of its third arc, Piers tightened his grip on the handle and brought the case to an abrupt halt. He leaned over to kiss his mother's beaming face.

Charlotte's fingers made a fist around the black velvet bag. "I'm sure Miranda will be impressed." She kept her voice light, her eyes cast down.

"Miranda?" Her mother's eyes darted between her two children, her nose confused by the scent of a new hunt. Piers glared at Charlotte who stared down at the velvet bag, tracing the edges of the rocks with her thumb.

Charlotte glared back. "Or have you moved on exclusively to rich widows?"

Piers's arm gripping the briefcase froze as he stared at his sister. "Bloody hell, Charlotte. What's that supposed to mean?"

"Only that while I'm doing my job, sorting out problems, you're apparently chatting up widows at charity galas."

"You mean while you're pestering everyone in New York for reports no one needs, I'm out there building a business!"

"Children!" cried their mother, anguished.

Charlotte and Piers glowered at each other, their mother's presence forgotten. Piers's usually complacent, even features were twisted with anger and surprise, and a red flush glowed underneath his unshaven chin. Charlotte met his look with a defiant nonchalance that masked her inward misery, trying not to see her mother's astonishment. Tears blurted from the edges of her eyes. She had destroyed Christmas. But it wasn't her fault, she told herself wildly; it was her mother's for fawning over Piers, and Piers's for lapping it up so complacently, and her father's for dying in an auto accident, and Patrick's for being so inscrutable and evasive, and Henrietta's for being such a snob, and even Horace's for ignoring her last night. Her tears began to swirl down her cheeks and the room became blurry. She felt rather than saw Piers's furious gaze and her mother's disappointment: It was unbearable. Dropping the velvet bag onto the faded carpet, she flung herself from the room·

Henrietta's miniature one-bedroom house, tucked into a mews street in south London, retained the ramshackle look of the horse's stable it had once been, with its crumbling bricks and oversized door. Looking at it now, Charlotte felt her first glimmer of optimism since returning to London after Christmas. It had been a grim two weeks. The new year had broken with unrelenting rain, transforming fields into lakes and trapping animals in mudbanks. In the short, dark January days, Charlotte had travelled to and from her job on tubes packed with sullen City workers whose wet raincoats filled the stuffy trains with the smell of post-Christmas depression and damp. In the office, her colleagues' expressions were inscrutable, showing no afterglow of the holidays. Even the office plant she had coaxed back to health had died during her absence, leaving a ring of dried-up brown leaves around its base. Charlotte had picked up the dead plant, including a strand of Christmas lights wrapped around its trunk, and stuffed it into the rubbish bin.

Only Patrick appeared, as ever, fresh and cheerful. A week in America – exactly which part was unclear – had left his skin more tanned than ever. He moved among his colleagues like a streak of white paint on a grey canvas, trailing a swathe of luminescence. Either ignoring or oblivious to the post-holiday stupor of his colleagues, Patrick circulated the office, slapping slumping backs and squeezing hunched shoulders. Charlotte had received her allotted share of attention as he bounded past her desk during his regular rounds, giving her a quick kiss on the cheek by way of a new year's greeting, and dropping an orange Hermès scarf box on her desk.

Charlotte pushed on the wide wooden door, which had been left cracked open, and stepped into Henrietta's sitting room. It was its usual mess of papers and books heaped onto a pair of faded sofas rejected by her parents. In the small room, the over-large sofas glowered at each other from opposite corners, like dowagers outraged by reduced circumstances. Charlotte smiled at the familiar sight, equally appalled and envious of Henrietta's mess; try as she might, she couldn't help but arrange her books in the neat, dusted rows demanded by her upbringing.

Henrietta appeared, undressed beneath a silk bathrobe and rubbing her wet blond hair with a bath towel. She gave her friend a kiss and Charlotte smelled a hint of gin on her breath. Henrietta had always started the drinking aspect of social events well in advance of anyone's arrival.

"Charlotte! So punctual, as always."

Henrietta waved a hand toward a sideboard crowded with liquor bottles and disappeared. Feeling subtly rebuked, Charlotte mixed herself a vodka tonic, heavy on the vodka, and wandered into the kitchen, where she was surprised to find no sign of food. Both the stove and oven were cold. As she was peeking into a pantry cupboard, Henrietta joined her, the V-neck of her black wraparound dress moist with dripping hair. In Henrietta's hand was a fresh drink.

"May I help?" Charlotte asked, gesturing to the empty countertops.

"No worries. The local grocer has started a delivery service. The food should be here any minute. They promised to send someone over by eight." The flat's buzzer rang. "That must be them now." Henrietta moved to the door and Charlotte overheard a burst of hilarity: "I thought you were the pudding!" Adrian and two of his friends walked in, carrying wine bottles and umbrellas, followed in another few minutes by two more friends. As the small room filled with damp bodies and noise, Henrietta kicked a few piles of books into a corner and switched on a tape of Madonna. The party began in earnest.

Sitting on a sofa next to a friend, Charlotte kept half an eye on the door as she waited for Patrick to arrive. He'd greeted the invitation with incredulity: *You want me to go to a dinner party of the friend who hated me?* he'd said, though without sounding particularly concerned. He'd agreed to come, however, and Charlotte watched for him now with wary anticipation. When he entered, she searched his face, relieved to find only curiosity. As always, he was impeccably turned out in a blue-checked shirt under a crisp navy suit and Charlotte ran her eyes over him, reveling in his fresh-faced good looks. She watched as Patrick greeted Henrietta with a tight smile before heading through the cramped space in her direction. Halfway across the room, Adrian intercepted him with his hand outstretched, his forehead prominent under his thinning blond hair. The two young men shook hands with an energy suggesting their mutual distaste.

"The financier!" Adrian said, his pale wrist moving up and down.

"The regulator!" Patrick responded, his tanned fist engulfing Adrian's hand.

Charlotte refocused her attention on her friend. Around them, Henrietta circulated with bottles of vodka and gin, her long blond hair now dry and swirling around her face as she plied her guests with drink. Yielding to a pleasant vodka-induced relaxation, Charlotte stopped monitoring Patrick and lost herself in conversation. When at last she left the sofa to join the others in the dining room, she found that Henrietta had left her a place between two of Adrian's friends, and assigned Patrick a seat at the head of the table between her and Adrian.

Henrietta distributed the chickens and salads and the party broke into conversation. Turning to her left, Charlotte asked her neighbor about his past year. His pale eyes brightened, and he embarked on a detailed description of his activities as a solicitor. Staring at his moving lips, Charlotte transferred her attentions to the other end of the table, where Henrietta and Patrick were trading comments about the foul weather. Henrietta's precise voice, accustomed to directing a classroom, cut through the small space easily, and Patrick's voice, equally loud and relaxed, dominated the quieter voices of the other guests. Charlotte heard Adrian join the conversation at the head of the table, which had now shifted from weather to Shorwell. Patrick, whose voice had become louder with drink, was regaling his listeners with imitations of W. Henrietta's voice came sailing down the table.

"You mean to tell me no one knows his real name?"

"Nope," said Patrick.

"But surely he can't sign documents with just an initial?" Adrian said.

"I guess he gets his lawyers to do it all for him. I wouldn't know. I'm just the sales guy." Patrick laughed easily.

"You must find us very simple-minded and straight-forward after the W.'s of Manhattan," Adrian said, "Given that we have actual names and identities."

"Not at all," Patrick responded, graciously. "I think you're – charming."

Charlotte noticed that her neighbor had paused and reached for his wine glass. She started to formulate a follow-up question but stopped when he resumed speaking. Charlotte inclined her head in his direction and smiled. Her attention returned to Henrietta.

"What I really find fascinating about Americans," Henrietta said, waving her fork in small airborne circles, "is their ability to invent themselves. We're so boring and stuck over here. Look at this table – all the same people we've always known, eating chicken off our parents' discarded china, cramming for tests to get into all the same schools our parents attended, so that we can hang the same class pictures on the wall of our loo! Whereas Americans have this massive country and can come from anywhere, and do anything, and be anyone, and no one gives it a second thought. It must be the most amazing sense of freedom, all that self-invention."

"That's the American dream," agreed Patrick, nodding his blond head as he neatly speared his chicken wing.

Henrietta put down her fork and took a sip of red wine, swirling the liquid around in the large glass. Charlotte shifted her weight uncomfortably. She knew the look Henrietta was giving her wine, and it boded danger. She abandoned any effort to listen to her neighbor.

"Your world seems so enviable," Henrietta said, putting down her glass and looking at Patrick. Her shoulders hunched forward under the thin knit fabric of her dress. "Look how amazing you've been: In six months from arriving, you've hired some the brightest people in the City – Horace Bloom alone being his year's most brilliant maths student, and you've got both the Cheethams, and who knows who else – and they're all working for you! And we don't even know who you are."

Patrick put down his fork and picked up a large cloth napkin, wiping his mouth slowly. Replacing his napkin, Charlotte saw him meet Henrietta's eyes. "I don't believe your immigration people asked for an FBI report when I landed at Heathrow. Unless it was in Latin, of course, in which case I might have missed it."

Adrian laughed uncomfortably and leaned toward Patrick from the other side. "Of course not. I believe our police force has just recently made the switch to English to protect our little island – ha ha."

Patrick turned toward Adrian. "Well then, I'm sure they're doing great. And I'm sure your friends can look after their own interests, too," said Patrick. He voice was hard, and he'd abandoned any effort to smile.

"Are they?" asked Henrietta. Patrick said nothing as he aligned his knife and fork in parallel lines on his plate. His face had grown atypically red with the liquor and heat. Patrick met Henrietta's eyes, and Charlotte held her breath.

"I'd say they're doing pretty well since meeting me. Look at Charlotte." Patrick, Henrietta and Adrian all turned in her direction. Patrick's voice, stripped of geniality, rose above all the other guests, who gradually fell silent as he spoke. "Hey Charlotte, aren't you doing well since joining Shorwell? Have you ever made so much money?" The usual teasing quality of Patrick's voice had turned into a hard sneer. "Tell your friends here the truth. What were you doing before with your fancy, elite education? Advertising biscuits? So now you're making a ton of money, travelling around and buying expensive clothes. Not bad for – what was it they called you when you had to have that operation for your spine? Char-Bar?"

Charlotte stared at Patrick, stunned. She stood up, felt a wave of nausea, and sat down again. Around the table, the guests sat mute and paralyzed, gazing downward at their plates.

"Patrick!" she said, "how could you?" She clutched the table to steady her trembling hands.

"How could I what? Defend myself in this snake pit of snobs who are all but accusing me of being a criminal, and a cradle robber to boot? You didn't seem so God-damned reluctant at my apartment last month. Why don't you tell your guard dogs down here *that*?"

Patrick stood up. He towered over the shocked, silent guests, and glared up and down the table, daring them to respond. His jaw was set in an angry upward tilt and he was breathing hard, his chest rising and falling under his tailored jacket. He inclined his head toward Henrietta.

"Thank you for the invitation. I'm afraid I have to go." He turned on his heel and left the room. No one spoke as the front door slammed. There was a collective exhalation from the remaining guests and slowly, the low hum of conversation returned. Charlotte's neighbor coughed once and turned to the person sitting on his other side, leaving Charlotte isolated in a pool of silence. She looked down at her plate and her untouched chicken slices, feeling her pulse throbbing at her temples. After a minute, she stood up and walked into the sitting room, where she began to dig through the raincoats heaped onto the sofa. From behind her, someone coughed lightly. Charlotte answered the cough without turning around.

"Don't speak to me, Henrietta," she said. "You purposefully goaded Patrick on. He's right. You're an unbearable snob. I can't believe you would do this to me."

Another cough, deeper this time, acknowledged her words. Locating her damp coat at last, Charlotte turned around to find Adrian. Under his large forehead, his pale eyes drooped with fatigue and worry.

"Adrian!"

"I'm so sorry, Charlotte. Henrietta can be a bit over the top on the protective front, especially when she's drinking." Adrian took a step forward to help her with her coat but she stepped backward, rebuffing him. She started to do up the buttons, yanking hard at each one as she worked her way up toward its collar.

"Well, never mind. I was ready to quit Shorwell anyway. It's really not such a good fit after all." Her attempted laugh emerged as an anguished, strained bark.

"Charlotte, I know you're angry – anyone would be – but you can't leave just yet. Or, I should say, I really hope you won't."

Charlotte abandoned her jacket and looked up, surprised. Adrian's expression gave nothing away. There was a long pause.

"Charlotte, there's something I need to tell you," Adrian said, gesturing to the section of sofa not covered by raincoats. They sat down and Adrian began, choosing his words carefully. "You know how I called your office the other day? It has to do with some questions about Shorwell. One of its clients lodged a complaint with my agency about its reporting and we're just looking into it. I've contacted my counterparts in America for some routine information, and my initial review has raised some questions." His voice trailed off and stopped. Charlotte sat next to him, perched at the edge of the sofa, looking down at the cover of *Tatler* magazine, where Princess Diana was posing in a backless dress.

"That's an even better reason for me to leave, then."

Adrian coughed. "It's slightly complicated. Usually these investment firms are a black box, and we have trouble gaining information. But with you here, and your brother in New York, we might be able to learn more." He looked at Charlotte. Her eyes were still cast down, refusing to meet his. "Also, if there is a problem, it may be that Piers is in an – awkward – position in New York."

Charlotte said nothing. From the dining room, they could hear loud conversation and laughter as the party renewed itself. The noise of their friends flowed toward their sofa, emphasizing their silence.

Charlotte lifted her head, meeting Adrian's eyes. "Piers might be in trouble?"

"We don't know yet."

"And my staying at Shorwell can help?"

"Possibly."

Charlotte looked back down, making no motion, listening to the raindrops slamming into the windows. Without speaking, she nodded, stood up and turned toward the door, feeling Adrian's eyes on her. As she walked outside, she flinched as the rain fell on her uncovered head and she paused to pull forward her hood, glancing up toward Henrietta's dining room window as she did so. From the dark, wet night, the brightly lit space looked like a stage set of a play well into Act Two, the actors deep in conversation and displaying a range of expressions all too easily read: hilarity, curiosity, amusement, boredom. Charlotte watched them as the rain plunked down onto her hood and rolled forward onto her forehead. As she watched, Adrian returned to the dining room and resumed his seat, slipping an arm around the back of Henrietta's chair. His face had wiped away all sign of the concern he had shown Charlotte a few moments before. From outside on the pavement, cold and anxious, Charlotte turned away and set off into the night.

12

The Path Not Taken

Jed sat in his office, staring at the numbers flickering on his screen. He squinted at the oil price and punched the enter key. The screen refreshed, but the price of oil remained the same. He swore at the screen and pushed enter again. The price reappeared, unchanged. He flipped to the spreadsheet that was open on his computer and plugged in the current market price for oil, closing his eyes while the values of his futures contracts were adjusted to reflect the new market price. He opened his eyes and scrolled down to the bottom of the spreadsheet. On his heavy, pallid face, two spots of red started to grow just below his eye sockets. *God damn it*, he thought. The contracts were tanking again, even after he'd rolled them forward and met his broker's most recent margin call. The futures, which had killed him all the way up as the price of oil skyrocketed during the Iraq invasion, were now killing him on the way down, as the U.S. troops moved into the Middle East and oil reversed course. The light on his phone flashed, showing an external line. He punched the key to pick it up on his speakerphone.

"Yes?"

"Jed, it's Pierre." The broker's voice, emanating from a trading room three blocks south of Shorwell's office, sounded weirdly intimate, as if Pierre's lips were touching the microphone attached to his headset. He pronounced Jed with a soft, French j: *zhed.* Jed glared at the screen and said nothing.

The broker's cultivated French voice spoke again. "Jed, I am sorry, but the margin on your account is too low. The usual backwardation of the contracts has moved into contango."

"Spare me the lesson in finance."

"And my _banque_ needs you to increase your balance to maintain adequate margin."

"How much?"

Over the microphone, Jed could hear a series of rapid key clicks and then a cough. "$26 million," Pierre said, with what sounded to Jed like smug satisfaction. "Or, I'm afraid, we will have to liquidate your position."

"I know the rules." Jed hung up, adding to himself, _you self-satisfied asshole._ Jed looked back and forth between the screen and the open spreadsheet on his computer as he thought. He was more annoyed than panicked; in his experience, there was always a pool of money stagnating somewhere amidst the ebb and flow of Shorwell's sloshing funds. He considered his options. He'd already tapped the cash accounts of the US clients to meet a previous margin call and didn't want to have to run them down to a level that might trigger an automated alert in the back-office. He had the back-office staff pretty well cowed by his reputation as the firm's star trader, but he didn't want to have to play that card unless absolutely necessary. He could tap the cash of the UK client accounts, but that would require currency trades and more headaches. His last option was to re-value the derivative positions of the UK clients and free up cash that way. If the clients even looked at their statements – which Jed very much doubted – they couldn't argue that the values were wrong, since there was no public market for the derivatives and no one knew how the hell to price them anyway. Who was to say that some broker hadn't shouted over some offer for them at the new, lower price? He could always re-inflate them when his bets started to pay off.

The margin call problem settled, Jed tapped a pencil against his screen as he considered how he was going to fill the hole left by the disastrous trade in oil futures. He needed something big, leveraged, and fast. Maybe he could squeeze some good ideas out of the traders. He turned his head toward the glass wall between his corner office and the long, parallel lines of trading desks running down the center of the floor. A group of traders in khakis and blue striped shirts – all of them with slicked-back hair, like W. – was laughing as one of them tried to pitch a nerf ball into a trash can perched at the far end of the room. The trash can, sitting on a stack of twelve empty pizza boxes, had a basketball hoop attached to its rim. Useless, he muttered. He stared at the ticker prices on his screen again, glancing at the prices of international equity indexes. What about Shorwell's analysts in London? Wasn't there one of them who was meant to be smarter than the rest? Patrick was always boasting about hiring some guy who was supposedly the rocket scientist of Oxford. Horace something. Tomb? Womb? Jed picked up an office directory lying on his desk and scanned the list of London employees. Horace Bloom, that was it. Sounded like a character from a children's book. Well, this Horace Bloom was about to dig him out of this hole.

Piers sat at the counter of a Midtown bar after work, listening to the Shorwell traders swap war stories. Eddie, a self-styled tough guy who claimed to be from the Bronx, was boasting about the time he'd cleared $500,000 from betting against a pharmaceutical company just before the FDA rejected its application to market a new drug. Eddie was on his third bottle of imported Belgian beer and was nursing both his drink and his story with care, giving the long version of his victory narrative. Piers had heard the story twice before; its details were unchanging, except for each rendition's upward valuation of Eddie's profit. The ambient noise of the dark bar was loud, and he found it hard to keep his attention focused on the story.

Concentration had generally been a struggle for him since his return from England. Accustomed to the dreary, grey damp of England, New York's freezing January cold had shocked him profoundly. His first inhalation of New York's biting, sub-zero wind-driven snow left him breathless and paralyzed. In short order, he had equipped himself with leather boots and a full-face wool mask, through which his eyes stared out in frozen shock. His colleagues, long hardened to the northeast winters, laughed at his get-up, dubbing it Sir Lancelot's armor. A new caricature appeared on the office white board of a knight jousting, his head, body and sword entirely covered by a black woolen stocking. Piers was too cold to care, buying himself a Russian fur hat to wear over his hood.

Eddie reached the pinnacle of his story, when the news of the FDA's decision hit the news wire. Piers turned his head away and scanned the rest of the room. A group of young women were drinking cocktails at a round table near the front door. A few solitary men were drinking at the bar, glancing between the group of young women and their own half-empty drinks. Piers looked toward the back of the room. A few tables had been pushed against the wall under some metal wall sconces that emitted a low, flickering light. A woman sat alone at one of the small tables, a book pulled close to her face. Piers couldn't see either her face or the title of the book from where he sat. She seemed totally immersed in its pages, oblivious to all the conversations around her.

Staring at her, it took him a few minutes to realize that he felt rattled, and few minutes after that to locate the source of his discomfort. It was her book. With a thud of slow-moving surprise, he realized that he couldn't remember the last time he had read a book. Certainly not since he'd been in New York; since his arrival, it had been only stock reports, the *Wall Street Journal*, and tabloids. Searching his memory, the only books he could recall were the Sherlock Holmes series his mother had given him for Christmas. He scowled as the image of Conan Doyle books merged into a picture of Charlotte accusing him of wasting his time in New York. He looked again at the girl, wondering which book held her attention in this loud, dark place.

Piers left his beer on the bar and strolled toward the men's room, which was located just beyond her table. He tried to read the book's cover as he passed. No luck: she had laid the book flat on the table's surface, and her straight brown hair obscured its pages as she leaned over it. Piers passed her and loitered in the men's room as he got ready for his next attempt. Moving very slowly, he passed her table again from the other side and paused. The angle of his body fell between the metal sconce and the book, blocking its light. The young woman glanced up, her chin angled to one side, her lips compressed into a frown. "You're blocking the light."

"Sorry," he said automatically. He meant to move, but didn't, immobilized by a faint tug of recognition. Where had he seen her before? It took him a moment to locate the memory: It had been the night of the Hamptons party. She had been serving drinks at the door, wearing an oversized white shirt and looking as though she'd never handled a bottle of vodka before.

She looked at him impatiently as this thought passed through his brain. She showed no reciprocal sign of recognition. She spoke again, very distinctly. "Would you please move?"

"Sorry," Piers repeated, "But I think I met you at a party in the Hamptons. Do you work as a bartender?"

She hesitated, as if reluctant to answer. "Sometimes. I temp for a catering company. Was that the party at the ridiculous fake French chateau with all those drunk guys jumping into the pool?"

Piers changed the subject. "What are you reading?"

She scowled and held up her book: *The Unbearable Lightness of Being*. The title meant nothing to Piers. "Well I guess I'm being useful, then," he said. She said nothing, but her look of irritation was replaced by confusion. Piers adopted what he hoped was a rueful smile. "I mean by blocking the light, which, according to your book, is unbearable." The eyebrows above the woman's guarded grey eyes rose a notch. She put the book flat on the table. Under her bulky black sweater, her torso shifted forward.

"You're clever," she said, grudgingly.

"Is that such a surprise?" Piers asked, stung by the implied insult. Her eyes flicked over to Piers's group of traders and back again to Piers.

"You're with those guys, right?" she asked. Piers nodded.

"Wall Street guys?" she said. Piers nodded again.

"That's why." Her tone was gentle, almost regretful, as if she was trying to soften the blow. Without thinking, Piers took a step backward. The light on the wall once again illuminated her book. He didn't know whether to be annoyed or amused. He gave her a tight, unsettled smile, and gestured to the wall sconce.

"Your light, uh—"

"Anna."

"Anna. Piers. Enjoy your book." She nodded, and Piers turned away. He had walked a few steps when he heard his name. He turned back. Anna had stood up and was looking in his direction. She was quite small, he realized, and dressed entirely in black, from her suede boots to the top edge of her black turtleneck. Under the pallid light, her small hand, poised on the book's cover, stood out, as if in a chiaroscuro painting. On the pale skin of her forehead, one worry line traced the gap between her eyebrows.

"Piers?" Her voice was muffled by the loud recorded music that filled the few feet between them. Piers leaned forward, straining to hear. "I'm sorry," she said, "I didn't mean to offend you."

"I'm much harder to insult than that," Piers said. "I have a sister who makes you look like a ray of sunshine." With a laugh somewhere between amused and bitter, Piers turned away and rejoined his colleagues. A few of them glanced in Anna's direction, but without much interest; her straight dark hair, bulky clothes and book all acted as natural deterrents. During Piers's absence, another trader had launched into a new story. The bar was crowded now, as the after-work crowd was joined by people who were hunkering down for the night, seeking refuge from the freezing streets outside. Every time the door opened, a gust of icy wind swept toward the bar, causing everyone to clutch their drinks and glare at the newcomers. Piers finished his beer and started to don his wool mask.

Eddy turned toward him. "Gonna brave it home?" he asked. Piers nodded and began to layer on his outer garments: thick black wool coat, navy wool scarf, black hood, fur hat, and leather gloves. In his full winterized costume, he felt like an assassin. Unable to make himself intelligible through the full-face mask, he slapped Eddy's back with his glove to say goodbye. As he turned to go, he saw that a tall man wearing a scruffy leather messenger bag was standing above Anna's table. Through the eye holes of his mask, he watched as the man sat down facing her, the solid bulky mass of his black coat blocking Piers's view of her face.

Piers headed out to the street, bracing himself for his first breath of icy air. It felt like knives cutting his throat. Moving quickly on the dark, empty pavement, he headed north up Sixth Avenue. Inside his clinging wool hood, his head was fogged from the noise, alcohol, and smoke of the bar, and he heard his own labored breaths. Quickly, he crossed ten streets, and found himself near his office building. He glanced up. It was mostly blacked out, but here and there a few offices remained lit. On a whim, Piers decided to stop by his office and ask Jed if he wanted to play squash; Jed always seemed to be there these days. Piers turned into the lobby and flashed his security card to the building's night guard, who nodded him through without looking up from his newspaper.

Exiting the elevator on the fiftieth floor, he stopped short, disoriented by the vision of the trading floor absent of people. The cleaners had not yet been in, and pizza boxes lay across the floor and trading desks, the smell of stale cheese still hanging in the air. Piers walked across the trading floor and turned toward Jed's office. Sure enough, Jed was in his usual position, staring at his computer through eyes that were barely open. Behind him in the nighttime darkness, the window of his office reflected his computer screen, a blurry sea of red lines. Piers walked down the hallway towards Jed, coming to a halt just outside Jed's door. Jed looked up. His eyelids flipped open and his normally phlegmatic face twisted with a spasm of surprise and fear as he bolted upright. After a split second, recognizing Piers underneath the black face mask, his fear turned to anger.

"Jesus Christ, Piers, you look like a fucking murderer. You scared the crap out of me." He sat down, his hands shaking.

Piers removed his hat and hood in one motion, revealing a thick mop of flattened curls. He grinned at Jed and sat down in a chair near Jed's desk. Jed flipped to a different screen on his computer, and the mirroring window behind him turned white. "Sorry, mate. I didn't mean to terrorize you. I was just wandering by and thought you might want a quick game of squash. I'll even let you beat me." Piers laughed, but stopped when Jed didn't join in. Instead, Jed was looking beyond Piers into the empty trading floor, his thoughts clearly elsewhere. Piers hesitated and tried again. "Squash? Hey, Jed, are you okay?"

Jed's heavy face turned toward Piers. His eyes were bloodshot, and the enlarged pores of his skin looked damp. Jed stared at him for a moment. Piers waited for a sardonic comment.

"Do you ever feel," Jed said slowly, "that things aren't going to work out?"

"Sorry?"

"Do you ever think," Jed repeated, keeping his eyes on the trading floor beyond his office, "that the game will go against you?"

Piers sat very still, trying to think what to say. He searched his memory. Fragments of pictures floated up – rowing races, his father at the dinner table, his final exams at university. No, he realized; he hadn't ever really, in the end, felt that way. He tried to think of something he could say and failed. Jed stared at him for a moment and nodded, understanding the silence. His heavy face was expressionless. Piers flailed for something to say. His voice emerged with false, almost desperate cheerfulness.

"Jed, you'll win. You're the smartest guy here."

Behind his bloodshot, weary eyes, Jed looked almost amused. "No way, man – that's W. He's so smart he doesn't even show up to do this crap." Jed turned back to his computer screen, dismissing Piers. Piers stood up, hovered awkwardly for a moment, and retraced his steps to the elevator. The security guard was still reading the same page of the newspaper. Piers plunged back out into the frigid cold, his enthusiasm for the gym gone. He raised his arm for a cab, wondering which game would be on ESPN when he got home.

By 7:30 a.m. on Monday morning, Horace was at his desk, listening to the voice mails that had piled up on his phone earlier that morning. As always, he had already read the *Financial Times* cover to cover on the Tube, a feat he achieved by folding each side of the paper lengthwise into thirds, accordion-style, so that he could turn its large pink pages without jostling the passengers crammed next to him. The thin Monday paper, filled with the left-over unused scraps from Friday's agenda and relegated to the paper's second-string editor, was an easy read during the forty-five-minute journey. Nothing much seemed to have happened over the weekend: John Major, the new prime minister, was boasting about helping the Americans push back the Iraqis from Kuwait; East Germans were pouring west through the demolished Berlin Wall; and the U.S. was bracing for a raft of poor economic data. The voice mails, left by brokers sitting in offices stretching from Hong Kong to San Francisco, were the usual combination of rehashed news and useless punditry. Horace listened with growing impatience to the series of half-awake, twenty-five-year-old voices reading from their scripts: a vast sea

of undigested, regurgitated data whose relevance was obsolete by the time it sloshed through his headset.

Horace drummed his fingers on the desk, erasing every message halfway through, waiting in vain for some nugget of original thinking or analysis to glow through the detritus. Not for the first time, he wondered how his love of math had led to this point. For years, his path had been determined by the straightforward, if unoriginal, objective of winning every math and science prize at school and university. It was a goal he attained without undue effort. As a child, he had simply realized, with the undramatic clarity that accompanied knowing he was shy, had brown hair, and liked books, that he understood numbers differently from other people. They were, in a way, his earliest friends: so steady and precise, so reliable – so different, in short, from the challenges of navigating social cliques or crushes on girls. When he looked at a page of numbers, he saw a staunch and loyal field of allies – toy soldiers who had all enlisted exclusively in his army. They had taken him straight to Oxford to study math, where he had won a first, and then to the City, where he had been bored stiff at an old British colonial bank before moving to Shorwell, an American upstart. And now he was listening to marketing stooges tell him why he should care that industrial production in the world's largest economy was weak. His forehead creased with contempt. What did they know? They probably couldn't even define regression, much less craft a multi-variable regression analysis.

A new voice drew his attention back to his phone. It was American, someone one he didn't recognize. He punched a button to re-play the message. *This is Jed Miles from the New York office. Could you call me when you get in?* Horace checked his watch, calculating the time in New York. It would be 3:30 a.m. there. He dialed the number Jed had left, planning to leave a message.

A tired voice answered. "Yes?"

"Jed? This is Horace, Horace Bloom. You called. Isn't it the middle of the night there?" Horace heard a sigh come through the line that might have been static.

"Horace, I hear from Patrick that you're the resident rocket scientist over there."

"Applied maths, actually."

"Whatever. I hear you're the best he's got. I have a proposition for you. I run a little hedge fund within Shorwell, just a private pool of money. It's done well, but I figure it can do even better with some new ideas. Long, short, whatever. Any currency, any exchange, any market cap."

Horace waited for Jed to continue, but the weary, terse American voice stopped. Horace spoke up. "No problem, Jed. When do you want these ideas?"

"Every day, starting today. You'll get a 2% cut of whatever profit your ideas contribute to the fund. And if you hit your target, your cut doubles."

"What's my target?"

"$50 million."

Jed hung up, and Horace sat staring at his desk, his mind spinning. Four percent of $50 million was $2 million. Not bad for a kid from a village in rural England who spent his teenage years reading Dostoevsky and logic problems. Finally, a challenge. Horace closed his eyes, feeling the adrenalin start to move through his body. Taking a deep breath, he opened his eyes, switched on his computer screen, and started to scroll through the day's stock charts.

When he looked up an hour later, the trading desk was full, and Patrick was standing next to their head trader, discussing the direction of the dollar against the newly created euro. Charlotte, he saw, was in her usual place in the corner of the room, her head bent over a stack of faxes. He glanced at her quickly, being careful not to catch her attention. The anger between them had faded, replaced by a habit of mutual avoidance, diligently maintained by each one's unyielding pride.

In his concerted effort not to speak to Charlotte, Horace had, to his surprise and discomfort, become even more aware of her motions. Today, glancing in her direction, Horace thought the tilt of her head seemed lower than usual, and her shoulders more slumped. She was staring at some papers on her desk, but Horace could have sworn she wasn't reading them. Everything about her position suggested depression, and Horace felt a wave of pity despite himself. The full loneliness of being the only woman in the office, with no friends, and a desk stuck in an isolated corner, struck him fully for the first time. It must be awful, his brain registered, before he reined in his empathy to focus instead on her ridiculous, smitten greeting of Patrick the morning after she'd asked him for help with the client reports. He saw again her look of delight and desire as she'd greeted Patrick, and he felt again a wave of irrational humiliation.

As Horace wallowed in his anger, Patrick entered the office and walked toward Charlotte's desk. Despite himself, Horace tracked Patrick's progress, bracing himself for Charlotte's rapturous welcome. To his surprise, Charlotte instead seemed to sink even lower in her chair, as if trying to avoid Patrick's glance. Horace let his eyes rest on Charlotte, puzzled, wondering at the change. After a moment, he forced himself to look away; their relationship, whatever it was, meant nothing to him. He looked down at the pile of company reports stacked on the left side of his desk. Two million dollars, he thought. His left eye twitched as the number passed through his head. Pressing his lips together, he extended his left hand and picked up the report on the top of the pile: 250 pages on British Petroleum. He turned to its first page, crushed its spine flat with his fist, and resolved not to look up until he had a stock recommendation for Jed.

At 9 p.m., Horace was still at his desk. The pile of company reports now sat on his right side, each one opened, its spine flattened, its contents read, digested, and critiqued. Over the day, his colleagues had come and gone, quietly leaving sandwiches by his side. The streets surrounding Shorwell's office were dark and quiet, enlivened by sporadic bursts of noise from pubs, whose fogged windows framed the silhouettes of drinking City workers. Charlotte, too, had come and gone from the office. Unlike the others, however, she had not returned home when she left the office. Instead, she had headed to the pub nearest the office, where she appropriated a table in the back room near the toilets. There, she'd hunkered down with a book and a half-pint of lager for three long hours, ignoring the curious glances of neighbors and waiting until she could be sure that the office would be deserted.

Adrian's appeal to her at Henrietta's flat had been followed by a phone call, in which he'd asked her to look for any documentation Shorwell maintained about its custodial arrangements with clients. *There's probably something on file on Patrick's computer,* he'd said. Torn between her desire to be free of Shorwell, which now seemed to her an absurd misadventure, and her anxiety about Piers, Charlotte had wavered for days before acceding to Adrian's request.

At 9 p.m., Charlotte finally left the pub and set out into the empty streets. In the silence, the tapping of her heels ricocheted off the facades of the empty buildings, unnerving her further. She stumbled on the uneven cobblestones as she hurried, muttering to herself, *calm down.*

Entering Shorwell's building, Charlotte tiptoed past a sleeping security guard and walked to the front door of the office. She dug an office key out of her purse and slid it into the lock, turning it clockwise. It stuck. Charlotte paused in surprise. Had someone locked the door from the inside? Trying again, she worked the key back and forth, flinching at the sound of metal grating against metal. She swore under her breath, and felt her hands start to sweat. She kept twisting the key, glancing behind her back every few seconds.

She was leaning forward, trying to gain more leverage, when the office door finally gave way. Unbalanced, she fell forward and flailed out her arms, clawing at the person in front of her.

"Charlotte, stop that. It's me!" Panicked and unhearing, Charlotte continued to wave her arms like a crazed windmill, her gold bangles clanging against one another in the air, her eyes unseeing. A man caught her wrists and Charlotte fell, her heel caught by a pile of wires. When she looked up, panting and shaking, Horace was staring down at her, his brown eyes wide with surprise. A red welt was rising on his pale cheek where she had scratched him, and his dark hair was matted to his forehead with sweat.

Charlotte's felt her fear slide into embarrassment and anger. "Horace! Why are you here? And why did you lock the door from the inside?"

"To prevent a crazy person like *you* from wandering in off the street. And as for what I'm doing here, I might very well ask *you* that question. Your fingernails are lethal." He touched the angry red ridge on his cheek. Charlotte and Horace glared at each other, unspeaking, before

Charlotte freed her shoe from the encircling wires and clambered to her feet. She smoothed her skirt with quick, harsh strokes.

"I'm just back to pick up some reports that we need for marketing," she said, not looking at him.

Horace didn't even bother to mask his incredulity. "At nine o'clock at night? That's ridiculous."

"More ridiculous than your being here at this hour? What are you doing, anyway?"

"I'm working on some new ideas for a guy in New York who runs an internal fund." His voice trailed off, and he tilted his head down, pushing the hair out of his eyes.

"Who?" Charlotte demanded.

"Jed Miles."

"Oh, I've heard about Jed. He's the one who produces the reports that Miranda faxes me – when she can be bothered, that is. And he's the one who travels around with Piers on sales calls. All roads seem to lead to Jed. Why is he calling you? Doesn't he have analysts in New York?"

"Not ones who are any good, apparently," said Horace, with a rare show of ego. Turning his back on Charlotte, he crossed the office to his desk and sat down, ostentatiously picking up a stack of papers. Charlotte watched his retreat and stood up, crossing the office toward her own desk and sitting down with an emphatic bump. She looked at her desk. In the abandoned office, the silence between them was smothering, and Charlotte realized that the televisions had been turned off for the first time in her memory, exposing the low hum of computers and an occasional muffled car honk.

Forced to play along with the charade she'd set in motion, Charlotte turned to the stack of month-end client reports in front of her. The Welsh Shipping report was on top, discarded after her conversation with Mr. Penry. She picked it up, hearing Mr. Penry's irritated voice: *And this last position, Miss Cheetham, doesn't show up on my Reuters terminal at all.* Charlotte turned to the last page of the report, where the alternative investments were listed under the sub-heading of derivatives. What was a derivative, anyway? Glancing at Horace, who was once again immersed in reading, Charlotte dug out the reference book she kept hidden in the back of her desk drawer: *A Beginner's Guide to the Stock Markets.* She turned to the index and looked up derivatives, turning to the relevant chapter. *A derivative,* she read, *is a security whose value derives from the fluctuations in price of an underlying asset. Most derivatives are traded over-the-counter and are unregulated.* Useless, she thought, shoving the book back into her desk drawer.

She squinted at the faxes, trying to make out the blurry series of letters next to the position that had offended Mr.Penry: GLD/FRT*12=O. Picking up the fax, she walked over to the Reuters terminal on Patrick's desk, where its cursor was blinking a dull green. She looked again at Horace. The welt on his cheek had turned purple and his eyes were trained on his reading, his imperviousness to her glacial. Sitting down in Patrick's chair, she typed in the list of characters and hit enter. *Error,* read the screen, accompanied by a sharp beep. Charlotte reentered the chain of symbols, swapping a 0 for O. *Error. Beep.* She glared at the terminal, frustrated. Without thinking, she called out to Horace. "Horace, I can't find one of the client's positions. Could you possibly help?"

Charlotte felt him hesitate before looking up, and she watched a veil of caution fall across his eyes as his thoughts shifted from his report to her. Slowly, he rose and took a few steps, perching behind her shoulder and staring at the Reuters terminal.

Charlotte twisted in her chair to look up at him. "I've been trying to look up the price of a derivative owned by the Welsh Shipping Fund. But when I type in its code, I get nothing. See?" Charlotte punched the code on the keyboard. *Error. Beep.*

Horace leaned over Charlotte to see the faxed report, running his bloodshot eyes over the blurry faxed page. He glanced between the page and the screen, checking Charlotte's entry. Perching his body on the edge of the desk, he started to type, explaining to Charlotte, "I'm just seeing whether it shows up on other exchanges." In the quiet office, the keyboard's clicks were audible as Horace's pale fingers moved across the keys. A series of error message appeared, each one accompanied by a tinny beep. *Error. Beep. Error. Beep. Error. Beep.* Horace's fingers stopped moving. He sat staring at the screen, a puzzled expression on his face, his hands resting lightly on the keyboard. He said nothing.

"Horace? What do you think?"

Horace continued to stare at the terminal as he answered. "I don't know, Charlotte." He continued to look at the screen, showing no sign of moving. Charlotte watched the rise and fall of his breaths under his blue wool pullover, the one he donned everyday once the workday was over, as if assuming his real identity. He turned his head toward her, fixing his reddened eyes on hers. "Charlotte – I don't mean to alarm you – but do you think there's any chance that something odd is going on in New York?" Charlotte's thoughts turned to Adrian, his pale eyes worried below his domed forehead and receding hairline. She hesitated, uncertain.

"I don't know," she said.

Horace nodded, keeping his eyes focused on Charlotte's. His left eye twitched, and he raised a self-conscious hand to cover it. "It gets worse when I'm stressed," he said.

"Are you stressed now? Do you think we should be worried?"

Horace continued to look at her, as if trying to make up his mind about something. Behind his quizzical expression, she could practically feel him weighing the pros and cons of a decision. Was he deciding whether to confide in her? Whether to help her? Her mind flashed to her first day in the office, when Horace had tried to explain the principle of standard deviation. She watched herself turn from him to Patrick, hearing again Patrick's mocking laugh. Silently, she cursed herself. How had she been such a fool? How could she have been so stupid as to ignore all his efforts to help her? She extended a cautious finger in the direction of his forearm, barely touching the rough weave of his sweater.

"Horace, look. I don't want to maintain this charade. I know we haven't been speaking – too much – lately, but I'd be so grateful if we could put that behind us, at least for now. I came here tonight because Adrian Whitely asked me to look at the files on Patrick's computer. I don't really know what I'm meant to be looking for – anything unusual, I guess. Will you help?"

Horace's eyes, focused on the finger Charlotte had placed on his arm, widened when she mentioned Adrian. Sitting above her, he nodded, his face carefully blank. Together they turned toward Patrick's computer. The screen was in sleep mood, an oblong figure eight careening across its surface, bouncing from edge to edge. Horace stabbed at a few keys.

"It's password-protected, of course," he said.

"Patrick hardly strikes me as a computer wizard," Charlotte said, "How about his name? Or Shorwell?"

Horace tapped at the keys. The oblong figure eight continued to flitter across the screen. He paused. "How about *your* name?" Embarrassed, Charlotte shrugged, feeling her face flush. Horace typed CHARLOTTE. The crazy eight continued its rotations. Charlotte stared at the screen, wondering what Patrick would choose when he first got to London. She saw him in his blank white bedroom, his torso twisted above hers as she tried to extract her earring from his shirt collar, the phone ringing in the next room. Her cheeks reddened further.

"Try Miranda," she whispered. Horace said nothing as he typed in MIRANDA. The crazy eight exploded into a frenzy of shooting colors which resolved into a row of files, each one named for a client. Horace clicked into a few files and scrolled through the spreadsheets and notes that emerged. They all looked entirely straightforward. He ran a search for files that had been used recently, ones that were stored on a back-up server, and anything suggesting unusual activity. Nothing. Charlotte didn't know whether to be relieved or disappointed. At the least, she would be able to tell Adrian that she had tried, and that he would have to pursue his investigation without her. Relief swept through her as she anticipated being free from Shorwell, and she turned to Horace with an almost cheerful expression as he shut down Patrick's computer.

"Adrian's on a wild goose chase?" she said. Horace shrugged.

"I don't know. But if Patrick's involved, he isn't doing it from here." He rubbed his bloodshot eyes before turning to Charlotte with a tired smile.

"I'm exhausted. This place loses its charm after eighteen hours. Want to join me at the pub? I just have to leave a message for Jed." Charlotte nodded and waited as he left a message on Jed's answering machine: a description of a shipping stock that would rise if oil prices kept climbing. He put down the phone and turned toward Charlotte.

"Let's go. Promise your talons will be sheathed?"

Charlotte stood up and waved her fingers in the air. "I promise. Let's go."

13

Outside Agitators

Piers shut the book in frustration. It was hard to concentrate while half-listening to the television pundit drone on about oil, and he was self-conscious about looking at a paperback novel while in his office. Moreover, he had no idea what the author was talking about. Turning the book over, he stared at the cover's black-and-white photo of Milan Kundera's face in profile, a grizzled chin under tired, lined eyes. Born in Czechoslovakia, he read, and now living in France. Piers glanced out of the window next to his desk. The grey fog of January hovered outside, obscuring the view of neighboring buildings. He tried to think of anything he knew about Czechoslovakia and drew a blank; it seemed impossibly far away from his Manhattan midtown office. His thoughts shifted to Anna. He'd returned twice to the bar where he'd met her, each time feeling an irrational wave of disappointment at the sight of her small, abandoned table. After the second failed effort, he'd gone to a bookstore to buy the Kundera novel. His phone rang, and he threw the book into the bottom of his desk drawer. "Piers Cheetham," he said.

"Hello Piers! It's me. It's been ages. How are things?" Charlotte's light voice sailed into Piers's ear, its vibration unleashing a wave of anger that reverberated through his body. He hadn't forgiven her for the terrible things she'd said at Christmas and he found that his anger was still white hot, just beneath the surface. He said nothing.

"Piers, I am sorry about Christmas – really, I am. I hope you'll forgive me. Can we put it behind us? There are more important things happening, Piers, and I need to talk to you."

Her voice took on a coaxing note, and Piers worked hard to keep his grudge unyielding. "What more important things?" he asked.

"Adrian – you remember Adrian Whitely, right? Henrietta's boyfriend? Well, he's working for Downing Street at the office that regulates investment firms, and I happened to see him, and he told me he's a bit worried about Shorwell –"

Piers cut her off with a bitter laugh. "So now that you've launched me into Shorwell, you want to pull me out? You've got to be joking. Isn't Adrian the short one trying to be an actor? You can tell him I can manage my own affairs."

"Oh Piers, I know it must seem that way, but I'm just trying to help."

"Thanks, Charlotte, but I'm absolutely fine. Perfect. Never better." Piers slammed down the handset and pushed his chair away from his desk. Swiveling toward his office door, he rose and headed toward Jerry's cubicle, instinctively seeking relief in a conversation about sports. Jerry had sisters; he'd understand. Piers paused as his peripheral vision registered Doreen, the receptionist, moving in his direction. He had never seen Doreen away from her desk in Shorwell's front lobby, and he turned to her in surprise as she shuffled toward him with awkward haste, her bulk swaying over high heels. She came to a pause outside his office, panting slightly. Her face was anxious under its layers of makeup: her red lips pursed, and the pupils under her fake eyelashes dilated.

She grasped his shirtsleeve with long red fingernails and spoke in a loud whisper. "There's a man to see you who says he's from the SEC. I tried to tell him you're not here, but he won't leave. What do you want me to do?"

Piers hesitated. "Send him back here, I guess. No, wait, I'll come get him and take him into a conference room." Together, they turned back toward the lobby. Piers could feel the traders' heads swivel toward them as they walked, but he kept his gaze forward and his expression blank.

He found the visitor tipped forward on the lobby's white leather sofa reading a tabloid. Piers studied him, relaxing as he assessed the man's cheap black suit and unkempt thicket of hair. Approaching the sofa, Piers deployed his most cut-glass British accent, "I'm told you wish to see me?"

The man tipped back his head and looked at Piers with eyes that were oddly small for his broad face, and hostile. He stood up. He was shorter than Piers by a head, but unlike most short men, he didn't roll back onto his heels and stand straighter when meeting someone taller, instead remaining comfortably slouched. He nodded at Piers. "Is there somewhere we can talk?" he asked.

Piers glanced at Doreen, who was gaping at the visitor. Silently, she nodded in the direction of the main conference room. Piers gestured his visitor ahead of him, and the two men walked into the cavernous, dim room, empty except for a gleaming conference table. Sitting down, the agent from the SEC pulled a wad of receipts and papers from his pocket and rifled through them until he found a card with fraying corners. He pushed this in front of Piers, who looked down: Joseph O'Brien, SEC. The gold logo of the government agency was stamped above his name along with a tiny picture of the scales of justice.

Piers smiled perfunctorily. "What can I do for you, Mr.," he hesitated, pretending to forget the man's name, and glancing down again at the card. "O'Brien."

The man ignored the question. "You're from England, right?" In his thick Brooklyn accent, you're emerged as *you-wuh*. "My granddad was there during the war. He went over from Dublin to find work and got stuck in London during the Blitz. He and his buddies used to bet on what the Germans would bomb every night. Some guys, they just have bad luck, you know? And some guys go out and find it." O'Brien sat back into the upholstered conference chair and dug into his jacket pocket. He extracted a pack of cigarettes and a plastic lighter bearing the insignia of the Mets. "Mind if I smoke?"

Smoking was against Shorwell rules. Piers shrugged. O'Brien nodded and flipped open his lighter. The tip of his cigarette glowed red for a moment, and O'Brien looked around for an ash tray. Finding none, he tapped his cigarette onto the tabloid in front of him. The acrid smoke drifted toward Piers. O'Brien coughed. "So, Piers-from-England, let me tell you who we are and what we do. The SEC is the government agency responsible for regulating investment firms. In the UK, our counterparts would be the Office of Fair Trading. Are you familiar with them?"

"No."

"Right. You will be. Our division just got a letter from them with some questions about Shorwell. They want our help. Apparently one of your UK clients has been questioning how you price your positions.

I've got the hedge fund beat, so it was thrown on my desk. I took the opportunity to look into Shorwell's recent filings and found some interesting stuff."

Piers, whose face and body had remained frozen during these comments, stirred. "For any organizational queries, I suggest you speak to my boss, who heads up the firm. Doreen can put you in touch with him."

The SEC agent took another drag of his cigarette and ground its stub into the tabloid with bitten-down fingernails. Piers watched the cigarette's dull red glow vanish into an article about a NYPD drug bust.

"W.? Oh, we know all about W. Your boss is a close – supporter – of the SEC. We've spoken to him in the past. How's his squash game these days?" Piers said nothing. "The problem we have, Piers, or rather, the problem *you* have, is that the legal documents Shorwell has to file with our agency give your name as the salesperson responsible for the funds whose pricing is an object of concern."

Piers's frozen expression melted, as a coughing fit overtook him. "Excuse me?" Piers said.

"Yeah, let me show you." O'Brien removed a piece of paper from his wallet that had been folded into eighths. He laid it in front of Piers and pointed to its bottom edge. "See there? That's your name listed as the party responsible for the Shorwell funds. And there's your signature, just there." O'Brien stabbed at the signature with a stubby finger.

Piers felt the blood drain from his face as he recognized the documents he'd signed in W.'s office after the Hamptons party. He bit down on the inside of his lips hard. Charlotte's words from the morning's conversation reverberated in his head – *Adrian thinks something's wrong.* He stared down at the page, saying nothing.

O'Brien withdrew the paper, speaking as he re-folded it. "Piers, I know you're new here. Let me tell you something, just as a friend, just because my family happened to come from your side of the pond. You're working for a clever guy – a clever chap, I guess you'd say. And this clever guy, W., has stitched you up nice and tight with all these legal documents. I bet you have no idea what you signed, right?" Piers said nothing. O'Brien nodded. "That's what I figured. Here's the deal. The SEC has been watching W. for years, but he's a slippery character. Every time we try to stomp on him, he peeks up through another hole. Like a gopher. Or a mole. You got those over there, right? So I'm here to offer you a deal – good for you, good for us."

O'Brien paused, glancing around the windowless, blank walls of the conference room. Piers felt the taste of panic rising from the base of his esophagus and swallowed hard, afraid he would vomit on the conference table. He forced himself to speak. "Mr. O'Brien, I don't know the history of your dealings with W. But it seems that this conversation should be with him, not with me." He paused, trying to suppress the bile burbling in his throat.

The man shrugged and started to fold the scorched tabloid in front of him around the ground-up ashes of his cigarette. Using his palm, he flattened the pages into a neat square and stood up. "Okay, buddy. You've got my card if you want to call me. But let me tell you, it's just a matter of time. W. has done a nice job pinning you down with legal bullshit, and I think you'll understand pretty fast that dealing with me is your best choice. But I'll let you figure that out." Piers remained seated, too shocked and nauseated to respond. O'Brien rolled the flattened tabloid into a cylinder and stuck it in his pocket. "I'll see myself out," he said.

The heavy door swung shut behind him and Piers sprinted toward the corner of the room, heaving vomit into the black fake-wood trash can. He remained doubled over, his temples pulsing, and wretched again. He stood up and wiped the sweat from his forehead with the back of his hand. *Calm down,* he told himself. *Try to think.* He had to talk to someone. He ran through the options in his head. Charlotte? Out of the question. Jerry? Useless. Jed? He sighed. It would have to be Jed. Who else was there? He left the conference room and went to the men's room, where he splashed his face with water and rinsed out his acid-tasting mouth. Staring into the mirror, he tried to reassemble his expression into one he recognized, before giving up and making his way to Jed's office.

Jed was in his customary position, glaring at the computer screen and stabbing at his keyboard. As Piers hovered in the doorway, he heard an English man's voice on Jed's speaker phone: *Trades at 20 times forward earnings, twice book but only three times free cash flow – and with the oil price recovering, should be a leveraged play.* When Jed heard the word oil, he swore and hit mute. Piers entered his office, standing just inside the doorway.

"Was that Horace?" Piers asked in surprise.

"You know him?" Jed's laconic voice had a dangerous edge of anger.

Piers inclined his head a fraction. "Slightly." He paused, waiting for Jed to stop glaring at his computer screen. "Jed, do you have a second?"

"No," Jed answered, continuing to bash at his keyboard. "Can it wait?"

"No."

Jed sighed, and turned his large head toward Piers. Under his glazed eyes, his pasty complexion was highlighted by two spots of red on either cheek, where small clusters of spiderweb veins had started to sprout.

"I just got a visit from a guy in the SEC," Piers said. Jed's face showed no reaction. His tired eyes remained just as hooded, and his torso didn't move. Piers continued. "He said that his agency has been investigating Shorwell for a while. They think W. is doing something illegal. He wants me to cooperate with him. He had a copy of the document we signed in W.'s office that day after the party. Apparently, the SEC gets copies of all the documents relating to sales people – I don't know. He said it implicated me in something – something irregular."

Jed nodded slowly, keeping his eyes fixed on Piers. "And you said?"

"I told him to talk to W."

A faint light seemed to flicker in the depths of Jed's eyes, like a fish darting in the water beneath a solidly frozen lake. Jed turned back to his spreadsheet. "Don't worry about it," he said, his eyes on his screen. "The SEC is always sniffing around and throwing out accusations to see what sticks. They hate guys who make money. They don't have anything on you. They're just testing the waters. Look at me – I've been here five years and I'm fine. This guy is picking on you because you're new."

Relief flooded Piers. He leaned forward toward Jed, craving reassurance. "Really? Are you sure?"

Jed nodded at his screen. "Absolutely. Hit the gym and forget about it."

"Got it. Hey, Jed – thanks." Piers hovered in the doorway for a last minute before turning away, a new energy animating his step.

When Charlotte entered the Shorwell office the morning after her late-night visit, she found that the cloud of anxiety that usually descended upon her each morning had dissipated. Surprised, she almost looked up in search of her psychological gloom. Where had it gone? As she walked toward her desk, not bothering to monitor whether the traders were watching her, she realized that it wasn't trailing her, either, or waiting to settle when she sat down. Fortified by her plan to quit her job as soon as possible, she no longer cared what her mute colleagues said or thought. The knowledge of her imminent freedom imbued her spirit with a new gust of energy.

She pushed aside the marketing and stock market reports piled on her desk and donned her phone headset, dialing into her voice mailbox. The first message was from the young woman in Wales. Her voice was lower than Charlotte had remembered, as if she'd matured from a soprano to an alto during the Christmas holidays.

"Miss Cheetham? This is Myfanwy Burton, from the Welsh Shipping Pension Fund. I'm sorry to bother you, but we're in a bit of a tizzy here and Mr. Penry asked me to ring you as soon as possible. He's in even more of a lather than usual, if you can believe it," – Miss Burton gave a conspiratorial chuckle – "because apparently his endless spreadsheets charting everything about our business – his great pride and joy, his *pièce de résistance* – haven't gone his way. He'd had it all planned out, you know: the price of running ships around the ocean, and what the employees cost (not a lot, I don't mind telling you), and the price of oil, and what our customers pay. Well, it seems that when the countries in the Mideast invaded each other – hardly the glamorous world of Laurence of Arabia, did you ever see that? – Mr. Penry bet the price of oil would go up. Then the Americans went in and the price of oil went down and you can't imagine Mr. Penry's rage. He'd made all sorts of bets – hedges he calls them – which were all wrong once the Americans got involved. So," said Miss Burton, taking a much-needed breath, "I'm afraid because of Mr. Penry's bad luck – and stupid, typically male decisions, as my mother said – we're having to sack lots of people and we need the money in our pension fund back. Mr. Penry would like you to fax us – hang on," Charlotte heard a rustling paper and then Miss Burton's voice, sounding more official, "*an up-to-the-minute valuation of our fund and a date by which you can wire the funds.* Such a bore. Anyway, I do hope everything is lovely up there in London. I am sure it is much nicer than here, anyway."

On this depressed note, Myfanwy Burton concluded her message. After her disquisition, the silence in Charlotte's ear was particularly deafening. Poor Miss Burton, Charlotte thought, what awful news. Filled with sympathy, she dialed Miranda's extension in New York, planning to ask her for the most recent valuation report of the Welsh client's portfolio, and for the procedure to liquidate the fund. She reached a recorded message saying that Miranda was away for the week. Charlotte frowned. She would have to call Jed directly. Locating his number in the Shorwell company directory, she dialed his extension.

"Jed here." His toneless voice seemed to emanate from a cave, and Charlotte realized that she had been put on a speaker phone.

She adopted her most professional demeanor. "Jed, it's Charlotte Cheetham from the London office. I believe you work with my brother, Piers?" There may have been a grunt, but Charlotte couldn't tell. "I've just had a call through from our shipping client in Wales. They're redeeming –"

"What?" The sudden volume of Jed's voice caused her to jump.

She began again. "Yes, I'm afraid they're redeeming. They need the most recent valuation report and want to know when the funds can be wired over." There was a long silence, and Charlotte feared that the connection had gone dead. Five seconds passed. "Hello? Jed?"

"Yeah, I'm here. Hey, Charlotte, look – I'll get back to you as soon as I can, okay?"

Jed pushed the end call button and swore. The Welsh were redeeming? They couldn't redeem. He had been using their account to meet the margin calls of his French brokers. This was going to be a book-keeping nightmare. It wasn't as though he couldn't raid another client's account to fund the Welsh, but it meant creating yet another series of faked documents. He just didn't have time for all the layers of subterfuge. Not when his own fund was cratering again. He stared at the stock charts of his fund's positions on his screen: red graphs whose crazed oscillations were his constant companions. He saw the red pictures all the time now. Even in the few hours that he closed his eyes and passed out on his desk – between 3 and 6 a.m., when the office was all but silent and abandoned – he saw the lines of the graphs and rows of the Excel spreadsheets dancing on the inside of his eyeballs, mocking him. The hole in his hedge fund was growing by the day, as the price of oil careened like a yo-yo trick.

His mind raced. He needed time to replenish his funds and dig his way out. He couldn't redeem the Welsh now. He would have to put her off. Gathering his energies, he considered his cards. His bets were going against him now but might turn around. Horace had made him some money and might make him more; his ideas weren't bad. W. was away, chasing some French girl in Morocco, and the phone connections from north Africa were spotty. Piers was in his pocket, now that the SEC had scared the wits out of him. His thoughts paused, as Piers's anxious face flashed through his brain. That was it. He would use Piers. He dialed Piers's extension.

Piers picked up on the first ring. "Jed – hey buddy! What's up?"

"Piers – your sister, Charlotte…"

"Charlotte?"

Jed heard the anger and defensiveness in Piers's voice and smiled to himself. "Yeah, Charlotte. I just got a call from her. One of her clients is redeeming, and she's asking for the most recent valuation report and for the funds to be wired over. I tried to explain to her that we can only redeem at quarter-end, but she just didn't quite seem to get it. I know she doesn't have an investment background, like us. I was wondering, Piers – I'm sorry to turn this into a family issue – but do you think you could talk to her for me? I'm snowed under right now."

"No problem, Jed. Consider it done." Piers hung up the phone and dialed Charlotte's office number in London, swearing under his breath. The phone call connected with the British Telecom network and he heard the long dial tones of England. He swore again with impatience, having grown accustomed to the shorter beeps of the U.S. After a minute, her voice mail message clicked on and Charlotte's familiar voice answered. Despite his bad mood, he couldn't help but notice the cool professionalism of her voice mail message. His anger intensified. There was something absurd, he thought, about a younger sister pretending that she was a professional; it was like one more stage in her childhood enthusiasm for dress-up. Fuzzy images without context or date crowded his brain as Charlotte's identities flashed before him. There was Charlotte dressed as a nurse after she watched the documentary about the Great War, her feet catching in a long white apron, her hair covered by a drooping white tea towel; Charlotte the mountaineer, doggedly trudging along a muddy path and tripping over their father's walking stick; Charlotte the mesmerist draped in gauze scarves and bead necklaces, hunched over a Ouija board; and, very briefly after her first communion, Charlotte the nun in a shiny white dress and veil. His mind flicked through the images in an instant as he half-listened to Charlotte's recorded voice: *Please leave a message and I will ring you back as soon as I can.*

Piers hung up without leaving a message. He didn't want to talk to her anyway. He wanted to help Jed – he *had* to help Jed, who increasingly seemed his only ally and support – but he didn't know why Jed couldn't stonewall Charlotte on his own. He sighed. When had it all become so twisted? For years it was simple: He'd led the way, and Charlotte had beamed in his direction, as, in his view, befitted a younger sister. In return, he had run interference when she had clashed with their mother; charmed or intimidated difficult schoolmates, as the case demanded; and encouraged her when her poems – too many and too dreary, in his unspoken opinion – fell short of her goals. When their father died, their bond had grown tighter as they sought out each other instinctively, sitting for hours in Charlotte's bedroom (warmer than his own), their individual pools of unhappiness bleeding together: Charlotte mesmerized by Gone with the Wind, and Piers plowing his way through Sherlock Holmes mysteries.

Piers rubbed his temples, trying to rid his imagination of a young Charlotte frowning over her book, one finger mindlessly twisting a dark strand of hair. He didn't need Charlotte now, he thought angrily. She was the one who had led him to this job, which was meant to be his path to glory and riches, and where he now faced a grubby SEC agent and a half-mute, exhausted colleague as his only ally. His frustration mounted as he considered his position, and in five minutes he had worked himself into a rage at the young woman on the answering machine who had replaced the adoring and loyal Charlotte of his childhood. He would leave her a message telling her to stop bothering Jed. It was the only choice: Jed needed her to back off, and he needed Jed.

He picked up his phone's headset and dialed Charlotte's number. It hadn't rung once when Charlotte's voice sounded in his ear.

"Charlotte Cheetham here."

The confident polish of her voice intensified his anger. "Charlotte, it's Piers."

"Hello Piers!"

Her surprised pleasure diverted him briefly, but he stayed the course, pushing away the love he felt for her with a huge, soul-destroying effort. "Charlotte, I'm calling because I just spoke to Jed. He said he tried to explain to you that he couldn't liquidate the Welsh account until quarter-end but that you didn't understand."

"He didn't say anything of the kind. He just said he was too busy to discuss it."

"Well, whatever. He just asked me if I could ask you not to bother him about it right now."

"Piers, they're my client. They have the right to redeem, and I am the person who is meant to help them."

Piers paused. There was no disputing the truth and reasonableness of this. He changed tactics, lashing out at Charlotte with venom intensified by the disgust he felt at his own behavior. "Charlotte, I know you don't have a background in investments," he said, his voice tinged with condescension, "But we can't just redeem the funds at any time. We are running a business with rules and regulations."

"Are we?" Charlotte's voice was quiet.

Piers exploded in an exhausted, ignorant fury. "Of course we are. What in the world do you know, anyway? Patrick hires you and suddenly you think you're some sort of investment guru? For God's sake, you're just a souped-up advertising girl Patrick fancied!"

Piers heard the swift intake of breath on the other end of the line and stopped short. He wished desperately he could withdraw his last sentence but it was too late: It hung between them, somewhere over the Atlantic Ocean, dripping its bitterness into the crashing waves of the sea. Piers braced himself for Charlotte's fury, almost hoping she would say something equally fierce, so that he could justify his words. But there was no answer from Charlotte, just silence. "Charlotte, please," he sputtered.

She cut him off. "Poor Piers," she said in the same quiet tone. "I'm sorry." She hung up. Piers stared at the phone receiver, his head whirling, the nausea in his gut building once again. Closing his eyes, he found Anna sitting in a circle of white light, staring at her book, oblivious to the world around her. <u>Anna</u>, he breathed, his body leaning forward as he tried to get closer to the image in his head. That's what I need, Piers thought, not knowing whether he meant Anna, or her book, or the two of them together; to him, they had merged to form one united ache of longing of some better, simpler, lost world. He watched Anna turn a page before the vision evaporated. Opening his eyes, he saw again his phone. His eyes shifted slowly from his phone to his desk, from his desk to the wall, from the wall to the window, and back once more to the phone, completing the full circle of his imprisonment.

14

The Rock and the Hard Place

New York City emerged from its frozen stupor with the same stunning speed that had marked its arrival. After months of bitter cold, the filthy snow banked up along the streets oozed gracelessly through the metal grates below, leaving a slimy residue of grime and pitted pavement in its wake. Overnight, the city sprang into new life. Lacy white and pink cherry blossoms emerged from trees which had looked all but dead the week before, their delicate scent carried across the city by gusts blowing off the Hudson River. The hordes of people trudging up and down the city's long avenues shed their armor of winter clothing like snakes molting old skin; overnight, women exchanged high-heeled boots for strappy sandals that highlighted their newly waxed legs and painted toenails. The whole city felt fresh and reborn in the glorious and sudden spring.

Piers alone remained mired in a blackness impervious to any outer regeneration. He registered the resurgence of bare skin and the flowering trees of Central Park and heard the laughter of the diners who poured into the café tables crowding every sidewalk, but he walked through it all untouched, an imposter in the city and in his own body. He saw his steps without feeling them and heard himself speak without being conscious of forming the words that emerged from his mouth.

O'Brien had not disappeared. He had continued to call every few days, speaking in a familiar, casual voice, dropping new hints with every voicemail of an ongoing investigation of Shorwell's activities. *We're finding out some interesting things, he said, and if you were willing to help us, it would be good for us and for you.* At first, panicking, Piers ran to Jed after each of these messages, but he stopped once Jed had three times given him the same answer, *He has nothing on us, don't worry about it.* But Piers couldn't stop worrying. He started to see his phone as a crouching animal waiting to pounce, and bile filled his mouth each time he saw its red light flash with a new voicemail. When W. finally returned to the office after a jaunt through north Africa, China and Japan ("You can't believe the geishas," he'd said), Piers practically welcomed the invitation from his office to meet him for squash, hoping desperately that W. would reassure him that nothing was wrong.

Piers arrived at W.'s club on a balmy Tuesday evening, feeling almost normal and hopeful, his hopes pinned on the next hour. Relieved of his heavy wool coat, he felt the fresh air on his skin like a forgotten friend. He was wearing his favorite polo shirt, an old one in which he'd pummeled friends from university in tennis games that now, from West 57th Street, seemed impossibly distant. He strode up the black pavement toward W.'s club, his gym bag banging against his side, his pulse racing.

He reached W.'s club and checked in. In the guest locker room, he looked around for Jed, but didn't see him. He threw his belongings into a small metal cubicle and re-tied his shoe laces. Glancing into a wall of mirrors, he saw that his bare legs looked skinnier and paler after the winter, and his cheeks seemed flushed even before he started the game. He looked down at his watch: 7 p.m. He rushed down to W.'s regular squash court located in the bowels of the club.

Piers found W. poised in a runner's lunge, his arms stretched straight up toward the ceiling, palms clasped together as if in prayer. The lean sinews of W.'s muscles strained against his crisp white shirt and shorts, and his skin was deeply tanned. The older man nodded at Piers without speaking and sank further into his stretch with long, controlled breaths. Piers glanced around at the bright white box crisscrossed in vivid red lines. From neighboring courts, he could hear rubber balls slamming off walls and men yelling. It was hot, and he realized that he was already sweating. W. transitioned from his lunge into a low squat, his knees bent, his arms angled upward.

W. glanced at Piers. "Chair pose. I picked it up in India. Try it – it's incredible for the glutes." Piers shrugged, embarrassed, while W. held this new position while counting under his breath. At twenty, he straightened up and began to whirl his arms like windmills, loosening his shoulder joints. Piers felt a slight gust pass him in the airless box. "OK, let's go." W. said.

Piers won the racket spin and headed to the right of the court to serve. The hard rubber ball cracked against the white cube like a gunshot and Piers, startled by the sound, sprang into motion. He won the first few points and began to relax, enjoying the feeling of his body in motion after the long, apathetic winter. The ball ricocheted back and forth against the cube's six surfaces, the two men in pursuit. After fifteen minutes, W. called a short break. Breathing hard, Piers drank some water and waited while W. stretched his hamstrings with a new yoga pose. They started again. The ball started to pick up pace, and Piers was alarmed to find that his muscles, dormant over the winter, were already tiring. W. took two points in a row, saying nothing as he ratcheted up his level of play, hitting the rubber ball harder with every point. Piers lost another two points and found himself gasping for air.

W. glanced at him. "OK?" he asked.

"Fine," Piers answered, his chest heaving.

W. served again, a fast backhand rail into a corner. Piers's racket missed the ball by a foot. Unnerved, he started to swing wildly, missing the ball as often as he found it. W. racked up five more points in swift succession. Piers glanced up at the glassed-in viewing area above the court, where Jed usually waited when he wasn't playing.

W. followed his look and shook his head. "Just us tonight, buddy."

After another ten minutes, Piers was down by another three points. His legs felt leaden, his chest hurt with every inhalation, and the sweat from his hands was causing the racket to slip. With every lost point, his concentration receded further. W.'s expression remained impassive as Piers's game deteriorated, but his racket seemed to pick up pace as he hit the ball with increasing force.

After Piers's racket missed the ball by a full three feet, W. paused. "Break?" he asked.

Piers, red with exhaustion and shame, nodded. The two men exited the court and crossed the corridor outside to a large water cooler. Piers filled a paper cone with water and collapsed onto a wooden bench. W. continued to stand, watching him. "Too many evenings out on the town? I remember my first year in this city. I gained ten pounds in the first month." W.'s fingers stroked his concave abdomen. "But you're still lean, Piers. If anything, you look a little gaunt. Anything troubling you?"

Piers shook his head. His curls had fallen in sweaty tendrils over his forehead, obscuring his red-rimmed eyes. He managed a half-smile in W.'s direction, not meeting his face. "No, I'm fine," he said.

"That's good. I wouldn't want the SEC to get you down." Piers's head jerked upward. W.'s mouth was impassive, but his eyes were narrow, watching Piers. "Doreen told me about O'Brien's visit. That guy's been on the SEC's hedge fund beat for years, trying to find some way to sock it to the rich guys while he grovels around on his government salary." W. lowered himself onto the bench, inches from Piers. The individual dark hairs on W.'s thighs were clear under the bright lights. W. leaned forward to massage his calf muscle as he spoke. "I'm sure he managed to scare you with some threat, right? That's what all those SEC guys do – insinuate a crime and threaten to throw you in jail unless you cooperate." Without warning, W. moved his hand from his calf muscle to slap Piers's knee. Piers jumped and stopped breathing. "What you need to know, buddy, is that O'Brien is bluffing." Piers took a tentative breath, and felt his shoulders sink a fraction. W. continued. "And if you even think about working with him, I'll send your mother, your sister, and all the London tabloids the video tape I have of you snorting coke and hooking up with your mermaid friend at my beach house. Did you know she has a lily tattooed to her left breast? The footage shows it clearly. It's a nice job. You can see every petal. The Brits I know are a little reserved, so my bet is that you wouldn't like the publicity." W. stood up and clapped Piers on the shoulder, holding it briefly. "I'm glad we had this talk. Let's call it a tie."

W. removed his hand from Piers's shoulder and turned toward the corridor. Numb, Piers watched him stroll down the corridor and disappear into the VIP area of the club. Piers stood up and walked to the locker room, where he undressed automatically and found a shower, turning its dial to the hottest setting. Under the scalding water, W.'s words echoed through his head: He was on film snorting coke and having sex – his mother would know – the tabloids would know. He needed an idea; he needed advice. Around and around his thoughts went as he searched for a solution. Frustrated, the only image that materialized in his brain was Jed. Maybe Jed would finally say something different this time.

Dressing swiftly, Piers left the sports club and walked the few blocks to his office. The balmy evening had sunk into darkness, but the soft, spring caress of the air lingered. Piers passed tables of sidewalk diners grasping at the last moments of the beautiful day. Piers walked past them in a daze, his head down, his stride hurried. Their pleasure in the evening seemed impossibly inaccessible.

The Shorwell office was almost entirely deserted. A sole cleaning woman threaded her way through the cubicles, aiming an aerosol can at anything in her path. Piers turned toward Jed's illuminated office and paused in surprise. Jed was not in his chair. Piers stared, realizing how he'd become used to Jed's flaxen head and glaze-eyed stare as an unchanging office feature. He walked down the hallway and paused at Jed's door, his eyes widening. Jed's swivel chair had been pushed away from the desk and white printer paper was littered across the floor. He winced as a smell of vomit drifted toward him, cutting through the office's overlay of disinfectant. Advancing a few steps, he stopped short. Jed's bulky body lay face down on the carpet beneath the desk, his chest rising and falling slowly, a rivulet of greenish bile leaking from his mouth. Piers leaned down and tapped Jed's shoulder. There was no response. With both hands, Piers wrestled Jed's body onto its back. One of Jed's arms fell against the base of the desk and a spasm of pain crossed his heavy, inert face. Piers glanced around the office, looking for something to prop up Jed's large head. Seeing nothing, he dug into his gym bag for his sweaty polo shirt and stuffed it under Jed's head. Jed began to snore.

Piers stood up, trying to make sense of the scene. Leaning over the unconscious body, he looked into Jed's desk drawer, which had been left open. Scrunched into a corner, next to a stack of yellow Post-it pads were two Ziploc plastic bags half-filled with white powder. Next to them, a lidless plastic bottle held four white pills. Piers looked again at Jed. Jed's shirt had pulled away from his pants, and a few inches of white flesh rose and fell steadily. Suppressing his revulsion, Piers knelt to pick up the papers lying around Jed's head, avoiding the ones closest to the vomit. He flipped through them. They were lists of client equity holdings, annotated by Jed with tiny letters and numbers. Piers squinted at the writing but couldn't make it out. Dropping the papers, he turned to Jed's computer and clicked on the mouse. The whirling spheres of the sleeping screen dissolved into an Excel spreadsheet. Piers scrolled to the top of it. *Gladiator Fund* was written in the top left box, followed by rows of stock positions, their cost basis and current value. Forgetting to breathe through his mouth, Piers inhaled sharply as he ran down the list of trades, all of them deeply under water, the value of their losses demarcated in a bright red font. He flinched as he reached the last line, a summary of the carnage: -85%, (-$210 million).

Piers glanced down, distracted by Jed's increasingly loud snores. His conversations with Jed came hurtling to him in disordered fragments: *I'll call my Hamptons broker... nothing to worry about ... this means you're on your way to serious money.* Piers turned his eyes to the wall two feet above Jed's head. His mind raced with unwelcome thoughts. Jed's fund was a wreck, and Jed had been lying about his trading prowess. If that was true, what else was? Were the funds' performance a lie, too? Was it all a house of cards? Piers's head whirled as he tried to absorb, for the second time that evening, the implications of new information. His courage failed; all he could think was that he had to get away, and now. He looked again at Jed, whose body had been seized by a fit of coughs. Piers was frightened by his desire to smother the coughs by strangling him – suffocating him – anything to silence him and expunge his existence from Piers's life. He grabbed the sweat-drenched shirt from under Jed's lolling head, which slammed down on the grey carpet. Jed's coughs stopped. Piers stared at him, clenching and unclenching his fists, before turning away. He marched down the empty corridor and took the express elevator to the lobby.

Outside, the night was lushly dark, the air tinged with the sweetness of the early plum blossoms. Piers hailed a cab, giving the driver his address before the door was even closed. He shut his eyes, feeling the cab's motion as it flew down Fifth Avenue. The image of Jed's ungainly body, gasping for breath, kept intruding on his thoughts. Go away, Piers said to the image. It remained. Go away, Piers shouted, this time out loud, flicking open his eyes just in time to see the driver glancing at him wide-eyed in the rear view mirror. By the time he reached his dingy street on the lower east side, he had a plan: He would head straight to the airport, buy a one-way ticket to London, and leave New York that night.

Piers bounded up the five stories to his apartment with a frenetic relief-fueled energy. Panting, he threw open his front door and turned straight toward his bedroom, intending to throw the contents of his wardrobe into a suitcase and head directly to Kennedy Airport. At the threshold to his bedroom, he paused as his brain registered an unfamiliar smell. He turned around and froze. In the far corner of his living room, O'Brien sat on his futon sofa, reading a tabloid and holding a cigarette. In front of him on the coffee table, the plastic lid of a take-out food carton was overflowed with dead cigarette stubs. With a languid, almost regretful motion, O'Brien closed the tabloid and looked up at Piers.

He smiled. "Nice place," he said, gesturing with the glowing cigarette. "I bet you can see Tomkins Square Park from here." Piers stared at O'Brien in shock. O'Brien extended an arm clad in a navy nylon jacket toward the chair facing the sofa, playing host. "Please, sit down."

Piers remained standing. His voice, when he found it, was a whispered croak. "How did you get in here? You can't just enter someone's home."

O'Brien smiled at Piers, his face relaxed. "The SEC works closely with the FBI and federal judges. White collar crime is hot these days – search and seizure warrants are no problem. But I apologize for smoking in your apartment. It's a bad habit, I know. My wife hates it." O'Brien dropped the end of his cigarette into the heap of stubs and sat back, crossing his right ankle on top of his left knee. He moved his hand to drum his fingers across his exposed ankle, all the while watching Piers. The young man continued to hover at the far end of the room, staring at him, unmoving.

O'Brien gave a little shrug. "So, have you figured out more about your employer by now?" Piers bit down on the inside of his lips. O'Brien nodded. "You know you're in the soup, right? Hey Piers, let me ask you something. Does the name Simon Hays mean anything to you?" Piers said nothing, and O'Brien continued. "He's your compatriot, Piers. Another Englishman who came to work on Wall Street. Do you know where he is now?"

"Where?" said Piers. His voice was still a whisper, barely audible against the car horns from the sidewalk below.

"In jail in New Jersey, convicted by an American judge and jury for breaking the law. Ten years in jail. But you know, he didn't have to be there. If he'd just cooperated with the authorities, he'd be back in England now, sitting in the pub." O'Brien shook his head back and forth, as if ruing the man's poor choices.

Piers swayed back and forth feeling sick. He gathered his nerves, his voice gaining strength as he spoke. "Whatever you've got on Shorwell, I'm not part of it. And I know you know that. Your fight is with W., not me."

O'Brien's eyebrows lifted a fraction. He rose from the sofa, and walked toward Piers, stopping one foot away from him. Piers's nose twitched at the intense stink of cigarette smoke that clung to O'Brien.

"Piers, I gotta tell you something. You're not leaving Shorwell or the U.S. until this is settled. Your name is on a no-fly list that the FBI maintains with the air traffic authorities. People on that list don't board international flights." Piers said nothing, staring beyond him to the barred window at the far end of the apartment. O'Brien spoke again, his voice quiet, his consonants crisp. "Piers, I've been hunting W. and other hedge fund assholes for five years. Five years of being dodged and taunted by these rich, entitled bastards. Now I've got one. Unfortunately for you, he's got you. Sorry about that. Basically, your only option is to work with us, if you don't want to end locked up like Simon Hays. I'll leave you think about it."

O'Brien stood up, and patted Piers on the shoulder. His short, solid body moved to the door in three strides, his nylon jacket straining against his wide shoulders as his hand reached for the doorknob. Hearing the door slam, Piers collapsed into a fetal position on the floor. Rocking back and forth, his whole body shaking, he started to cry, his sobs mingling with the shouts of the revelers below, celebrating the spring night.

15

Reluctant Partners

L istening to her phone messages at work, it took Charlotte a few
minutes to recognize Piers's voice. It wasn't just the Americanized
inflections that threw her; it was also the irregular, staccato rush
of words, the long pauses, the cracks in his speech as he seemed to be
gulping back tears, all of it punctuated by the eruptions of honking
cars. She played his message again and again, trying to glean more of
its meaning through the payphone's hissing connection: *Jed's fund –
O'Brien from the SEC — FBI no-fly list.* By the fifth playback, she could
see him standing in a glass box in the middle of Sixth Avenue with cars
rushing past him, his eyes bloodshot, the palm holding the handset
damp with sweat.

Saving Piers's message, she let her eyes wander around the office as
she considered what to do. The most obvious person to call would be
Adrian, she figured. He owed her a favor, given that she'd tried to help
him by searching Patrick's computer, even if she hadn't found anything.
Moreover, he was Henrietta's boyfriend, and their fathers had been in
school together. Presumably he could be trusted? Charlotte picked up
her phone and dialed Adrian's office. She could hear him speaking to
someone else as he picked up the phone.

"Adrian Whitely here."

"Adrian – it's Charlotte Cheetham. Sorry to bother you, but it's
important."

"No worries, Charlotte. What's wrong?"

"I've just picked up a message from Piers. It was over a payphone,
and a bit garbled. He said someone – O'Brien? – from the SEC had visited him and was – I know it sounds absurd – threatening him. Given
what you told me the other night, I thought I should tell you. I was

wondering, could you possibly reach out to someone in New York? Piers sounded worried. In truth, he sounded terrified."

"Of course, Charlotte. I'll see what I can find out. I'm sure it will be fine." Adrian hung up and sat up straighter on his uncomfortable government-issued chair, his eyes brightening, feeling a hint of the adrenalin that used to flood him before walking on stage in university productions at the Oxford Playhouse. He'd specialized in advisor roles, both comic and evil: Othello's Iago, Peter Whimsey's butler, King Lear's Gloucester. He had a knack for sidling up to the leading man and whispering in his ear while remaining perfectly audible to the audience. At first, his job in government had seemed a departure from those days, but he'd quickly come to realize that the Office of Fair Trading was not so different a stage from the Oxford Playhouse after all. Some of his old acting tricks had started to slide back into his repertoire, such as the long pauses before making a point, and angling his torso toward his audience while balancing on the balls of his feet. His voice training would be useful, he hoped, when he entered the House of Commons as a young MP one day.

Adrian glanced at the only decoration in his narrow grey office, a framed photograph of John Major, the new prime minister, looking eager to please. Hadn't his father been in vaudeville? Drawing a blank, his thoughts returned to Charlotte. Her appeal was the most interesting problem to have come his way since joining the agency the year before. His job of reviewing the documents of newly arrived foreign banks was tedious and held little political upside, given that Downing Street had explicitly lured to London the very firms he was tasked with regulating. Adrian very much doubted that there would be any political will to threaten this new-found golden goose of tax revenues, whatever he discovered. He'd enjoyed a flurry of excitement when the Welsh Shippers had contacted his office with a question about Shorwell, but his preliminary investigation had yielded nothing, and the standard inquiry letter his office had sent to the SEC had gone unanswered. Now, however, Charlotte's call presented a new angle. Who knew what prizes, both political and personal, might be won?

Adrian stood up from his desk and stretched his narrow frame to its full height, 5'8". He had never been tall enough to win the role of the romantic hero. He ran his fingers through the roots of his blond hair, a habit he'd developed to gain an extra half-inch. Sitting down again, he dialed the main number of the SEC in New York, asking for Agent O'Brien. There were a few clicks, and Adrian heard a man coughing on the other end. It was the long, gagging cough of an inveterate smoker. The hacking paused.

"O'Brien here."

"Ah, Mr. O'Brien." Adrian adopted his most polished and plummy accent. "This is Adrian Whitely in London's Office of Fair Trading. Your counterpart across the ocean, one might say."

Another series of coughs greeted this suggestion of professional fraternity. Adrian paused until the refreshed gagging stopped. "Mr. O'Brien, I will come directly to the purpose of my call. It seems that one of our citizens, now working in New York, has been visited by the SEC in connection with his work at a financial firm. He mentioned your name. Here in London, we were hoping we might be able to help – both him and, of course, your efforts." Adrian paused, and waited for O'Brien to say something. He thought he could hear the crinkling of newspaper pages turning in the background.

"Who's the guy?"

"Piers Cheetham. I heard from his sister, whom he called after your recent visit."

"His sister?"

"Charlotte Cheetham. She works at Shorwell's London office."

The crinkling stopped, and O'Brien's voice became louder, as if he had pulled the receiver to his mouth. "She does? Who'd you say you are again?"

Adrian took a deep breath, considering what angle to take. The man in New York didn't have to know that he was an entry-level government agent. He scanned his memory for the right tone and landed on the brisk condescension he'd perfected when playing Henry Higgins in a school production of *My Fair Lady*. "Adrian Whitely, from London's – Downing Street's – Office of Fair Trading. We monitor financial firms in the City and are responsible for tracking down and prosecuting financial misconduct. We have, in fact, been looking into Shorwell London over the past few months for possible irregularities with their incorporation documents."

"What have you found?"

"Just a few papers suggesting that their corporate governance structure is unusual. The man heading their London office, an American, is named as an independent contractor, rather than the firm's American CEO or the Chairman of the Board."

"Oh, you won't find W. anywhere, believe me."

"Pardon me?"

"W. Head of Shorwell. Slippery as a cat. Morals of a rat."

Adrian considered momentarily whether he could offer his credentials as a former Shakespeare actor to this would-be poet to further their relationship. Cat/ rat was more doggerel than poetry, he reflected, discarding the idea.

O'Brien interrupted his thoughts. "Look, Mr. Whitely, we might be able to work out a deal. Piers seems like an okay guy. I don't want him. I want the crooks he's working with. If you can get this sister to produce some internal documents showing the way they're screwing over their clients, I might work out a deal." Startled, Adrian said nothing. When O'Brien continued, his voice was slower, and sly. "Think of it this way – it's a win/win. You get your guy, I get mine. You can make your career from it. No offense, but you sound about fifteen years old. So this might make your bosses – Downing Street, right? – take notice. What do you think?"

Adrian's Henry Higgins took on an offended tone, as if Eliza Doolittle was purposefully mauling her vowels. "My primary concern, Mr. O'Brien, must be the smooth regulation of our financial institutions. Any personal motive would be quite secondary, I assure you. But in the interest of helping a British citizen, I will certainly consider your suggestion. Shall we speak in, say, a week or so?"

As Adrian delivered this speech, the rustling in the background started again. Adrian waited, and then coughed. "Mr. O'Brien? Shall we speak again in a week?"

"What? Oh – sure. No problem. I'm in no rush. But your buddy Piers might be."

Adrian heard a callous laugh and then a click, as O'Brien put down the phone. Adrian stood up and walked toward his office window, staring at the building next door, a 1960's concrete cube thrown up to fill in the gaps left by the Blitz. He considered O'Brien's offer. It wasn't a bad idea, really, and there wasn't any risk in it. He could play the white knight to Charlotte, which would please Henrietta, and Piers Cheetham would owe him a favor. He was lingering on a vision of Charlotte, her eyes filled with tears of gratitude, when his phone rang.

"Adrian? It's Charlotte. Have you spoken to anyone yet?"

"Two seconds, Charlotte." Adrian placed his hand loosely over the mouthpiece of his phone and said to the empty space in front of his desk *I'll be right with you*. It was a technique he used regularly to ensure maximum efficiency from all callers. He uncovered the phone. "Sorry, Charlotte. Yes, I've been in touch with the appropriate people. I might be able to help."

"Really? That's wonderful."

"I've had a word with O'Brien, the one who visited Piers. It seems he's not after Piers particularly—"

"Thank goodness!"

"He seems to be using Piers in order to reach the senior man. W.? He's convinced that Shorwell is doing something illegal. He thinks there must be computer documents in London that prove it. It comes down to this, I'm afraid: he's willing to help us if we can give him some indication of Shorwell's fraudulence."

There was a long pause. Adrian could hear Charlotte's labored breathing at the other end of the line. "Adrian, I've looked through Patrick's computer. There's nothing there."

"Well, check again. Perhaps if you have a really good look-around you'll dig up something. Patrick strikes me as a particularly slippery fellow. No offense to your friendship with him, of course." Adrian coughed apologetically.

After a long pause, Charlotte answered, not bothering to hide her skepticism. "I'll see what I can find."

Charlotte hung up and stared across the office. At 2 p.m., the usual afternoon torpor had settled over the room. The only noise was the periodic eruption of papers from the fax machines, and the TV pundits' inexhaustible stream of commentary. Charlotte no longer heard either. She looked across the room toward Patrick, who was typing on his keyboard, his face uncharacteristically concentrated. His blond hair was combed away from his unlined forehead, and his shaved jaw was tilted upward as he stared at his screen. The pressed fabric of his pin-striped shirt crinkled slightly as his hands moved across the keyboard. A wistful, almost nostalgic sigh moved through Charlotte as she remembered meeting him for the first time. He had seemed so well-scrubbed and energetic, so shiny and new, so – <u>American</u>. She stared at his scrubbed skin and clear blue eyes. Did they hide the furtive machinations of a criminal? Was it all a genial façade hiding a sordid narrative? Arrogance, manipulation, callousness – these qualities were now known to her. But her imagination faltered at a deviousness beyond them; try as she might, she just couldn't envision Patrick plotting the downfall of the clients they'd visited together.

Picking up a blank piece of paper, she wrote in careful cursive, *Piers: Options*. She moved her pen down an inch and wrote *1. Search Patrick's computer again. 2. Ask Horace to search New York computers remotely (if possible). 3. Try to get Miranda to send me all documents from NY.* She paused at option 4, glancing toward Patrick's desk again. He had stopped typing and his face had relaxed. He glanced up, catching her stare. Smiling, he called out, "How's your corner, Charlotte?" Charlotte gave him a feeble wave and returned to her paper. She looked at the 4 and then wrote, *Enlist Patrick's help.* Slowly, she put the cap on the pen, stowing it and the paper in her desk drawer. She walked over to Patrick, who was now standing at the center of the trading desk, reading out loud from a tabloid. All around him, the traders looked up at him, mesmerized.

"Get this," Patrick said, holding up the tabloid. "Pop star eats hamster each morning for breakfast. 'Two slices of toast, a vole, and Bob's your uncle, says Rockin' Rob.' God, I love the press over here." Patrick laughed and caught sight of Charlotte, who had joined the group, shuddering at the tabloid's photo of a tattooed man in spandex, holding a rat by its tail.

"Patrick, could I have a word?" Charlotte felt the heads of all the men turn in her direction. She ignored them, keeping her eyes fixed on Patrick's smooth golden head. He nodded and gestured her toward the glassed-in conference room at the side of the trading floor. Charlotte pushed aside a stack of plastic carrier bags and half-eaten ham sandwiches as she sat down. Patrick took a seat opposite her, saying nothing, a guarded quality shadowing his face. Charlotte faltered, feeling the enormity of her decision weigh upon her like a knife. What if there was a scam and he was part of it? What if confiding in Patrick would backfire, and put Piers in an even worse situation? She closed her eyes for a moment, forcing herself to breathe, trying to steady her thoughts. When she reopened her eyes, Patrick was still looking at her, waiting. "I've spoken to Adrian Whitely," she began. Patrick said nothing. "You know – Henrietta's friend, the one in the regulators' office."

"Your friend from the dinner party," Patrick said, keeping his eyes trained on her.

Charlotte flushed. "Yes, that one. Patrick – I'm sorry about all that. It's all water under the bridge now. I'm afraid there's a real problem. Not silly ones like – like all that." Charlotte glanced through the glass door separating them from the traders. In Patrick's absence, she saw, their spirited moment had passed, and they'd reverted to their usual silence. She looked again at Patrick, who had remained quiet and still, like an animal waiting to decide which way to spring.

Charlotte began again. "It's Piers. He called me from New York. He's scared. The SEC have visited him and told him that Shorwell is engaged in some sort of fraud, and that they're going to hold him there until he gets them the evidence they need."

Patrick's eyes widened, and his face lost any trace of amusement. "Fraud?"

"I don't know," said Charlotte, "But that's what he said. So I called Adrian Whitely, because I thought that maybe, through his connections, he could help – and he called someone called O'Brien at the SEC in New York..." She trailed off, as the enormity of the situation overcame her again. Patrick continued to stare at her. His expression gave no indication to his thoughts, and he said nothing as she wiped a tear away with the back of her hand. "Adrian told me that he can help Piers only if he – Adrian, that is – gets proof that Shorwell is doing something illegal. He seems to think that I can find something like that in this office and that you will know where it is."

There was a long silence. The color had drained from Patrick's tanned cheeks, like a scrim being lowered over a canvas. Charlotte felt ill, wondering what she had set in motion.

"He thinks I have something showing Shorwell's doing something illegal?"

Charlotte nodded. Patrick sat without moving, his torso frozen against the black upholstery of the conference room chair. His face was tight but composed. Charlotte could feel the tension within him as he considered. He gave nothing away, and Charlotte started to chew on the inside of her lip. Was he planning to tell W. what she had said? Agonized, she waited, watching his face. He avoided her gaze and looked beyond her into the trading room. A few minutes passed in silence. When at least he spoke, the pupils of his blue eyes seemed to have shrunk into pinpricks, which he turned onto Charlotte's flushed, tearful face.

"Do *you* think I'm a con man?" Patrick asked. His voice was level, devoid of its usual ironic note.

Charlotte looked down at the table. "No."

"But you're not sure," he pursued, his voice flat and hard.

"Patrick, I don't know what to think anymore. And—"

"–and I'm your only hope?" Patrick nodded, as if answering his own question. He looked her squarely in the face, his blue eyes hard. "Look, Charlotte, I don't know whether Shorwell is a scam or not." Charlotte stared at him, trying to read his thoughts, desperate to know whether he was telling the truth. She watched as he read the uncertainty in her face, his nostrils flaring. "Jesus, Charlotte, why are you so reluctant to believe me? Do I look like a crook? Is that really what you think?" Charlotte flinched under his unbroken, impassive stare. He continued, his voice quiet. "You may think, along with your snobby English friends, that I'm some American hick who doesn't come from anywhere, who can't speak a word of your useless Latin, who's helpful for getting rich and getting laid, and who can be laughed at for your amusement. But you can tell all those entitled friends of yours that I am not a criminal. And I'm not stupid either. And," continued Patrick, the color in his cheeks darkening and his words coming faster and faster, even as his tone remained calm, "I haven't worked my ass off in order to get brought down by some scumbag in the SEC who is making his reputation off W. So you need to tell me exactly what you know, and what your decent, but – let's be honest – not overly bright –" Charlotte winced, but Patrick continued,

202

mercilessly, "brother of yours knows." Patrick rose from his seat, still holding Charlotte's gaze. "Have you told Horace? He'll be useful."

Charlotte nodded. Patrick's face was absolutely solemn. For the first time, Charlotte felt she was seeing the real person behind the charming, inscrutable façade who had been such an object of fascination to her during the past year. He stood above her, not speaking. In the stillness, she could almost feel the anger moving through his body.

She broke the silence. "Let's work on it tonight, okay?"

Patrick nodded. He walked toward the door of the conference room and opened the door, hesitating. Holding it ajar, he turned back toward Charlotte. "Not that it matters, but do you have any idea how hard I have worked to get here? Do you know how many crap jobs I've taken and how many idiots I've flattered? Do you have any clue, Charlotte, what it means to grow up with no money and claw your way up to the big leagues? No, of course you don't. Well, let me tell you – if this is a scam, I am going to be the first one out. And you can be sure I'm not going to let it all get taken away by some goddamn flunky at the SEC."

Patrick marched through the open door and returned to the traders' desks. Charlotte watched their heads lift at his approach. She saw him go over to Horace, sitting at the furthest desk from the conference room, and whisper something in his ear. Horace nodded and glanced in her direction. Then Patrick moved toward the center of the room, his face resuming its usual genial expression. Charlotte watched as he made a remark that caused all the traders to look up, their faces illuminated with pleasure. Patrick's eyes swept over the group as he monitored their reactions. Then his own smile faded, and he sat down at his own desk, his eyes again utterly serious.

Later that evening, Charlotte, Horace and Patrick returned to the conference room. At 9 p.m., the office was empty and quiet except for the patter of the television pundits floating overhead, whose ceaseless chatter had shifted from the price of oil to the forthcoming U.K. elections. Smells of cleaning fluid and stale sandwiches lingered in the stagnant air. The three young people sat at the round wood table, equidistant from one another, a tense silence hanging over them.

Charlotte broke the silence, alternating her gaze between the two men, omitting any preamble. "Adrian needs a document indicating that Shorwell is doing something illegal. I think we should review what we have, and what we might get. The only thing I can think of so far is the report that Miranda faxed through for the Welsh Shippers." She glanced at Patrick when mentioning Miranda. He met her look with a blank expression. She continued. "As Horace already knows, the report lists a derivative which doesn't seem to exist on Reuters. It suggests, but doesn't prove, that Jed might be making up positions to manipulate the value of the client's fund. What else do we have?" She poised a ball point pen on a yellow legal pad and waited.

Horace spoke next, looking at Charlotte. "Jed's hedge fund. Every once in a while he sends through numbers about what it's worth so that I can adjust my position sizes. The numbers careen all over the place. It just doesn't make sense, unless he has massively leveraged bets I don't know about. It seems like the size of the fund fluctuates separately from its holdings."

Patrick shook his head, impatient. "None of this is enough. It's way too circumstantial. There's no way the SEC will bite at that." Patrick's words hung in the room, his skepticism filling the silence. His usual look of humor had evaporated, leaving a hard, tight surface of anger. Glancing from Charlotte to Horace, he continued, "If Shorwell is co-mingling and raiding client accounts, there will have been instructions about how to move the money. Why don't we call the custodial bank, posing as a client, and get the bank to send us a history of money transfers?"

"I thought of that," answered Charlotte. "I already tried calling Shorwell's custodial bank, the one whose name is listed in the marketing presentations." Patrick and Horace turned toward her in surprise.

"And?" prompted Horace.

"I got a voice mail – a woman saying she would ring me back. She never did. I tried to reach an operator but the phone went dead."

"Well, let's go there in person," said Horace, warming to the chase. "Charlotte, why don't you ask Piers? He's right there."

Patrick gave a snort of contempt. "We're relying on Sir Lancelot to get this done? Jesus Christ. We may as well just send the SEC a Valentine's Day card."

Charlotte glared at Patrick. "Do you have a better idea?"

"I do, actually. As long as we're relying on your brother's sleuthing capabilities, I suggest you get him to break into Jed's computer. Jed's the one producing the valuation reports, right? And the one running the hedge fund. So if there's a scam, Jed has got to be part of it. He may look like a stocky narcoleptic, but his arrogant brain is working nonstop. Horace, can you break into his computer remotely?"

Horace shook his head. "I can try, but I think it's unlikely. Charlotte, can you reach Piers and ask him to get into Jed's computer? I think it's our best bet." Horace looked at Charlotte, who nodded. Without a word, Patrick stood up and turned to leave.

He was almost at the door when Charlotte spoke. "Patrick – what about Miranda? Should we talk to her?"

Patrick turned around and looked at Charlotte, the faintest shadow of his usual grin across his face. "You want to compare notes on how I fall short?" He shook his head. "No, she wouldn't know anything. She's not really an operations person, so to speak." Patrick turned again toward the conference room door, leaving it open behind him. Charlotte and Horace watched through the glass walls in silence as Patrick left the office, the main door closing behind him with a muted click. Charlotte exhaled and looked at Horace, whose long fingers were tapping the table with a syncopated rhythm. She strained to hear the song he was humming under his breath.

"Horace?"

Horace stopped humming, his fingers paused mid-air. His tired brown eyes met hers. "Yes?"

"Do you think Patrick knows more than he's telling us?"

Horace's fingers resumed their silent beat, his head nodding in time to the unheard melody. He played a few silent measures before answering. "I have no idea, Charlotte. But we don't have a lot of options, do we? So it's a moot point." He looked up, his clever eyes brightening under their veil of fatigue. "But sitting here isn't going to help. Come on, let's get a drink. You can't help Piers tonight." Horace pushed his chair back from the table, keeping his eyes fixed on Charlotte, whose face remained twisted by worry under her thick brown hair. Rising, he walked a few steps to the back of her chair and rested his hands lightly on her shoulders. Leaning forward, he spoke softly into the crown of her head.

"He'll be all right, Charlotte." Charlotte tilted her head forward in a shallow, mute nod. She sighed, feeling the weight of his hands on her shoulders. She stood up and turned a wan face to meet his.

"I could use a drink," she said. "Probably two."

Horace chuckled, and swept his arm toward the door in a mocking bow. "Let's make it three. After you, madam sleuth."

Patrick stepped out of the black cab in front of his south London flat in a sour mood. At 10 p.m., the street was deserted. Beyond the embankment, the Thames lay dark and quiet, its water illuminated in patches by a line of newly installed fake Victorian lampposts. A smell of fish from the industrial warehouse next door wafted over – the same warehouse that his estate agent, a rather beautiful and very young woman, had promised would be pulled down within months of his arrival the year before. *You can't believe the speed of gentrification in this area,* she'd said to him breathlessly, eyes wide beneath her billowing hair. Another lie, he thought, ducking into the lobby of his building, exchanging the smell of dead fish for one of new carpet.

Jabbing the button to call the lift, he stood frowning. The events of the past week had thrown his characteristic buoyancy under a cloud and shaken his immutable narrative of success. It wasn't, he reflected, as though he hadn't faced his share of frustrations and snubs in ten years of clawing his way up the corporate ladder. Back-stabbing colleagues were part of the game, and he'd taken on their salvos in stride. At times, he'd almost welcomed his rivals' challenges as an opportunity to prove the superiority of his code of conduct, one which demanded a cheerful and even-keeled response when others lost their cool.

Over the years, his emotional self-control had led him to see his career as a version of the Chutes and Ladders game he'd played as a child. It was his own morality play, based on his personal version of merit: impatient and undisciplined rivals slid down chutes created by their own inadequacies, while he clambered up the next rung and waved them a cheerful goodbye. With cleverness and tenacity, his qualities had propelled him far from the back office of the third-string brokerage firm where he had started his ascent. Unlike W., whose mythic rags-to-riches story demanded a suitably humble beginning, Patrick had suffered a real one long enough to know that no one who had spent years filing back issues of S&P company reports, and buying coffee for the people who read them, would brag about it. The people he knew who had started at the very bottom stayed quiet about their sordid origins.

Patrick entered his flat and let the door slam behind him. The sound echoed down the silent corridor, lined with other doors whose occupants he had never seen. His flat was completely silent, and he found himself yearning for the sirens and sidewalk mayhem that had so irritated him during his years in New York. Flicking on the lights and the television, he poured himself a whiskey and settled down to watch the late-night NBA game on ESPN, but quickly grew irritated by the basketball players, whose vigor and grace made him feel even more exhausted. He gazed at them blankly with dry eyeballs, before letting his back slump against the back of his sofa.

Staring down at his hands, he tried to calculate his potential losses. His bonus? His salary? The money vested in his retirement account? His whole career? Anger and fear collided in him; his playbook hadn't prepared him for this. He punched the flat grey surface of the sofa cushion beneath him, which bounced back smartly. Taking a gulp of whiskey, he tried to steady his thoughts, but found that his nimble, clever mind was uncharacteristically numb, his imagination stuck in a filing room in suburban Long Island with floor-to-ceiling grey filing cabinets and rectangular fluorescent lights hanging from chains overhead. A metal table in the middle of the room was stacked with company reports printed on cheap paper. There were hundreds of them, all needing to be filed – reports from rating agencies, brokers, analysts and economists. On the floor, piles of unopened manila envelopes held yet more reports. For the two years of Patrick's time there, the pile had never shrunk.

Patrick shook his head back and forth, physically dislodging the filing room. It yielded to scenes from his years at Shorwell: his first day at Shorwell; his first meeting with W., all elation and opportunity; his first years at the trading desk, joking with the guys who sat next to him for ten hours at a stretch, their motions and smell as familiar to him as his own; the times W. had clapped a hand on his shoulder, calling him his *numero uno*; and his first sight of Miranda, as she strutted by the trading desk in a tight black skirt and high heels, her cool blue eyes surveying the traders. In his memory, he looked at her irritated, impatient expression. Then, picking up his tumbler of whiskey, he crossed the room to the phone which sat on the carpet next to a wall jack. Miranda picked up after four rings.

"Miranda, it's Patrick."

"What do you want?"

"Charming as ever, I see. How about 'how are you' as a start?" There was no answer. Patrick's vision of Miranda on the trading floor, one hand perched on a jutting hip, dissolved into a picture of her scowling across a café table, complaining that he'd been ignoring her. "Miranda, I need your help. Is something going on over there?"

Miranda's voice dripped with disdain. "Why should I tell you?"

"Because we're friends?"

Miranda snorted. "Right. I – don't – think – so. Jed said that you and Little Miss Beatrix Potter Charlotte Cheetham went home together after the—"

"Oh please, you don't believe anything Jed tells you."

"Sounded pretty plausible to me. He said—"

"Whatever Jed said is crap. But even if it isn't – and it is – how about helping an ex-friend?"

"I don't help ex-friends."

"How about ex-more-than-friends?"

"*Especially* not them."

Patrick's voice rose as he lost patience. "Christ, Miranda, could you just tell me if something's up? We're on the same side, remember? We're the ones who've fought our way up, not the spoiled brats who do fuck-all between paychecks." There was silence. Patrick's voice softened, and he pulled the receiver closer to his mouth. "Hey, Miranda, do you remember going to that restaurant last spring down in Tribeca? Remember laughing at the bankers eating those three-pound steaks, the ones that didn't even fit on their plates, and how the steak juice dripped onto their $5000 suits? Remember, Miranda? And we said we'd—"

"Stop, Patrick."

"We said that when we made it to the top of the greasy ladder, we wouldn't act like a bunch of frat boys who got their jobs through connections. Remember what we said? C'mon, Miranda." There was a low hum of static on the other end of the phone. "Miranda, babe, I *know* you remember. We said—"

"Stop, Patrick." Her voice was barely audible.

"We said we were going to win the game by being smarter than all those assholes, and that when we did, we would go to the best restaurant in the whole city, not some ridiculous steak house. So if I – and you – are about to lose everything we've worked for, I want to know. And as my ally, or ex-ally, or ex-friend, or ex-more-than-friend, which even you have to admit was pretty hot, could you please tell me what the fuck is going on?" A long silence met this speech. Patrick could practically feel Miranda's brain whirring under her thin blond hair, weighing her response. He waited, knowing better than to speak. He could almost see her narrow shoulders sag forward over her bony collarbones when her deflated voice finally emerged.

"Patrick, I don't know what's going on. It's just getting weird around here."

"What do you mean?"

"Creepy. Weird. Whatever. Jed started sending me lots of different versions of client reports and biting my head off if I sent clients the wrong one. And he's in his office all the time, scowling at the screen hour after hour without blinking. I swear – I watch him from the hallway and he doesn't even see me. And he has started to lock his door from the inside. How paranoid is that? And it's not just Jed. Your hire, Piers, is wandering around the office looking less and less like a big boy scout and more like a haunted wreck, and I heard a rumor that some guy from the SEC visited him." Patrick tugged at the synthetic fibers of the carpet as he listened, his mood darkening, his breath growing shallow. This wasn't the information he had wanted.

"Patrick? Are you there?"

"Yeah. I'm here." He thought furiously, his brain leaping toward exits. "Look, Miranda – I have an idea. I'll come back to New York as soon as I can manage it. Together, we'll figure out what's up. We'll be a team again, the two of us against the do-nothings. Okay?" Patrick waited for a response, but Miranda said nothing. He forged ahead, ad-libbing seamlessly, leaning on the instinct that had so far never misled or betrayed him. His voice gained pace. "I can't do it without you, Miranda. You're crucial. You and I both know that if something's wrong, Jed has got to be at the center of it. So I need you – *please, Miranda* – to figure out what his computer passwords are. I guarantee it's the key."

Another five seconds passed before Miranda spoke. "Even if I decided to help you, Patrick Connolly, which I may or may not, there is no way we can get into Jed's office. I told you. He is always there. And when he's not, he locks the door."

"Angela has the keys to everyone's office, right? And access to the passwords? Aren't you two friends? Take her out for a drink or something. You can bond over – I don't know – whatever women talk about when they're together."

"How guys are assholes. Anyway, remind me why I should trust you? Or help you?"

"Fine. Don't trust me. But if this thing blows up, you're out of a job too, and it's back to the New Jersey suburbs, right? The strip malls, fat people, your mom's house?" Patrick lowered his voice and spoke each word carefully, infusing his voice with a whispered intimacy. "Miranda, doll, if something is really going wrong, we have to work together to salvage something out of it. We'll be stronger as a team. You know me – I'm the guy who lands on my feet. If you join me, we can land together. And whatever I can make out of this, I'll give you half, okay? And I *always* make something out of nothing. You know that. It's my specialty." Patrick waited for the words to sink in. He knew better than to speak again; he knew just how hard he could push Miranda before it would backfire. After ten seconds he heard a labored sigh from the other end of the phone. He smiled to the empty room. He knew that noise; it was the one she'd made after he'd convinced her to come back to his apartment for the first time.

"Okay," she whispered, and hung up.

Patrick went into his kitchen and put his empty whiskey tumbler in the sink. He took a glass bottle of Belgian craft beer out of the refrigerator and returned to the living room. The TV was still showing the NBA basketball game. He looked with approval at the players running up and down the court, lunging toward the ball. He nodded. Game on, he thought.

Piers stood in the middle of lower Sixth Avenue, trying to hear his sister's voice over the honking of yellow taxis swerving toward the center median, where he stood at a payphone half-covered by plastic. It had begun to rain, and he balanced the phone's receiver between his ear and shoulder as he tried to open a cheap black umbrella that he'd bought from a street vendor for five dollars. Its release button stuck, and he flung it into the gutter, partially blocking a drain.

Charlotte's voice was urgent. "In the marketing materials, the bank's address is 30 Mercer Street – that's Soho, right? Its name is First Trust Bank of Manhattan. Just say you're a client and ask for a transcript of all the money transfer instructions for the past year. Hopefully that will show us whether Shorwell has been moving money between client accounts or not. If that doesn't work, then you'll have to break into Jed's computer."

"What?"

"Jed's computer. Patrick thinks that if there's a scam, he's in on it. You have to get into it and look for anything suspicious."

"Oh, that'll be fun." Piers's note of sarcasm blasted through the static on the line. "Hang on, Char." Charlotte heard a man in the background yelling at Piers: *Hey kid, I gotta use the phone, too* and Piers's terse response: *Fuck off, buddy.* Charlotte flinched.

Piers returned to Charlotte. "There's no way I can break into Jed's computer. He keeps his office locked all the time, even when he leaves for five minutes. But I'll try the bank and call you back. Just a sec," Charlotte heard him yell at the man again, *I said find another fucking phone!*

"Char, sorry, but I have to call you back." Piers slammed down the receiver with a force that caused it to bounce off the hinge and fall, careening back and forth on its metal cord. Piers turned in the direction of Mercer Street, muttering the address Charlotte had given him. It sounded familiar, somehow.

He walked east, trying to move quickly through the sidewalk, now crowded with umbrellas, the biggest ones emblazoned with the names of investment banks. He veered right and left, threading his way through the lingering, gaping tourists and contemptuous, glaring locals. After fifteen minutes, Piers reached Mercer Street. He stopped, glancing back and forth as he tried to find a street number tucked into the unbroken line of restaurants, clothing boutiques, and galleries.

Spotting a building with Ionic columns that seemed plausibly bank-like, Piers set off, but was disappointed to find its front window full of mannequins in neon clothing, their fake hair bright red and pink. He turned away. The rain was falling steadily now, and the drops ran down his neck into his collar as he scanned the buildings. After a few minutes, he spotted a building whose sandstone façade was engraved with the number thirty. He stopped and peered through its large front window, misted over with condensation, making out two rows of black leather chairs and sinks. A tall woman stood behind a chair, flicking a comb through the blond hair of the woman seated in front of her. Piers stared at them, puzzled: 30 Mercer was a hair salon. After a few minutes, the standing woman stopped her combing and turned to look at Piers, whose large fuzzy outline hovered just outside the window. Her red heels covered the distance between them quickly. Cracking open the door, she stuck out her head, glaring at Piers.

She pointed her comb at his neck. "May I help you?"

Piers squinted at her, puzzled. "I've met you," he said, ignoring her look of impatience. "Wasn't this an art gallery?"

Her look of irritation deepened. "Yes, and now it's a hair salon. Do I know you?"

"I work at Shorwell Capital. I think you sold me a painting. Aren't you a friend of W.'s?"

"You could say so. W. owns this building. I switched from art to hair. Anyway, I'm busy." She let go of the heavy door, which started to swing shut. Piers grabbed it.

"Sorry," he said, "But do you know whether this was ever a bank?"

The woman turned on her heel with an amused expression. "Nope. That's one business I *definitely* haven't done."

Piers heard a peal of laughter as he retreated to the sidewalk. Without thinking, he headed toward the nearest subway station, pounding down its wet, grimy steps and dropping a token into the turnstile. The station's dirty tiled walls dripped with rainwater leaking from above, and the moist air smelt like decay. A train screamed into the station and Piers pushed his way in, automatically sweeping his eyes up and down to check for anyone overtly crazy. Slumping onto a plastic seat, he let his head flop forward as the train lurched forward. Charlotte's voice became a soundtrack accompanying his thoughts: *Jed's computer... Patrick is convinced...*

The train reached Midtown and Piers exited. It was still raining, and he could feel the damp rising through the soles of his shoes as he walked along the pavement toward Shorwell's offices. Piers nodded to the security men at the front lobby's desk as he walked toward the bank of elevators. Usually, he felt impatient as he was propelled up fifty floors, but today the trip seemed instantaneous. He entered Shorwell's lobby to find Doreen immersed in a paperback novel. She glanced up at his entrance, her eyes widening as she took in Piers's wet hair and suit.

"Honey, don't you have a raincoat? You're gonna get sick."

"Doreen, I need to see Jed. Is he around?"

"Nope – just went out. I gotta say I was glad to see him leave. Seems like he's pretty much living here these days."

"Did he say when he'd be back?"

Doreen gave a short laugh. The dome of her shellacked red hair vibrated. "Since when did Jed talk? Do you want me to page him?" She reached out to her switchboard with a finger covered in gold rings.

"No – no – Jed needs a break, absolutely. Please don't page him."

"Okay, hon. Whatever."

She ran her eyes again over his dripping clothes and then looked back down at her novel. Piers walked to the trading floor. At 4:30 p.m., the stock market had closed, and the traders had started to leave their posts monitoring their computer screens. With pale faces and glazed eyes, they filed out past Piers, making arrangements to meet at a sports bar later that evening. Piers nodded at them as he moved toward Jed's office. As Doreen had said, Jed was absent and his office looked aggressively empty, like a portrait painting whose subject had wandered off. The door to the office was closed, as always, and Piers tried its handle. It turned. He paused in surprise and glanced behind him toward the empty corridor. Silently, he slipped into the office, seated himself in Jed's chair and tapped on the computer mouse.

The screen woke up to show the spreadsheet of hedge fund positions Piers had seen the night that Jed had been lying unconscious at his feet. Piers didn't bother checking how much Jed had lost since then. Instead, he went directly to the main menu of the computer to open the firm's internal email system. He scanned the subject headers of each message, tapping rapidly at the down arrow as he searched for something interesting. Nothing. Piers suspended his finger over the keyboard. He kept looking. Perspiration was starting to break out on his forehead, and his sweat mingled with the rain that still clung to the damp hair falling over his eyes. He started to breathe more quickly. Surely there would be correspondence between Jed and the custodial bank? He ran a search on First Trust Bank of Manhattan. The computer froze, and he could hear the mechanical clicking of the hard drive as it searched. A box appeared on his screen: *No results match your search.* He swore softly and ran a new search under the words "money transfer." Again, the computer screen froze as the hard drive began to squeak and hiss. *Come on,* urged Piers.

He glanced up again and froze. Jed had just turned the corner from the lobby to the corridor, and was headed toward his office. Jed's head was down, and he stared at the grey carpet as his heavy legs moved across the floor. Piers leaped up from his chair and bounded toward the door, reaching it just as Jed raised his head. Jed's expression darkened as he registered Piers, and he halted in surprise. He eyes scanned Piers's face, taking in the wet hair, the dripping clothes, and the look of panic. His own heavy, pale face was immobile, his extra flesh hanging from below his eyes and jaw in soft layers. His large frame stood blocking the corridor, motionless as a wax statue. He stared at Piers, saying nothing.

Piers spoke first, his voice emerging as a strangled croak. "Hi Jed. I was looking for you. Charlotte – my sister – needs a client report, and Miranda isn't returning her calls. I thought I'd come ask you directly."

Jed continued to say nothing as he pushed his way past Piers, throwing his briefcase on the carpet with a thud. He sat down at his desk and moved the computer mouse. His email messages appeared where Piers had left them. Jed turned his head toward Piers. His puffy round eyes narrowed. "Did you touch my PC?"

"No."

"I didn't leave it on this."

Piers shrugged, holding his palms up to the ceiling in a gesture of wonderment. "Don't know, Jed – I'm not a computer expert. Anyway, can I get a client report for Charlotte now that you're back?"

Jed continued to stare at Piers. Piers held his gaze, refusing to look away. The sound of a vacuum cleaner hummed behind Piers, signaling the end of the day.

Without looking away, Jed spoke. "No. Have your sister call me directly."

Piers nodded, saying nothing. He retreated down the corridor, forcing himself to keep his steps at a sedate pace. He felt Jed's eyes on him as he moved. Once inside his own office, he found that he was shaking uncontrollably. He sat in his chair, staring at the neon print from the art gallery-now hair salon, seeing again the blond woman wielding her comb like a knife as she spoke to him, Jed's look of pure hatred, and O'Brien, crouched over a tabloid. No bank – no documents – he had failed. He stared at his shaking hands as if they belonged to someone else, with equal measures of pity and contempt. He thrust them in his pockets and stood up, almost falling at the wave of nausea which hit him. He flung himself out of the Shorwell offices, down the elevator and into the city street, where it was still raining, and now dark. Headless of the rain falling on him, he started to move west, straining in the dark to make out the outline of a phone booth to tell Charlotte the bad news.

16

Saving Piers

"So Jed walked in on Piers as he was searching his computer? So much for that." Patrick gave a harsh chortle and tilted his blond head toward the nearest TV, where an anchorman pointed to a map of Iraq, as if preparing his viewers for a geography quiz. A ticker tape of commodity prices scrolled beneath the map. Charlotte, sitting opposite him at the conference table, gave full vent to her anxiety-fueled irritation.

"And I suppose you think it was Piers's fault that Jed returned when he did? What would you have done, Patrick? Thrown on an invisible cloak?" She glared at him as the anchorman dragged his pointer across Iraq's border to Kuwait. Horace held up his palms.

"This isn't getting us anywhere. Here's where we stand: the custodial bank is a hair salon; we have nothing to give Adrian; and Jed is unlikely ever to leave his office unlocked again. Any bright ideas?" Horace directed his question at Charlotte, who abandoned her glare at Patrick to meet his eyes.

"I think we should make a set of assumptions about how the scam operates," she began.

"*If* there's a scam," interjected Patrick, his head still angled toward the TV.

"For the purposes of getting Piers out, let's assume there is one," persisted Charlotte. "We could craft a few plausible messages using the internal office system about pricing or trade execution or moving money between funds – I don't know. Something that seems not quite right. And then we could deliver them to Adrian."

"What's Adrian's background, anyway?" asked Patrick, glancing at Charlotte.

"He was in acting school before giving it up for government. Henrietta told me he has political ambitions."

"Jesus Christ, what a bunch of amateurs. Acting school? Is that a typical prerequisite for politics around here?"

"Wasn't Ronald Reagan an actor?" asked Horace. Patrick swiveled his head toward Horace.

"That was ages ago, and besides, he came from California, so it doesn't count. No one takes California seriously."

"Right, I'll remember that," Horace laughed. He turned toward Charlotte, his face losing its flicker of levity. "Charlotte, I know you'll do anything to help Piers, but I don't think we can risk submitting faked documents to the SEC, even if they can't reach us over here. It's too dangerous. And the last thing we want to do is become crooks ourselves as we deal with potentially real ones." There was a pause as Horace's words sunk in. Patrick turned back to the television and Charlotte stared down at the table, a laminated piece of particle board painted to mimic wood. She traced her finger slowly along its fake whorls, thinking about what Horace had said. She looked up.

"How about sending him something real, then? Not just the valuation report from the Welsh Shippers, but also one of Piers and Jed's sales presentations. Piers is always bragging about how potential clients fall at his feet when he and Jed show them graphs of Shorwell's historical returns. If there is a scam, mightn't it show up in those numbers? It would give him something to chew on, at least." Horace hesitated, his face conflicted.

"I don't know, Charlotte. It could work, I guess." His voice was unconvinced. "The main thing is to give the SEC enough of a pretext to search Shorwell's computers, at which point they'll probably find more. Or not. But it might give us a chance to get Piers out." Charlotte's eyes dimmed as she registered his lack of confidence. She looked at Patrick and back again at Horace.

"Do we have a better idea?" No one spoke. A muted thud signified the onset of the building's ineffectual heating system. Turning his head away from the TV, Patrick stood up.

"Right. I guess that's it then. Personally, it seems like grasping at straws to me. Anyway, I'm going. If I'm about to lose my bonus – and possibly my job – because of an over-eager SEC agent, I'm sure as hell not spending eighteen hours a day in this room." Patrick shrugged on his navy blazer and reached down for his briefcase, grasping its handle with tight knuckles. Raising his other hand to his brow, he gave Charlotte and Horace an ironic salute before turning on his heel. When the main office door shut behind Patrick, Charlotte stood up and walked around the table to Horace's chair, lowering herself carefully onto its plastic arm and covering his long fingers with her own shorter ones. She let her head fall heavily to one side, banging Horace's ear.

"Ouch!" Horace feigned outrage. "I suggest, Miss Cheetham, that you don't mar the contents of this head. It's about to be pressed into service to rescue your feckless brother."

"*Terribly* sorry," Charlotte answered. "I hadn't realized your brain was so delicate." She rested her head against his, sinking the side of her body into his shoulder. Horace turned in his chair toward her. His face, amused and weary, was inches from her own. His brown eyes crinkled upward at the corners when he spoke.

"We can't all be as infallibly clever as you," he said, "Some of us simply – try – harder." He leaned forward to kiss her lightly, before re-settling his weight forward to kiss her again, this time not so lightly. He pulled away, his cheeks flushed. "Not that this isn't delightful, Charlotte, but I don't think it's going to save Piers." Charlotte, whose eyes had been half shut, reluctantly reengaged with the scene around her. She nodded, and slid off Horace's chair, sweeping her hair off her face and yanking her skirt back into place.

"You're right. Let's go dig up all the marketing documents we can find and send them all to Adrian. And then, perhaps –" she paused, blushing.

"Yes?" Horace prompted.

"And then, perhaps—" we can resume the more compelling part of this evening," Charlotte said, kissing his brown hair and leaving the conference room.

O'Brien sat in his New Jersey office staring at the package Adrian had sent over from London. It had arrived that morning by special courier, a large white envelope containing a cover letter and some documents. O'Brien looked at the letter first, a heavy, cream-colored paper whose letterhead announced in flowery cursive *Office of Fair Trading, Salisbury Square, London.* Underneath, scrawled in a cramped hand, was a brief note: *Hope this will prove of interest. Will be in touch. A. Whitely.*

O'Brien frowned as he noted the small insignia of a bejeweled crown stamped into the upper right-hand corner of the paper. He ran his index finger across the crown, feeling its raised surface and leaving a smudge of dirt on its edge. His frown deepened. His department didn't have the budget for engraved stationery; he didn't even have a budget for a decent printer. He'd worked his whole career at the SEC without ever seeing paper like this. And now this kid Adrian something-or-other was sending him documents with cover letters stamped with engraved crowns. Wasn't the Office of Fair Trading his counterpart over there? By his reckoning, people on his side were supposed to pull down the rich, not be one of them.

O'Brien put down the offending letter and picked up the other documents in the envelope: a valuation report of a fund called the Welsh Shippers Pension Fund, and a glossy Shorwell brochure. He turned to the brochure first, glancing through the paragraphs. It looked like the usual verbiage spewed forth by all the hedge funds he was meant to be monitoring. His face shadowed as he read the usual words: *spread, variation, asset, deviation, volatility...*

He glanced up, bored. In truth, he had never understood what it was these hedge fund guys really did. His lack of understanding didn't really bother him. No one knew how they worked, he figured; they purposefully made their trades impenetrable to anyone outside their money-printing meccas. With only partial information of infinitely complicated trades, the regulators were in an impossible position and the hedge funds knew it. The regulators knew it, too, but they wouldn't admit it to themselves or to anyone else.

He looked at the graphs of the Shorwell funds' historic returns. They looked weirdly high and consistent – never falling, even in down markets, and returning more than 10% each year. It seemed unlikely, but was it illegal? He put the report down on his desk, picked up his phone and left a message for a colleague reputed to be a math whiz: *Hey man – O'Brien here. Could you look at some hedge fund returns for me and let me know if you think they're real? I've done my own analysis but I want a second opinion.*

O'Brien relaxed into the gray vinyl of his desk chair and looked at the wall across from him. During the five years he'd sat in this office, he'd plastered it with memorabilia: his degree from CUNY School of Law, take-out menus from a local Chinese restaurant, and the schedule of jazz bands at a dive bar around the corner. Dominating the center of the wall was a large poster of King Kong looming over the Manhattan skyline at night, his furry fist raised as he clutched a piece of the Empire State Building.

O'Brien stared at King Kong's familiar, hairy face. Over the years, though O'Brien wouldn't have admitted it, the unlovely monster had become his most constant companion and even, at times, his greatest source of inspiration. The powerful, hairy torso and expression of yearning and confusion on the beast's face touched his heart, and never failed to reinvigorate him. O'Brien stared up at King Kong, his fist resting on Adrian's letter. *Five years,* he thought. *Five years of my life. Is it possible I've got one of these guys?* Closing his eyes, he imagined himself in front of his colleagues, his head tilted forward in a show of modesty as the SEC's commissioner read out a commendation of his work. He saw himself taking the podium – its faulty microphone functioning, for once – and making a speech about his long study of the hedge fund industry, the effort's frustrations and impediments, near victories and missed opportunities. He would conclude with a short homily on the values of hard work, perseverance and the inevitability of victory to those on the side of morality. In his imagination, he admired his face bathed in a golden light of victory, his wrinkles gone, his bald spot miraculously regrown.

He paused in his vision. If only, he thought, he could get something that implicated W. more explicitly. His thoughts turned to his recent visit to Piers's apartment, the young man's face white and shocked, his hands trembling. The vision aroused in him no sympathy; as far as he was concerned, Piers and his kind were exactly the group of people he'd dedicated his life to erasing. He indulged in a vision of Piers caught in a fishing net, flapping on the boards of a boat, and considered whether to let him go. The power he felt in controlling another person's fate was too rare a pleasure to yield without consideration. He thought it over as the netted Piers flapped in his head. He'd make one more demand first, he decided, before releasing him back to his country of engraved crowns. O'Brien stood up and diverted his incoming calls to voice mail. Pulling on his nylon jacket, he headed out to Piers's apartment.

Two hours later, Piers walked down Second Avenue at dusk, feeling a glimmer of his former self after joining his colleagues for drinks. The liquor had relaxed his muscles, and his stride felt loose as he walked through the city's darkened streets. Looking around, he could almost remember the city as he'd first experienced it – its air of novelty and excitement, its implicit promise of adventure. He turned into his own street and glanced up automatically at the window of his fifth floor apartment, freezing when he saw that it was illuminated. Had he left a light on that morning? As he stood staring, a man's silhouette moved into view: O'Brien. Instinctively, he reversed direction, sprinting east and ducking into a corner bodega, where he walked straight to the furthest corner. He looked up to find himself surrounded by hundreds of sex videos for rent, arranged on floor to ceiling metal shelves. A sea of near-naked women in postures of erotic passion stared out at him from under their plastic covers. Still panting from his sprint, Piers halted, trying to calm his nerves. Another customer looking at the videos glanced at him with a disgusted look, grabbed a video and left. Piers's eyes darted from one video to the next as his mind raced. *I can't stay here,* Piers thought. *O'Brien will be there all night.* He left the shop and retraced his steps until his apartment was again in view. O'Brien's silhouette had disappeared.

Piers walked up the five flights of stairs, not bothering to find his key in the pocket of his trousers. He knew the door would be unlocked. As he mounted the stairs, the smell of cigarettes became more and more pungent. Reaching his own door, he closed his eyes and swung open the door. A haze of smoke enveloped him.

O'Brien sat on his sofa. His short fingers curled around a near-dead cigarette and his heavy torso, encased in its nylon jacket, crouched over the NY *Daily News*. Piers let his door slam shut behind him with a loud thudding noise and the metallic rattle of safety chains. O'Brien continued to read and smoke, ignoring the noise and Piers. Piers stood, staring down at him. After a minute, O'Brien finally looked up, his narrow eyes casually running up and down Piers's body, taking stock of him.

"Hey there," O'Brien said, as if Piers were his roommate. "How are you?"

"Fuck off," said Piers.

"No need to be like that," said O'Brien. "Have a seat. Oh, sorry – I guess I've got the only seat here. You didn't do much furnishing, did you?"

"Fuck off," Piers repeated.

O'Brien looked at him, nodding slowly. The light of fake joviality faded from his face. He ground out the cigarette he was holding and tossed it onto a mound of dead stubs. "Have you thought about my request?" Piers said nothing, continuing to stare down at O'Brien, who was now leaning into the back of the sofa, looking relaxed. Piers nodded. O'Brien's small eyes glowed.

"I knew you'd see sense. I came prepared." He reached a hand into the pocket of his nylon jacket and extracted a cardboard box, placing it on the tabloid. He eased its top off and extracted a metal rectangle which he held up to Piers. "This is a Sony M-909 Micro-cassette recorder. It features voice activation and auto-reverse. It is the very latest in furtive voice recording technology, and the world's smallest tape recorder. Guess its dimensions." He raised the tape recorder higher, his face beaming with pride. Piers said nothing. "C'mon, Piers, just guess," O'Brien pleaded. "Just one dimension – its width. It's the *very latest*." Piers relented.

"One inch?"

"Nope," said O'Brien, waving the recorder in a small loop. "Guess again."

"Three-quarters?"

"*Half* an inch," said O'Brien, turning the box on its side with a flourish. "*Half* an inch. It cost $495. Not chump change. The SEC paid up for this baby. And you, Piers Cheetham, are the first to get to use it."

"I'm honored," said Piers, with heavy irony.

O'Brien nodded, oblivious to Piers's tone. He stroked the side of the tape recorder, tracing small circles with a stubby index finger. A thicket of hair burst from his skin just above his knuckle. The circles slowed, and O'Brien looked up. He held the recorder out to Piers with a regretful air. "Here," he said, "Take a look. I'll show you how it works."

Piers took two steps to retrieve the tape recorder from O'Brien's hand, grimacing when their skin touched. Recorder in hand, he retreated to his position by the door. O'Brien watched him, and Piers suppressed a desire to let the small metal object crash onto the floor.

"Maybe you'd better sit on the ground while you're handling it," O'Brien said. His eyes, focused on the tape recorder, missed Piers's look of contempt. Piers lowered himself onto the wooden floor. He looked at the small metal box, with its tiny Sony insignia and row of buttons. He pressed one and a miniature tape cassette emerged. "Looks pretty straightforward," he said.

"The beauty of it is in the miniaturization of the electronic components," O'Brien said with a defensive tone. "I'll leave it here with you. Take it out for a few test spins, okay, until you're totally comfortable with its capabilities. When do you think you'll see W.?"

"He asked me to play squash with him Wednesday," Piers said.

"Wednesday? Fine. I'll be here when you get home from work. Does 6:30 p.m. work for you?"

"Sure."

O'Brien stood up, yanking down on the ribbed hem of his jacket. He took a final look at the tape recorder. "Take good care of that thing," he said, gazing at it with anxious eyes.

"It will be my main concern," said Piers.

"Good." O'Brien made a wide circle around Piers and disappeared into the corridor, letting the door slam behind him.

"He wants you to what?" Charlotte, sitting in her flat with Horace, strained to hear Piers's voice. He seemed to be calling from a bar. She could hear the hum of a crowd and a jazz band somewhere in the background.

"He wants me to tape W. – to wear a hidden wire and record him saying something illegal," Piers said again, shouting into the cup of his hand which he held over the plastic receiver. "He showed up at my apartment again yesterday. He says he won't let me out of the country until I do it. But Charlotte – there's no way. W. will never fall for it. I don't know what to do." Piers's voice, sounding raw, trailed off as he fought to catch his breath. Charlotte could feel his fear and desperation careen through the wires and she tried to stay calm, thinking desperately.

"Piers – let me think – please – can you call me tomorrow? I'll have a plan by then." There was silence on the other end of the line. "Piers, tomorrow, please? Same time. I promise."

"Okay, Charlotte. But please – please – get me out of here."

Charlotte replaced the receiver and sat, staring at the phone. She bit down on the inside of her lips and drew her eyebrows together. A new vertical line between them deepened as she considered. She looked up at Horace, who was sitting across her room reading <u>War and Peace</u>. His brow was furrowed too, but she knew it was because he was deep into the battle of Borodino. Compared to the French army's winter retreat from Moscow, he'd just remarked, Shorwell was small potatoes.

"Horace?" Charlotte ventured. His eyes stayed firmly engrossed on the page as they moved swiftly from left to right. "Horace? That was Piers. We have another problem." Charlotte watched as he dragged his gaze away from the page, looking preoccupied and confused as he adjusted from the Russian battleground to Charlotte's flat in London. He closed the book, leaving his finger inside to mark his page.

"That was Piers. O'Brien visited him again. He got the documents from Adrian, but now he's saying he wants Piers to get W. on tape. But that's impossible." Charlotte crossed over to the sofa and sat down next to Horace, tilting her head down toward his novel. The Penguin edition's cover showed a group of Russian soldiers in long red and black wool coats standing on a snowy road. It looked very cold, and she couldn't tell whether the painting was meant to be before or after the battle. Struggle and conflict, she thought, staring at the picture, it never changes. Horace looked up from the book and met her eyes.

"You're tired," he said.

"We all are," Charlotte answered with a fierce quality. "But being tired isn't the problem. Being hunted and held in New York by a SEC agent is. Poor Piers." Horace draped an arm around her shoulder and she let her body slump into his side. The nubby texture of his wool sweater scraped against her cheek, and she could feel his breath rising and falling. She settled into his warmth, yielding to the comfort of his presence, letting the exhaustion of the past months settle on top of her like a thick, mummifying blanket. She sat next to Horace, saying nothing, barely breathing.

Her mind slowed to a crawl, wrapped in the woolly smell of Horace and numbed by the months of stress. How had it gone so wildly wrong? As a teenager, waiting for her life to begin, she had felt her own existence bleached and depleted by the golden halo cast by Piers's charmed existence. For years, she had nurtured her private grievance, begrudging him his shining place in the sun, and the glowing admiration her mother lavished on him. Reflexively, she reached down into her familiar well of resentment, waiting for a few drops of her childhood frustrations to lubricate her usual thoughts. She paused and realized with surprise that the well had run dry; all her years of silent grievance had drained away, somehow, when she wasn't paying attention. Her envy of Piers, so long a constant, small knot inside her heart, a touchstone around which she had oriented her childhood narrative, had melted when she hadn't been paying attention. Now, sitting on the sofa, Horace's silent, calm body against hers, she felt flooded instead by her dormant love for her brother, and fears for his safety. She longed to turn back the clock and restore the rightful order of things, launching him back into his position of casual preeminence, from which he could once again dispense charm with the unthinking generosity of those who have been given and expect everything. Charlotte lifted her neck a fraction from Horace's sweater and spoke upward in the direction of his ear.

"Piers was always the one whose life was perfect," she said, and flopped her head back into his side. She felt Horace nod above her, saying nothing. The arm around her shoulders drew her more closely to him. She sighed and fell into a deep sleep.

"Here's the thing," Charlotte said. She was sitting once again in the Shorwell conference room, with Patrick directly across from her and Horace at her right-hand side. She directed her comments to Patrick, whose eyes were cast down toward an old *Sports Illustrated*. He was twirling a ballpoint pen in his left hand, and Charlotte tried to keep her voice from rising in irritation as the pen clattered onto the table after each failed effort to spin it on his thumb.

"Adrian told me that O'Brien called him, pleased about the documents we sent. He's having them analyzed. But now O'Brien is saying he won't let Piers out unless he has another piece of evidence against W. He wants Piers to get W. on tape saying something."

"Like what? 'Sorry guys, did I happen to mention the whole thing's a scam?'" Patrick laughed bitterly, and let the pen skitter across the polished surface of the table.

"He wants W. saying something on tape," Charlotte repeated. "I don't know what, and I'm not sure it matters. And from what you've said, W. is too clever to get caught saying anything anyway." There was a long pause as no one said anything. Patrick returned to his efforts to spin the pen, and all three of them watched it fall from Patrick's thumb onto his magazine, coming to a halt on top of an interview with a British soldier just back from Kuwait. Charlotte started to twist a large strand of brown hair around her index finger, yanking it violently. She stared at Patrick's bowed, golden head, once the object of desire and now a source of irritation and anger. Didn't he realize that Piers was stuck, and that this was a moment of crisis? She opened her mouth to speak, her lips starting to curl around their opening sounds of fury, when Patrick lifted his head in her direction. She closed her mouth.

"I think the only thing we can do is keep going," he said.

"What do you mean?" Horace asked.

"It's simple," said Patrick, "Or the concept is, anyway. I go to New York and tape a conversation with Piers in which I pretend to be W. and say something questionable. O'Brien thinks he's listening to the real W. People always hear what they want to hear. O'Brien wants to hear W., so he'll think I'm W. Then I stay in New York, Piers gets to leave, and O'Brien looks like an idiot. That's it." Charlotte shook her head, incredulous.

"Patrick – that's a bold idea – but can you pull it off? Can you sound like W.? And won't O'Brien know?" Patrick shrugged, and held his palms up to the ceiling. His face wore its customary expression of unconcern, no line of worry marring his tanned face. If anything, he looked more relaxed and fit than usual, a Greek god dropping in from a celestial playground to learn about the earthly concerns of bumbling humans.

"I don't know, Charlotte, but we don't have a better idea. And I'm a damn good mimic. It's one of my main talents. Adrian thinks he's an actor?" Patrick snorted. "Give me a break. Watch this."

Standing up, Patrick swept his hair straight back and patted it into place against his head. He unbuttoned the cuffs of his pressed shirt and rolled back each sleeve neatly, displaying two muscled forearms. With a graceful motion, he sank into a deep runner's lunge while lifting his arms above his head, palms clasped. He fixed Charlotte and Horace with a haughty, condescending stare.

"Warrior pose," he said to his audience, stretching his vowels to mimic W.'s New York intonations. He sunk another few inches toward the carpet. "Picked it up in Madras. Mind/body control is everything if you're gonna win. Bet you can't do this." Patrick lowered his hands to the carpet on either side of his bent knee, jumped both of his legs backward and hoisted them into the air. Finding his balance on his arms, which wobbled only slightly, he continued to speak while holding the handstand. "The sky's the limit, guys, even when you're upside down. Did I ever tell you I was a circus acrobat as well as a rock star in college? The girls loved me."

Walking on his hands, Patrick took a few steps forward before lowering his legs back down to the carpet and standing up. Charlotte and Horace broke into applause, and a pleased smile crossed Patrick's face, now red and flushed with exertion. He tipped an imaginary hat to Charlotte and gave a short bow. He stood at the table grinning and breathing hard, before collapsing back into his chair.

"The fact is, we don't have much of a choice. And frankly, I wouldn't mind socking it to that bastard O'Brien. He can't be too much of a genius. And, come to think of it, I wouldn't mind helping to nail W. too, if it turns out that his games have just caused me to lose a ton of money."

Patrick's voice grew angrier as he spoke, his face losing the animation of the previous five minutes. Charlotte shivered, practically feeling the temperature drop as the hilarity of Patrick's acrobatics was once again replaced by fear and anxiety. She felt Horace's eyes rest on her from his position at the table. She could feel him weighing Patrick's idea. She turned to him, widening her eyes in a silent question. His brown eyes were bloodshot and glazed with fatigue, and his mouth turned down at the corners.

"It might work," he said, slowly, without enthusiasm. He turned to Patrick. "Would you like me to join you?"

"No, thanks, Horace," said Patrick. "No offense, but I don't see what you could do over there anyway. You can keep Charlotte company over here. When it's all over, we'll get together for a big victory party in the country. You two can choose which of your magnificent country mansions we'll use."

"Oh, they're not so magnificent," Charlotte said automatically.

"Oh yeah?" Patrick looked at her from across the table. "You should see where I grew up. It would fit into your front hall." He rose and began to gather his belongings scattered around the table, stowing his magazine, notebook and pen into his briefcase, and closing the case with a click. "Well, I'm off," he said, swinging his briefcase down to his side. "I guess this is goodbye. Not exactly what I'd envisioned, but hey, that's life. I'll call from New York."

Without waiting for a response, Patrick glided out of the room. Charlotte watched him as he marched toward the exit, pausing only slightly to take once last glance around the office. In profile, his face looked like the senator on a Roman coin, proud and unflinching. The office door slammed shut. Without speaking, Charlotte and Horace stretched out their arms to join hands, gripping one another as though their linked bodies would be the ballast keeping them tethered to their small, safe space, protecting them from the dangers circling outside.

Charlotte closed her eyes, letting down her guard in Patrick's absence. When she opened them again, Horace was looking at her, unsmiling.

"What do you think of Patrick's plan?" he asked.

"What do *you* think?"

Horace dropped her hands and shrugged. "Honestly, I don't know. I have to admit, I'm impressed that he offered to do it. Who would have expected Patrick to go out on a limb for someone else?" Charlotte said nothing, covering Horace's hand, now lying on the table, with one of her own. His skin felt dry and cool and she ran a finger over his knuckles with a ragged nail.

"You know, it would be incredible if O'Brien fell for it," Horace said.

Charlotte let her hand rest, motionless on top of his. She nodded. "I know."

They sat there for another moment, silent. The office was in a half-light and deserted. From the traders' horseshoe, the chairs had been pushed back at odd angles, and newspapers were strewn across the floor. It was as lackluster and featureless as a thousand other corporate offices but Charlotte felt almost nostalgic as she glanced around, thinking of the hundreds of hours she had spent hunkered down within its walls. She looked at Horace, whose thumb was tapping a rhythm onto the back of her hand.

"Horace? What are you going to do when this is all over?"

His thumb paused in its motion. He thought for a moment before speaking. "Assuming we're all not thrown in jail, you mean? Take a holiday, I think. Somewhere far away, with every novel Tolstoy and Dostoevsky ever wrote. Maybe Chekhov too, come to think of it."

"I thought Chekhov wrote plays."

"Then I'll take his plays." Horace's thumb resumed its light syncopated tap on Charlotte's hand. He watched it for a moment, and then paused, still looking down at their linked hands. "And what will you be reading?"

"Where?"

"On our holiday, Charlotte. *Obviously.*"

He turned in his chair and smiled at her. With both hands, he leaned toward her chair and pulled its arms against those of his own so that the two chairs were touching, forming a small, tight rectangle encircling them both. He put his hands on her shoulders and pulled her toward him, pausing to brush away the tight cylinder of hair falling in front of her lips, and kissed her. Charlotte leaned into him, her hands on his knees. When they parted, his glance was amused. "I'll be hoarding all the Russian literature, so you'll need your own, I'm afraid. I don't think this relationship extends to my books yet. Why don't we go to dinner and then to a bookstore? We'll start your collection." Charlotte smiled and leaned forward, feeling the rough stubble of Horace's cheek as they kissed. Pulling back slightly, she put both hands on his shoulders and stared at him. His tired eyes met hers with a questioning look.

"I have a better idea," she said, gripping the worn threads of his sweater. "Let's skip the books and go back to your flat."

Horace's eyes widened, displaying red lines streaked across his eyeballs. His mouth opened in surprise before curling upward. "Brilliant idea, Charlotte." He covered her hands with his own and gripped them as he glanced around the office. "But I have to ask – when this is all over and done with, will you still consent to know such a dullard like me?"

"Don't be ridiculous, Horace," she retorted, a pink flush of pleasure suffusing her cheeks. "You're not a dullard. At least – you're the best of the male dullards, if one has to choose."

"Your compliment overwhelms me," Horace laughed, raising one of her palms and placing a light kiss in its center. "Let's go find the swiftest of all London's black cabs."

17

Miranda Rights

At 2 p.m. the next day, Patrick stood in the corner of the street-level lobby of Shorwell's New York office. He had come straight from JFK but looked neatly groomed, as always, courtesy of the showers and pressing service of the British Airways business class arrivals lounge. Only the faintest shadows ringed his blue eyes. Standing behind an enormous potted palm, he watched fifty floors of Midtown workers flow past him as he waited for Miranda. After his year in London, he was newly struck by the beauty of the New York women rushing past, their hair perfectly highlighted, their short skirts flaunting their unforgiving diets and exercise regimes. Patrick felt his head spin from some combination of fatigue and desire. *I forgot how gorgeous the girls are here,* he thought, his eyes flitting from one woman to another, his pulse quickening. *What the hell was I doing in London?* A skinny, freckled woman in a black suit with a plunging V-neckline stopped directly in front of him. Patrick started. "Miranda!" He leaned forward to kiss her, but she dodged his lips and his kiss landed in the air two inches beyond her left cheek. Taking a step back, she glared at him.

"Don't think that I forgive you just because I agreed to meet you, Patrick. I'm only doing this because you're giving me half of whatever you manage to get out of this, remember? And knowing you, you'll get something."

"I'm delighted to see you, too."

"Hah."

Together, they turned toward the elevators and glided up fifty floors. Doreen's eyes widened when she saw Patrick, but she said nothing, simply nodding to Miranda. Miranda nodded back and motioned for

Patrick to follow her to Jed's office. They walked quickly down the corridor.

"Where is he?" Patrick whispered, swiveling his head behind him.

Miranda said nothing until they were inside Jed's office, the door shut. "He finally left to get his lunch, and Doreen called the building's security guy to disable our bank of elevators. She's dating him, so it's no problem. He promised her thirty minutes before he'll have to listen to the other floors' complaints. You owe Doreen $500 for that, by the way; I bargained her down from $1000. That's not including the $100 I shelled out for drinks for her. And I got Jed's latest password, too – Doreen was named the system administrator when the whole thing was upgraded last year. Here." Miranda handed him a piece of lined paper, torn out of a notebook. Patrick glanced at Miranda's loopy cursive: *Gladiator1991*. He shook his head with incredulity and Miranda's mouth registered a very faint smile as she watched him. "I know," she said, "Pathetic, right?"

Miranda sat down in Jed's chair, perching herself on its very edge, her nose wrinkling with distaste. Patrick remained standing, leaning over her as she started to tap at Jed's keyboard. Patrick watched her manicured oblong red nails fly across the keys, remembering when he'd kissed each one on a sidewalk outside a West Village bar after they'd gone out for drinks for the first time. He recalled the desire he'd felt then with detachment, as though envisioning someone else's life. Now, her polished nails filled him only with impatience. He glanced up at the empty corridor and back to the screen.

Miranda's fingers paused. "I'm into his personal emails. Looks like he has a dealer. Does he do drugs?" Patrick shrugged, uninterested.

"Can you search for anything with the subject heading Money Transfer?" he asked.

Miranda nodded and resumed her rapid typing. Another ten minutes passed as Miranda tried various keywords. They all came up blank. Patrick, whose eyes continued to flick back and forth between the screen and the corridor, made an impatient noise. Miranda's fingers came to a halt and she twisted her neck around to stare up at him, her pale blue eyes flashing with suppressed triumph.

"Sorry, Patrick, looks like your plan to outwit Jed isn't going to work." Patrick ignored her smug tone, wracking his brain for ideas. He glanced around Jed's office, its walls unadorned, its one shelf empty except for a dead plant. What did he know about Jed? Stocky, sleepy, arrogant Jed, who grew up in the 1970's and 80's, no doubt mocked and despised by his classmates. He tried to remember his own childhood; what were the social outcasts of his class doing? Dungeons and Dragons? Rubik's cubes? Star Wars? He thrashed his memory, trying to see past the glow of easy popularity that had illuminated his own schooldays.

"Try Darth Vader," he said to Miranda. She snorted and typed in Darth Vader. The mechanical disk drive under the desk whirred briefly before displaying a list of six emails, all of them addressed to someone called VaderShorwell. Miranda paused in surprise. *Whatever*, she muttered under her breath. She clicked on the first email, leaning into the screen to read it, Patrick's head right above hers. It was one sentence, dated from six months ago: *Hey Vader, I need $20 million moved from the Utah Engineers into the special fund. Usual terms. Darth.* She clicked on a few more, all to the same person, all with instructions to shift money from client funds into other funds. She twisted her neck around to look up at Patrick.

"What do you think?" she said.

"I don't know. Who's Vader?"

"Someone in the back office, I guess. Jed started down there, remember? He's their hero for getting bumped up to the trading floor."

Patrick nodded. "It sure looks like he's moving money around illegally and this guy is getting a cut. Could you print them all out?"

Miranda nodded and started to send them to the nearest printer, located in the copy room half-way down the corridor. She was sending the last email to the printer when there was a sound in the corridor. Patrick looked up. Jed was rounding the corner holding a large deli bag, sweating from climbing fifty floors of stairs. Behind him, Doreen rushed forward unsteadily, her high heels swaying and her hands flapping. Before Patrick had a chance to say anything, Jed entered his office and yanked back on the chair Miranda was using. Shocked, Miranda fell off its edge, banging her forehead against the desk and landing on the carpet. Jed leaned toward his computer, seeing the list of emails. He stood up, his face twisted, his heavy eyes directed in fury at Patrick, who had just helped Miranda to her feet. She scurried out of the room. Patrick met Jed's look, his face impassive.

"Who's Vader?" Patrick asked.

Without speaking, Jed dropped his deli bag on the desk and swung a fist at Patrick, landing a punch on Patrick's chin. Patrick, gasping, lurched backward before regaining his balance and aiming a punch at Jed's midsection. The men flailed at each other, trading punches, falling over the desk and the chair, as Doreen watched from the doorway, her mouth open. Jed, tired from his hike up fifty floors of stairs, faded first, doubling over when Patrick landed a sharp kick into his knee. Jed grunted in pain and paused, his heavy torso heaving for breath. Patrick sprinted to the copier room where Miranda was standing over the printer, which was laboriously printing out each email on a separate piece of paper. Grabbing the five emails already in Miranda's hand, he gave her a quick kiss.

"Thanks, babe," he said, "I'll be in touch." He ran out the door. Miranda, her forehead bleeding, picked up the final email and followed Patrick out of the office.

Charlotte sat on a velour banquette, a small leather travel bag tucked behind her feet, her eyes fixed on the door. At 5 p.m., the low-ceilinged Midtown bar was just starting to fill with people released from the office buildings on Sixth Avenue, their eyes brightening at the sight of the glowing liquor bottles lining the walls.

Charlotte dabbed a cloth napkin into her ice water and dabbed it onto her forehead and temples. She had lost track of how long she had been awake since taking a plane from Heathrow early that morning. The hours that had passed since she'd crept out of Horace's lumpy double bed at 3 a.m., careful not to disturb his low, even snores, were now a mangled blur of cabs, airports, and still more cabs. Since reaching Sixth Avenue, she had lingered in a series of cafes and delis, all within the shadow cast by Shorwell's soaring building. Only once had she left their tables to sneak into Shorwell's office to leave a note on Miranda's desk. Now, dotting her eyelids with the wet napkin, she fought to stay awake as she stared at the door, willing Miranda to arrive.

Mumbling under her breath, she tried to rehearse her lines: *Miranda, I know we didn't get off on the right foot, but I really need your help, I'm sorry about Patrick* – maybe she shouldn't mention Patrick. She started again: *Miranda, I know we got off to a bad start, but I need your help, it's about Piers...it's about Jed... it's about Patrick.* In truth, she wasn't sure what she needed from Miranda. Last night, staring at Horace's back, she had been unable to sleep, her mind stuck on an image of Patrick balanced on his hands, his gleaming black loafers pointing at the ceiling. Was it likely, she thought, that O'Brien could be fooled by a false voice recording? And why would Patrick offer to run the risk? Surely he'd look after his interests before those of Piers, for whom he'd made his contempt all too clear. He certainly wouldn't put himself on the line for her sake, she thought, squirming; presumably his contempt for her was only just shy of his feelings for Piers. These thoughts had exerted a stranglehold over Charlotte's brain for an hour before she had concluded that Patrick's motivations were too uncertain to be trusted. She would have to go to New York herself and beg Miranda to help her find something – anything – that O'Brien might accept.

Charlotte found herself looking at a woman poised at the entrance of the bar, her thin lips frowning under oversized black sunglasses. Lanky, straw-colored hair flopped onto the shoulders of her fitted black jacket, whose deep V neckline fell from two sharp collarbones covered by freckled skin. The woman thrust the sunglasses onto her head and rested a hand on her hip as she stood blinking into the dim room, letting her eyes adjust. Charlotte stared at her from the banquette, uncertain. This woman's face was pointy and haggard, her cheeks bloodless. She looked ten years older than the woman Charlotte had met in a bar less than a year ago; there was no trace of the gleaming, glossy actress who had screamed across the bar for a drink. The woman caught sight of Charlotte and her frown deepened. The disdain was unmistakable: Miranda.

Miranda walked the length of the room, her bare white legs and knobby knees stalking across the floor like a giraffe. She reached Charlotte's table and stared down at her, making no move to sit. Charlotte rose, reeling from the fatigue which swirled around her head like an invisible mist.

"Thank you for coming, Miranda. I know you didn't have to." Miranda lifted her eyebrows a notch in response, saying nothing. Charlotte turned to the waitress who had materialized at the edge of their table and asked for two mojitos. She turned to Miranda. "I remember you liked them when I met you. I hope you still do." Grudgingly, Miranda sank into the chair facing Charlotte's banquette, glancing down at Charlotte's travel bag.

"Is it a New York field trip for the whole London office?" Miranda asked.

"No, I think just Patrick and I are here. But we traveled separately," Charlotte hastened to add, seeing a dangerous flicker in Miranda's eyes. "He doesn't know I'm here. I'm trying to avoid him, actually."

The waitress returned with a tray bearing two tall glasses sprouting mint stalks. Charlotte and Miranda watched in silence as she placed them on the table. The waitress glanced between them as she worked, obviously discomfited by two women sitting in silence. Charlotte dug into her wallet and held a credit card out to the waitress, who hesitated, as if there might be some mistake. "We'll start a tab," Charlotte said, stretching the card further toward her in silent appeal. The waitress shrugged and took the card, turning back to the bar.

"You've learned a few things," Miranda said. Charlotte took a sip of her drink. The cold liquid slid down her parched throat. She felt her shoulders fall an inch. She began again.

"Miranda, I know you have no reason to help me."

"None," said Miranda flatly, stirring her drink with the mint.

Charlotte nodded. "But I'm desperate to help Piers, I guess you know that the man from the SEC is after him?" Miranda gave a non-committal shrug as she continued to mash the mint against the side of the glass before dropping the wet spring onto the table. Lifting the glass, she drank the whole mojito in several long gulps. She replaced the glass on the table and met Charlotte's eyes. Her own were hard and devoid of emotion.

"Let me guess. You need me to find some documents that will prove that Shorwell is a scam." Charlotte's mouth dropped open and her hand, holding the icy mojito, froze midair. Miranda scoffed. "What, you think you're the only one using me? You're the second request today. And you're too late. I already handed over the only documents I could find to

Patrick. Another person who has no right to ask me a thing." Miranda picked up her empty glass and stood up without a word. She walked over to the bar, returning moments later with two large tumblers of a transparent liquid. She placed one in front of Charlotte. "It's straight vodka. I figured we may as well lose the girly drinks and cut to the chase. I put them on your tab." Miranda took a large sip. Small patches of pink had started to appear in her hollow cheeks, shadowing their concavity. Her wrist wobbled as it descended to the table. Charlotte leaned forward.

"Miranda, I just want to say I'm sorry about Patrick. I didn't know he had a girlfriend."

"Neither did he, apparently," said Miranda.

"And there's nothing between us. It was just a stupid infatuation on my part. Patrick can be so – I don't know – charming." Miranda said nothing, stirring her vodka with a cocktail straw. They sat in silence, each woman conjuring up a different image of Patrick, each one lost briefly to a moment of desire, now recalled through the shadow of disappointment. Charlotte's image dissipated first, replaced by one of Horace's bare shoulder, rising and falling. She looked up at Miranda.

"Do you have a brother?" Charlotte asked. "Or a sister?"

"What?"

"Do you have a brother or a sister?"

"No. I had a cat once, but he got eaten by a coyote." Charlotte wasn't sure whether this remark was intended to be ironic. She decided to play it safe. "I'm sorry. How awful for you. Well, the thing is about siblings is – whether you love them or hate them, or both love and hate them – you're a bit stuck with them. They're part of you, however much you might like to think otherwise. You don't just get to jettison them when they're difficult, or disappointing, or in trouble. So, I'm afraid I just don't have a choice. And I know it's not your problem, but it would mean so much to me if you'd help." Miranda looked at Charlotte speculatively.

"How much?"

"Sorry?"

"How much would it mean to you?"

"What do you want, exactly?"

"I want to get out of here. What's London like, anyway? I've had it with New York."

Startled, Charlotte paused as she thought quickly. "Why don't you come for Easter? I'm sure my mother would be delighted to have you stay until you can find a place in London. You're a ballet dancer, right? Maybe we could introduce you to someone who manages the ballet at Covent Garden. You could help." Miranda nodded slowly, considering.

"Fine. I'll do anything as long as it's not Shorwell or near Sixth Avenue." She drained her glass and thumped it on the table.

"More vodka?" Charlotte asked.

"Sure," said Miranda, "no ice."

The bar was full now, and the mood festive, as people moved through their second and third drinks. Charlotte forgot her exhaustion as she kept pace with Miranda's drinking; her capacity for liquor had escalated over the past twelve months, and she felt only somewhat tipsy as she embarked upon her third drink. Miranda became less guarded with each glass, and her movements more fluid. Charlotte could almost feel Miranda's tension as it rolled off her body and dissipated around the room. When Miranda was mostly finished with her third drink, her cheeks now fully red and her neck tilting almost to her shoulder, Charlotte tried again.

"What do you think, Miranda? Will you help me?" Miranda plunked her glass on the table, looking almost relaxed. "Sure, why not? As it happens, I saved one of the questionable emails for myself." She reached down into her bag lying on the floor, and withdrew a folded piece of paper, handing it to Charlotte. Charlotte scanned the few lines and looked up.

"Who's Vader? Isn't that the name of the Star Wars villain? The one whose breathing sounds like a vacuum cleaner?"

"Yup. Aren't men sad? But it's all I've got. Another drink?"

Patrick stood on the ground floor of Piers's apartment building. He recalled Charlotte's woeful tale, months before, of the depressing apartments she'd toured in New York, and the address of the one she had recommended to Piers. He glanced around the dim lobby, unimpressed. Despite the poor lighting – two of the three overhead lights were out – a layer of grime was all too visible on the tiled floor, as were the mold spots growing up the grey cement walls. A stack of flyers for take-out pizza and nail salons sat on a rusted metal radiator. Piers was paying $2800/month in rent, Charlotte had said. Piers quickly multiplied this figure by the likely number of apartments in the building. Not bad, he thought, his spirits lifting. A rental building might be a good investment someday.

Seeing no chair, he sat down on the cleanest of the steps leading to the second floor, carefully lifting the flaps of his suit jacket so they wouldn't be crumpled. For the first time since arriving in New York, he let himself relax. The fight with Jed had been unpleasant, but nothing he couldn't handle. He recalled it now, seeing Jed's heavy head reared back on his shoulders, lines of red spiderwebs rising through the unhealthy pallor of his cheeks, his large hand making a fist. Even through his initial alarm, Patrick had recorded Jed's loss of poise and slovenliness with contempt, mercilessly noting the untucked shirttails, the unshaven jaw, the folds of his neck sagging into his shirt collar. Unimpressive, Patrick thought, smoothing the fabric over his bent knees and flicking off an errant piece of lint.

He opened his briefcase and removed the documents Miranda had printed out, re-reading the emails. It wasn't much, but it was better than anything Piers would be able to dig up for O'Brien, he figured. All he needed was enough of a hook to get O'Brien to hire him as an inside source to Shorwell and give him time to figure out how he could salvage his own position. The SEC had a reputation of paying its whistle-blower sources well, and that should tide him over until he figured out his next move. He looked at his watch. Wasn't O'Brien supposed to be here now, on his way to retrieve the tape from Piers? Patrick envisioned Piers sitting upstairs with his blank tape. What an idiot Piers was, Patrick reflected, to say he'd try to get W. on tape; W. was inaccessible, and Charlotte and Horace were fools, or desperate, or desperate fools, to believe the SEC would fall for a faked tape. He dismissed them all with a shrug as his thoughts hummed along. He was pleased with his progress over the last twelve hours; so far, he seemed to be navigating this latest series of obstacles as well as possible, and with any luck, he might conceivably come out ahead. How bright could this O'Brien be, anyway? Putting the papers back in his briefcase, he pulled out a tabloid and turned to the sports section.

O'Brien sat in the back of a yellow cab, immobilized by the crowds of people flowing past it at the intersection of Astor Place and 4th Avenue, all of them indifferent to the horns blasting in their direction. The skin-tight jeans of a teenage girl brushed against O'Brien's window, and she barely glanced down. O'Brien was seized by irritation at her indifference, arrogance and youth, now decades behind him. He checked the digital readout of his watch: 6:20. His pulse quickened as his prey neared, and he turned his eyes away from the side window and toward the back of his driver's bald head, anticipating the moments ahead. He ran the scene that lay ahead of him like a movie that had already been made: himself bounding effortlessly up the five floors to Piers's overpriced, under-furnished apartment; striding in without knocking, and holding out his hand for the microtape player – its absence had been a source of anxiety. He smiled to himself as he rehearsed his triumph, before realizing that the cab had stopped and the driver's head had twisted around to watch the smirks and smiles move across his face.

"$17," the driver said, looking at him warily.

O'Brien dug into his pocket, withdrawing a crumpled $20. He handed it through the plastic divider to the driver, who offered him $3 in return, handing the bills through the plastic window with the very tips of his fingers.

"I need a receipt," O'Brien scowled. The driver flicked one to the backseat and slammed shut the plastic window. O'Brien slid his bulk across the bench seat and heaved his way onto the sidewalk, slamming the door behind him and running up the steps to Piers's building. Entering the foyer, he paused. A blond young man in an immaculate blue suit was sitting on the third step, reading the *New York Daily News*. O'Brien stared at him. He had never seen anyone in the lobby before. The young man looked up with an easy smile.

"Mr. O'Brien, I take it?" Patrick stood up with a graceful motion, dropping his tabloid to the floor.

"Who are you?"

"Patrick Connolly. Shorwell Capital. I believe you're on your way to see my colleague Piers Cheetham?" O'Brien said nothing. "I'm glad to meet you. May I take a few minutes of your time?" Patrick glided across the foyer and shook the half-extended hand of O'Brien, who remained frozen in the entranceway, his broad face startled and suspicious. Patrick fixed him with cheerful blue eyes. "I understand that you've been – encouraging – Piers to find some evidence suggesting that Shorwell is engaged in questionable business practices. I'm here to offer you some documents that might fortify your case."

O'Brien repeated his question. "Who are you?"

"Patrick Connolly. I've been at Shorwell three years, two in New York and one in London. Please." Patrick gestured to the stairwell where he'd been sitting. Together, the two men sat down on the third step. Patrick removed the documents from his briefcase and held them as he spoke. "I think I can help you with your investigation. First of all, I know everyone in both offices. Also, crucially, I'm on your side."

"You are?"

"Yes. I know I may look like one of these hedge fund guys you've been tracking all these years – five, right? – but actually, I come from a little town in upstate Minnesota."

"I'm from Jersey."

"Same thing – Jersey, Minnesota – the point is that I wasn't born with a silver spoon stuck in my mouth either. I bet you've worked your ass off to get where you are today." O'Brien thought of all the days he'd sat in his office eating Chinese food from cartons, staring at his King Kong poster. He nodded slowly, and Patrick nodded along with him. "Right, so you know that most these hedge fund guys don't deserve these crazy payouts. I'm here to make you a deal. I'll stay at Shorwell and be your inside guy. Together, as a team, I guarantee we can take down W. And just to prove my sincerity, I'm willing to share some documents that implicate his senior lieutenant. You can think of them as an appetizer to future information." Patrick handed the emails in his hand to O'Brien, who squinted at them in the half-light.

"Who's Darth? Who's Vader? Is this some sort of joke?" O'Brien started to rise from the step, his face angry. Patrick put a firm, restraining hand on O'Brien forearm. The older man lowered himself down again.

Patrick took back the pages and stowed them in his briefcase as he spoke. "They're code names for our senior traders. I think you'll find that my information is far superior to anything our friend upstairs can provide. Needless to say, he wasn't able to get W. on tape."

"You're pretty well-informed," O'Brien said grudgingly. "Why are you doing this?"

"As I mentioned, in the spirit of being on the right side. And because I understand that the SEC has a very generous whistle-blower payout policy. I have no doubt that we could both meet our objectives if we collaborated."

O'Brien hesitated. "You think you can get evidence against W.?"

"I think I can get you a lot closer than Piers. What do you have to lose?" A loud car honk from the street punctuated Patrick's question. Patrick stood up and brushed down the fabric of his suit jacket. "Do we have a tentative deal? If so, I'm happy to draft an agreement to send over to your office."

O'Brien hesitated as he considered the proposition, trying to assess its downside. He didn't see much. This guy seemed a lot smarter and better informed than Piers, whose utility had always been as an entrée, anyway. And the documents Patrick had shown him were more definitive that anything he'd seen yet, and certainly better than the questionable performance data Adrian had sent through. O'Brien stood up and yanked down on the elasticized waist of his nylon jacket. Reaching into his pocket, he pulled out a business card with fraying corners and handed it to Patrick. "Send me your terms and we'll talk," he said.

Patrick smiled at him. "Perfect. I'll get them to you today." Picking up his briefcase, he shook O'Brien's hand again and glided out the door.

The sun was sinking into the Hudson river by the time Charlotte emerged from the subway on the Lower East Side. She hurried through the streets, her feet racing through the shadows cast by the stunted leafless trees in planter boxes. The subway from Midtown had inexplicably stopped just outside the 14th Street station, and she'd been stuck below ground for an extra twenty minutes before it started up again. It was now 6:50 p.m., twenty minutes after O'Brien was supposed to be collecting the tape from Piers.

Reaching her brother's street at last, she raced up the building's stairs and entered the foyer that O'Brien and Patrick had left only twenty minutes before. Barely pausing for breath, she climbed the five floors to his apartment and knocked. She heard slow footsteps, before the door opened with a rattle of safety chains.

Charlotte froze at the ravaged version of Piers that stood on the threshold. A ragged stubble covered his chin and his dulled eyes sank into half-circles of puffy skin. His own look of shock made his destroyed features even more exaggerated, almost grotesque. His face showed no pleasure in seeing Charlotte, and she repressed a pang of hurt. For a long moment, the siblings stared at each other, unspeaking.

"What are you doing here?" Piers said.

"I'm here to help. I said I would, remember? I have something for O'Brien. Wasn't he supposed to be here?"

Piers nodded and took a step backward, gesturing to a middle-aged man sitting on the sofa, a cigarette in his hand. Charlotte ran her eyes over him before stepping in his direction with her arm outstretched. Her voice rasped from the exertion of climbing the stairs, but she spoke with confidence.

"I'm Charlotte Cheetham, Piers's sister." O'Brien nodded casually, without bothering to rise. *What appalling manners*, Charlotte thought automatically, taking another step forward. "I have something for you." She withdrew from her purse the email Miranda had given to her and handed it to O'Brien, speaking in a rush as he glanced at it. "I think you'll see that it shows—" O'Brien glanced at the paper and started to laugh. She paused, insulted. "Don't you want it?"

O'Brien let the paper drop onto the coffee table in front of him. "Maybe. What do you want in exchange?"

"To let Piers go home."

O'Brien shook his head. "Sorry, can't do. Piers is stuck here until further notice. Didn't he tell you? He's on a no-fly list controlled by the

FBI." O'Brien ground out his cigarette and pushed his hand through his thinning hair, shielding his eyes from Charlotte as he spoke. Charlotte stared at him, watching his motions and trying to make eye contact. She said nothing. O'Brien stood up and patted the thin nylon of his jacket pocket, through which the outline of the tape recorder could be seen. O'Brien continued to look at the floor. "Sorry the tape didn't work out, Piers. I'll be in touch."

O'Brien left, banging the door. Charlotte said nothing as she listened to his steps clatter down the corridor and start down the staircase. Avoiding Piers's eyes, she glanced around the small apartment. It was a mess, his clothes heaped onto the floor and take-out cartons littered across the coffee table. A baseball game, muted, played on the television. Without speaking, Piers headed back to the futon sofa and slumped onto it, leaving Charlotte standing, her overnight bag at her feet. She looked around for a chair and, seeing none, lowered herself next to him on the sofa. Together, they watched the baseball players run silently around the diamond field.

"Piers?" she ventured. Her brother didn't turn to look at her. She tried again. "Piers? Let's go home."

"I can't. You heard him. I'm on a list." His voice was unsteady, cracking over the monosyllables.

"I think he's bluffing. He made that motion people make – you make – when they're not telling the truth." She spoke softly but steadily. Next to her, Piers nodded slowly. A tear started to roll down his cheek, and then another. Embarrassed, Charlotte said nothing as she put an arm around his back. Piers leaned into her, crying harder and harder. Charlotte sat very still as her brother cried. When he stopped sobbing, he sat up again, staring down at his hands.

"I'm sorry, Char. It wasn't supposed to end this way." Charlotte nodded, keeping her hand on his arm, lightly touching his sleeve. Piers wiped his eyes with the back of his hand and turned his face toward hers. Under his haggard, exhausted eyes, there was a very faint glimmer of hope. "Do you really think we could just leave?" he asked.

"I think he's just bluffing," she repeated. "There's nothing to lose, anyway. Let's go." Standing up, she glanced around his small room. She grinned. "What a mess," she said, with a teasing quality. "You've really let down your standards since moving to New York."

Piers looked at his sister with the barest hint of his old humor. "I know," he said. "What would mother say?" He stood up and walked to his bedroom, where he started to throw the contents of his drawers onto his bed. "Let's get out of here," he said.

18

Crossing to Safety

Charlotte and Horace walked along the wet field, their strides matched and their hands clasped loosely together. The wide cuffs of their waxed green raincoats brushed one another, melding the drops of rain which clung to the cloth. Their knee-high wellington boots made a soft swishing noise as they moved through the tall grass. In every direction, undulating horizontal lines of field, hedge and wall rolled to the horizon, their outlines blurred with mist.

Miranda trudged behind them, plowing through the wet earth with an uneven gait punctuated by muttered curses. Having snubbed Charlotte's offer of flat-heeled rubber boots, she was now engaged in a furious battle against the Sussex mud. The high, sharp heels of her black boots sank like anchors into the wet earth with each step, and she yanked her feet forward with defiant fury. After three miles of fogged fields and damp hedgerows, Miranda's patience had worn thin.

"Are we headed anywhere in particular?" Miranda called forward to Charlotte's wet green raincoat.

"Not really," answered Charlotte, without turning around. Miranda absorbed this information as they continued down the path, Charlotte and Horace silently and smoothly, Miranda with a violent lurching motion behind. Miranda tripped on a rock and swore at the wet grasses soaking her trousers. She cursed.

"Is this some sort of English thing, walking through the rain and getting drenched for no reason?"

Charlotte laughed and stopped, turning to look behind her. Miranda's blond hair was streaked across her face in bedraggled strands – she had refused a hat – and her cheeks were red with the exertion of fighting the mud. Away from Manhattan's urban backdrop, standing furious in the dripping field, she looked about twelve years old.

"I guess," answered Charlotte.

"I can see why Piers chose to sleep in," Miranda snorted.

Piers had retreated to his boyhood bedroom for the two weeks since he and Charlotte had returned to England. They had left New York immediately following Charlotte's arrival. She had been right: The border officials at JFK had stamped Piers's passport without a second glance; if there was a FBI no-fly list, Piers wasn't on it. Charlotte and Piers had sat through a bumpy and sleepless flight in silence, Charlotte limp with the exhaustion of the past two days, and Piers distant and removed, a depleted and unrecognizable version of himself. From Heathrow, shivering in the unseasonably frigid weather, they had traveled directly to their mother's house, where Piers had claimed a stomach bug and sequestered himself in his room. A week later, Miranda had joined them, arriving at the local train station in a narrow skirt and heels, followed by a porter hauling her pile of suitcases.

Charlotte, Horace and Miranda rounded the corner of a long field and found themselves joining a gravel lane lined by trees, wide enough for them to walk together. The sun, straight overhead at noon, brightened a patch of rain clouds above them. Miranda, now walking easily in her ruined boots, glanced around, shoving her dank, blond hair behind her ear.

"I heard from Patrick," she said.

"Has he left New York?" Charlotte asked.

"Nope. He's back at the office consolidating his position now that Jed's been dragged in for questioning by the FBI and SEC."

"You know," said Horace, "Jed left me one last voice mail right before you came back from New York."

"He wanted another trading idea?" Charlotte's voice was incredulous.

"No. He wanted me to know that he was going to spend the rest of his life plotting how to retaliate when this is all over." Charlotte shivered and gripped Horace's hand more tightly.

"Let's go home," she said. "I think Mother's waiting for us with Easter lunch."

An hour later, Charlotte stood in the center hallway, waiting for Miranda to descend. Her hand began its habitual descent down the side of her head before colliding unexpectedly with her chin, newly exposed after a recent decision to lop off most her hair. She turned to see Miranda looming above her at the top of the staircase, clutching at the banister as she navigated the uneven stairs. Miranda's narrow legs, semi-visible through the diaphanous material of her dress, gingerly descended each creaking stair. She reached the landing with a thump and glared at Charlotte. "How many people have died coming down that staircase?" she demanded.

"We use it to weed out house guests," said Charlotte. "We're hoping for our very own ghost." She ran her eyes over a pale expanse of skin emerging from Miranda's sleeveless dress. "I should warn you that Mother doesn't heat the house past February. No one has ever braved the dining room in fewer than three layers."

"Then I'll be the first," Miranda said carelessly. "You can tell your mother it's an American thing."

They found Horace in the dining room hunched over a book propped up on the sideboard. Behind him, the table had been laid hastily for Easter lunch. A faded tablecloth sprouted embroidered daffodils beneath two tarnished silver candlesticks, and three domed platters lined the table. Charlotte picked up an opened bottle of white wine and filled two glasses, handing one to Miranda, and placing a second on top of Horace's book, forcing him to look up. From behind, she heard her mother in animated conversation with Horace's parents as they filed into the room, discussing the stretch of unusually cold weather. Piers followed last, his face grey from lack of exercise and his blond curls plastered to his forehead. Avoiding everyone's eyes, he walked directly to the table and picked up a new bottle of wine. The guests sank into chairs and began to tuck into the food without ceremony.

"I've just had the most awful news from Lady Philippa," began Mrs. Cheetham, handing her daughter a platter of sliced lamb obscured by a thicket of fresh rosemary.

"Yes?" answered Charlotte, handing off her platter of potatoes to Horace.

"Her water pipes in London froze and burst during this terrible patch of weather. Something to do with turning off the heat? I didn't quite catch the details. I'm afraid your basement area has been flooded. She wanted to know when you'd be back. She mentioned that your desk and bookcase are absolutely drenched." Horace, still holding the plate of potatoes, swiveled toward Charlotte.

"Oh, Charlotte – all your poetry notebooks – I'm sorry." Charlotte envisioned her stack of writing journals, their lines of poetry now blurred into amorphous blobs. She said nothing, waiting for an emotion to accompany this image, like the clap of thunder after a bolt of lightning. To her surprise, none arrived. She waited for another moment, just to be sure, and met Horace's anxious eyes.

"You know, I was planning to move onto prose anyway," she said to him. "More fun."

The guests fell comfortably into conversation, their spirits lubricated by the wine and food. The room was cozy and warm, its windows steamed over with the heat of the corner fireplace which had been pressed into service in the unusual cold. Only Piers remained quiet, focused on his plate and refilling his glass of wine at twice the rate of everyone else. Sitting midway between her brother and mother, Charlotte chatted with Horace's father while monitoring her mother's glances down the table at Piers. Over the past weeks, Piers had deflected and dodged all references to New York, and the siblings had maintained an instinctive and complicit silence on the year's events. With a mother's instinct, however, Mrs. Cheetham felt the absence of some critical piece of information, and Charlotte could feel her gathering momentum for an attack, buoyed by the wine and the presence of her friends. Sure enough, her mother's brittle consonants now shot down the table, past the candlesticks and salt cellars, and rising above the other conversations.

"Piers, darling, when will you have to go back to New York?" Charlotte, Horace and Miranda all froze. Piers said nothing as he continued to chew on a bread roll, swallowing it with a large sip of wine.

"I'm not going back, I don't think." He said it mildly, not meeting his mother's widened eyes.

"But Piers, after you've made a such a success of it!" There was a general silence as all four Shorwell employees stared at their respective plates. Piers coughed.

"It was a bit dull, actually. You remember Patrick, who was here last Easter? He's likely to leave too, for greener pastures."

"That terribly amusing American boy?" Mrs. Bloom asked. She turned toward her son. "Horace, wasn't he heading up your office? Who will take his place?" All heads swiveled in Horace's direction. Horace raised his brown eyes first toward his mother, and then toward Charlotte. His cheeks had turned pink with the wine and heat of the room, and he hesitated before speaking.

"I believe I'm next in the queue. I got a message from New York yesterday. But really, Shorwell feels a bit limited in its opportunities just now. I was thinking of opening my own fund instead, provided I could find the right staff." Horace glanced down at his napkin before turning toward Charlotte. "I was hoping, Charlotte, you might consider joining me?" He looked intently at her as he spoke, ignoring the others, who were watching in silence. Charlotte pushed her hair behind her ear with a shrug.

"I don't know. I might consider it. But I'd need a raise."

"Charlotte!" remonstrated her mother from the head of the table. "Is that appropriate? At Easter lunch?"

"Of course," said Horace, nodding.

"And a promotion," added Charlotte.

"Really, Charlotte!" repeated her mother.

"I was thinking," said Charlotte, ignoring her mother and keeping her eyes focused on Horace, "Of co-director, perhaps." She placed her left hand on top of Horace's, which was resting on an embroidered spray of blooming flowers. "How does that strike you?" Horace turned his palm upward to clasp hers in a firm grip.

"Done," he said. "I'll call the lawyers."

About the Author

Clarissa Swire held senior positions at financial firms in London and New York City. A graduate of Stanford University, she lives with her family in Northern California.